THE CLARITY

THE CLARITY

A Novel

KEITH THOMAS

LEOPOLDO
& CO

ATRIA

New York   London   Toronto   Sydney   New Delhi

LEOPOLDO & CO

ATRIA

An Imprint of Simon & Schuster, Inc.
1230 Avenue of the Americas
New York, NY 10020

First Leopoldo & Co/Atria Books hardcover edition February 2018

LEOPOLDO & CO/ATRIA BOOKS and colophon are trademarks of Simon & Schuster, Inc.

For information about special discounts for bulk purchases, please contact Simon & Schuster Special Sales at 1-866-506-1949 or business@simonandschuster.com.

The Simon & Schuster Speakers Bureau can bring authors to your live event. For more information or to book an event, contact the Simon & Schuster Speakers Bureau at 1-866-248-3049 or visit our website at www.simonspeakers.com.

Interior design by Dana Sloan

Manufactured in the United States of America

10   9   8   7   6   5   4   3   2   1

Library of Congress Cataloging-in-Publication Data

Names: Thomas, Keith, 1975- author.
Title: The clarity : a novel / Keith Thomas.
Description: First Atria Books hardcover edition. | New York : Atria/Leopoldo & Co., 2018.
Identifiers: LCCN 2017036133 (print) | LCCN 2017045123 (ebook) | ISBN 9781501156953 (ebook) | ISBN 9781501156939 (hardcover) | ISBN 9781501156946 (softcover)
Subjects: LCSH: Women psychologists—Fiction. | Memory—Fiction. | Girls—Fiction. | BISAC: FICTION / Horror. | FICTION / Suspense. | FICTION / Mystery & Detective / General. | GSAFD: Suspense fiction. | Mystery fiction.
Classification: LCC PS3620.H6293 (ebook) | LCC PS3620.H6293 C58 2018 (print) | DDC 813/.6—dc23
LC record available at https://lccn.loc.gov/2017036133

ISBN 978-1-5011-5693-9
ISBN 978-1-5011-5695-3 (ebook)

To the memory of L. P. Davies, whoever you were

AUTHOR'S NOTE

THE HISTORY OF World War I is peppered with tragic and fascinating stories. There are, no doubt, many men who died just after the declaration of Armistice on November 11, 1918. George Lawrence Price, a Canadian, and George Edwin Ellison, a Brit, have both been recognized as the last British soldiers to be killed on the muddy battlefields of the First World War. Their stories are devastating, their deaths even more so. I have combined aspects of both men's lives and demises in the following novel.

1

THE WORLD IS a wasteland.

And Private George Edwin Ellison is on patrol.

Fingers numb, body battered, he pushes his way through a blackened field that was once a school yard. The wind is fierce. He pulls up the collar on his jacket to block it out but it finds the holes, the tears, and worries at his skin the way the biting gnats did on the rust-colored banks of a nameless Belgian canal. Bites he still scratches; bites he suspects will never heal.

George counts his steps, a time-killing habit. A distraction.

Each footfall a crunch on ruined earth.

A solitary beat in the nothingness.

Behind the village school building, he finds the charred body of a horse. Its forelegs fused with the blackened pile of the school's chimney. Beelzebub's chariot, he thinks with a chuckle before moving on. He's seen worse. Smelled worse. Truth is, he's been lucky. It is day 1,566 of the war to end all wars and he still walks, still has the use of his hands, and the ability to remember home. Not like Richards from A Company. Not like the limbless American he found in an alfalfa field. The war was supposed to be the last spasm of hatred, the last night before a dawn of reason. Only instead of a spasm, it'd become a cancer.

Surely, the world couldn't handle another day.

As he counts out his steps, George thinks he hears the chanting of the villagers who'd welcomed them into the devastated hamlet.

But likely it is just the ceaseless rush of the wind through the naked trees.

George rounds the school building and waves the all clear to the rest of his platoon. As they move toward the canal, he picks up his step. The cold has seeped into his bones, and he recalls fondly how he warmed his fingers beside an oil-drum fire that morning. He wishes he could hold that heat like water, rub it like a salve on the numbness overtaking his body. Thinking of the fire conjures up images of home and of his grandmother's butter tarts. He sees his son, James, smiling as he waves goodbye in the doorway of their Edmund Street house. And he sees his wife, Hannah, on the night before he'd left: her cherubic face glowing over their last rationed candle, tears sparkling on her cheeks.

George had carved her image on the back of his pocket watch.

A smiling, cherubic face done in a simple, amateurish style.

Folded and worn, the watch has survived the worst of Ypres, Loos, and Cambrai; a scrap of metal that dodged bullets and survived mortar rounds. George knows that bodies are the weakest link. He's watched so many men die. So many men suffer. Yet he is still here. Still marching, still counting out steps. Sensing his brief surge in optimism, the exhausted sky breaks open further and lets loose a deluge.

George slows, head hung low under the battery of cold rain.

Behind him, the platoon falls into formation. The guys who have faith—the ones who believe in something more than mud, fog, rain, and fire—they follow closely. For them, George is the lucky one. Their rabbit's foot. Their dream catcher. He is the one who always keeps walking, pushing forward ceaselessly, on automatic, when they all would gladly crumble.

Sixty-five feet from the canal, Major Ross halts the Fifth Royal Irish Lancers' approach. In the middle of the road, rain spattering their faces, George kneels down in the muck beside Private Frank Price.

George points to several cottages across the canal.

"What do you think?"

"Don't like it," Price says. "We're sitting ducks here."

Eyeing the loose bricks on the house's façade, George says, "Good spot to stick a rifle." After a minute of watching through the rain and mist, he stands and squeezes Price's shoulder. "I think we should check those houses. Let's get some guys."

With three machine gunners in tow, they cross the bridge.

Major Ross yells after them: "Hold there, boys. We'll be across in five minutes."

Every step across the bridge is slicker than the last, and the water churns beneath them, festooned with tree limbs, trash, and the bloated bodies of what once were sheep. On the other side, they approach the house carefully, each holding his breath, each as close to George as they can possibly be.

Reaching the first house, the machine gunners push their way through a broken door to the dark interior. One of the gunners, Robinson, shouts out a warning, "Ne tirez pas! Ne tirez pas!" Robinson has shouted the phrase in every village, every town. Even though they all knew the French rarely had weapons, it had become Robinson's mantra, his way of staying sane.

It works.

In the kitchen they find three elderly Belgian men with broken smiles and blackened hands. George checks the back room, while Frank and the gunners talk to the old men. There are Germans near, the old men say. Just outside.

That's when the roof comes apart.

At first George thinks it is a building collapse. He ducks down, ready for the spine-breaking timbers to hit, but when they don't, when all that falls is a fine mist of brick dust, he knows they are under fire. An angry buzzing comes next, as slugs careen around the house, ricocheting off the walls. Dodging bullets, ducking low, George scrambles into the kitchen, where the gunners fire through the windows.

Frank grabs George's sleeve.

"We have to get out of here!"

George says, "We need to hold this position till the rest get here."

Frank drags George out a side door and, crouched low, the rain suddenly renewing its attack on their already drenched clothes, they zigzag to a low brick wall at the rear of the house. The narrow cobbled streets look clear, the houses around them empty. George points to a hill three hundred feet to the north. There, a German machine gunner reloads his Maschinengewehr.

Price says, "I don't think we can take him. We should turn back."

"We have two minutes to hold here."

George looks down at his pocket watch to see that the hands have stopped. He's confused; he'd just recently wound the watch. It should be working. But he is even more confused by the tiny red droplets that lie in a line on the glass surface of the watch, like red rain as crimson as blood.

The time is stuck at 10:55 a.m.

George hears the clatter of gunfire but it is a world away. Like thunder a few villages over. It doesn't last long. He turns to see Price hit the muddy earth, a bloom of mud and debris flying overhead. And then George falls backward, only very slowly. The watch in his hand remains as still as its arms. The rain has stopped. The air thick, heavy like a blanket. A heartbeat later and George finds himself staring up at the sky.

Robinson leans over him with a look of terror.

It is 9:29 a.m. and the numbness starts to move across George's body.

It crawls from his fingers, up his arms, and from his toes to his thighs. It is not the stinging numbness of the cold. Not the impersonal numbness of the rain. It is like falling asleep. Like being a child, sinking into a place of enveloping comfort. It is like falling asleep with Hannah in his arms. With that thought, George's breathing slows. And an overwhelming, almost suffocating peace comes over him.

Robinson reappears.

"You're gonna be okay, mate," he says, but the expression on his face says something else. "Doc'll fix you up. You'll see. We'll get you home right quick."

The sun comes out.

George hears distorted shouting. More of the guys in his platoon appear; they stand over him, helmets off. Robinson leans down again, close to George's face.

"God damn. It's over, George," Robinson says, the tears on his face running lines through the caked-on dirt. "The war is over. It's fucking armistice."

It is 9:30 a.m. and George Edwin Ellison is dead.

The very last British casualty of the First World War.

The sun throbs overhead.

The rabbit foot, the dream catcher—his luck has run out. And as George's body settles into death, his pupils dilate, becoming two black pools that widen until they consume the whole world. All that is left is darkness.

And in that darkness, a small voice screams.

2

THE SCREAM WOKE Ashanique Walters before she realized it was coming from her own mouth.

Two days ago, she'd turned eleven, and the balloons from her party had deflated and lined her small bedroom floor like dark stones. The door to her bedroom was half-open and out in the living room of her mother's small apartment she could see the television flickering. An infomercial for a blender ran on mute; white people with cosmetic smiles mugged for the camera as they pretended to enjoy a smoothie that looked like it was dredged from the bottom of Lake Michigan.

Ashanique had never felt her heart beat so quickly.

A week ago, she'd gone over to a friend's house and played with her pet bunny. With her heart racing, Ashanique remembered how the bunny squirmed when she'd held it. How her friend's mom had told her that if the rabbit got too scared its heart would beat so fast it would burst. Ashanique's face was slick with sweat, her skin cold despite the blankets, and she worried her heart might burst.

Reaching down to adjust her sheets, her fingers came away wet.

Sticky.

Ashanique pulled down her blankets. There was a dark stain on her pajama bottoms between her legs. Blood. She ignored it and climbed out of bed and headed to the pile of books in a corner. There she found a pencil box filled with crayons beneath a tattered hardcover copy of *Goodman &*

Gilman's Manual of Pharmacology and Therapeutics. She carefully peeled the wrappers off the sticks of colored wax and then, in the half-light, began drawing on the walls. . . .

. . .

Ashanique's mother, Janice, found her standing on her bed thirteen minutes later.

Confused, still half-asleep, Janice turned on the lights.

Ashanique blinked in the instant brightness as Janice looked over the drawings that covered the walls, even the corners of the ceilings.

"Did . . . did you see this, baby?"

Ashanique nodded.

Janice took Ashanique's wax-covered hands and squeezed them. Then, leaning down, she locked eyes with her daughter. Only, they weren't the same eyes she'd tucked into bed a few hours earlier—something had changed. There was a maturity behind them, a knowing that went beyond the girl's years.

"Ashanique, everything's going to be okay. . . ."

"That's not my name."

Janice took a deep breath and let it out slowly.

"What's your name?"

"It's George. What's wrong with me?"

"Nothing's wrong. Nothing's wrong, baby girl."

Janice held Ashanique tight, but Ashanique pulled away.

"I don't want this. . . . I'm scared. . . . I'm scared I don't know who I am. . . ."

"Everything will be okay, all right? You have to trust me. I know this is scary. You feel like you're upside down. But this thing that's happening to you, in time you're going to understand it. I'll tell you what I know in the morning, about the others. But, right now, you know those caterpillars Mrs. Carol got—"

"Who's Mrs. Carol? I don't know that person. . . ."

Fighting to keep her voice from trembling, Janice ran her fingers along the back of Ashanique's neck and said, "They were ladybug babies but they didn't look like ladybugs, did they? No, they looked like little ugly caterpillars with spikes. But then they transform. They curl up and put a little black shell

'round themselves. They don't know what's happening. You think they decide when the transformation starts? *Nah*, it's programmed in their blood. It
happens when it's time. And when that little black shell opens, what comes
out of it?"

"A ladybug comes out. . . ."

"That's exactly right," Janice said. "A beautiful ladybug."

3

WITH HER DAUGHTER passed out in bed, a glass of water and a Tylenol later, Janice sat on the couch with her stopwatch in hand.

She tried to calm herself, but her heart was doing its own thing.

Been waiting for this since the girl was born, and now you're going to freak out? Had a decade to get your ass ready, girl. Don't fall apart now that it's time.

The only art Ashanique ever brought home from school were messes of wet paint and blurry ink stamps. Ashanique's teacher said it wasn't the girl's calling. Mrs. Adams had even joked about maybe a career in medicine, since Ashanique clearly had a doctor's handwriting.

But what Ashanique had done was ... impossible.

She'd transformed her room into a panorama of hell.

Using crayons and finger paint, Ashanique had painted smoking ruins of buildings that loomed over crushed bodies and rivers of blood; horses, their manes on fire, ran across fields of spent bullet casings; soldiers with machine guns blasted away at faceless crowds. And in one inky corner near the ceiling, there was a realistic pocket watch with red crayon droplets on its glass face. The time on the watch was 10:55 a.m. The watch appeared broken, and Ashanique had carefully drawn a crude smiley face beside it. Janice had no idea what any of it meant, but she had no doubt about what she'd have to do next.

On the couch in front of the flickering TV, Janice started the stopwatch and then, laying it down on the seat, she reached under the couch to pull

8

out a secondhand laptop from its hiding place. Her hands shook as she opened the laptop. To counter the shaking, she balled her fingers into fists and closed her eyes. Then she gave herself to the count of ten to calm down.

You're in control for once, she thought. *This is you in control.*

Janice opened her eyes and turned the laptop on. It took forever to boot up and then even longer to connect to the neighbor's Wi-Fi. But not because it was a slow machine, it was because Janice had to mask her connection via a series of convoluted encryption programs.

When the stopwatch hit two minutes and thirty-six seconds, Janice opened a Tor browser. It was her access to the "dark web," the Internet's perennial boogeyman—its darkest alleyway, its deepest forest. As with most things, the truth was a lot less sensational: Tor was a tool and the dark web merely another side street. Albeit one largely populated by drug dealers, political dissidents, conspiracy theorists, and jaded degenerates.

Janice clicked her way to a website that consisted of nothing more than a black page with a list of dates and what appeared to be military operations. The dates went back to the mid-1980s and continued up until the early 2000s. The operations, things like "unconventional warfare" and "direct action," were marked as "carried out" and designated with qualifiers like "success" or "failure."

Moving the cursor to the left-hand corner of the site, Janice clicked on a tiny star. It opened a new window, a live chat room. She typed:

Biogenesis3: My daughter's Null. I need to come in.

As Janice waited for a response, she glanced at the stopwatch.
Another forty seconds had passed.
Come on. . . . Come on. . . .
Then, a digital chime sounded. Someone else had entered the chat room.

SEATTLE_UNDO: been forever, 51. how can we trust you?
BIOGENESIS3: You don't have to. Send someone.
SEATTLE_UNDO: will have to discuss this with dr. song
SEATTLE_UNDO: do you have the solution?
BIOGENESIS3: No. But did you forget who you're talking to? What I've sacrificed? We all moved here. Into the lion's den.

BIOGENESIS3: It's too early. Just now happened.
SEATTLE_UNDO: is your daughter stable?

Janice looked up from the laptop at her daughter's room. The door was shut, the apartment dark. Outside, a car screamed around a corner. Dogs barked. The apartment's thin walls did little to keep the sounds out, but they faded quickly.

Janice typed:

BIOGENESIS3: For now.
SEATTLE_UNDO: we will be in contact when we have asset there.
BIOGENESIS3: Hurry. You know what this means.
SEATTLE_UNDO: we know

Janice logged out.

The stopwatch hit four minutes.

She powered down the laptop and then slid it carefully back under the couch before she headed to the bathroom.

There, in the brutal glare of an unshielded lightbulb, Janice studied her face. Her brown skin was chapped, cheeks sallow, and her eyes deeply bloodshot. It was nearly five thirty in the morning, but the haggard look on her face wasn't from exhaustion or worry.

I'm getting worse, Janice thought. *Only a few years before Dr. Song's gonna have to sleep me like the others. Wonder what that's like, living in a dream like some fairy-tale princess until Prince Science comes along to fix you.*

For a moment, just between heartbeats, Janice saw a man reflected in the mirror. He was tall and white. His head was shaved and he wore a salt-and-pepper beard. Janice could see a scar on his forehead. His aquiline nose had been broken sometime in the past and it bent slightly to the right.

Janice closed her eyes and took a deep breath.

When she opened them, the man was gone.

Janice pulled out a medicine pack from the cabinet over the sink. Then she punched two yellow-and-white capsules stamped METROCHIME from their protective silver blisters and popped them into her mouth. She'd been taking these drugs for seventeen years and they went down easy. Drugs on board, she crouched and reached behind the toilet, and pulled out a plastic bag bound with duct tape to the underside of the toilet bowl. Inside was a Glock 17—9 mm. Janice ejected the magazine, counted the bullets, and then reloaded it, all in one smooth motion.

Nine seconds. You're getting rusty, girl.

Rusty. Worn. Built to degrade. Staring down at the gun in her hand, Janice considered what it would be like when the capsules stopped working. When Dr. Song gave her that permanent IV and put her adrift into her own mental abyss. Before she even knew what she was doing, Janice put the muzzle of the Glock in her mouth. It tasted like old silverware. She imagined the contents of her head spattering Pollock-style on the green tile of the bathroom floor. But the thought passed quickly. If nothing worked, if the voices got to be too loud, if Ashanique was lost or Dr. Song found, there would be time enough to end it quickly. Always disappointed in her pessimism, Janice forced herself to be positive: *You're acting a fool. Let the medicine work. Let it do its job,* Janice told herself. *Ashanique has the solution. You know in your heart of hearts that she does.*

Janice took the gun from her mouth and wiped her lips.

It's so early. You're just stressed and losing your cool.

Can't lose your cool. Can't ever lose it like that again.

Janice stood and tucked the Glock into the waistband of her sweats.

Looking back at her reflection, she flashed a toothy smile.

"Let's go, Fifty-One. You can do this."

4

THE LECTURE HALL was full.

Looking out over the faces of the two-hundred-plus undergrads scribbling in their notebooks, Matilda recognized only a handful. They were two months into the semester and most of the kids hadn't yet attended a lecture.

But they were certainly there for hers.

Of course they are, Matilda thought.

She knew the reality of it: the undergrads weren't there for her speaking skills or even to hear her hypotheses. Matilda wasn't like her mentor, Dr. Clark Liptak. She could never push away the lectern and wade up into the seats like a rock star. No, the coeds weren't crowding the seats to catch a glimpse of the department's hottest professor. Or be razzle-dazzled by academicspeak. They didn't want to hear her lecture on the atomic correlate of memory or synaptic plasticity. They were sitting in the half-light, sharpened pencils at the ready, recording apps open on their phones, because of the topic. It was the message that brought them, hardly the messenger.

"How many people in this room believe in life after death?"

Half the hands went up.

Matilda had done this lecture fifteen times in the preceding two years. And every time, the number of students who believed in the hereafter decreased.

Guess what, Maddie, another five lectures and it'll just be the homeschooled kids at the front of the hall with their hands up.

12

"Ghosts?"

Half the hands stayed raised. The biggest showing she'd seen.

Most of the undergrads, Matilda found, rejected their parents' clouds-and-sunshine heaven but went whole hog on ghosts. She chalked that up to pop culture. All the ghost-hunter reality shows, the now near ubiquity of Halloween. If she were a sociologist, she'd have called it trading one fable for another.

"How about reincarnation? The rebirth of the soul in a different body?"

Only six kids kept their hands up.

"Well, today we're going to talk about past lives," Matilda dived in. "About what that term means, why we want to believe in past-life regression therapy, and the pitfalls of hypnotism."

Matilda dimmed the lights and put up the first slide.

It was a droll *New Yorker* cartoon she'd inherited from her undergrad adviser, a badly cropped and overpixelated image of two men sitting at a desk across from each other. The bubble over one guy read, "I'm here to learn more about reincarnation." The other guy's bubble read, "Welcome back!"

The slide got a few chuckles.

"Belief in reincarnation is as old as civilization itself. Even though my esteemed colleagues in the physics department two doors over tell me that time doesn't actually exist, everything we do is dependent on it. We are creatures of time. Locked into seasons, driven by cycles. The clock rules everything we do, from the minute we're born to that final second before we die. As humans, we're always looking to rise above nature. Bust out of our earthly bonds. To break the stranglehold time has over us? That'd be the ultimate."

The room was silent, focused.

The undergrads weren't scribbling in their notepads. They were leaning forward, breathing slowed, fixated. Everyone—from the freshman with the broken leg to the sophomore with the pierced eyebrows—was tractor-beamed on slides, ratcheted in on Matilda's voice. Unlike Early American English Literature, where they had to dissect a poem by a recluse holed up by an algae-choked pond, this was the kind of lecture the students were happy their parents were paying for.

Another slide flashed on the screen:

New Age artwork of an oak tree spinning in outer space.

Cheeseball, Matilda thought, *but effective.*

"The idea that we're not the end of a line but a continuum is a universal one. Every human culture, throughout history, has built itself on the foundations of the cultures that came before it. Civilizations don't just spring up ex nihilo, out of nothing. They are carried forward. They are built with our grandfathers' and grandmothers' bricks. That's poetic, but you get what I mean. We are nothing without our pasts."

The next slide popped up.

In it, a 1950s-styled woman reclined on a couch. She had black hair cut short and her eyes were closed but she wasn't asleep.

She'd been hypnotized.

Matilda said, "This is Virginia, a housewife from just down the road. In the midfifties she began recalling the past life of a nineteenth-century Irish woman named Bridey Murphy. Her case was one of the very first modern past-life cases. It's a benchmark, one that came to define thousands and thousands of others. And, yes, she is hypnotized in this picture."

The slides continued to click by.

Photo after photo, face after face.

Normal people. Old and young, black and white. Matilda scrolled through their stories as she rattled off their names. "This woman recalled a past life as the pharaoh's daughter.... This man was the reincarnation of a decorated World War Two fighter pilot.... She was once a general in the War between the States.... All of them recalled the lives of people they could not possibly have been related to. You'll be surprised to learn they all shared one thing in common: a therapist. A therapist consciously, or more often unconsciously, caught up in his or her patient's stories."

There was an audible sigh from the audience.

Already, she was letting them down.

"But, of course, it's not just that the therapist is primed to find past lives in a subject. Turns out, people who most often claim to have past-life memories also believe in reincarnation. They want the memories. They want to feel as though there's something bigger than themselves, that they are more important that just a sales clerk or a lawyer."

She went on. Slide after slide, point after point. Matilda never lost sight of her goal: These undergrads weren't going to walk away well versed about the Bloxham tapes or with deep knowledge in neurolinguistic programming. But they would become better critical thinkers. Matilda's job, the real reason she was standing at the podium, was to shake these kids' foundations just enough to ensure they walked out of the room a little dazed. And she was feeling it; she was in the zone. On track to have her best lecture yet.

Until the door at the back of the hall opened and Clark slipped inside.

God damn it.

He stood against the wall, hands folded neatly behind his back. Matilda noticed he was wearing the suit she made the mistake of telling him he looked really sexy in. She knew it would never come off after that. Her mistake. He was even growing out his beard. She had to admit it looked good and added to his already distinguished, late-forties, in-his-academic-prime air, the same air that had attracted her to him eighteen months ago.

"That's why," Matilda continued, distracted, "we often find that the past lives people claim to recall are typically grandiose. No one wants to have the past-life memories of a Russian peasant or a Neolithic hunter. They want the memories of kings and queens. Of powerful people, respected people they would rather be like. Who would you rather have a conversation with? The ghost of Einstein or the sad specter of some failed businessman?"

"If it was real . . ."

Matilda looked up to see one of her sophomores, the boy from Wisconsin who stayed late after every class with reams of questions, the same one always looking to poke holes in her theories. He stood and finished.

". . . then what would that mean for your chemistry research? If there's evidence of some sort of afterlife, then maybe memory isn't a biochemical thing. Maybe it's a spiritual thing and that's why people remember past lives? You know, like people have kind of been saying for thousands and thousands of years."

"I, uh . . ."

And, just like that, Matilda was thrown off.

It actually wasn't because of the Wisconsin kid's question (really, it was more of an emotivistic statement) or his overconfident tone. It was the memory that flashed into Matilda's head. The memory she never realized she'd had.

For a split second, Matilda saw her mother, Lucy, in the kitchen putting the finishing touches on a BLT stacked high with bacon and heirloom tomatoes. Matilda had been in high school at the time, and Lucy was showing the first signs of the neural degeneration that would slowly take her mind apart, brain cell by brain cell. In her memory, Matilda sat on the kitchen counter, putting the utensils Lucy handed her into the sink. Lucy laughed to herself and said, staring down at the sandwiches, "What if one day scientists prove that being spiritual is just another mental illness? What if they make a pill to treat it?" The comment came out of the blue. Lucy hadn't attended church since she was six and lived in Iowa. Matilda asked her mother what she meant, but Lucy just shook her head and suggested she was just getting old.

She was forty-three at the time.

Flashing back to the classroom, Matilda stared out at her students but didn't see them. She pulled a Post-it Note from her purse and scribbled a few shorthand notes about the memory. As she did this, she distractedly tried to wrap up the lecture.

"I think that question is . . . not worth answering actually. It presupposes that this is a . . . Okay, listen, I have sat in on hundreds of past-life regression-therapy sessions. I've personally done in-depth interviews with seventy-five people who claimed to have vivid memories from a past life. I have yet to see a convincing case. Regardless of mechanism, be it spiritual or chemical, the fact remains that our memories end when we end."

Tucking the Post-it into her purse, Matilda looked up to see Clark wink.

5

AN ELECTRONIC CHIME broke the tension.

The students were up and out of their seats and choking the stairs before Matilda had time to mention that the next week they'd be discussing operant conditioning. She pulled her hair back in a ponytail. Two weeks ago she'd dyed it blue. The class got a kick out of seeing it, and her graduate students seemed to think it spoke to her rebellious nature inside the institution. They considered Matilda *that* professor, the one willing to rock the boat and contemplate outsider ideas. Well, they'd find out soon enough that when it came to science, she was as much a traditionalist as the others. She just did things with a little more color, a little more verve. As Matilda gathered up her papers, Clark walked over and pecked her cheek.

That's new, she thought. *He must want something.*

"So how was it? Tell me honestly."

"Good," Clark said. "You have their attention, that's clear."

"I threw in the Barnum-effect thing last minute. Not sure it added much."

"It didn't."

Barely hiding her frustration, Matilda stuffed her papers in her messenger bag. They went in wonky and got caught in the zipper, but she didn't have the patience to sort them out. Clark got the hint. Thinking he knew exactly what to say, he leaned in and whispered, "You look stunning."

"That's great, but I'm actually going for professional."

"You're young. Professional is dull. Come on."

Clark put his hand on Matilda's shoulder, gave it a soft squeeze.

They'd been having sex for ten months. It began the way these sorts of affairs always did, with naïveté traipsing into the darkened woods of hedo-

17

nism. She'd caught Clark's eye during one of his infamous subjective validation lectures, infamous because he'd always end them with a demonstration. A sacrifice. He'd pull some poor grad student up onstage and break them down—tear apart all their core beliefs; leave them psychologically shrunken and traumatized. The audience ate it up. And after the psychological bruising had worn off, the victim always became a true believer. *Always.* A week after the lecture, Matilda stopped by Clark's office in a skirt shorter than she normally wore, with her hair up, and asked him about a 1998 paper he'd written on the Dark Triad of Machiavellianism, psychopathy, and narcissism. His eyes wandered. She was there to impress.

It worked.

Forty weeks, two weekend getaways, and six crying jags later, here they were—the most open secret in the psychology department. The sex was good, but his lies were terrible. It amazed her that a man so practiced in how the mind works wouldn't be able to juggle his own deceptions.

Matilda hated being the other woman. Hated the hot swell of shame she felt when she caught a glance of the family photos on Clark's desk. No matter how lifeless, how unloving his marriage was—and he insisted it was "at the organ-donation stage"—the idea that she was breaking something, even something already broken, was unsettling. Still, she'd never felt so *enjoyed* before. For Clark, this affair with Matilda was like the first full meal he'd had in years.

As they stepped out of the lecture hall, into the teeming hallways, Clark scratched at his chin. It was a familiar nervous affect, one of his blatant tells for when he shifted into passive-aggressive mode—his worst mode.

"So I got a call yesterday I'd love for you to check out this afternoon."

"Let me guess, a parent calling about their daughter?"

Clark said, "Yes, but not what you're thinking."

"I'm thinking she experimented with 'shrooms, had a nasty trip, wound up in a psych hold over at U.C. Med and her father is threatening to sue. Dean Gilovich wants you to mediate, do some of your patented angry-parent whispering?"

Clark laughed and touched her hip. "That's my sexy hate machine."

Matilda pushed his hand away. "Yuck. You know I hate that."

Clark apologized as they stopped at an elevator bank.

"Look," he said, his voice a lower register to not-so-subtly communicate his displeasure at being reprimanded, "this is outside the U. It's a favor for a friend. And, yes, by friend I mean someone who's given very liberally to the campus and our program in particular."

"So another nutjob?"

"I thought you were going for professional? The girl was in a car accident. She wasn't drunk or anything. She's a good kid. Got knocked out, concussion, the works, and woke up recalling her time aboard a merchant marine vessel at Incheon."

"You know traumatic brain injury stuff is unreliable. I can't do anything with a case like that, Clark."

"Please. Just see her. For me."

"I still haven't gotten through last quarter's Gardner essays. There's that proposal for the APA, and Teresa and I are still crunching numbers on the assisted-living study. Todd and I are heading over to the Marcy-Lansing Apartments this afternoon, and that always leads to . . . Anyway, just feels like every free hour between here and March is well accounted for."

The empty elevator arrived and as they stepped inside, Clark pulled Matilda close and crushed his lips against hers. She melted, even with his newly emboldened whiskers tickling her cheek, and his left hand clenching her ass.

"First off," Clark said, as he let her go and adjusted his tie, "it'd be doing me a huge favor. I have back-to-back meetings all week. Then there's the whole Aspen deal on Saturday, and I was hoping to get a few runs in. Second, and most important—"

"So it should have been first."

"I was building the dramatic tension. Anyway, despite your pooh-poohing, it's right up your alley. You need more structural stuff in your work. Turn that chemist side of your brain loose on it. How about tomorrow morning we meet up early? I'll bring coffee and doughnuts, we'll meet at your office, and I'll tell you everything there is to know. Then you can decide. But I think you'll love it."

The elevator stopped. The doors slid open.

Matilda stepped out, but Clark stayed inside, hands holding the doors open.

"You know," he said, "you shouldn't be too harsh on the spiritual kids. I've often found that, at the end of the day, we all end up hoping for something more than just this life. If I were to die tomorrow, you bet I'd be spending my last conscious moments praying there's a heaven. Or thinking of your great ass..."

With that, Clark let the elevator doors close.

The last image Matilda had of him was a blurry grin.

6

MATILDA'S OFFICE WAS a shrine to memory.

Though it was small—exactly ten feet by fifteen feet, and she had measured it several times—it was packed tight with all her thoughts. There was a heavy oak bookcase stuffed with psychology volumes, notebooks, and bound journals. Most of which she'd inherited from her predecessor: a tenured professor who shared a love for the smell of old books. Even though Matilda hadn't thumbed through half the hand-me-downs, she frequently sat in her office and gazed at them. Bookshelves were little shrines to knowledge, her mother used to say. She assumed with some certainty that the bibliophile in her was a direct product of her genetics. The one and only fact Matilda truly knew about her father—or "drive-by sperm donor," as Lucy called him—was that he collected first-edition, signed hardcover books.

But it wasn't the books that people who stopped by Matilda's office noticed first. It was the walls. Or, rather, what was covering them: Post-it Notes, file cards, and scraps of paper. They made the walls look like they were growing multicolored bark. And all that paper went at least half an inch deep. It was so thick and ubiquitous that Matilda worried about the structural integrity of the room.

Cutting a chunk out of one of the walls and viewing it sideways would provide a cross section of Matilda's mind. She'd been in the office two years and each "stratum" of paper would reveal a different aspect of her work: from her first proposals to lab setup to experiments and data collection. The very bottom layer would reflect her initial thoughts on the chemistry of memory. That was Matilda's true passion—the core of her drive. She wanted to find the neurochemical pathway that explained how memories were made and stored.

And she would not stop adding to the walls until she did.

Despite the appearance of the office, Matilda was not messy. She was a fastidious thinker. Her mother used to say she "never met an idea she couldn't categorize" and almost threatened to have the saying (which she'd coined) crocheted and framed.

Matilda tacked the note about Lucy up on the wall, just over her desk.

Then, after shaking off her frustration with Clark, she let out a deep sigh and settled down into her well-worn desk chair. Mentally running through the rest of her day, Matilda let her eyes rove across the walls before settling on an organic molecule drawn on lined paper. It was glutamate, the most common neurotransmitter in the brain. The shape of it resembled a fish. One of Matilda's juniors drew it for her a few months earlier. He was very nervous when he handed it to her. A big chemistry nerd with a crush on his prof, it was the only sort of love letter he could craft. And, of course, she adored it. Glutamate. Matilda liked how the word had a distinctive onomatopoeic resonance. To her, it sounded like someone chewing gum. *Glutamate—glu*, Latin for "sticky stuff" and *ate*, meaning "from a salty acid."

As Matilda turned the word over in her mind, she remembered why she found it so curious: her grandfather, Norbert, used to mumble something similar.

"*Gloyb yo gloyb nit*," he'd say. "*Gloyb yo gloyb nit.*"

And just like that, Matilda was six again and climbing the narrow stairs in her mom's old house to the second floor. In her memories, it was always autumn. The light was diffuse and the stairs creaked.

Grandpa Norbert's room was at the end of the hall, just past the tiny green-tiled bathroom. Matilda's mother's father had moved into their house when she was three. All she knew about Grandpa Norbert was that he was from a faraway country where they didn't speak English, his wife had died in a war, he didn't seem to like children, and he only ever came out of the bedroom to use the bathroom and stare down at her like a shadowy statue from the top of the stairs.

Matilda was thankful her bedroom was on the ground floor beside her mother's. Unlike most of her school friends, she was not scared of the basement—it was the upper story that hid a potential monster.

In Matilda's memory, Grandpa Norbert's door was open a crack and she was desperate to peek inside—she had only ever seen inside Grandpa Norbert's room once, just a few weeks earlier, when her mom was sick and asked her to bring him some hot tea. Then, Grandpa Norbert had been in bed, a lump snoring beneath rough blankets. Matilda placed the tea on his dresser, and when he coughed, clearing his throat like something at the Chicago zoo's big-cat exhibit, she ran. A timid child, Matilda had recently learned to be scared of three new things—thunderstorms, spiders, and jaguars. Jaguars were the worst. Her school friend, Annie, had terrified her at recess with a story about a jaguar dragging a Brazilian woman from her bed. "And," Annie delighted in saying, "they only ever found her feet."

Matilda approached her grandfather's door very slowly, cautiously, and peeked inside. She saw his bed, the rough blankets in a scrambled pile, the dresser, and, most disturbing, his worn and muddy leather shoes. Just as she was opening the door farther to look at the closet, Matilda heard the toilet flush in the green-tiled bathroom.

Her heart nearly exploding, Matilda raced into Grandpa Norbert's room and slipped underneath his twin bed. It wasn't until she'd pushed herself up against the wall, her clothes covered in dust and cobwebs, that she realized the mistake she'd made—she should have turned and run downstairs. If she had been fast, and she was a very fast runner, she could have passed him in a blur.

Now she was trapped.

Matilda watched through a narrow rectangle of light under the bed as Grandpa Norbert shuffled into the room. She could see his bare feet—toenails thick and yellowed by fungus, and veins snaking around his joints like thick worms.

Grandpa Norbert mumbled to himself, "... *momzer ... barchot shonnen ... zolst lingen in drerdi ... veshat laphu na ushi ...*"

Matilda heard him go through a paper bag. She cringed when he dropped a black skeleton key on the floor. It was one he wore on a string around his neck. Mom told Matilda it was for the closet in the bedroom. She wondered what he kept in there—the bones of children? A jaguar he'd smuggled from the zoo? Possibly.

"*A brokh tsu dayn lebn ... hoch mast osten ...*"

Matilda held her breath as Grandpa Norbert's gnarled hand appeared and snatched up the fallen key. She could see numbers tattooed on his forearm in faded ink. They reminded her of spider's legs. Matilda exhaled slowly as he crossed the room and unlocked the closet door. She had to remain calm.

From her vantage point, Matilda could see the closet was filled with canned food. Stacked neatly, can upon can, it created an aluminum wall that reached up to the ceiling. There was no obvious organization to the cans. Peas sat on clams; yams were tucked in beside peaches. As he stood there looking in, Grandpa Norbert spun several of the cans around to better see their labels. He continued to mumble. Matilda was fascinated by the cans. Mrs. Cartwright, her first-grade teacher, once told her that she should bring an extra snack to school, one to put in her desk for "a rainy day." Matilda wondered what rainy day Grandpa Norbert was waiting for.

Maybe it will be a flood.

"Hundert hayzer zol er hobn, in yeder hoyz a hundert tsimern, in yeder tsimer tsvonsik . . . pul shecken . . . vot ma'ya vi'zitka . . ."

Mom told Matilda that Grandpa Norbert's talk was his own language. It wasn't what he used to speak where he came from; it wasn't what his wife who died spoke. Mom said it was mostly Yiddish, some Russian, and a lot of it made up.

Regardless of what it was, it sounded scary.

Grandpa Norbert closed the closet door, and Matilda listened intently as he locked it. Then, she heard the bedroom door open and then close. She moved to get a better angle but couldn't see Grandpa Norbert's feet anymore. Carefully, sliding on her belly like a seal across the Antarctic ice pack, Matilda emerged.

And Grandpa Norbert was standing right there, just off to the side of the bed by the dresser. He had tricked her.

Matilda wanted to scream but couldn't.

Grandpa Norbert's face reminded Matilda of a wild animal. The kind that rampaged through a forest, howling as it ran. His eyebrows were bushy and unkempt explosions of hair that overhung deep-set glacier-blue eyes; his lips were hidden behind his scraggly beard.

"Hit zikh, du host zikh shoyn eyn mol opgebrit!"

"I'm s-s-sorry, Grandpa," Matilda stuttered, backing away. "I didn't mean—"

Matilda turned to run, but Grandpa Norbert grabbed her and placed something in her hand. When she finally wrenched herself free, she ran downstairs and didn't stop running until she was safely outside in the small backyard, beneath the sweeping "hair" of the dying weeping willow. After she'd caught her breath, she opened her hand to see what Grandpa Norbert had placed there.

It was a black, polished river stone.

She cried looking at the stone and cried when Lucy came home and made her go up to Grandpa Norbert and apologize. Grandpa Norbert was taken to the hospital for an ulcer two weeks later and died twenty-four hours after he was admitted. Matilda never learned where the stone had come from or why her grandfather had given it to her. But she kept it on her desk throughout school. She knew it was buried somewhere beneath her papers on her desk. She leaned forward to look for it when she was startled by a knock at the door.

Todd Garcia-Araez stuck his head in.

He was a thirty-year-old assistant professor of psychology from Baltimore. Tall and chubby, with a mop of red hair, Todd loved the clinical aspects of his job. And, unlike Matilda, he found endless satisfaction in promoting talk therapy. Real talk therapy, as he liked to call it. Old-school. Todd even had his office decked out with a leather armchair. The type nineteenth-century therapists had in their book-lined bureaus. And plants. He had a lot of plants.

"You ready to go?"

"Yeah," Matilda said. "Just, uh, just give me a minute."

"Okay. I'll be outside, warming up the ride."

Todd closed the door.

Matilda dug around her desk for the stone. She found it under a stack of newsletters. She touched it to her cheek.

It was warm.

7

CLOUDS THREATENING RAIN hung low as Todd's Volvo station wagon pulled into the parking lot outside the Marcy-Lansing Apartments.

He killed the engine and grabbed a file folder from his backpack. Flipping through the pages, he read off the visits for the day.

"Following up on the self-harm thoughts that Tanisha told us about. There's Shana and Derrick too. We really need to talk to their aunt about some of the abuse stuff. Would be good to fill them in."

"We ever hear back from Chicago welfare on Jamir?" Matilda asked.

Todd looked over his notes. "Still waiting."

Matilda turned to the apartment building. Its gray hulking bulk sat low in the late-afternoon shadows. She scanned the floors, eyes falling over boarded-up windows and the telltale charcoal marks where past fires had licked the bricks. The apartments were built in the mid-1970s. Perhaps back then its builders saw great things ahead like ambitious futures for the residents they hoped to pull out of poverty. As well-intentioned as they were, they were also very wrong. For the vast majority of the two thousand people who called Marcy-Lansing home, it was yet another ghetto to escape. Only this one went up instead of out.

"You ready?" Todd asked.

"Yeah, let's go do some good."

As they made their way inside, Matilda and Todd passed a huddle of young boys milling around the entrance. Tight denim, black ball caps, and

26

puffy coats, the boys—none of them older than fifteen—smoked cigarettes, cursed, and laughed loudly. The tallest of them, with a knit cap and freckles, stepped in front of Todd.

"Where you think you're going, bro?"

"We're from the university," Todd said. "We're here to visit a few people."

"What people?"

"*What people?*" one of the boys parroted. "You all doctors or something?"

"Yes," Matilda said.

The boy with the cap looked her up and down, "Maybe I need a physical...."

A few of the other boys laughed, gave high fives. Cap stepped up to Matilda. His head cocked to the side, he stared at her hard. His smiled revealed the glint of his gold fronts. He was close enough that Matilda could smell the menthol cigarette on his breath. Instead of shying away, she stepped even closer, inches from his face.

"What's your name?"

"Huh?" Cap asked.

"What's your name?" Matilda said again.

"Shit." Cap stepped back, looked over to his friends to read their faces. They were transfixed. No help. "Why you want to know?"

"I think I know you," Matilda said, reading the microexpressions dancing across Cap's face. He was compressing his lips, squinting. Very nervous.

"Your mom's Raenice, right?" Matilda continued.

"Yeah. So..."

"So...She asked me to talk to you. Said she's worried about you. You're having trouble sleeping. You should talk to me about it. I can help."

Cap blinked rapidly as he ground his teeth.

Tight as a coil, tension hung in the air.

"Ha," Cap laughed, breaking the moment. "I'm just playing with you, lady."

He stepped aside and let Todd and Matilda pass.

Matilda nodded to him. "Seriously, if you need help, I'm here."

"Nah, I'm good. I'm real good."

As Cap and his friends laughed and tossed their cigarettes, Todd and Matilda traversed the small apartment lobby to a graffiti-festooned elevator.

"You handled that well," Todd said after the elevator doors had closed.

"They're just kids."

"I've seen 'just kids' beat a man unconscious for his shoes."

At the ninth floor, they navigated a narrow series of hallways lined with doors to apartments. Most had new locks installed, and there were trash bags sitting outside half the doors. As they walked, Matilda looked over at a box of old toys by one door. In and among the ratty stuffed animals and broken electronics were Barbie dolls that had been colored with markers to make their skin black.

Matilda and Todd stopped at a door near the end of the hall.

They caught their breath before knocking. The day's first case would be a rough one. Behind the door was a thirteen-year-old heroin addict. The kid had tried to stay clean, but his father was in jail and his mother's boyfriend routinely assaulted him. During their first meeting, the boy told Todd and Matilda he had no future. That no one listened to his worries, his fears, or his dreams. Matilda noted dozens of cuts on his arms from where he'd dragged a naked razor blade across his flesh.

"Ready?"

"Let's go."

8

GABI DE LA CONDI was hearing the voices again.

They told her that this, *this* was it.

This is what you've spent the last eighteen years waiting for.

Gabi zigzagged through the crowds of shoppers; their clothes were still beaded with raindrops and the smell of their perfume and cologne and hair spray and breath mints was nearly overwhelming. Gabi had to stop by the food court to dry-heave into a trash can. As she caught her breath and wiped saliva from her lips, she noticed a boy, no older than eight, staring at her over his lunch. A little boy with freckled cheeks and olive-pit-colored eyes, just like . . .

"Mommy," the boy said, his mouth half filled with pizza crust, "what's wrong with that woman over there?"

The boy's mother, a pretty woman who looked existentially exhausted, refocused her son on his food. "It's not nice to stare," she said.

Gabi didn't want to think about the freckled boy she knew. The one they'd damaged so badly he had to be kept in a cage like an animal. Gabi closed her eyes and pushed away the worst of the memories.

Focus, the voices told her. *Today is the day.*

Riding the escalator to the second floor, Gabi noticed the big toenail on her left foot—thick, curved with fungus—was sticking out through the unstitched leather of her falling-apart flats. The voices didn't even need to tell her she was losing it.

She already knew.

But if there was anything she prided herself on, it was being tough. Tough in the way Father Broderick at the All Saints orphanage taught her to be. She knew the dictums: you never fall, you roll; you don't take a punch, you slide into it; illness is only an opportunity to improve your immune system; loss makes for a cleaner house. *Being so desperately poor that your shoes are falling apart on your feet?* she asked herself. *Yes, that's true commitment. This is because I am the cause. I am the reason we're still alive. The reason we've gotten to this moment.*

And, yeah, she had had to sacrifice her dignity. Numerous times. She had to put up with an unbearable amount of scorn and hate and shit. She knew that anyone in her situation would go a little crazy. It had been fifteen years. *Or was it seventeen?* Gabi couldn't recall the last time she'd slept in a bed with clean sheets.

Upstairs, Gabi found her mark examining suits at Macy's.

He was a businessman with unnaturally tan skin and marbled hair that was crisp with gel. Judging by the coat haphazardly slung over his shoulder and the fact that one of his loafers was untied, Gabi knew he'd be easy. And so she moved quickly, weaving through a crowd of loud teenagers, before bumping into the businessman hard enough to knock him off-balance. He turned to her, ready to shout, but choked on any ounce of ambitious rage he might have had when he saw her face. The disheveled, filthy look got them every time.

"I'm sorry," the businessman said. "You okay?"

He didn't hang around for an answer. Instead, pulling his coat tight to his chest, he melted into the passing crowd. Gabi made her way toward the dressing room with the businessman's cell phone, a Samsung with a large touch screen that had clearly been shattered and replaced several times. But that didn't matter, at least not for what Gabi intended.

As she walked, Gabi took the phone apart with a sure hand and near-military efficiency. She dropped the stuff she'd sell later in the left pocket of her coat; the rest—the GSM antenna, the Wi-Fi adapter—she slid into her right. Impressively, the cell was cannibalized within fifty-two seconds. Gabi would make a few bucks from the parts but it was the SIM card she was after, the access to a working line.

Stepping into a dressing room, Gabi locked the door and settled onto the tiny stool tucked into one corner of the room. The mirror was streaked, and Gabi avoided catching a glimpse of herself in it. She didn't want to know how matted her hair was, how dusky her skin had gotten. In the immediate silence, without the crush of passing voices and the atmospherics of air recycled through endless vents, the voices came back, chanting their simple chorus:

Look, Gabi, look at what you've become.

Gabi pushed the voices away and pulled an indented MetroChime capsule from her pocket. She chewed it between her left molars, the good ones, before she got to work on the Raspberry Pi phone in her purse. It was a smart design, a hand-built smartphone with a touch screen. A little clumsy, sure, some of the soldering was rather ugly, and the 3-D–printed case she'd made at the library didn't exactly snap on tight. But it worked, and it was untraceable. Gabi slid the stolen SIM card into her DIY phone. It took a second to come online. As it did, the voices hummed in the background. Gabi pushed her big toe back into her shoe and considered shoplifting a pair of sneakers on her way out. Seconds later, the phone was ready, the SIM card active; Gabi had only one phone number memorized. She dialed. Two rings later, a woman's voice answered, distorted by disguising tech.

"Yes."

"It's Gabi. You got the message about Fifty-One?"

"Yes."

Gabi cleared her throat and pulled up her coat sleeve. She had three watches on her left wrist. All displayed the exact same time. She tracked closely as the seconds clicked by. "They need a route to Dr. Song," she said into her cell. "Contact Dirk. He can send Childers. You do know what this means, right? This is it. This is what we've been waiting so long for."

"Of course."

"Excellent."

Hearing someone moving down the narrow aisle just outside her dressing room door, Gabi ended the call. Then she leaned down to peek through the two-foot gap at the bottom of the door. Seeing nothing, Gabi took the Raspberry Pi phone apart. She slammed the screen against the wall and cracked the SIM card in half.

Done, the voices said. *Told you this was the day.*

And that was exactly when a head appeared in the gap under the door.

A man's head, bald with no facial hair. Not even eyebrows. Gabi recoiled, her adrenaline kicking in before the terror did. The baby-faced man held a gun in his right hand and aimed it at Gabi's chest as he smoothly pulled himself through the gap under the door. As her hands started to shake, Gabi was struck by how easily the man could torque and stretch himself like a gymnast. She was dumbstruck even further to see how tall and thin he was when, fully inside the changing room, he towered over her. The man wore a hoodie, athletic sweatpants with reflective stripes, and latex gloves.

This is the devil, the voices in her head said, *come to get you, Gabi.*

"Where is Fifty-One?" the man asked.

Gabi could hardly speak. Her throat was so dry, collapsing in on itself.

"Where is Fifty-One?"

"I don't— I don't know."

Gun still leveled on Gabi's chest, the man reached into his jacket pocket and pulled out a syringe filled with clear liquid. As the man bit the safety lid off the top of the syringe, the voices chanted, *He's the devil. . . . Devil come to get you. . . .*

"Where is Fifty-One?" the man asked again.

"I'm telling you the truth—I don't know," Gabi said. "I haven't seen her in decades. You have to believe me."

He'll take your heart; he'll take your eyes. . . .

The man moved quicker than Gabi expected. In the space between heartbeats, he'd shoved the gun into her gut, pressed his left forearm up against her throat, and forced her back against the mirror. With her throat pinched, Gabi felt faint. She couldn't push the man off. Her hands scrambled across his hoodie, her nails searching desperately for any exposed skin they could sink into.

"You're going to have a heart attack," the man said. "It'll be caused by a coronary spasm. One of the arteries that feeds blood into your heart is going to clamp down. Real tight. It will be painful, feel like someone just hit you in the chest with a sledgehammer. But you'll die within seconds."

He'll take your heart. . . .

Gabi gasped. Her vision blurred and the world spun around her. For the first time in fifteen years, she was happy to hear the voices. *You're going to be okay*, they told her as they repeated Father Broderick's favorite saying: *Every end is a new beginning.* As her body went limp, the man took the syringe and stuck the needle into the soft, red corner of Gabi's right eye. Then he calmly depressed the plunger. The clear liquid burned as it went in. Gabi's sinuses were suddenly on fire and, even as weak as she was at that moment, she bucked and kicked.

"Good," the man said. "Fight it. Fight it."

Gabi fought. And that was when the real pain hit. Her body wracked by a tsunami of ragged nerves, the wave of agony washed over her and stole the very breath from her lungs. Gabi's eyes went wide as she spasmed once and heard her incisors break as her jaw clamped down too tight.

The man let Gabi fall to the floor of the dressing room.

Lying there, a final spasm shook her limp body before she was still.

In her last milliseconds of existence, the voices, the ones that had taunted and cajoled her for half her life, suddenly fell silent. Gabi's oxygen-starved brain did the only thing it could think to do—it scrolled back through images, searching desperately for the few moments when she was happy.

It found sunshine . . . a beach . . . a welcome hand . . .

• • •

Rade cracked his neck, peeled off his latex gloves, and then emerged from the dressing room, closing the door carefully behind him.

On his way out of the Macy's, he folded his gloves carefully before sliding them in a pocket of his hoodie.

Five minutes later, Rade was hot-wiring a black SUV in the mall's parking garage when a Latino man with a ponytail noticed him.

"Yo! The fuck you doing?"

Rade sat up and looked the man over.

"That your car, man? Don't look like your car."

As Rade stepped out of the car, Ponytail stepped closer to look into the SUV's interior. Rade's tools were laid out on the front passenger seat in a roll-up leather case. It was the kind of kit a professional thief carried around.

"Oh, hell no. Can't let you do that—"

But Ponytail stopped short when Rade dragged a box cutter blade across the softest part of his throat, just above the Adam's apple. The wound was barely visible, like a long pink paper cut, before the blood welled up, bubbling out. It happened so fast, Ponytail had no final movements, no noise: just wide-eyed, horrible shock.

Ponytail crumpled at Rade's feet.

Pocketing the box cutter, Rade got on his cell and, as his call rang through, reached into the SUV to gather his tools. A deep-voiced man answered.

"Talk to me."

"Northgate Mall. I need all camera feeds wiped from four fifteen to five. And I've got collateral disposal on the fifth floor of the parking garage."

"What about Fifty-One?"

Rade crossed the garage to another SUV.

"Twenty-Two wouldn't talk. But she did make a call on a burner cell. Home construction. Must have snagged a SIM off someone, possibly someone in the mall. We need to look at police reports, someone calling in about a lost cell. We trace the calls made with its SIM card and we move forward."

"Dr. Sykes asks that you be more careful, Rade."

"More careful how?"

"You're not a Viking. This isn't a slaughterhouse. Make them cleaner. We can't have questions. You already know all this."

Rade hung up the cell and slid it into his pants. Then he pulled a code grabber from a hoodie pocket to read the SUV's remote keyless entry signal. It took two tries but the doors to the SUV unlocked. Rade climbed inside, unrolled his hot-wiring kit, and got to work.

Fifty-six seconds later, the SUV's engine roared to life.

9

MATILDA AND TODD were leaving a patient's room on the seventh floor when an older lady with braided hair pulled Matilda aside.

"Can I talk to you, please?"

The woman's eyes darted. She clearly had a secret.

"Of course."

As Matilda followed the woman down the hall, toward the stairs, she turned and waved back to Todd. "I'll meet you down at the car in just a few minutes," she told him. He looked confused. "It's fine," Matilda assured Todd.

The woman brought Matilda into her neat apartment at the end of the hall, beside the elevator. It was homey, with a couch covered in plastic, dozens of framed photos of family, and several oil paintings of Jesus. There were potted plants in every corner, mostly wandering Jews and ferns.

"It's about Janice's daughter," the woman said, "something's wrong with her."

"Okay."

"My neighbor, Janice. Her girl, Ashanique, she just ain't right lately."

"Can I ask your name?"

The woman glanced back over her shoulder, at the door to her apartment. It was shut, though she was still clearly nervous, obviously trying to tell Matilda something she shouldn't be. "I'm Carol. But that ain't important. It's Ashanique. You need to just talk to her, see if she's all right. Last few days, she seems off. Different."

35

"How old is Ashanique?"

"Eleven. Her momma has me watch her after school when she's at work. She's very protective, Janice. Ashanique's her only child, and even though she's tough with the girl, she'd do anything for her. That's what's got me concerned, you know? Ashanique ain't acting herself, and when I brought it up to Janice . . . Shit, well, she basically told me to just mind my own business. But I know Ashanique. I know something's wrong."

"Is Ashanique home now?"

"She's upstairs," Carol said. "I can bring you up there."

As they made their way up the stairs, Carol told Matilda about the family.

"Never seen the father, but Janice is a good mother. Don't get me wrong, this place, it takes discipline to raise a child right. You got to have your hand on them, if you know what I mean. Temptation to do the wrong thing every day. A lot of bad people. A lot of desperate ones too, Lord. . . ."

Matilda followed Carol onto the ninth floor, where they stopped at a door marked 915. Carol said, "She ain't gonna want to talk to you. Not at first."

"I understand."

"I wouldn't bring you up here if I didn't think it was the best thing for her."

Carol pulled a key from her purse and unlocked the door. Stepping inside, she called for Ashanique. The apartment was stripped down to the bare essentials. Secondhand furniture and a few standing lamps. A window fan spun lazily.

Matilda's cell buzzed in her coat pocket. It was Todd checking in. He sent a text telling her that he didn't like the idea of her being alone in the building. He wanted to know where she was and if he should come back in.

Ten minutes, she replied. I'LL BE OUT SOON.

Todd sent the quizzical-faced emoji.

Followed by: FIVE MINUTES.

Carol knocked on a bedroom door at the back of the apartment. It was only when she saw the door that Matilda realized there was no art on the walls of this apartment. No family photos, no color. The door to Ashanique's room looked as though it belonged to a different family. Its surface was a riot of drawings. Pencil, pen, finger paint, Wite-Out, charcoal—the little girl who lived behind it had used everything she could think of to create a complex mural of half-glimpsed shapes and strange figures. It was like viewing a car crash through a thick veil of fog.

"She done this just the other day," Carol said, reading the surprise on Matilda's face. "Stayed up all night to make it."

Looking closely at the drawings, Matilda could make out soldiers, hills, trees, and a horse; its blackened body merged with the ruins of a building. It was clearly drawn with a child's hand but there was a macabre power in the simplicity of the sketches. Something akin to a middle school *Guernica*.

"This is why I came to you," Carol told Matilda. "She needs help bad."

The bedroom door opened, and Matilda stood to see Ashanique.

She was struck by the girl's gaze: like looking into the eyes of a much older person. Matilda had never believed the old aphorism about the eyes being the windows to the soul. It smacked of New Age cheesiness. But with Ashanique's eyes, Matilda felt as though she were looking into the eyes of her grandfather. They were deep, wild pools of experience. Unbroken. Vivid.

"Ashanique? My name is Matilda. Is it okay if we talk?"

"Ashanique's just one of me," the girl said.

10

ASHANIQUE'S ROOM LOOKED just like her door.

Every surface crawled with crayon, pencil, and paint. Every inch of the room was ornamented by drawings of war and violence. Soldiers marched across the walls. Explosions sent spirals of black smoke into churning blue-gray clouds. There was blood and there was fire and there was rain. Matilda could not believe the varying styles of the artwork—from crimpled, highly detailed illustrations (she could make out the broken teeth in the mouth of a screaming soldier) to loose, abstract swathes of panicked, chaotic forms that suggested paroxysms of rage.

Matilda had never seen anything quite like it.

"Want to sit down?" Ashanique asked.

The girl dragged a school chair with an attached tray from the corner and set it beside her bed. Matilda sat. Despite the mania covering the walls, the bed was neatly, almost expertly, made. Perfect corners. The kind you could bounce a quarter off of. On one of the pillows was a drawing of a building, like a military base, ensconced in a snowy pine forest. Matilda smiled at Ashanique.

"My name is Matilda Deacon. I'm a professor and social worker."

"I've seen you here before," Ashanique said.

"Is your mother around?"

"No."

"And who watches over you when she's gone?"

"I'm old enough to take care of myself. But if she has to, Mrs. Carol looks after me."

Law required Matilda to talk to the parent, with the exception of an emergency situation. If she were to encounter a child in immediate danger, she could intervene. Clearly, Ashanique didn't appear to be in any physical distress, but Matilda was desperate to understand what was going on. It wasn't such a leap, in her mind, to assume that the girl's psychological condition was deteriorating.

It was bending the rules, but she technically could classify it as an emergency.

"Okay," Matilda continued. "That's good. My work involves talking to children. Children who might be having troubles, things that they worry about, things that keep them awake at night. Is there anything worrying you, Ashanique? Mrs. Carol says she's concerned you might not be feeling well."

Matilda glanced over to where Carol had been standing, but she was no longer in the room.

"I'm feeling fine," Ashanique said. "At first, I thought I might be sick. I was scared when it started. But now, now I think I understand what's happening."

Matilda leaned forward. "What is happening?"

"The people inside me. They aren't silent anymore."

"What people, Ashanique?"

"There are so many." The girl chuckled. "George was first. I didn't know why, but I think now it's because he died in shock. He didn't know what hit him. That made a big difference. The others, they've been coming back slower. At first they're just these echoes, but the more they show me, the stronger they get."

"Have you told your mother about these voices?"

Ashanique nodded. "She tells me not to worry about them."

"But are you worried?"

"No. Not anymore."

"Do you mind if I make some notes?"

Ashanique shrugged as Matilda reached into her purse and pulled out a notepad and pen. She scribbled a few key words—*auditory hallucinations? endaural phenomenon?*—to guide her thoughts later. She didn't want to admit that the case was unusual. In her experience, every past-life-regression case initially felt like it could be something she'd never seen before. But then, after a few minutes of directed talk, they always fell into established categories. *Always*. Matilda knew that mental illnesses were like snowflakes—no matter how unusual the expression of the pathology was, every illness could be categorized.

Still, Ashanique's condition instantly *felt* unique. Not only did the girl seem preternaturally calm and collected, but she also didn't speak like an eleven-year-old girl. She phrased things like an adult and used uncommon terminology. Ashanique spoke like someone very well-read. It was possible, Matilda considered, that the girl had been coached. Maybe she was just a good actor. Maybe this was scripted.

"What do these voices tell you?"

Ashanique thought for a second. "Their stories. Life stories. But it sounds silly saying they *tell* me these things. They don't tell me. They don't show me either. I just know them. Like when you wake up and open your eyes and even though you've been dreaming about something crazy, you know you're in your room. You know that the dream was just a dream. I know their stories."

Matilda wrote down: *dream vs story*.

"Can you tell me George's story?"

Ashanique nodded. "But it's sad."

"I understand."

Ashanique was quiet for a moment before she said, "Why do you want to know all this? I tried to tell Mrs. Carol. She didn't want to hear it. I tried to tell a few of the other kids who live around here. Like the boy next door. Him, the rest of them, they said I was crazy, that I'm talking like I'm sick or something. Why do you want to know about this so bad? Mrs. Carol make it sound really terrible or something?"

Matilda folded her arms in her lap. "Okay. Like I said, I'm a professor—"

"Of what?"

"Psychology."

"You're not a doctor . . ."

Matilda cringed at that. It was a sore point. One she'd battled before.

"No, I have a PhD in psychology." Matilda felt as though that would be saying enough, but she couldn't help herself. Even if Ashanique didn't care, she needed to prove herself, to defend her choices. "I knew I wanted to go into research, so I did a duel PhD in neuropsychology and chemistry. I talk to patients because I like people and it's something the university encourages. We enjoy getting out into the community and helping where we can."

"So what do you want to know?" Ashanique asked.

"Tell me about George. All these drawings you've done—"

"He did them."

"Okay," Matilda said, correcting herself, "all the drawings that George has done. I see people fighting. I see fire and horses and . . . it looks like cities in ruins."

"The people are soldiers. George was never a very good illustrator. He drew small doodles for his kid sometimes but . . . this stuff is different. These are overwhelming." Ashanique pointed to a corner near the window. "That is the battle of La Bassée . . . and over there is Lens and Armentières. And up on the ceiling is what he saw at Wieltje. That last one is significant. I don't know if I'm pronouncing it right, but it's a village where George saw the gas being used the first time. . . ."

Ashanique's careful French struck Matilda; the girl had either heard the names of these villages and towns before, or someone had taught her how to pronounce them.

"What gas?"

Ashanique pointed over her shoulder at a crayon triptych above the bedroom window. Soldiers could be seen lying on the ground, scattered like blown leaves. Their faces, though scrawled in a child's hand, were twisted into tearful howls.

"Phosgene," Ashanique said matter-of-factly. "Typically mixed with chlorine."

"And where did George read about that?"

"He didn't. He saw. He was one of the lucky ones to have a gas mask."

Matilda looked past Ashanique at the drawing.

"People always assume it's the chlorine," Ashanique continued. "But it wasn't. The chlorine was bad all right, but phosgene was a terrible irritant to the lungs and the mucus membranes. Most of the exposed soldiers survived the gas attack at the Third Battle of Ypres. The ones who didn't, they suffered something awful."

Ashanique's expression was one born of experience. It was the crimped, pained face of someone talking plainly about something that, under any circumstances other than the dilution of time, would have been unbearable.

Matilda excused herself for a moment and pulled out her cell to text Todd. She sent him the room number and told him to come up. Immediately. Then, reaching into her purse, Matilda pulled out a small video camera. She knew she was bending every ethical rule imaginable, if not outright breaking them. But she needed proof, photographic evidence, that what she was hearing was as real as it felt. Trying to calm her excitement, Matilda told herself that there had to be a trick: *There is simply no way this girl is what she seems. You need to break the illusion down, make sense of it. You're being played, girl.*

"Is it okay if I film our interview?"

"Do you usually film your interviews?"

"Only the ones that I need to revisit."

"So you believe me?" Ashanique asked.

"I believe that you're telling me the truth."

"Fine," Ashanique said.

Matilda set the video camera on the tray. Leaning in to look through the viewfinder, she lined Ashanique up within the digital frame. As she did so, she noticed that the girl was smiling but still anxious. Ashanique toyed with several colorful plastic bracelets on her left wrist—one red, one green, one yellow, and another red. Matilda wondered if this was the very first time that anyone had really, truly listened to Ashanique's story.

"Do you show it to other people?" Ashanique asked.

Matilda shook her head. "No. Just for me. It's transcribed, though."

"And who does that?"

"Someone at the university."

"Someone you trust?"

"Of course."

"Good," Ashanique said. "Because some of what I'm going to tell you is disturbing. Some of it is going to make you very uncomfortable. I just want to make sure you don't get in trouble for it."

"I won't."

Matilda pressed record.

A little red light flashed on the back of the video camera.

"Here we go," Matilda said, more for her own comfort than the girl's.

11

11.13.18

Transcription #098.19

Dr. Matilda Deacon / Employee Number 34-7609

The following transcription is of an interview with a female eleven-year-old subject, AW, re: her belief that she is experiencing "past life" recollections.

AW is a healthy girl. African American. Oriented to time and place. Appeared calm and willing to answer questions. Mother was not present, but AW's caregiver approached me. She was quite concerned about AW's behavior—suggesting it was an emergent situation.

Note: I have a consent form on file signed by AW's mother—Janice Walters—for social service work in the Marcy-Lansing Apartments. Consent was collected by my colleague Dr. Todd Garcia-Araez, eleven months prior to my visit. There are no records of Dr. Garcia-Araez ever speaking with AW or Janice.

RE: past lives: AW is stringent in her conviction that these recollections are the result of inherited memories—though she describes them as "people" who exist inside her.

DR. TODD GARCIA-ARAEZ comes in around minute three.

00:00:15

DR. DEACON: Can you tell me about George?

SUBJECT AW: George Edwin Ellison was a British soldier in World War I. He was the last British casualty of the war.

DR. DEACON: What unit was he with?

AW: Fifth Royal Irish Lancers. A private.

DR. DEACON: And when did he die?

AW: He was killed by a sniper's bullet at 10:55 a.m. on November 11, 1918. He died at 10:59 a.m. It was raining. He didn't hear the shot. He fell backward. The rain was hitting his face.

DR. DEACON: And you . . . experienced this?

AW: Every second of it. As if it was this morning.

DR. DEACON: Does that scare you?

AW: At first it did. More from the shock.

DR. DEACON: This was a violent death. I would imagine that would be quite frightening to see, let alone experience.

AW: Yes, but you have to put it in perspective. George came from a long, long line. He knew it would continue beyond him. At that last second, he knew. . . .

DR. DEACON: How? How did he know that?

AW: I don't know. It was in the last milliseconds. The very last images in his brain. He saw them. He saw me.

DR. DEACON: He saw you? In 1918?

AW: Yes.

DR. DEACON: You do know that some people will have trouble understanding that, right? That some people will suggest that this is all information you learned. Or were taught. That maybe this stuff just got mixed up in your head. Sometimes, we conflate dreams with reality. There have been studies—research studies—showing that nearly 50 percent of the memories we have are inaccurate. They're either distortions or they're made up.

AW: That's because science hasn't caught up with this yet. It's like that saying about the elephant and the blind men.

DR. DEACON: That they can only describe one part of the animal. A trunk. Big ears. A tail—

AW: And it sounds like a fairy-tale creature when you only talk about parts of it. But when you see it as a whole, you understand it's . . . reasonable.

DR. DEACON: And you can see these memories the same way?

AW: Yes. (pause) But it's not just seeing. I feel it. I know it. Anyone can know the facts about George. Stuff that was in the papers. He was a miner. Had a wife and a child. I can tell you everything about George. But it's not so much me telling you the facts. It's the feelings. And he . . . felt so much.

DR. DEACON: What did he feel?

AW: George looked at the world different from the way you and I do. He sometimes would stop dead in his tracks. . . . They'd be marching—his regiment—and he'd stop and just stare up at the sky. All the other guys bumping into him, they'd think he was crazy. He wasn't. He was looking at the clouds. The way the light bounced off them, the way they moved and shifted shape. That captivated him, but it was more than just the visual. It was the way it felt. Staring up into the sky, seeing the clouds, he was in awe of it. . . . The feeling he had was astonishment. . . .

DR. DEACON: At clouds?

AW: Sounds silly. I know—

DR. DEACON: It doesn't. No, I didn't mean— Clouds can be striking. The sky can be inspiring. Some people can find beauty in the smaller details, the things most of us either ignore completely or take for granted.

AW: That was George. He appreciated the little things.

00:03:12

DR. DEACON: Do you know what cold reading is?

AW: No.

DR. DEACON: It's a skill that some people have. Mind readers. Magicians. A way to tell what someone is thinking. To expect their answers and their choices but reading their body language, their facial expressions—

A door is heard opening. AW looks off camera.

DR. GARCIA-ARAEZ: Sorry.

AW: It's okay. We were just talking.

DR. GARCIA-ARAEZ: Is it all right with you if I sit in?

AW nods.

AW: Are you going to ask me questions too?

DR. GARCIA-ARAEZ: Not unless you want me to.

DR. DEACON: Getting back to where we were. Are you telling me these things because you think they'll impress me?

AW: Of course not. You wanted to talk to me.

DR. DEACON: Yes, I did. I'm trying to help you.

AW: I don't need help. Not any help that you can give me. I've seen the elephant, Doctor. I don't think that makes me crazy. (pause) I'm not doing any cold reading. Or whatever. I'm telling you what I know. You can look it all up online—everything about George—but that won't convince you, will it? And you need to be convinced.

DR. DEACON: I don't think it's that cut and—

AW: George carved a smiley face on the back of his pocket watch. It was a gift from his uncle. Nothing too expensive, but that pocket watch saw George through the war. It kept him sane. He was thinking of his kid one night. There was a break in the shelling, the air stank of sulfur and the sky was lit up like it was on fire, but for the first time in days, there was a moment of silence. He carved the smiley face in the back of the pocket watch then. It wasn't like an emoji. He wasn't an artist or anything, but it was more detailed than just a circle, a curved line, and two dots. It was something to make his kid happy, a present to him. He died looking at it three weeks later. . . .

DR. DEACON: What do you think all this means? Beyond having this information, beyond seeing and feeling these things, what does it mean to you?

AW: Do you believe in synchronicity, Doctor?

DR. DEACON: I suppose it depends. There are competing definitions. But I do believe in meaningful co-incidences.

AW: The Night Doctors say synchronicity is real.

00:07:39

Dr. Deacon gasps and then is quiet. AW leans forward. Silence until:

00:07:42

DR. DEACON: The Night Doctors. Where did you hear that?

AW: I've seen them. In my memories. George didn't see them. He was dead before they came. But the other ones did. I was drawing a picture of it before you came here.

DR. DEACON: What other ones?

AW: I remember them all. All the way back. They were scared. My old selves, they were terrified. . . .

DR. DEACON: Of the Night Doctors?

AW: Yes.

DR. DEACON: Are you scared of them? Does someone here or at school hurt you? Maybe someone you trusted? Maybe someone your mother knows?

AW: I should be scared of them, but I'm not. They will be looking for me. I know that now.

DR. DEACON: Why will they be looking for you?

AW: Because of what happened in that place.

AW turns around to the bed and picks up a drawing of a square black building in a forest by the ocean. There is snow around the building.

DR. DEACON: What happened there?

AW: Something terrible. I can't see the details yet.

DR. DEACON: But you will eventually, you think?

AW: Yes.

DR. DEACON: I would very much like to hear about that then.

AW: You're a nice person, Doctor. I know you're trying to help me. But if you do, the Night Doctors will find you. They find everyone. . . .

There is a rustling sound before recording stops.

00:10:21

End

12

"THE HELL IS going on in here?!"

Janice stormed in, incensed.

Ashanique jumped up and ran between her mother and Matilda as Matilda shoved the video camera back into her purse.

"Mom, it isn't—"

Ashanique stopped short when she saw the fury in her mother's eyes.

She knew, instinctively, that Janice's rage wasn't because of Matilda's being there—it was because Ashanique had broken her mother's trust. And trust, as Janice had explained since Ashanique was old enough to understand the word, was the glue that kept a relationship between mother and daughter strong.

Without trust, well, you had nothing.

Ashanique wanted to defend herself. She wanted to tell her mom that she wasn't a part of this—Matilda came in because Carol brought her. But she knew that wasn't the full story. The full story was that Ashanique wanted to talk, that she was desperate to tell someone about what was happening to her. And she wanted Janice to know that Matilda was a sweet person, a person who would listen without judgment. Or fear. But the words never left her mouth.

"I need you to leave," Janice told Matilda. "Right the fuck now."

Todd stood at the front door and held it open as Matilda gathered her stuff and formulated apologies. "Mrs. Walters, I'm sorry. Carol asked me to talk to Ashanique because she was worried. I don't know if you remember, but you signed a release form when my colleague and I came a few months ago—"

"Doesn't matter. I didn't approve this."

"That's what I'm telling you—"

Janice pointed to the door.

"I need you out. Now."

．　．　．

Janice had spent two hours stuck in traffic.

Work had been hell, and she was getting worse.

The headache that had trailed her home blossomed during her commute. Every red light, every time the bus driver tapped his brake, the discomfort grew—what began as pinpricks behind her eyes had metastasized into a throbbing mass of white-hot pain. Janice tried to defuse it with ibuprofen and MetroChime—exceeding the strongest dose Dr. Song had recommended—but they did little to help. Dr. Song had warned Janice that at her age it would be only a matter of months before she'd need to begin IV treatment and possibly a year or two before the "long nap."

Fuck that, Janice had thought at the time. *Not me. Not now.*

Truth was, Janice's condition had never affected her work. But that week, she'd been able to cut hair only four days. The other three she was shaking in bed. It took everything in her to not look like the complete mess she was.

The most recent memory that had crept into her head was profoundly disturbing. Luckily, it was choppy, as half-formed as the mind that made it. When Janice pieced the memory together, she saw her own feet, twisted by disease, clumsily stomping through mud thick with the scythe-like rib bones of cattle and grinning human skulls. She held a human femur, one end sharpened into a fierce point, in her left hand. Its tip was bloodied. The afternoon's headache brought the memory with it and further strained Janice's already tenuous hold on her patience.

And that was before she found Matilda in her apartment.

While Matilda kept trying to explain herself, all Janice could think of was the gun in the bathroom. She knew people had killed for far less. But she couldn't do it. No matter what the memories might suggest, she wasn't a killer.

"I'm going to go, okay," Matilda said, backing out of Ashanique's room and heading toward the front door, where Carol stood, red-faced. "But I really need to talk to you about your daughter. Please, there is something—"

"No."

Janice followed Matilda through the living room.

"Not going to happen, Doctor."

"But there is something going on with Ashanique. Carol's not making it up or being overreactive. I think it would be really, really valuable for both you and Ashanique if you brought her by my office at the university. Just to talk through some of what she's told me. I think this is very important."

"She makes things up," Janice said. "Reads a lot of books."

"I understand that—"

"No, you don't. She's telling stories to impress you. And it worked, didn't it? Ashanique likes to show off how smart she is 'cause she's an incredibly smart girl. And the people at her school don't get her. But I get her. Don't doubt that for a second. I get her as clear as anyone else. And I'm telling you to forget it."

Matilda pulled her business card from her purse.

Eyes steeled, Janice ignored her and placed her hand on the doorframe.

Matilda looked back at Ashanique.

The girl was embarrassed and scared. Janice could see it, and her face softened, though only slightly.

"We're good," she told her daughter. "They're leaving now. We're gonna be just fine."

Matilda handed her business card to Carol and stepped into the hall.

"Don't ever come back," Janice threatened.

The door slammed shut hard enough to rattle the frame.

13

"WELL, THAT WAS exciting. You okay?"

Todd looked over at Matilda as he eased the Volvo onto the interstate.

After they'd returned to the car, Matilda spent the first few minutes in silence, scrolling through websites on her phone.

"Jesus, there was something seriously unhinged about that woman. Think she was on something?"

Matilda wasn't listening to him, despite her looking up from her phone. She gave Todd a blank stare.

"Sorry, just . . ."

"It's okay. Lot to process."

"It's all real. All of it."

Matilda had pulled up everything she could find on the life and death of George Edwin Ellison. And everything Ashanique had said checked out— every fact about his place of birth, his regiment, his injuries, and his family. With one exception: Matilda couldn't find any mention of a smiley face etched into the back of George's pocket watch. The pocket watch existed—it was housed in the Canadian War Museum in Ottawa and there were even pictures of it online. But the smiley face wasn't among them. Matilda found it curious; Ashanique had made quite a deal of the engraving, hammering it hard in her retelling of George's life.

"Maybe the girl just read the Wikipedia entry."

"No." Matilda shook her head. "She wasn't reciting— Hang on. . . ."

Matilda called the War Museum. She made her way through various museum staff before being directed to the voice mail of one of the curators. She left a detailed message asking about George Edwin Ellison's pocket watch and a "family legend" about there being a picture on the back. She felt silly when she hung up the phone.

"Wow. You're serious," Todd said, looking over at her.

"I've never seen anyone like her."

"Come on." Todd laughed dismissively. "The girl's cute; she's got a great affect. I wouldn't be surprised to find out she was older than she looked, you know? This sort of thing happens. The girl's a great actress, the mom's coaching her, and they fool a bunch of people, people like you, into getting them things. Hooking them up with meds and tests—I've seen it happen. Stone-cold, sociopathic, I'm not talking Munchausen by proxy or folie à deux—"

"Janice didn't even want us there. You saw how she reacted."

"Exactly, that's part of the scam."

"Todd, you're talking crazy. I do think Janice is hiding something, but it's not about some scam to get drugs. That's silly. And jaded. No, something real is happening with Ashanique—maybe high-functioning savant syndrome or an odd manifestation of ideasthesia. Whatever it is, Janice knows what's going on with her. She just doesn't want to talk about it."

"I think you're spooked. Blindsided."

"Will you just stop?"

Matilda sank back into her seat with a sigh. She wasn't sure why she was so unnerved. Everything Ashanique had told her, all the details—like the names of the battles George had fought in—were impressive, but what Matilda couldn't get out of her head were all the things the girl only hinted at.

"Okay, so I was being obnoxious." Todd picked up the conversation again. "How about this: You've seen how many of these cases? Mostly they're adults and mostly they're terrible actors. So it's not surprising that you find a kid like this, an African American girl in a low-income apartment complex, and it's a bit shocking. That's the trick, though. She's using your expectations against you. Using those internal biases to put you off your game."

"I wasn't off my game."

"I didn't mean it that way. But I do think you're being played. The whole thing was too good to be true. It wouldn't surprise me if Janice was at one of your classes, maybe sat in and took a shit ton of notes. Ashanique hit all the boxes, avoided all the traps. She's good. Really good."

Matilda pulled a tea tree oil stick from her purse and rubbed some into her temples. The cooling effect was an instantly relaxing distraction.

"That stuff stinks. The girl said *Night Doctors*, right? That was weird."

"She did. It was weird for someone her age."

"You seemed taken aback by it."

"I did?"

"Yeah, you did. Why?"

"I've heard it before. An . . . an old client."

"Fill me in, Maddie. I don't know what Night Doctors are."

"I don't know that much, honestly," Matilda began, "but they were pretty much boogeymen from the South; 1800s legends, mostly forgotten today. At the time, they were as bad as anything. There were stories going around African American communities that if you were out late or wandered into a part of town you weren't supposed to be in, the Night Doctors would get you. They'd perform hideous experiments, cut you up, and then use your body to train medical students."

"Damn . . ."

"Most of those stories were actually spread by the Klan. Trying to keep the black communities living in fear. But the truth is, a lot of African Americans ended up on the autopsy slabs of medical schools. Medicine was taking off; the days of the field surgeon were in the rearview mirror. They needed bodies to train on."

"Shit, you're saying the stories were true?"

"There was a huge jump in grave robbery around the time the Night Doctor stories were spreading out across the South. I'm saying it's not a big leap to suggest that sometimes being dead wasn't a requirement. We're talking about a culture that saw black as less than human."

Todd mulled that over as the Volvo hit the exit ramp.

"Okay," he said, "so maybe the folklore continued to today in some communities. But you're not actually suggesting that Ashanique believes there are physicians in scrubs and masks stalking the streets looking for people to dissect? Like roving gangs of killer doctors."

"I'm not suggesting anything."

14

AS SOON AS she got back to the office, Matilda searched her archives.

I know I've heard it before. . . . It's here somewhere.

There was nothing on her walls about the Night Doctors, at least nothing out in the open. Matilda spent a few chaotic minutes combing through her file drawers. Despite the number of folders she'd stuffed into each one, they were all labeled and correctly organized. Matilda had a rule she'd learned from Clark: Never touch something more than once. It was basically a riff on the old "stitch in time" chestnut, but she saw the logic in it. With so many ongoing projects, she didn't have time to waste relabeling files or sorting papers. But there was no file about Night Doctors.

It'll be on your computer, Maddie.

Ugh. Great. The computer. . . .

The department IT guy, a bearded dude with a nose ring, sighed loudly the last time he had been called in to install more RAM on Matilda's desktop. She actually had to get special approval from the department for the procedure. Rather than just upgrade her computer, they decided to keep adding RAM until they couldn't. When the IT guy had finished, he awkwardly mentioned one of the department's upcoming classes on reducing digital clutter.

"You know, to streamline your machine," he said. And added, "You have a ton—like a real ton—of stuff on here. Cleaning it up would make it function better. Move fast. It's almost kind of a hazard." Then he looked up at the office walls.

Matilda told him she was happy with the speed of the machine, thank you.

The IT guy left with another sigh.

Matilda's voice mail was an example of the clutter that had him so concerned. She had 223 folders of voice messages. Each one was labeled with a date. They were downloaded automatically from the messaging system into her email in-box. Matilda didn't save every voice message she received; that would be crazy. No, instead she "deconstructed" approximately 75 percent of them. Deconstruction—her own term—consisted of pulling important information from the message, typing it out, and then saving it as a text file before tossing the message itself.

Running a search, she found the voice message she was looking for in a folder named T. V. #2449-293. The message (kept whole rather than being deconstructed) had been left for her approximately sixteen months ago, around eleven on a Tuesday night. It was labeled T. V. 8-21(1). Matilda had listened to the message the following morning and returned the call. But she got no answer.

She found out why a few days later.

Matilda got up, closed the door to her office, and put on headphones. Plugging them into her desktop, she leaned back in her chair and listened to the wounded voice of a ghost.

Hearing Vang again was unnerving and deeply painful.

Hi, Dr. Deacon, it's me. I know I said I wouldn't call again for a while but . . . kinda clichéd to say, but things are getting worse again. I know. I, uh, I started smoking again, and, well, no surprise here, but I got sick. Went into the hospital and— You got that, right? I mean, they sent over those medical records? They should have. Anyway, that was bad enough but what made it worse was the fact that they had me in a psych hold. I was really, really out of it. Like real bad. I couldn't talk, so they didn't know about the fact that I had a head injury when I was a kid. I wish I could have at least told them that. It explains why I can't remember worth shit.

Being in the hospital and being off the drugs, the memories just came barreling on back. Total knockdown. Like being hit by a tsunami. They must have thought I was totally insane, hearing me howling and shit— It was bad, Doc. The usual ones came back. I, uh, had the memories about being on a fishing boat. That's actually a calming one. He had six children by two different women, which is kind of nuts but . . . So I also had the one about the Native American woman who got attacked by wolves. Memories like that are exactly why I smoke, you know? Shit, I keep calling them memories, and I'm sure you're shaking your head listening to this. They're not memories, okay? Visions is what I need to call them. I'll get there, Doc. Serious, I will.

Anyway, I'm calling 'cause I seriously need your help. I had this moment of enlightenment. I don't know what triggered it. Maybe it was something I heard or something I saw but . . . I honestly think it's a real memory from my childhood, Doc. Like from before the accident or whatever damaged me. And it's really fucked-up. I don't know who else to tell about it, so, sorry, I'm putting it on you. Don't listen to this before you go to bed, okay? It's like the—

The voice recording was cut short. Matilda assumed Vang had been cut off by the messaging system, but she didn't actually know how long a message someone could leave. Regardless, he called back about two minutes later and left a second message. In her files, it was titled T. V. 8-21(2). Matilda pressed play and closed her eyes. Readying herself for the shock to come.

Got cut off there. Not sure where I stopped but, um, I was saying that this memory is from me. Like the actual me, only as a kid—a little kid. Before the foster homes and shit. I'm this little scruffy Hmong kid running around the streets of . . . Damn, I don't actually know what town, but it's maybe Mexico or Puerto Rico. Words are in Spanish. There are palm trees and beaches. I don't know what I'm up to but it's clear that I've got no one. Ha! That shit didn't change much, did it? I'm totally a street kid. An urchin or whatever. Living with a bunch of other street kids, stealing things and begging for change. That's me. And I'm maybe like six years old. This is in the seventies. It feels like the seventies. I see really old cars and people wear super-lame clothes.

I'm running around these streets when I get hit by a fucking car! Some asshole totally hits me. I'm not that messed up by the accident. I don't have anything more than some scrapes and some nasty bruises. But this car just totally drives off. Asshole. That's not even the part I was warning you about, Doc. It's what comes after that. Most people, they get run over somewhere— especially a little kid—and the police show up. Sure enough, a crowd gathers around me. Then an ambulance comes. This nasty old ambulance. I'm actually psyched, 'cause going to the hospital means getting a bed to sleep in, and I've been sleeping on the streets up until this point, and it means getting an actual, bona fide hot meal.

The thing is I don't go to the hospital. The ambulance takes some really funky turns and winds up outside the city. I'm strapped down in the back, but I get one arm free and sit up enough to see that we're in the countryside— farms and everything on either side of the road. But it isn't until we pull off the street and into the driveway of this little house that I really start getting scared. And there's just this one phrase that's rattling around in my head: Night Doctors. Beware of the Night Doctors.

Matilda opened her eyes and stopped the message for a moment.

Just hearing those two words again was startling.

God damn it, Dr. Deacon, why weren't you paying attention?

Matilda actually had done some reading about the Night Doctors after she first heard the message. But she was convinced Theo Vang suffered from paranoid delusions and schizoaffective personality disorder. It didn't help that he'd had some serious head trauma as a kid and was addicted to methamphetamine. Theo was a very, very damaged man. And no one would have blamed Matilda for dismissing his memories. She had tried to help him, but his concerns were simply too unbelievable to take seriously. Of course, hearing his voice again, she regretted her judgment.

Matilda pressed play, and braced for the rest of the message.

I know it when they wheel me into the house. There's a surgery-looking setup in there. A white room; all clinical, like a lab or something. And, crazy as it seems, there's a big machine there. It looks like a telescope. Only the ceiling isn't open to see the stars. It's crammed in there, and wires and cables and things are lying all over the floors. They wheel me on this gurney, or whatever, and they strap down my one free arm. And ... there are other kids there. Other ones they took. Shit, this is hard to talk about without ...

Anyway, it's scary as hell. And I start screaming, 'cause I know that the
Night Doctors won't heal me, they're gonna hurt me. And then . . . they do.

Matilda stopped the message and took off her headphones. As she did, her gaze fell on a printout half covered by Post-it Notes on the wall just over the computer. She knew what it was but needed to see it nonetheless. Matilda needed to have that moment, to feel those emotions. She needed the tears that would follow.

The printout was an obituary from the *Chicago Sun-Times*.

On it was a photo of a haunted-looking, fiftysomething Hmong man. His name was Theo Vang, and he had jumped off the roof of his halfway house five hours after leaving Matilda the voice messages.

15

DIRK BOGRAD WOKE up screaming.

He was still at work, sitting behind the front desk at Sargent International Bank. He hadn't realized he'd fallen asleep. It looked bad, the security guard bolting upright at his post—sweating, heart racing. Unfortunately, he wasn't alone in the lobby. A woman walking past stopped and glanced over at him, concerned.

"I'm okay," Dirk said. "Just—just the chair slipped is all. . . ."

As the woman exited the building through the revolving door, Dirk caught a distorted reflection of himself in the window opposite his desk. He was ashen. Blinking several times to pull himself together, he leaned down and opened the Velcro top of his lunch bag to remove a silver pill case. Dirk shook two yellow-and-white MetroChime capsules out. He chewed them quickly before washing them down with a sip of cold coffee.

"God damn," he said out loud to no one, "you're falling apart."

Dirk had been a security guard at Sargent International for fifteen months and he'd never fallen asleep on the job before. Not once. Even with his sleep patterns and the crushing boredom of his job, he'd always maintained a professional attitude. He certainly couldn't afford to lose another job. Not with his wife going down in her hours at the clinic and his son hoping to go to camp again.

Pull it together, Dirk, you've got a lot of people depending on you.

An hour later, shift over and no additional embarrassments, Dirk was ready to leave. A phone buzzed in his backpack as he packed up. Dirk was startled. He kept his cell in a case on his belt; the buzzing, however, was from the flip phone he'd gotten in the mail two months earlier, the one that had never once rung. Looking around and seeing no one nearby, Dirk pulled the flip phone from his bag. There was an encrypted message written out in a substitution cipher on the small screen. With the package had been a letter from Dr. Song. Written to resemble a friendly sales pitch, there were hidden messages embedded in the letter—it took Dirk an afternoon to decipher it using the key his brother had given him. The long and short of it was simple: he needed to keep the flip phone with him at all times. If it rang, answer. If a text came through, read it.

So it begins, Dirk thought. *Here we go, bro.*

Dirk unfolded a scrap of paper from his wallet. It was a grid with letters in tiny boxes, all done in a microscopic font. He laid it flat on the desk and slowly, methodically decoded the text message from the flip phone.

51's daughter is Null. Chicago, Marcy-Lansing. 915. They need a path to Dr. Song. Send Childers to meet them at the museum in two nights.

So this is spy craft, huh?

Using the flip phone, Dirk texted the decoded message to the only number in the phone's contacts. A Chicago-based number but one he wasn't familiar with. As soon as it was sent, Dirk followed the directions he'd been given and snapped the cell phone in half. He tossed it and the handwritten decoded message into the lockbox under his desk. They'd both be industrial shredded in the morning. Simple.

Dirk leaned back in his chair and nodded to himself. The process was certainly easier than he'd expected. He had to admire the organization's commitment to secrecy and protocol. He figured, you couldn't be too careful in today's screwed-up world. Dirk wasn't sure if he'd ever get another flip phone in the mail, but if he did, at least he knew how the whole thing worked.

Easy enough.

Dirk grabbed his things and tossed his keys to Billingham as the guard walked in, the zipper on his pants down. Billingham was an old guy, maybe in his late sixties, and Dirk didn't give him any grief. Reminded him of his father, in a way. Always late and never really pulled together.

On his way to his Passat, Dirk got a text from his wife, Beth.

Dinner's going to be a little earlier tonight. Ok? Your friend Jeremy stopped by. Said he was in town on short notice.

As he drove home, Dirk thought about the message some more.

Jesus, he thought. *Jeremy. I haven't seen that old bastard in years. What the hell would bring him to Indianapolis? Must be garbage with his wife again. Dude could never keep it in his pants.*

Dirk laughed out loud about that. For the twenty minutes that remained of his ride, he didn't yell at slow cars or honk his way into the exit lane. For the first time in what felt like years, he was actually excited to entertain at home. He just hoped Beth had cleaned the place up. At least a little.

But when Dirk stepped into his suburban ranch home, his face dropped.

Beth had tears running down her cheeks. Hunter was scared pale.

And the man in the hoodie at the dinner table, sitting between his wife and teenage son, wasn't Jeremy. Dirk had never seen this man before. Not at work, not at the gym. As Dirk walked across the room, carefully dropping his coat on the couch, he studied the man's face and became instantly incensed.

What the fuck is this? Some guy got the wrong house?

He was ready to lay into the guy when he noticed two things: First, the man at the table with his family was totally bald. He didn't even have eyebrows. He was tall and thin, maybe in his midforties, but odd-looking, for sure. And two, there was a small, clear box sitting on the hutch behind the table. The box was vibrating, making the sound an old dot-matrix printer made.

"Just who the hell are you?" Dirk asked.

Beth looked up at Dirk. Her eyes trembled in their sockets.

If this fucking guy has touched her . . .

The man at the table stood up. He wore latex gloves, like the kind you see at the hospital, and held a gun. Dirk was no expert, but he guessed it was a Sig Sauer.

"Sit," the man said.

Dirk sat, panic breaking out the sweat on his forehead.

"Where is Fifty-One?" the man asked.

Dirk shook his head. He didn't understand just what the hell that was supposed to even mean. He looked over at Beth. She was so pale. So frightened. And Hunter, the poor kid was audibly grinding his teeth. Dirk knew he needed to put a stop to whatever was happening. Clearly, the guy in the hoodie was there to rob them *or worse*. . . . Thinking back through his security guard training, the conflict-resolution lectures and crisis management slideshows, Dirk quickly formulated a plan of attack. But the clear box sitting on the hutch interrupted his thoughts and timing. It dinged loudly, the way a convection oven would.

"Where is Fifty-One?"

"I don't know what you're talking about, man," Dirk said. "Seriously. I don't know who Fifty-One is, and I don't know who you are. I'm asking you nicely, please get out of my house right now and leave my family alone."

The man in the hoodie turned and fired. A bullet whizzed just over Dirk's right shoulder before embedding itself in the wall behind him. A fine plume of drywall dust wafted past Dirk as he reflexively shuddered.

"I'm going to ask one more time. Where is Fifty-One?"

Dirk swallowed hard.

"I honestly don't know. I'm telling you the truth. . . ."

As Dirk spoke, the man reached back to the clear box and opened its lid. The box was a 3-D printer. An advanced model, not on the public market yet. He reached inside and pulled out two freshly printed rubber gloves. The man in the hoodie held the gloves up to the dining room light.

Dirk could see fingerprints on the tips.

"I've been directed to keep things clean," the man said. "So you're going to be killing your family tonight. I took your prints off the tumblers in the kitchen and had them printed on these gloves."

The man pulled the printed gloves over his medical exam gloves.

Dirk pushed back from the table, fast as he could. He was going to take this motherfucker right here, regardless of the costs. He figured that if he could dodge the man's first shot he could get ahold of the gun, maybe wrestle it out of his hands.

We'll see who's the real badass then.

But Dirk was slow.

Before he'd moved a foot, the man in the hoodie turned, the gun barked, and blood Rorschached across Hunter's chest. The teenager gasped and fell backward. Beth screamed like she would scream forever. The man shot her in the neck and blood drizzled the table as she tumbled backward to the floor.

Dirk couldn't even move. Could hardly breathe.

Calm as ever, as though he did this sort of thing on any given evening, the man in the hoodie pulled a cell phone from his back pocket and placed it on the table in front of Dirk.

"I need you to enter the phone number you sent a text to tonight," the man said. "You remember, don't you? You used a shitty flip phone."

"I—I don't think I can—"

Dirk couldn't help but stare down in horror at the bodies of his wife and son. It had all happened so quickly, he wasn't even sure of what he was seeing. *Those are just dummies,* he told himself. *Beth and Hunter went out for dinner. I'm just dreaming.*

The man in the hoodie snapped his fingers to get Dirk's attention. Dirk was crying uncontrollably, tears dripping all over his shirt as he picked up the cell phone and, hands shaking, typed in the number as he remembered it.

Dirk handed the cell to the man in the hoodie.

"This is correct?"

"I—"

The man leaned forward and pressed the Sig Sauer to Dirk's temple. Dirk planned to close his eyes but, once again, he was too slow. The gun kicked, the bullet burrowed through Dirk's brain, singeing the cerebral cortex as it traveled, and exited the other side of his head enshrouded in a fine mist of blood.

Dirk's body slumped onto the table.

. . .

"How's that for clean?" Rade asked the corpses.

He was packing up the 3-D printer when a sudden, urgent pounding on the front door caught his attention. Rade stopped what he was doing and slowly opened the front door to see a middle-aged Indian woman standing on the porch in a sari. She looked quite concerned—frantic, even.

"I'm sorry—I live next door and heard— Is Mr. Bograd here?"

Rade opened the door, and the neighbor stepped inside. She was shaking, her eyes darting. As soon as she saw the bodies, the Indian woman's face began to curl into a mask of horror. Rade shot her in the face before she could scream. The Indian woman stumbled forward and collapsed, face-down.

Shit. Now Rade had a problem.

Dirk couldn't very well have shot and killed the neighbor because, as an autopsy would determine, he was dead before she arrived.

Rade picked up a leather briefcase he left by the front door and opened it. He removed a pair of stainless steel, surgical-grade forceps and carefully dug the bullet out of the Indian neighbor's head. Luckily, her skull had fractured and the bullet was relatively easy to find in the resulting mess. Rade walked over to the dining room table and carefully pried the bullet from the wall where Dirk had been sitting.

Rade switched the two bullets.

The scene was set: the Indian neighbor heard the shots, she ran over, and then Dirk, depressed, angry, broken, shot her before he shot himself.

Good enough.

Satisfied, Rade left.

16

EVERY TIME MATILDA walked into the Stonybrook Assisted-Living Facility, she felt a deep pang of regret.

Sometimes, she'd sit in one of the upholstered armchairs near the front desk and watch visitors sign in as the harried receptionist, a young woman with tattoos on her neck, fielded a near-constant barrage of texts from her zebra-cased cell phone.

Most of the visitors were like Matilda, adult children, seeing their frail and forgotten parents. The ones who visited most often, the weeklies, even dailies, had a businesslike demeanor. They were checking emotional boxes, following up on promises they had made when their parents' minds were stable. The people who came by a few times a year, the children who lived out of state or just couldn't stomach seeing the destruction Alzheimer's had wrought, arrived with stuffed animals and flowers. They brought in framed pictures of grandchildren and mementos. Burdened by their loss, these visitors dreamed of somehow shaking their loved ones from their long, long slumber.

Only it never happened. Once gone mentally, there was no coming back.

Matilda didn't know where she fell on the visitor spectrum. She came to see Lucy three times a week and she often brought meals. Every now and then she'd bring a gift—jewelry, flowers, little things she'd pick up at the Friday art market in Daley Plaza. Yet despite the frequency of her visits,

Matilda still reacted emotionally when she came through the front doors. She cringed; a lump would form instantly in her throat. It wasn't that the fake cinnamon-and-vanilla smell of the place or the dark furniture and dim lighting conjured up nostalgic memories. It was because she knew Stony-brook was a way station—life inside its carefully temperature-controlled walls provided a temporary, gentle easing into the infinite dark waters of death. And everyone who walked through its doors could sense it.

Matilda knew it was different in other countries. People died at home, not in quiet simulacrums of domestic life. Her friend and colleague Tamiko, a neuroscientist at the university, had told her that in Japan, and other Asian countries, the elderly moved in with their children. They cared for their grandchildren, cooked, and cleaned. And when they grew frail or de-mented, their children took care of them in turn. When the end came, it almost always came at home, surrounded by family.

After Matilda signed in at the front desk, she grabbed a freshly baked almond butter cookie from a tray beside the coffee and water pitcher. She ate it as she made her way through the lobby where two women, Francine and Rosa, frequently sat across from each other and watched TV.

As Rosa knitted, Francine thumbed through a three-decade-old issue of *National Geographic* with a photo of a scuba diver on the cover.

As she walked past, Matilda waved.

"Any luck on the article?" Matilda asked.

"Not yet." Francine frowned. "But I think I'm getting closer."

Two weeks earlier, while Matilda was waiting for Lucy to finish a rehab session, Francine explained that she was going through the seventy-five-plus back issues left behind by another resident. Francine was looking for an article from the mid- to late-1980s about a shooting at a nursing facility. The story had haunted her and she was desperate to read it again. Francine often joked that she had a morbid streak. Thinking on it, Matilda didn't re-call ever reading an article like that in *National Geographic*; it seemed to be outside the magazine's purview. She suggested that perhaps the article was in *Time* or *Life*.

Francine was certain it was in a *National Geographic*.

Matilda found Lucy in her bedroom. Lucy was seventy years old, tall, very thin, and had let her hair grow out to shoulder length. She wore smudged glasses. When she was younger, in Matilda's earliest memories of her mother, Lucy kept her hair cut short around her slightly cherubic face. Lucy had always looked at least ten years younger than she was. *Baby-faced*, people called it. Lucy hated the phrase.

Lucy didn't look up when Matilda walked in.

"I can't find it," she said, hands scouring the clothing in the top drawer of her dresser. "It was there yesterday. I saw it just before dinner."

"What are you looking for, Mom?"

Lucy looked up, a bit confused. Her eyes played across Matilda's face, as if she were trying to sync the features with the few memories she still had. For a split second, it looked as though Lucy was going to smile, to walk over to Matilda and melt into a hug, but the look of recognition passed just as quickly as it had arrived. Frowning, shaking her head, Lucy turned back to the task at hand.

"Can I help you?"

"It's a brooch," Lucy said. "My aunt gave it to me—"

"Aunt Deborah," Matilda said. "It's at the bank."

Lucy looked up, eyes quivering.

"Matilda . . . You're here?"

Matilda took Lucy's hands in her own, squeezed them.

"The brooch is at the bank, in a safety-deposit box with Grandma Helen's jewelry and Dad's papers. It's all there. All protected. Have you eaten dinner?"

Lucy glanced over at the clock on her wardrobe.

"I wasn't hungry earlier," she said before turning again to the dresser. "I just was so certain I saw my brooch this afternoon. You wouldn't believe some of the problems we've been having here recently. The woman next door . . ."

Lucy lowered her voice.

"The woman next door has been stealing things—"

"Mom, no one is stealing from you."

"She has been. I woke up in the middle of the night. There was a noise in my room. And I saw her. She was right here, going through the drawers, looking for valuables. I got up and I yelled at her. She screamed back at me and scratched my arm. Right here, scratched me with her nails. . . ."

Lucy pulled up the sleeve on her sweater to show Matilda. Her arm was very thin and her skin mottled with aging bruises, but there was no visible scratch.

"It was here. Must have healed already."

This was exactly the thing that killed Matilda. This was why she sometimes stopped and sat at the entrance to Stonybrook to catch her breath. These horrible moments, running on five years now, crushed her. Seeing her once-strong, once-brilliant mother reduced to a paranoid shell filled Matilda with sadness. It went beyond mourning the loss of the woman who shaped her life. Matilda had many years to deal with that loss, and she'd worked through it as gracefully as she could. No, a lot of the exquisite despondency that made her chest tighten came down to seeing her own future. Truth was, she knew that unless she could unlock the chemistry of how memories were formed, stored, and protected, she would follow Lucy into the inescapable maze of forgetting.

"Why don't we get something to eat? The café is open for another fifteen minutes or so. When I was coming in, I saw they're serving roast beef tonight."

Lucy considered.

"I do like the roast beef."

As Matilda placed her purse and coat on her mother's bed, she noticed a pile of clothing in the corner of the room. The closet door was open and the hangers were bare. Every article of clothing—coats, dresses, scarves, and hats—had been unceremoniously dumped onto the floor. Momentarily lucid, Lucy noticed Matilda's worried gaze and walked over. She placed a hand on her daughter's shoulder.

"I suppose I got a little carried away," she said, "I was sure I saw that brooch."

It took Matilda five minutes to get her mother out of the room.

Lucy insisted on finding a purse to carry, protesting that she was going to pay for the meal. Matilda couldn't convince her otherwise. Though the purse was empty, save for a few tissues, Lucy happily put it over her shoulder and followed her daughter down a hallway to the dining room, where they sat alone at a table beside a large window. Outside was a small courtyard where medical assistants smoked and checked their cell phones.

They made small talk until Lucy detoured into a tirade about the thief she was certain had been stealing stuff from her room. Matilda listened, appreciating her mother's wit and word selections but ignoring the mentally unbalanced rage and nonsensicalness of it all. She knew Lucy just needed to vent—this was her mother's new reality. It may have been paranoid and confused, but Matilda needed to respect that, for Lucy, the emotions were very real.

When they'd finished eating, Matilda escorted her mother back to her room in the memory unit. She helped Lucy into her nightgown and then brushed her hair while Lucy sang old French folk songs, songs she still remembered vividly from her sabbatical in Toulouse in 1984.

After tucking her mother into bed, Matilda curled up in a chair.

There, she fell asleep watching Lucy's frail chest rise and fall, rise and fall, as her mother drifted into a nostalgia-haunted REM sleep.

17

ASHANIQUE LAY IN BED with her headphones on.

No music played, just a muffled white sound—a combination of Ashanique's own breathing and the dull but constant thrum of the city outside.

The headphones weren't actually plugged into anything.

The jack was tucked under Ashanique's pillow.

Janice had gotten the headphones secondhand from a thrift store she passed regularly on her commute home. She and Ashanique went a few times a month, largely for coats and shoes, but frequently eyed the electronics in a glass case by the register. There were the usual decades-old castoffs: the five-disc CD player, the ancient Nintendo Game Boy, the portable DVD player with a cracked screen. More and more, headphones were showing up. None of the fancy brightly colored ones Ashanique noticed on the street. But, a month ago, when Ashanique saw the ones that were still in the box and advertised "noise-canceling" on the side, she begged her mom to get them. White and black, they cost fifty dollars.

Janice said she'd think about it, but she stopped by the store on her way home from work a week later and bought them. Though there really wasn't an occasion, she gave them to Ashanique for an early half birthday. Ashanique was delighted and danced around the apartment wearing them like earmuffs. The Marcy-Lasing Apartments were never quiet and the noise-canceling feature was a godsend. Around 10:00 p.m., when Ashanique typically went to bed, the noises began. The couple in the apartment right above theirs fought for hours. He'd throw things against the walls. She'd scream and stomp her feet. Sometimes, their arguments got so heated that Ashanique would sleep on the couch with a pillow over her head. But it wasn't just the sound from above: at night the apartment complex seemed to come to life.

Once, Ashanique had caught a few minutes of a PBS nature show about the Ecuadorian jungle. In the show, a camera tracked a jaguar as it made its way through a moonlit landscape. The narrator mentioned how loud the tropics got at night—how every nocturnal animal shrieked and chittered and howled as darkness fell. The Marcy-Lansing Apartments were the same. All the tensions, all the worries, all the anger that the residents had kept bottled up during the day spilled out when the sun sank from sight. All that tension emerged in shouts and whistles and echoing laughter, in fists pounding against doors, in dog barks in stairwells, in the blare of car horns, and the constant throb of window-rattling bass.

For Ashanique, putting on the noise-canceling headphones and then closing her eyes was like falling through a trapdoor into a snowbank of silence. Invigorating and, simultaneously, palliative.

After the first few nights of using the headphones, Ashanique began to hear things in the digital hum. Voices. Songs. Birdcalls. Things like that. At first, the sounds were soothing, like listening to her mom whisper on the phone in the other room. There was a security in the sound—the feeling that when she closed her eyes, when she let the world just take her, her mom was watching, listening in. But as time went on, the sounds embedded in the white noise took on a more ominous quality. She heard sounds like footsteps, creaking, and laughter. She knew it was just her mind making stuff up, but with George's memories suddenly pouring into her head—and other, richer memories right behind—she wasn't so sure anymore. Maybe, she wondered, what she was hearing were the echoes of other people's lives.

The door to Ashanique's bedroom opened and Janice walked in.

She sat on the edge of the bed and gently took the headphones off.

"Hey, baby girl. You doing okay? No cramps or nothing?"

Ashanique shook her head.

"And the things you've been thinking?"

"I'm okay, Mom."

"Good. Listen"—Janice took a deep breath in and released it slowly, like she had just taken a drag of a cigarette—"I think it's about time we moved to a new place. It's loud here. Doesn't exactly have the best neighbors most of the time. Things haven't been so great at work lately, and I thought, maybe if we moved out of the city a ways, just for a while we—"

"This is about the doctor who came here, isn't it?"

"No. No, hon. I'm not mad about that anymore. This is about you and me. Things are going to change, like I told you. I know you understand. Everything will work out just fine, but it might be a bit crazy for a while. I might be a bit . . . saltier. But you know it's just stress, right? That I don't mean it. It's not personal."

"Yeah, Mom."

Ashanique slipped the headphones back on and rolled onto her side. Janice rubbed Ashanique's back, her fingers playing along the girl's spine. After a few minutes, she got up, switched off the lights, and closed the door.

With the door closed and her body relaxed, Ashanique fell asleep quickly.

. . .

Janice woke at 3:00 a.m.

She could hear someone in the hallway outside the apartment.

Suddenly keenly awake, Janice got up off the couch and slipped the Glock 17 out from its hiding place in the bathroom. Safety off, she tiptoed to the front door as silently as possible. Her heart already a jumble, her sympathetic nervous system approaching overdrive, Janice peered through the peephole into the darkened hall just outside her front door.

Get ready, girl. They're here.

Two men stood just outside the door. They wore dark coats, but she could see green scrubs beneath. Even with their faces barely visible behind surgical masks, she knew why the men were there and who they were looking for. One of the men pulled a lockpicking kit from his coat and approached Janice's door. Slowing her breathing, she readied the Glock.

Night Doctors.

Those two words pummeled themselves into Janice's brain.

More than twenty years on the run, more than fifteen different apartments, more than a dozen different names, and here they were. She knew it was because of Matilda. And that was because she'd been lazy, gotten too comfortable, too secure. *Now it's come back to bite you in the ass.* There was a trail now—an invisible thread connecting Janice and Ashanique to the outside world.

It needed to be severed. And fast.

But first, they needed to survive this night.

Janice took her finger from the trigger, tucked the gun into the back of her sweatpants, and ran, bare feet padding quietly as a cat's, to the bathroom. The number of locks on the door, including a complex magnetic lock, ensured she had a few minutes. Maybe even five. Eventually, the Night Doctors would get frustrated enough to just kick the door down.

In the bathroom, Janice removed a loose tile from the wall, reached inside the hole behind it, and pulled out a plastic bag filled with MetroChime—the pale-colored pills in silver blister packs. Janice stuffed the bag into her pocket and grabbed a windbreaker on her way to her daughter's room. As she passed the front door, the knob rattled. Janice considered putting a bullet in the door and seeing if she hit anyone on the other side, but it was too risky.

Janice gently woke Ashanique and covered the girl's mouth.

"I need you to grab some clothes and your shoes."

Ashanique went wide-eyed seeing the Glock in her mother's hand.

"I need you to do it as quick as you can, okay?"

Ashanique nodded.

Janice let her go and Ashanique got out of bed and, eyes still glued to the gun, gathered clothes—jeans, underwear, two T-shirts. As she grabbed her things, bundling them into a plastic bag from her desk, Janice could hear voices whispering behind the front door. Her heart raced, her hands shook from the adrenaline. A ragged noise began, like metal being filed against metal. Like teeth grinding.

"Who are they?" Ashanique whispered.

Janice just shook her head and put a finger to her lips.

As silently as possible, they crept toward the back of the apartment.

Then came a sharp, loud rap on the front door. It was not a human fist knocking but the sound of locks being punched out. *Pop. Pop.* Janice heard the metal locks hitting the floor. The brutal crunch of breaking wood filled the interior of the apartment. Janice imagined one of the men had grabbed a fire ax from down the hall and now he was chopping his way inside.

"We need to move fast, baby."

"I'm scared."

"I know, I know."

Janice wrenched open the window behind her bed, overturning the two frail potted plants Ashanique had been trying to revive since she found them in a dumpster two months ago. Neither pot shattered, but the thud was obvious.

Within seconds, they were on the fire escape.

As Janice helped Ashanique through the window and closed it, she looked back and caught a glimpse of the Night Doctors scrambling into the hallway. They both held knives; long filleting blades that glinted in the half-light like silver fish at the bottom of a murky stream. Janice had seen what those knives could do. Even though she had been a child at the time, the memory was lodged deep into the core of her being—the knife was drawn, it cut the air like a whistle, and then it slid across a perfect expanse of bare flesh, leaving a red and glistening wave in its wake.

Don't go back there, Janice told herself, *not now.*

Janice turned her attention back to the fire escape.

Ashanique was in front of her, scrambling down the rattling metal steps. Janice followed; she did not look back again. When their feet hit the cold asphalt of the alleyway, they ran toward the sounds of traffic.

This was the moment she'd spent years preparing Ashanique to face. In fact, they'd played out this very scenario only a week earlier.

Janice was proud of how Ashanique held herself, how focused she was. When Ashanique was six years old, all her school friends were giggling in gymnastics or taking piano lessons while she was learning urban survival skills. How to filter and purify water, escape an evasion, handle firearms, and take apart pens to make lockpicks.

She would need that strength and training for what was to come.

18

RADE STOOD NAKED before the floor-to-ceiling mirror, wearing only wireless headphones.

Philip Glass's "Facades" played at maximum volume as Rade scanned his body. He did this every day, though he wasn't particularly vain. He was looking for corruption, for the animal breaking through.

The hotel room around him was spotless.

He'd inspected it carefully before the room's actual occupant, a businessman from Ohio with sagging jowls and clubbed nails from ulcerative colitis, returned from a dinner at the chain steakhouse across the street. Rade surprised him and, nude, wrestled him to the ground before he broke the fat man's neck between his thighs. He stuffed the man's body into the bed frame beneath the mattress and sprinkled it with the sodium hydroxide he'd ordered from a soap manufacturing supply store.

Rade prided himself on being meticulous.

He considered his work an extension of himself: the long shadow he cast out into the world. Rade wouldn't go so far as to say what he did was art. He wasn't pretentious. Well, at least not *that* pretentious. But this thing he did, it was a calling, and he took it very seriously. Staring at his face, violins sawing back and forth to a metronome rhythm in his ears, Rade couldn't help but consider himself handsome. It wasn't the hard edges of his face or the brutalist plugs he called eyes, it was the gravitas. It was the awesome power—a sort of biblical sway—that seemed to radiate from him.

I am the next stage, he told his reflection, *crushing the base.*

Rade noticed a blond hair poking up on his left shoulder. It was only visible in direct light and he had to roll his shoulder to see it properly. Maybe two centimeters long. Rade picked up a pair of medical tweezers from the nightstand by the bed. He plucked the hair carefully, ensuring it didn't break off at the root. Holding it tight in the tweezers, Rade examined the hair with the dutiful gaze of a scientist.

This is my battle.

Each hair a soldier to destroy.

Each hair an inch of ground to take back.

To win the war, he just needed to clear the hangers-on from his head.

Rade walked the hair over to the toilet, dropped it inside, and flushed it away. As he watched the water spin in the porcelain basin, he ran his hands over his hairless arms. His skin was soft and warm. He touched his face, his fingers tracing the supraorbital ridge where his eyebrows had once been. The skin there was so thin.

Rade did not consider himself human.

It was not something he admitted openly.

Rade didn't know what he was exactly—a spirit? A demon?—but he was certain that he was trapped in a hairy, vile body. One that sprouted hair in the most unlikely of places; that shed skin and grew useless nails; that oozed foul liquids; one plagued by strange, unnecessary urges.

Rade looked out at the world, the civilized world of cities and cars and tablet screens, and saw only apes poking away at technology they didn't understand. He saw gibbering, wide-eyed hordes of animals on the highway, and he cringed at the very thought of being surrounded by them in elevators, malls, and sporting events. Even the best and brightest luminaries of the scientific world or the champions of literature were just less hairy monkeys scratching at ingrown hairs, struggling with bowel movements, and salivating over bulges.

No, Rade was sure he wasn't human.

He was lighter, cleaner, and more efficient. And he was changing his body, redesigning the brute his mind was trapped inside, to become . . . *something more.* Rade was pushing into the chrysalis stage. Whatever his final form would be—and he had many ideas, ranging from the next stage of human evolution to a being composed entirely of light—it would finally make him feel whole, comfortable on this planet.

Rade returned to the floor-to-ceiling mirror with a duffel bag in one hand and a bowl of hot water in the other. This was his process. His ritual.

"Facades" began again, on a perpetual loop. Watching himself, his movements careful and calculated, he opened the duffel bag and removed a scouring pad and surgical soap. He applied the soap to the pad and then dipped it into the water before he cleansed himself. Every inch of exposed skin was scrubbed. He washed his penis but had no urge to masturbate; he looked at the organ between his legs the same way he'd look at his earlobe: a weird evolutionary adaptation for a bestial creation. Sure, the organ's purpose made sense and he'd indulged it in every way imaginable—from the most innocent pleasures to the most decadent horrors. Regardless, he now saw the pinnacle of joy as moving free of his physical form. And that time would come soon. He was sure of it.

Twenty-two minutes later, Rade stepped from the shower and toweled off.

His skin was bright red. Scoured.

Rade walked back into the main room and stood naked before the immensity of the night. The moment was broken by the buzz of his cell phone. Returning to the duffel bag, he kneeled down beside it and removed a single latex glove. He pulled it on, slid off his headphones, and answered the cell.

"Rade."

"Fifty-One is on the move," a woman's voice said.

"Where?"

"Washington Park."

"And what is near there?"

"The university. We expect they're heading to the medical center."

"She have the girl with her?"

"Yes."

Rade hung up and dropped the cell phone on the bed.

As he pulled off the latex glove, he noticed a tremor in his right hand: his index finger twitching with a life of its own. Suddenly furious, Rade grabbed his index finger and twisted it. Hard. Ignoring the pain, he closed his eyes, took a deep breath, and let the air out slowly. As his lungs deflated, he refocused himself. In his mind's eye, he saw a clock inside his chest; a series of overlaid gears, each ratcheting into synchronization. When he'd visualized each gear turning in perfect alignment with the gears in front and behind it, Rade opened his eyes.

His index finger stopped twitching.

Rade walked back into the bathroom and pulled two MetroChime capsules from a pillbox tucked into his shaving kit. He chewed them carefully, enjoying the resulting bitter mush. He knew he had to go—back into the morass of humanity, back into the animal fray.

Soon, he told himself, *soon. . . .*

It was only a matter of time before his body's infantile rebellions stopped; only a matter of time before he could ignore the constant babble of his older selves.

Rade was certain his next incarnation would be as a being of light.

19

MATILDA WALKED DOWN the hallway to her office wishing she'd showered. She'd had a fitful, awful night.

Every time the heat kicked on in Lucy's room, the resulting snap-and-rush sound shook her from a sleep as tasteless and dry as expired crackers. Matilda finally left around 5:00 a.m. She pulled her mom's blankets up and kissed her on the forehead—Lucy lay still, her lower lip trembling.

Matilda was nearly to the highway when she realized she wasn't actually tired—sore, yes, but very much awake. Her brain firing on every neural cylinder it had. She drove to work outside of herself: what psychologists refer to as self-hypnosis, her conscious brain unaware of the traffic or the stoplights; her body in full control of the car; her mind focused on Janice and Ashanique.

What is their story? What is Janice hiding?

After she'd parked in the garage, Matilda did a cursory search to see if Janice had a social media presence. She found the woman had no digital history at all. Matilda tried the university's electronic medical system. The only thing she turned up was a poorly scanned PDF copy of Janice's signature on a "consent to treat" form and a HIPAA notification. Both collected by Todd eleven months earlier. It was enough to cover her ass if Janice showed up ranting and raving about HIPAA violations and wanted to talk to the review board or file a complaint, but gave her precious little to work with. There was one curious thing: there were timestamps for each instance the

PDF had been viewed. While it had remained unmolested for almost a year, someone had looked at it three hours before Matilda got to it.

Who would look at a consent form in the middle of the night?

Reaching her office, Matilda unlocked the door and stepped inside. She was eager to get onto the system from her desktop and see if she couldn't drum up some information on who exactly had access to the PDF and why. With her first class two hours away, she figured she had time enough to do some deep digging.

She was wrong.

Ashanique was sitting in Matilda's chair at her desk. The girl was on the desktop playing Minesweeper. As Matilda stood there, eyes wide with shock, Ashanique spun around and smiled. That was when Matilda noticed Janice sitting in a folding chair in the corner of the room beside a mountain of file folders.

She had a Glock pointed at Matilda.

"Come in and close the door," Janice said. "Ashanique, move."

Ashanique got up out of the chair as Matilda, heart racing, closed the door behind her.

"Janice," Matilda said as she crossed the room to her desk, eyes locked on Janice's, "I know you weren't happy with me talking to—"

"Sit," Janice said, motioning with the gun.

Matilda sat and turned the chair to face Janice. Ashanique was sitting behind her mother, her face a storm of emotions. In that instant, Matilda understood why Janice appeared to have been erased from the web—she was in hiding, on the run from something, and Ashanique was caught up in her mother's whirlwind.

Janice said, "I need you to erase everything on the university system about my daughter. Every note you've taken, every medical record. I don't want her name, even her initials, to appear on a single form. Understand?"

"Yes." Matilda nodded. "But Ashanique needs help, Janice."

"Not from you. Delete the files."

Matilda looked past Janice at Ashanique.

"Are you okay?" she asked the girl.

Ashanique nodded. Though she appeared relatively calm, Matilda could see the anxiety and fear in her eyes. The girl was strong, incredibly brave, but

Matilda could tell Ashanique was just barely holding it all together. As much as she prided herself on having a consistently professional mien, there was something about Ashanique that brought out a powerful, almost feral maternal instinct in Matilda. Every fiber of her being joined in a cellular chant: *You need to protect this girl.*

"She's fine," Janice said, sensing Matilda's protectiveness.

She turned Matilda's chair back around with her foot.

As Matilda logged in, she noticed her hands were shaking. She had never had a gun pointed at her before. That wasn't as disturbing as the steeliness in Janice's eyes, however. The way she held the gun was so . . . proficient. For the first time in a very long time, Matilda worried that she was going to die in her office. Previously, she'd imagined that she'd have a heart attack after spending too many grueling weekends grading exams at her computer. But a bullet in the back was something else entirely. She wanted to panic, to scream until security came running and smashed down the door, but she knew that wasn't the way out of this.

Stay calm. . . . Just do what they say and breathe. . . .

As Matilda logged in, Ashanique glanced up at all the Post-it Notes. Cautiously, the girl read what she could, gently lifting the papers and looking underneath. As Matilda brought up her patient databases and medical records, Ashanique paused and pointed to Theo Vang's obituary.

"I know this man," Ashanique said to Janice.

Matilda shivered. "What?"

"I've seen him," the girl said. "In my mind."

"Not now," Janice snapped. "Let's finish this."

She leaned forward and tapped Matilda on the shoulder, pointed to the computer. Ashanique's frightened expression on her mind, Matilda tried to focus on the databases and files, deleting every mention of Ashanique (even if it was de-identified). Though it took only seconds, Matilda dragged the process out as long as she could. She knew a security guard usually rounded her floor around seven. If she could hold Janice off until he showed up, knocking at her office door, to nod and say good morning, then maybe she'd get Ashanique out of this thing with only a scare.

Forty-six minutes. Come on, you can do it.

"Where is the pharmacy?" Janice asked.

"Downstairs. First floor, but it doesn't open for another hour and a half."

"We need some medication."

"I don't— I can't really help you with that."

"You have an ID, right? One that opens doors."

Matilda said, "But not the pharmacy doors. I'm just research."

"We'll see. . . ."

Matilda turned around to face Janice. She hoped that her pleading look would be enough to convince Janice that she was serious, that this . . . *this* had to stop here, with no one getting hurt.

"Please, Janice," Matilda said. "Think of Ashanique. She shouldn't be seeing this. She should be getting some help. I know you think you're doing what's right, that you're protecting her but—"

Janice leveled the Glock on Matilda.

"Everything I do is for my daughter."

20

AS SUSPECTED, MATILDA'S ID didn't unlock the pharmacy door.

Matilda had suggested as much, but Janice needed to see it herself. Despite Ashanique's radiating tension and Matilda's shaking hands, Janice was utterly calm. Gun at Matilda's back, she cleared her throat and considered her options.

"Someone who works here will be in—" Matilda began.

"No time," Janice interrupted. "Move aside."

Matilda stepped to the right as Janice slipped a set of small stainless steel lockpicks from her back pocket. They appeared hand-machined.

"Come here, kneel down," Janice said, motioning to the space between her and the door. "I'm not going to hurt you, but I can't take any risks, clear?"

Matilda, the shaking in her hands getting worse, the fist at the back of her throat threatening to block her airway completely, kneeled down in front of Janice. As she did, she again caught the trembling fear in Ashanique's eyes.

Matilda mouthed, *It'll be okay.*

Ashanique didn't appear convinced.

As Janice worked, Matilda studied her closely. The woman's nonverbal clues gave away nothing; she was in complete control of her body. Matilda might have chalked it up to drugs, but she suspected it was training. Not military, not gang. The only people she'd seen who were that controlled, that insanely focused, had been new intakes to cult deprogramming sessions.

Click. The door unlocked.

Twenty-three seconds and Janice was done.

Janice tucked her tools into her pocket and motioned for Matilda to get up.

"We need a particular drug, okay?" Janice said. "It's called MetroChime."

"I'm not familiar with it."

"You'll look it up in the system. I know they have it here."

Matilda led Janice and Ashanique inside, through the tall shelving systems filled with carefully organized bottles, trays, and boxes. Matilda stopped at a computer. Her badge unlocked the home screen, allowing her access to her patients' files but not the pharmacy's dispensing software. Janice stood over Matilda, her impatient energy filling the room.

"I don't have access to this."

"Find a way around," Janice said. "The drug is for blood cancers. It works on chimeric antigen receptor T cells. It's phase three; there are trials ongoing here. Check research files. Make it happen, Matilda."

Matilda tried to log into the clinical research databases. She'd had access in the past, when she was called in on some pediatric trials, but it had been a long time. She doubted her approval was still valid. The passcodes would have been updated as well. Matilda knew it wasn't going to happen.

"It won't work," Matilda said. "Listen, Janice, please just—"

"Move."

Janice shoved the gun into Matilda's face.

Ashanique cringed.

Fighting the urge to jump up and try and overpower Janice, even if it meant taking a bullet to the chest, Matilda slowly got up out of the chair.

"There are other ways to get what you want," Matilda said. "I can talk to someone in the department; we can get you help. But Ashanique doesn't need to be here. She doesn't need to see you doing this."

"You need to shut the fuck up," Janice said as she took the chair.

Matilda moved back beside Ashanique. And as she did, their hands touched momentarily. It sent a warm, electric sensation up Matilda's arm and over her shoulders. She took Ashanique's hand in her own and squeezed it tight.

While Janice's lockpicking skills impressed Matilda, her hacking talents were actually surprising. Janice opened and closed programs with dizzying speed, diving into the guts of the operating system. Matilda's eyes, however, were fixed on the gun. Janice had placed it on the desk beside the computer. Out of her hands, the gun looked smaller. Oddly softer. Matilda couldn't stop her brain from conjuring up scenarios where she swiped the weapon to the floor and kicked it away. Or, even more ludicrous, where she grabbed the gun and leveled it at Janice.

As each scenario played out on the membrane screen of her mind, she asked herself: *Would you pull the trigger? Would you kill this woman in front of her daughter? Does it matter? This is your only chance. You want to live, right?*

Matilda found herself shifting her weight forward, her body unconsciously pushing itself toward the gun.

"Unit fifteen, shelf two hundred and one," Janice said, grabbing the gun and spinning from the computer, as Ashanique pulled her hand from Matilda's grip.

Unit fifteen was in the far-left corner of the room near the refrigerated medications. Janice found shelf 203 a few feet off the floor. The MetroChime was two shelves below. Janice grabbed two marked boxes and opened them. Stuffing blister packs of the drug into her coat pockets, Janice paused to hand a few back to Ashanique. The girl put them in her pants pockets.

"No, baby," Janice said. "You need to take two right now."

Matilda interrupted. "This is experimental—"

She stopped when Janice again stuck the Glock in her face.

"You shut up. Take them, baby. "

Ashanique pushed two of the yellow-and-white capsules through the silver blisters covering them. Janice kept the barrel of the handgun steady, inches away from Matilda's forehead.

"They don't taste too bad," Janice told her daughter. "Just go ahead and put 'em in your mouth and chew 'em up. You'll feel better right away."

Eyes on Matilda, Ashanique placed the capsules in her mouth.

Matilda nodded to her, hoping to project stoicism.

"It's okay," she whispered.

Ashanique chewed the capsules, her face pinched at the bitter taste.

Matilda had no idea what the cancer drugs might do, what sorts of side effects they could have. Phase III meant they'd made it through animal testing and a small cohort of human research. It meant MetroChime, whatever it actually was, had been approved for more extensive clinical testing. But none of that meant it was safe. Matilda knew that only a quarter of drugs actually made the move from phase III into general sale to the public. And chances were this T cell receptor cancer drug wasn't approved for use in children.

Wheels turning on the assumption that she'd get out of the pharmacy alive, Matilda tried to mentally calculate how long they'd have to pump Ashanique's stomach. At the same time, she knew it was likely that two capsules wouldn't have much of an immediate effect. Even more, Matilda suspected Janice had been taking them herself—*How else would she know about the drug?*—and doubted the woman would purposefully poison her own child. No, Janice surely believed MetroChime worked. *But to treat what?*

The back door to the pharmacy opened.

"Matilda?"

Matilda's body jumped at the sound of Clark's voice.

Janice tightened her grip on the gun. Matilda could see she was readying for the kickback, her shoulders narrowing and her soul going numb.

"I can make him go away. Please, trust me," Matilda whispered.

Janice shook her head.

"He doesn't have anything to do with this. *Please.*"

Clark's shoes squeaked on the tile floor. Matilda knew exactly which ones they were, the sneakers that he rarely wore, the ones his daughter, Amanda, told him were hip. Clark thought they were too shiny, too brightly colored, and told Matilda he worried people would look at him and assume he was some midlife-crisis sap desperate to hold on to his rearview mirror youth. She didn't have the heart to tell him he was right, that was exactly how the shoes looked.

"Yo, Maddie? You back here?"

Maddie . . . God, Clark, please be careful.

Janice nodded to Matilda. "Make him leave."

"Thank you. . . . Thank you. . . ."

Not wasting a millisecond, Matilda stepped out from between the shelving units. Clark waved to her and walked over, all early-morning, overcaffeinated smiles. "What the heck are you doing down here? I came in to meet you early like we'd planned and, uh, saw you vanishing around a corner. Figured I'd follow you down . . ."

Clark looked over Matilda's shoulder.

"You with someone? Pharmacy's not exactly open—"

"Clark, I can't talk right now. Can you meet me in my office?"

He read her face, the panic she was trying to hide.

"You okay, babe?" Clark asked.

"Yes, yes. I just— Meet me upstairs."

Matilda didn't see the shadow slide up behind Clark, but she saw the rubber-gloved hand reach across his neck. The sight was so suddenly incongruous that she couldn't process what was happening. She saw a straight razor in the rubber-gloved hand. The folding kind barbers used in old-timey shops, but sleeker, sharper.

Eyes bulging, Clark wheezed as the razor drew a perfect red line that bisected his throat. The line opened like a second mouth. It was filled with the brightest blood Matilda had ever seen.

Clark folded, his shocked gaze locked on Matilda's.

No. No. No....

Matilda wanted to scream.

She wanted desperately to explode in panic.

But she was utterly immobilized with horror.

There was a man in a hoodie and tapered athletic pants standing just behind Clark. He was extraordinarily bald and his skin gleamed in the buzzing fluorescents like a freshly waxed bowling lane.

He winked at Matilda.

"Where's Fifty-One?"

21

LIKE MOST PEOPLE, Matilda had mentally toyed with terrifying moments.

She'd indulged in weird daydreams born of bad headlines that quickly twisted into survival fantasies. Every time she'd played out the scenarios—whether in the midst of a mass shooting or being chased by an armed man—she took risks, bold risks, to ensure her own survival. But that moment, when the threat actually materialized in hideously cold reality, when the blood was pumping like thunder in her ears, she thought only of Ashanique.

"Run!"

Before the man in the hoodie could so much as wink again, Matilda spun and ran back toward the aisle where Ashanique was huddled. Janice stood in front of the girl, the Glock aimed at Clark's killer.

Without a word, she pulled the trigger.

Matilda ducked and turned to see the bullet slam into a cabinet to the right of the man. Despite the shot, he continued walking toward Janice.

"You have to run," Matilda said as she stumbled over to Ashanique and grabbed her arm. Then, she turned to Janice. "We need to go right now!"

Ignoring Matilda, Janice fired again.

The man in the hoodie dodged right, the bullet screamed past him.

"Please, Janice, we have to go!"

The man in the hoodie picked up speed, began running toward Janice. Seeing the predatory expression on his face, the cold fire in his eyes, Matilda knew he would not stop. Even with a bullet lodged in his lungs, if Janice were lucky enough to hit him, he would thunder forward with a cosmological certainty.

Get the fuck out of there.

Matilda dragged Ashanique toward the front door to the pharmacy. The girl was crying, her head turned back toward her mother, but she didn't slow. Matilda knew there was an alarm by the entrance. One she could trigger with her badge.

They'd had so many campus drills, so many intensely boring security presentations, that she knew the stats by heart—campus police would be on the scene within three minutes. However, three minutes sounded like nothing when she was in a classroom with a hundred other restless employees. But when a killer was chasing after her with a blade, it quickly became a lifetime. For a moment, Matilda thought about how she'd tell Clark about the morning's encounter—she imagined him putting a shock blanket over her shoulders while she sat in the back of an ambulance, the way loving people do on television—but then images of Clark's open throat, his desperate eyes, flashed before her.

Jesus, Clark...

Pushing aside the images, Matilda rounded a corner and collided with a medical cart. She remained upright, but the cart smashed back against a wall, boxes, syringes, and bottles scattering across the tile floor. Reaching the front of the pharmacy, Matilda directed Ashanique to scramble beneath the counter.

"Stay here, back as far as you can go. Stay hidden."

"What about my mom?" Ashanique asked from under the counter.

"I'm getting us out of here. Getting us safe."

"My mom, Matilda..."

Matilda couldn't answer; she needed Ashanique to be focused. They weren't safe yet. Not by a long shot. Matilda swiped her badge on the alarm pad by the door. Sirens instantly screamed to life.

Three minutes, Matilda repeated to herself. *Just three minutes.*

Then she ducked down beside Ashanique and wrapped her arm around the girl and held her tight. She wanted to reassure her that she was safe, that the nightmare was over. But she knew she couldn't. So she just enveloped Ashanique and let the girl melt into her, the only safety she could be sure of.

Seconds later, Janice barreled around the corner, Glock in hand. She glanced around the room for a moment before ducking down to peek under the counter. Her eyes locked with Ashanique's.

"I think I hit him," she said.

"Mom, I don't want to run anymore."

Janice calmly got to her knees and crawled under the counter to her daughter. She took Ashanique's right hand in her own and squeezed it before she leaned in and touched the tip of her nose to the girl's.

Ashanique began to cry.

"No, baby," Janice said, gun still gripped tight in her left hand. "It's going to be okay. We're going to be just fine. You have to do something for me, though. You have to listen. Can you do that for me?"

"Yes," Ashanique said, voice breaking.

"Police will be here soon, Janice. Just a couple of minutes."

Janice ignored Matilda, focused solely on her daughter.

"What's happening in your head—the voices, the people—is only just starting. You have to take the medication every four hours. Have to be exact. If you go too long between doses, you'll get a headache. Skip one and the headaches will get much worse. Miss more than three and there's no going back."

Ashanique pulled the capsules from her pocket to look at them.

"What if I like the memories? What if I want them?"

"No, baby," Janice said. "The memories are bad. Tell me you get that."

Ashanique nodded.

Janice continued, "Tomorrow afternoon, you need to have Matilda take you to the library at the International Museum of Surgical Science by four p.m. Don't forget. Can't be late, okay? Someone named Childers will be waiting there for you. You trust Childers, understand? No one else."

"You're gonna be there too, right?"

Janice bit her lower lip before she kissed Ashanique's forehead. The girl's eyes were turbulent and teary; Janice stabilized them with her own steeled gaze.

"I love you," Janice said. "Always will."

"Mom . . . ," Ashanique squeaked.

The sound of her voice crumbling under the weight of pain and distress nearly broke Matilda. She unconsciously wrapped her arm tighter around Ashanique, trying to stabilize the girl against a psychological cataclysm.

Janice said, "I need you to remember that I love you more than anything. Everything I've put you through, all the moving, all the medications, all the difficulty was because I needed to keep you safe. All I ever wanted was for you to be okay, to live a good life. That is why I have to leave now. Even if you forget what I look like, and you will, remember my love for you."

Ashanique called out as Janice pulled away.

Matilda held her back as the alarm shredded the air. As Ashanique screamed and struggled, Matilda watched Janice vanish around a corner.

Scattered gunshots quickly followed.

With every distant pop, Matilda cringed and Ashanique cried louder.

"They'll be here soon," Matilda said. "We're safe. We're safe...."

She realized she was saying it, almost chanting it, more for herself than for Ashanique. Matilda needed it to be true. She needed to believe this wasn't how her life was going to end. Just a day earlier, every cell of her being was coded with a singular goal—find the key to memory. Ashanique switched it all up. She was now the only thing keeping Matilda going; that shift, rooted in the primal core of her being, wrenched her focus toward a new goal: *You have to save this girl's life.*

"We're safe. I've got you."

Ashanique's cries subsided and she settled, but only momentarily.

The spasms began with a violent jerk as the girl suddenly wrenched her head back. Her eyes rolled to white, her teeth chattered. Matilda held her as tightly as she could, worrying Ashanique might bite off her own tongue and praying—for the first time in a long time, honestly, sincerely praying—security would arrive.

Just before she passed out, Ashanique opened her eyes, pupils widening.

"I see everything," she said.

Matilda held the girl and whispered half-remembered psalms.

"You will take refuge under his wing.... No harm will come to you...."

She felt silly saying the words out loud, trying to peel back the decades to find language that made sense. Matilda wasn't religious, but in that moment, it felt like the only thing to do. There was peace in it.

Matilda heard more gunfire.

Then shouting, running.

Seconds later, campus police officers appeared. Guns drawn, the radios at their hips rattled with static and panic. An officer with light-brown eyes crouched down by the pharmacy counter and looked over at Matilda and a limp Ashanique.

"It's over," she said. "You're safe now."

22

RUNNING.

Heart pumping.

Tunnel blind.

Branches whip the young boy's face as he races down the narrow trail. The other hunters are close behind him. He hears his uncle's rapid breathing. The musky scent of the tiger is strong, hanging like a vapor over the trail. He sees its tail in every creeper, its stripes in every shadow.

This is his moment.

His to own.

Around him, the forest pushes in. Birds call and scatter. Monkeys shriek in the low-hanging branches. The trees buzz with life. Every leaf hides an insect. Beneath every stone, a snake. The hunters know this trail but not like the boy. He's spent his life memorizing its turns and straightaways, navigating each stone and root.

The boy is twelve today.

His celebration is this hunt.

He wears a simple length of fabric tied about his hips. In his hands is the push dagger his uncle made for him. It has never pierced flesh, but the young boy is anxious to use it. In his mind, if he kills this tiger, he will be a strong man like his father. If he fails, he will be a simple villager. He's seen how their lives are measured by their kills. The boy's bare feet slap against the hard soil as he carefully dodges every approaching obstacle.

The boy and the hunters run through a field of shoulder-high grass before scrambling after the tiger as it winds its way down the rocky side of a steep gorge. A river churns far below. The hunters stop at the edge of the gorge, but the boy follows the tiger down—he is fleet, his balance uncanny.

Reaching the waterline, the boy jumps over boulders, slick with moss and washed by constant waves, before cornering the tiger in the roots of a vine-choked tree. The hunters egg the boy on from above.

He pulls his push dagger from his knotted sarong. The beast flashes its teeth and hisses. Heart racing, breath caught in his throat, the boy moves closer. The tiger lashes out with razor-tipped paws. The boy dodges but catches a claw on his thigh—it leaves a long, paper-thin gash.

The boy stabs with the dagger; the tiger lunges.

It slams into the boy, and the watching hunters shout as both tiger and boy tumble into the fast-moving river. They are swept into the river, tumbling, head over feet, in the choppy, dark water.

Two miles downstream, the river widens and slackens.

The boy is first to claw his way out onto the muddy bank. He rolls over, hacking up lungsful of water, and stares back at the river.

Birds flock overhead, their screeching echoing through the jungle.

The boy's heart slows, his breathing steadies. He is just pulling himself up when he sees the tiger paddling toward him. The boy freezes. It shakes off the water, eyes locked on him. The boy doesn't dare turn his head. The tiger growls once before leaping over the boy and vanishing in the forest behind him.

The boy falls backward and sighs.

The sun is reflected in his dark eyes just as . . .

23

THE BOY'S EYES became Ashanique's eyes.

The tiger and the river and the forest melted away, and all she saw were the bright lights of the ceiling spinning overhead like exploding constellations. She found herself lying in a hospital bed with an IV in her arm. The clear tape used to keep in the IV hurt, her skin was stretched around it, and the blood under the tape, a tiny puddle smooshed flat, discolored her skin.

Ashanique was alone.

The door was closed. Outside, she heard nothing. As though the very planet had stopped moving. Wherever she was, it seemed safe. Safe enough. Ashanique closed her eyes for a few moments and replayed the jungle chase. As it came rushing back, her pulse quickened. . . .

The jungle foliage crushing in . . .

The tiger jumping at her, its teeth flashing before . . .

A bomb explodes . . .

Clods of dirt fly skyward . . .

A British soldier falls, mouth gushing blood . . .

Ashanique's eyes snapped open.

She had to breathe slowly to calm her pulse, to stop her heart from bursting like a rabbit's. Calming down, she looked around the room. It was small, the bed enclosed by all manner of medical equipment—some of it on, most of it not. Despite the presence of the machines, deep down, coiled somewhere in her chest, was the soft, glowing feeling of knowing she was not sick.

No matter what Matilda said.

No matter what the doctors who hooked her up to the machines thought.

She wasn't sick, not sick like someone with cancer or a brain disease. Whatever was happening to her was organic . . . a process that felt determined and inevitable but at the same time familiar. Intimately so. Whatever was coming to life in her was integral. Ashanique also knew, intrinsically, inexplicably, that her mother was out there, alive, and that the bald man with no eyebrows was coming to kill her.

He had come for her mom. Ashanique was next on the list.

The Night Doctors always found their patients.

That is why Mom told you to run. Why she told you never to trust anyone except Childers. Go to the museum. Get there by sunset tomorrow.

With her uneasiness quickly rising, Ashanique pulled up the edge of the tape over her IV. The skin came up with it, the tiny, invisible hairs too. It hurt and the flesh around the IV was quickly turning red. But Ashanique knew she didn't have a choice, she had to push through the pain. Gritting her teeth, she pulled the tape away from her wrist. The IV came out with the tape, the long catheter emerging with a bubble of blood. Ashanique staunched the wound with the edge of the pillowcase.

Then she swung her legs around the edge of the bed and got up.

She was woozy for a moment.

The last rivulets of blood running down her arm tickled.

Ashanique found her clothes in a bag on a chair in the corner of the room. Dropping the pillowcase, she slipped out of the thin hospital gown and into her clothes. Fully dressed, shoes slipped on, she peeked outside, into the hallway.

It was empty.

Moving quickly, eyes to the ground, Ashanique walked out of her room and into the hall. She headed to her right, hugging the walls with her shoulder. Though she had no idea where she was going, she assumed this hospital was like most hospitals—stairs and elevators would be readily available.

The hallway ended, branching to the left and right. But twenty feet away, directly across from her, was a service elevator. It could only be accessed with a badge or a key, and there was an armed security guard standing in front of it, distractedly looking at something on his cell phone.

Ashanique mentally replayed the image of the bald man splitting open Matilda's friend's throat. She replayed the heavy gush of blood. She replayed the bald man's emotionless expression. His merciless speed.

Ashanique had to get into that elevator.

The intersection was busy. There was a nurses' station to her right, where two men and a woman, all clad in green scrubs, sat and talked. To her left, a man restocked a cart stacked high with folded bed linens. He had earbuds in and was nodding his head in time to a silent beat.

Ashanique figured she'd just walk over, as calmly as possible, press the call button, and hope the guard left her alone. It was risky.

What if he notices you? Asks you what you're doing?

How are you going to talk your way past him?

Think, silly. Come up with something good . . . something believable. . . .

Ashanique remembered the Indian boy and the tiger. While his memories didn't surge back, the sensation of them did. Looking over at the security guard, her eyes tracking his movements, she noticed subtle things about him—the fact that one of his shoulders slouched lower than the other, that he had coffee stains on his pants and orthopedic shoes. Things she never would have noticed two days ago—things she never would have cared about. But now, here, she saw them and put them together as though she were assembling a puzzle.

You're going to take him, a voice inside her head said. *He'll drop easy.*

Ashanique unconsciously balled her hands into fists.

She was a passenger in her own body. Someone else, someone older, someone dangerous, had taken over. The voice was strong, cold.

You bring the guard down and then get into the elevator. If you hurry, we can be out of here before the alarms even go off. You need to find Childers. Dr. Song can help you; he can help all of you and stop the Night Doctors and their killer.

Ashanique moved, every muscle taut, ready to spring, but just as she crossed the carpeted intersection, the security guard's radio blurted a static fart. He grabbed it and walked away, talking. Never even noticing her.

But Ashanique was in motion now.

As she walked to the elevator, Ashanique grabbed a ballpoint pen from on top of a crash cart parked against a wall nearby. With each step, she took the pen apart. Unwinding the pen's tightly coiled spring to pick the elevator lock, Ashanique stepped up to the elevator, hands unnaturally still. A heartbeat before she inserted the unwound spring, the doors whooshed open. Two doctors stood inside, staring at her. Both wore blood-spattered scrubs and medical masks.

Night Doctors.

Ashanique didn't think. She didn't plan what happened next, her body simply reacted. She swung the pen's ink cartridge hard into the first doctor's side; embedding the sharp tip of the pen in between his ribs like a small black arrow. The doctor screamed and collapsed backward into the elevator. But Ashanique didn't see that, she'd already turned, already started to run in the opposite direction.

Right into Matilda.

Seeing Matilda's face was like seeing the shore after being dragged, tumbling, by a riptide out into the dark sea. Ashanique ran to that shore, her composure breaking down, her strength crumbling away with every emotion-choked breath.

Matilda opened her arms to Ashanique.

"It's okay, I've got you."

"I need to get out of here. He's coming for me."

"You're safe," Matilda said. "You're safe here. The doors are locked and there are guards on every floor."

"I got out of my room easy."

Matilda looked over Ashanique's shoulder at the elevator, where several nurses were helping the injured doctor over to a chair. Security guards, their radios a riot of robot voices, raced over, eyes pointed in Ashanique's direction.

"The man isn't here anymore. The police are after him, okay?"

"And my mom?"

"I promise you they're looking for her, as hard as they can. As soon as the police hear something, they'll tell us."

Ashanique let go of Matilda and turned to the elevator. She watched as a nurse pulled the pen from the doctor's side. "She's going to be okay, right?"

"I'm sure she will."

Three security guards, hands on their weapons, were walking over.

Ashanique looked at Matilda, eyes swimming with tears. "I didn't mean to hurt him . . . I—I thought he was one of them. You understand, right? Please. Please tell them that I didn't mean it. That I'm just so confused."

Matilda waved off the security guards.

"Just give us a minute, please," she said.

The guards stopped a few feet away.

Matilda kneeled down and Ashanique followed. Heads close, eyes locked, Matilda asked, "Do you need to talk?"

"Yes. But not here."

"I understand," Matilda said. "Are you hungry?"

Ashanique nodded.

"Great."

Matilda looked down at Ashanique's wrist.

She noticed the oozing bruise where the IV used to be.

"The doctor's going to be okay. It was just a misunderstanding. You've been through . . . Well, you've experienced something this morning that most people never see. And shouldn't."

"You saw it too. It was your friend."

Matilda nodded, swallowing hard.

Ashanique watched a single tear form in the corner of Matilda's left eye. As it slid down her cheek, the girl reached up and wiped it away. Matilda smiled.

"Do they have pancakes here?" Ashanique asked.

"Yes. Very good pancakes."

"Can we go?"

Matilda stood.

"Yes, we can go."

24

KOJO OMABOE WAS looking for the cathedral patterns in a cherrywood board.

The bearded forty-five-year-old homicide detective was working on another end table. This one was for his neighbors, Morris and Barbara Thomson. They'd been excellent neighbors, watching out for his place when he'd been away and keeping an eye on his son, Brandon, though they didn't need to. *Neighborly* was how they described themselves. He figured that went a long way in today's world. And he wanted to reward them for it.

Like always, the cherry end table ended up a transitional piece.

Though Kojo wasn't instinctively drawn to any contemporary style, he found his hands made simple forms. He was minimalist by nature. When he looked at the wood, he never saw complicated pieces. He saw plain geometric shapes, mostly angled. It was not the sort of work his family would have expected.

Kojo's grandfather Ekow came from a long line of woodworkers in Aburi, Ghana. While Kojo had inherited Ekow's artistic bent, he didn't get his lighter skin tone or squat stature. Kojo was dark and tall, with broad shoulders and a permanently furrowed brow. Kojo had never met his grandfather, he only knew his face from his mother's photo albums, but he grew up surrounded by Ekow's work—there were masks on every wall and stools in every corner of his family home. Ekow'd made the traditional items for the souvenir market: Akan masks, Ashanti stools, mortars, fertility dolls, and drums. Despite being immersed in the culture, Kojo didn't come up thinking he'd make masks, dolls, or furniture.

He didn't think he'd be a cop either.

In high school, all the aptitude tests he took suggested he'd be an engineer or a physician. He had a thing for numbers and an intensely rational mind—his father had taken him to see *The Return of the Jedi* when it first came out; Kojo was ten. After the movie, his father asked him what he thought. Kojo said, "The spaceships wouldn't have really moved like that. There's no air in space." His parents were delighted and took to calling him Professor. The nickname certainly fit. Kojo had been a serious boy. Kids on the block had other nicknames for him, of course: from the innocuous "Poindexter" to the scalding "faggot." He let them talk, not ignorant to their taunts but not deterred either. But when he fought, which he rarely did, they got the message quick. Kojo's father had done some amateur boxing as a young man. He taught his son to always keep his hands up and head tucked.

"Key to winning a fight," his father told him, "is keeping their fists from your jaw. They hit your jaw, you'll drop."

Kojo's high school grades were good. There was even talk of college scholarships. And he was ready to take them, ready to fully dive into the "white world" in Wisconsin or Maine. But senior year, Kojo's mom got sick with sickle cell anemia. She went into renal failure just two days after his eighteenth birthday. She died six months later. Kojo's father took it badly. He drank himself into a stupor nearly every night. So Kojo spent his last year of high school taking care of the house, the meals, everything. He never went looking to be a cop, the academy came to him—there was a recruitment drive at the library. He'd been having a bad day and completed an application more out of frustrated boredom than anything else. Regardless of his attitude, he took the application seriously. Recruiters noticed he filled out every single comment box with blocks of carefully worded text (he even fixed two seemingly innocuous typos)—first time they'd seen that since creating the new application ten years prior.

That should have been their first warning sign.

In his garage, Detective Omaboe found the cathedral pattern in the cherrywood board. He spun it around and started to sand it down when he heard a crash, like a pan dropping onto a kitchen floor. He turned off his sander and, listening carefully, opened the door to the detached garage. It was quiet outside and early enough that the expressway wasn't yet choked with traffic. There were no sirens. As he stood in the doorway, looking across the street at the boarded-up windows on the old Hayder place and wondering if the tattered pink condemnation letter would ever fall off the front door, he heard the clattering sound again.

It was coming from his house.

Kojo scrambled across the backyard and opened the patio door.

"Brandon?"

Another crash. This time something shattered.

"Shit."

Kojo rushed into the kitchen to find his twelve-year-old son in a rage. Brandon was a big kid, easily half of Kojo's weight, and he was putting all of it into smashing the pots and pans onto the tile floor.

Seeing Kojo, Brandon began to cry.

"No!" Brandon wailed.

"It's okay." Kojo walked over, draping an arm around his son. "This is something we can fix. Not going to be a big problem, all right?"

"No. . . . No. . . . No. . . ."

His face puffy with tears and impotent rage, Brandon tried to wrench away from Kojo. But Kojo held tight, locking his hands around his son's waist. Brandon fought at first, his fists hammering down on Kojo's back. But Kojo only held him tighter. The doctors had explained that deep pressure touch sometimes helped kids with Down syndrome relax. Within seconds, Kojo could feel Brandon's racing heartbeat slow as his crying softened. His breathing normalized.

"It's okay," Kojo kept repeating. "It's all gonna be okay."

Brandon unwound in his father's arms, the tension dissolving away.

More and more, until Kojo could loosen his grip.

"You cool, now?"

"I'm cool," Brandon said.

Kojo let Brandon go. The boy slumped to the floor, and Kojo lay down beside him. He lifted up his son's chin so they could see eye to eye.

"What's going on? What's got you so upset?"

"Where's Ophelia? She's not here."

"I know, son. She's on her way."

"I want her here now."

"Come on."

Kojo stood and pulled Brandon up. Still wobbly with emotion, the boy shuffled over to the kitchen table and sat down with a sour face. As Kojo picked up the pots and pans, he examined several cracked tiles on the floor. Not a big deal. He could replace them over the weekend.

"Listen, buddy, I need for you to come find me when you need something, all right? You call me on the radio or you come find me. We talked about this just the other day, remember?"

"I couldn't find the radio."

"Well . . . it was in the living room earlier this morning. Did you look there?"

Brandon shook his head. "I'm hungry."

"Of course." Kojo bristled.

He wanted to throw the pot through the kitchen window. He would've loved to see it turn the pane of glass into a spiderweb before it jettisoned into the humid morning air and bounced with a tinny clang onto the driveway.

Instead, Kojo placed the pot on the counter and walked over and kissed Brandon on the forehead. As he did, he closed his eyes and took in his son's scent, a mix of coconut (lotion that Ophelia put on him), sweat, and the sweet, cloying smell that was unique to Brandon. It reminded Kojo of *prekese*, a Ghanaian spice with a sugary, fragrant aroma that he recalled from the gingery iced tea brew his grandmother would sip on hot days.

"I miss Mom. She's not coming back, is she?"

Kojo cleared his throat. "No, Brandon. You know that."

"She's dead is why."

"Yes."

Yesterday Brandon had begged for Constance to come back. He told Kojo he'd clean his room; he'd even clean the bathroom with a toothbrush like he saw someone do on a TV show. When Kojo reminded Brandon that his mother died five years ago, it took twenty-eight minutes for Brandon to still his frustrated shaking and calm down. Kojo knew he couldn't get caught up in that loop again.

"So what do you want to eat?"

Brandon thought for a second as he rubbed the last tears from his eyes. "Cereal," he said.

"The loops or that other junk?"

"That other junk."

Kojo filled a bowl with shockingly neon-colored cereal, added skim milk, and then placed it in front of Brandon with a spoon. Brandon reached for the spoon but paused. He looked up at Kojo and grinned.

"Thank you, Dad."

Brandon's smile hit Kojo like a meteor every time he saw it. All the horrible things that had passed before his eyes, the memories that woke him screaming—the dead woman with her legs eaten to nubs by rats, the child with his hands nailed to the dinner table, the unidentifiable drowning victim with skin that sloughed off like sheets of phyllo dough—all dissolved instantly. Kojo could never envision living without that smile. While the woodworking was an effective salve for existential worries, Brandon's smile was the only true cure for Kojo's world-weariness.

Watching Brandon eat, Kojo poured himself a bowl of the sugary stuff and was taking his first bite when his cell phone vibrated on the kitchen counter. Kojo calmly placed the spoon back down and answered the phone.

"This is Detective Omaboe."

Brandon quietly repeated Kojo's words as he chewed a mouthful of cereal.

"Got a ten-seventy-one at the university hospital," a brusque voice intoned. "Carson and Briggs are already en route, but Chief figured you need to be there too."

"Casualties?" Kojo asked.

"Casualties?" Brandon said.

"Several," Dispatch confirmed.

"I'll head out soon."

Kojo hung up and turned to Brandon. He was already getting upset again.

"Daddy has to work, B," Kojo said, shaking his head.

"I know that."

"Doesn't mean I don't want to be here with you."

"I know that too."

Kojo got up and patted Brandon on the shoulder.

"Finish up, dude."

Ophelia arrived at the house a minute later. She was a Ghanaian immigrant who had immigrated to Chicago several years earlier to be with her adult children and three grandbabies. The rest of her family, two sisters and three brothers, lived in Accra. She had told Kojo that she did not anticipate returning to Ghana to see them for many years, if ever. He told her he'd help any way he could. At the time, she just smiled, thanked him, and said, "You already have so much on your plate."

When Ophelia walked into the house, Brandon jumped up from his cereal and ran to her. He hugged her long and hard and told her that Kojo yelled at him about throwing the pans. Ophelia, her singsongy accent thick but clear, told Brandon that it wasn't good to throw pans.

"You know better than that," she told him.

Brandon nodded, then looked back at Kojo.

"You need to get dressed proper, Dad."

25

MATILDA WATCHED ASHANIQUE tuck into her second round of pancakes.

"These are pretty good," Ashanique said.

The girl was starving.

Matilda, however, couldn't take a single bite of her food.

Clark's demise kept running through her head.

Yet she couldn't cry. She couldn't feel those emotions anymore.

Earlier, while hospital staff ran a few tests with Ashanique, Matilda took a moment to grieve with colleagues in one of the psychology department meeting rooms. Clark's secretary of fifteen years broke down sobbing, knees buckling. Matilda calmed her, though inside she felt a spreading numbness. She knew it was trauma too—sometimes the body can be in such a stage of emotional siege that it chooses to shut down, to conserve resources like tears and breath. Sitting in that near-empty meeting room, Matilda thought: *This is what it means to move on. This is how a heart becomes hardened.*

Ashanique took a break to chew, then swallow, before she asked, "What did the cops mean when they said I was poisoned?"

Matilda didn't realize Ashanique had been conscious during the events following the incident in the pharmacy. After security had arrived, and shuttled Matilda and Ashanique to safety, they were taken across the building to the ER, where doctors pumped Ashanique's stomach. Matilda called in an oncologist she knew. He assured her the MetroChime wouldn't harm Ashanique, at least not in the doses she'd taken. Matilda had been assured

107

that Ashanique was given propofol via IV drip during the procedure. What-ever recollections the girl had, Matilda assumed, were either figments or the drug had been ineffective.

"They were worried about the drug your mom gave you."

"They shouldn't have been," Ashanique said. "She took it all the time."

"What do you remember after . . . ?"

"It was gross."

Matilda laughed, the stress of the morning easing.

"The cops came in and talked to you," Ashanique said. "I heard them ask you about how you knew me. Why they thought that man would be after my mom."

"Yes. I told them I didn't know the reason why."

"But you mentioned the Night Doctors. . . ."

"I did. I thought it was important."

Ashanique chewed her food in silence for a moment.

"I warned you, though," she said.

"That man in the pharmacy, was he one of them?"

Ashanique shrugged. Matilda sipped her coffee and then leaned back and watched people eating, milling about the cafeteria. A day ago, this place was banal—just another unfurnished link in the averageness of her day—but the creeping unease that had settled into Matilda's gut trans-formed it. Now, every movement, every scrape of fork against plate, every cash register chime, raised her hackles. The world around her was newly pregnant with danger. "I'm not going to have to throw this up, right?" Ashanique asked.

Matilda turned her attention back to the girl. "No," she said. "You can eat as much as you like. Your stomach feels okay?"

"It's fine."

Ashanique put her fork down.

"My mom's never coming back, is she? I can tell. If she were, she'd be here by now. I've been watching the doors to this room. Looking at the hallway over there, thinking I might see her. But I won't."

"You don't know that," Matilda said.

"I feel it, though."

Ashanique leaned to her right to look over Matilda's shoulder.

"Here they come again."

Matilda turned around in her chair to see two uniformed police officers approaching the table. Matilda was hopeful they had news about Janice. Maybe they'd caught Clark's killer and she could start grinding the edges off the fear.

Clark's gone, Maddie. Don't be selfish. Think about his wife, his kids . . .

"Dr. Deacon? We need you and Ms. Walters to come with us. Sorry to interrupt your meal but . . . it's important we do it now."

"Is this about my mom?" Ashanique asked.

"You'll need to discuss everything with the detectives."

Six minutes and two elevators later, Matilda and Ashanique found themselves in an administrative wing of the hospital. They were separated. Matilda escorted Ashanique to a meeting room where several nurses were waiting. She gave the girl a kiss on the forehead.

"I'll see you soon, okay? Don't worry. They're just going to ask you a few questions. Tell them everything. They only want to help."

Ashanique seemed anxious to be separated from Matilda, but she went into the room without raising a fuss and sat down at the table with the nurses. They immediately moved closer to comfort her as the door was closed.

Matilda followed an officer to a small conference room that overlooked a parking lot. Outside of the table and chairs, the only other thing in the room was a spider plant, its soil dry and cracked. The plant's leaves were yellow, blackened at the tips like they'd been burned. Matilda wished she had her water bottle, the one she got at a conference two years ago and kept under her desk. She considered getting up to bring the plant over to the bathroom, suddenly convinced she had to save it too, when a detective stepped into the room.

He sat down across from her, a cup of coffee in hand.

"My name is Kojo Omaboe. I'm a homicide detective with Chicago PD. I was called in to get your side of what went down earlier this morning. That was a very traumatic event. You need anything?"

"No, I'm okay. Thanks."

Matilda was struck by Kojo's bearing. Unlike the dozen or so cops she'd already seen that morning, she sensed a deep-rooted worldliness to him. It wasn't just his name or his dark skin. It was his demeanor. The other officers had been visibly shaken by the attack. Matilda could sense their discomfort; they radiated nervous energy. As a psychologist, Matilda understood why. Even people exposed to stress-inducing situations for years, decades even, can't override their body's natural inclination to downshift into the fight-or-flight response. The heart races; the skin sweats; the eyes dart.

But Kojo exuded a grounded calm that was reassuring. Rather than losing himself in his anxiety, Kojo seemed to be the type of person who could step outside his own body and say, *You're anxious. Let's not be anxious.*

"Great," Kojo said. "Should we begin?"

"Okay."

Kojo placed a tape recorder on the table and pressed record.

26

IN THE MATTER OF:

INTERVIEW WITH:

Deacon, Matilda

INVESTIGATIVE SGT: KOJO OMABOE #2716 / Chicago Police Dept.

VOL. 1 of 2

NOVEMBER 14, 2018

TAPE 1

00:00:28

KOJO OMABOE: Today's date is the fourteenth of November 2018. The time is 8:57 a.m. What I'd like to have done is, I'm going to identify myself and then have you tell me your name. I am Kojo Omaboe, homicide with the Chicago PD. Dr. Deacon?

MATILDA DEACON: Matilda Deacon.

KOJO OMABOE: As you can obviously tell, this is being recorded. Is it okay if I call you Matilda, Dr. Deacon?

MATILDA DEACON: Yes.

KOJO OMABOE: At this particular time, do you have any medical conditions that you know of?

MATILDA DEACON: No. Not now.

KOJO OMABOE: Do you take any regular medication?

MATILDA DEACON: Blood-pressure meds. Runs in the family. I also have a prescription for Prozac. Haven't taken it in several months. Probably expired. Is this important? I just— Uh, there was a shooting this morning.

KOJO OMABOE: I know. We're getting to that now.

MATILDA DEACON: Okay.

KOJO OMABOE: Are you feeling okay, right now? Do you think there might be anything affecting your ability to think clearly at the moment?

MATILDA DEACON: Other than seeing someone I know—knew—very well have his throat cut right in front of my face?

KOJO OMABOE: I understand. It's a formality, Dr. Deacon.

MATILDA DEACON: Sorry. I— It's been a stressful day.

KOJO OMABOE: You are a professor here, at the university. How long have you been teaching?

MATILDA DEACON: In the psychology department, it'll be six years. I did my graduate work here too, though.

KOJO OMABOE: Outside of teaching, you do research? There's a lab listed here in your file from HR.

MATILDA DEACON: Yes, in conjunction with the medical school. Neurology. It's basic research. Nothing clinical.

KOJO OMABOE: But you do see patients? Says here you go to the Marcy-Lansing Apartments once a month.

MATILDA DEACON: Yes.

KOJO OMABOE: That's how you came to meet Ashanique Walters?

MATILDA DEACON: Yes.

KOJO OMABOE: When did you first meet her?

MATILDA DEACON: Um, a day ago. I was at the apartments, seeing patients with Todd—

KOJO OMABOE: Dr. Garcia-Araez?

MATILDA DEACON: Yes. We usually go together. We were wrapping up the day when I was approached by a woman, uh, Carol. Don't know her last name. She asked me to look in on a girl she was sitting. She said the girl was sick.

KOJO OMABOE: This was Ashanique?

MATILDA DEACON: Yes.

KOJO OMABOE: And, in your determination, was she sick?

(PAUSE)

MATILDA DEACON: Possibly. We talked for only a little while. I found her to be a very smart, very convincing young woman. If she's mentally ill, I'm not sure what the diagnosis would be. It's too early to say.

KOJO OMABOE: Do you think, uh, Carol had a good reason to ask you to see Ashanique?

MATILDA DEACON: Yes.

KOJO OMABOE: You said she's not obviously mentally ill.

MATILDA DEACON: It's a complicated situation. Diagnoses like these take time. I would have to run a number of tests. This isn't like doing a swab and prescribing a pill. But, uh, but there's something very special about the girl. . . .

KOJO OMABOE: I understand. And you also met Janice, the mother, at this interview?

MATILDA DEACON: Yes.

KOJO OMABOE: I was told that the girl's babysitter, a, uh, Mrs. Carol Malone, said Janice was not happy that you were talking to her daughter. She kicked you out?

MATILDA DEACON: She was furious.

KOJO OMABOE: Why do you think that was?

MATILDA DEACON: I'm not really sure. At the time—

KOJO OMABOE: But looking back, knowing what you know from the incident this morning, why do you think Janice Walters was so upset that you were talking to her daughter?

MATILDA DEACON: She was involved in something. I can see that now. Ashanique was wrapped up in it, not directly but . . . Janice was convinced that my talking to Ashanique had exposed her to some mortal danger. She was deeply paranoid.

KOJO OMABOE: And that's why you told the other officers that Janice asked you to delete all the files related to Ashanique from your computer?

MATILDA DEACON: Yes. I think so. She had a gun too.

KOJO OMABOE: Can you tell me what your relationship with Dr. Clark Liptak was?

MATILDA DEACON: He was a colleague—my boss, in certain aspects. He oversaw a lot of the research I've been doing.

KOJO OMABOE: And you got along? You weren't angry at him about anything?

MATILDA DEACON: Not at all. . . .

(PAUSE)

KOJO OMABOE: I'm sorry. Do you need a tissue?

MATILDA DEACON: No, I'm okay.

KOJO OMABOE: And the man who killed him, have you seen this man before?

MATILDA DEACON: No. Never.

KOJO OMABOE: Thinking back, do you recall him saying anything to either Janice or Ashanique?

MATILDA DEACON: Like I told the officers, he only said one thing. He said, "Where's Fifty-One?"

KOJO OMABOE: Does that mean anything to you?

MATILDA DEACON: No.

KOJO OMABOE: Do you think that this man had anything to do with Janice's paranoid statements? That, perhaps, this man was part of the conspiracy she was convinced was out to get her and Ashanique? Why she wanted names deleted from the university files?

MATILDA DEACON: I don't know. It's possible. But that's your job, right? To find Janice, find the killer.

KOJO OMABOE: Yes, of course. And I take it very seriously.

MATILDA DEACON: Ashanique needs to be admitted to the hospital, okay? Her mother was giving her an experimental cancer drug. I have no idea why. But it— She needs to be evaluated by a physician. Kept under watch at the hospital.

KOJO OMABOE: Social services is already involved. Some good, very caring people. Trained just for situations like these. We're going to take good care of her, Doctor. If she needs medical attention, she'll get it.

MATILDA DEACON: She does. Trust me. When can I see her again? Can I come by this evening?

KOJO OMABOE: Let's talk about that later. I can see you and the girl have a bond. But after a thing like this—there is a lot to discuss.

MATILDA DEACON: I understand. Just, uh, please let me know when I can visit.

KOJO OMABOE: Will do. (Pause as Det. Omaboe writes something down.) Earlier, you said there is something special about Ashanique. Why do you feel that way?

MATILDA DEACON: I . . . Well, I don't know exactly. Like I said, she's a complicated case but there's something unusual in her demeanor, in her understanding of her own condition. That sounds like academic speak but . . . I'd very much like to talk to her again.

KOJO OMABOE: I'm leaving you my business card. Feel free to call me anytime, okay? If something comes up. If you remember something you wanted to mention. Or you're worried. There will be an officer doing regular patrols near your residence for the next forty—

MATILDA DEACON: You don't actually think—

KOJO OMABOE: I want to take every precaution, okay?

MATILDA DEACON: Okay. . . . Do you have— I don't know how to ask this without sounding cheesy but—

KOJO OMABOE: Leads? We're following up on everything we have. There are a lot of cameras in the university. We'll find this guy, okay? We'll get him.

MATILDA DEACON: There is one other thing.

KOJO OMABOE: Okay.

MATILDA DEACON: The man who killed Clark, he winked.

KOJO OMABOE: Winked?

MATILDA DEACON: Yes.

KOJO OMABOE: He winked at you?

MATILDA DEACON: Yes. After he killed . . . Why? Why do you think he would have done that? I've never seen him.

KOJO OMABOE: I don't know, Dr. Deacon. I don't know.

27

12:30 P.M.

DECEMBER 12, 1761

TROITSKE ESTATE

MOSCOW, RUSSIAN EMPIRE

SNOW FALLS ON *the elm trees lining the entrance to the vast Troitske Estate.*

Smoke curls from the squat chimneys of the numerous thatched houses that border the estate. Despite the high humidity and numbing cold, peasants from the villages around Troitske are working their fields, their tools scratching at the cold soil to prepare it for spring. In a field, workhorses whinny. A dog's bark pierces the brutal sky. Every living thing knows the coming winter will be harsh.

There is movement along the road to the estate. A carriage, ornate in its decorative elements, speeds toward the massive main house. The driver is a narrow-shouldered man with a face beaten by scars. Inside the carriage: a single occupant. Darya Nikolayevna Saltykova is twenty-eight and resplendent in royal garb. She was widowed two years ago, when her husband, Gleb, died. Though he left her the wealthiest widow in the empire, she never really loved him. She was just a child when they were married, and she found him, the nobleman, cold. He was always brusque with his advances. Never touching her, never kissing her, just forcing her legs apart and using her the way he used the village whores. He was nothing like Nicholas. Nicholas appreciated her. He read her poetry and tasted her sex.

Before Nicholas she was a ghost, an empty woman haunting her own life, a shadow trailing behind her sons. Nicholas brought her to life. For the first time, she felt a passion for something—a hunger that only he satisfied. It was wicked and she knew it. When they were together, her flesh became frenzied.

Her sex throbbed and burned. She needed to consume him entirely. To pull him so close that they would merge, melting into each other the way a steel bar vanishes into the smelter's pot. . . .

But Nicholas is gone. Gone five months now. Run off with the girl, the one with full lips that all the servants gossiped over. She was seventeen and her body was taut. Nicholas was supposed to die. The cunt was supposed to bleed at his feet before he was set alight. It didn't happen. Her servants failed, and now Nicholas and his child bride were as far away as Saint Petersburg or Paris.

When Darya had learned of his infidelity, she fell to the floor of her sitting room. Her eyes rolled into her skull and her mouth spat and her limbs writhed like serpents. Darya's closest servant ran for the physician, who later diagnosed her with the "shaking disease."

It was born of ill humors, so he bled her. For two days and nights, she lay in bed with leeches growing like blackberries on her arms. Then came the honey and the vodka. Darya was sick, vomiting every few hours, for another two days. Though she recovered, she was not the same. The seizures had broken something inside her body. She thought of a large clock, its insides so complex and everything about it perfectly weighted and balanced. If just one gear were to shift, the whole thing would be off. A gear had shifted within Darya.

Even now, five months later, Darya thinks of Nicholas and the lust returns. There is a heartbeat between her legs. As the carriage bumps along the road, jostling her, she feels the heartbeat quicken. She knows she'll have to slake its thirst. And only blood can satisfy this fire. The Slavs have legends of blood drinkers. They call them upyrs *and say these unclean souls roam the countryside, preying on people traveling alone or unfortunate enough to cross their paths. Darya does not believe in such fairy tales. Her need is not supernatural. For her, blood is power. Pain is pleasure.*

She scans the passing fields. Many peasant girls work the soil. Most of them are thick creatures made heavy by toil. But there is one young girl, with glossy red hair, leading a goat along the elm trees. She is singing. Darya tells the coachman to stop the carriage. Immediately. He obeys; he has done this many times before.

Seeing Darya, the girl pulls the goat closer and stops her singing.

Darya opens the carriage door and leans out.

"Hello. Do you know who I am?"

The girl, shy, hangs her head. The goat bleats.

"Come now. Don't be shy."

"You are the mistress," the red-haired girl says, "from the estate."

Darya smiles. "I have need for a new servant girl. Someone to care for the animals. Do you love your goat? I have many that need caring for. You should come to the house with me. Over lunch we will discuss the animals. I love them dearly, but I have had so much trouble finding someone whose heart is as pure as yours. I need someone to sing to them and show them love. Does that sound like something you would enjoy?"

The red-haired girl glances back over at the fields.

"Yes," she says, turning to Darya. "That sounds beautiful."

"Excellent. Tie your goat to a tree. I won't keep you long. We will go and sup at my house and you can tell me of the songs you like to sing. I may be a widow, but I am not that much older than you. Most of my servants are hags. They don't care about singing or animals. I long for a friend to share my passions."

The peasant girl ties her goat to the nearest elm tree and pats it on the head. She whispers something in its ear. The goat bleats before turning to the grass at its feet. With the scarred coachman's assistance, the red-haired girl climbs into the carriage and sits down beside Darya. As the coach lurches into motion, the girl looks down at her filthy clothes. Darya notices and leans forward and pats the girl on her knee.

"Don't worry," Darya says, "we'll get you cleaned up. Tell me your name."

"Liliya," the girl says.

The ride to the house takes another twenty-seven minutes. During that time, Liliya sings the folk stories her mother taught her. Her voice is good; it's high-pitched and ethereal and fills the interior of the carriage. The coachman weeps silently hearing the red-haired girl's voice.

At the house, the coachman stops the carriage and opens the door for Darya and her companion. A coterie of servants greets them at the stairs. Once inside, hot tea is poured and incense is burned. Darya knows Liliya has never seen such wealth. She stands in the enormous house's foyer, staring up at walls that seem to rise into the very sky. Paintings hang in abundance. A thousand gold and silver candles burn in glistening chandeliers. An army of servants stands at the ready, their eyes cast at the red-haired girl's feet.

"I have a music room," Darya tells the girl. "Do you want to see it?"

Darya leads her down a long corridor, to a staircase that descends into the very earth. In the basement, torches burn and light dances on the arched ceiling. Darya shows the girl to a small room, and she steps inside with a smile that quickly disappears.

The room is empty, with only a drain in the center of the floor. No music books. No instruments. Liliya turns around. There is confusion on her pretty face, but it soon gives way to fear. Darya knows what Liliya sees in her eyes.

Cornered, Liliya screams and claws the wall behind her. Darya closes the door. She pulls a fire poker from a rack on the wall and strikes the girl, beating her until the skin of her palms tears and Liliya's back is split open, her white spine gleaming.

The murder is over in only a matter of seconds.

Darya drops the fire poker to the floor and then, her arms and legs shaking with an orgasmic pulse, she opens the door to the room. Her servants are waiting. They come into the room with towels and buckets.

Satiated, Darya walks slowly back upstairs to one of the palace's showers. There, standing on the ornately tiled floor, she allows her servants to undress her. Then, stepping onto stools so they stand above her, the servants wring the bloody towels over Darya's face and arms. She bathes in the coagulating blood. Moaning in ecstasy, soaking up the intense cocktail of chemicals bathing her brain.

Darya closes her eyes.

28

WHEN DARYA'S EYES opened, they were Rade's eyes.

The same bottomless black, the same alien gaze.

Rade splashed water on his face and leaned in close to the bathroom mirror, the only finished bathroom in the entire apartment complex, and stared through the protective plastic warping his image. He noticed that he had missed a hair, a tiny, fragile thing barely the length of an aphid's antenna, on the left corner of his upper lip.

Rade considered taking off his gloves and plucking it by hand but didn't want to risk having the hair break off. That would be a pain, and he'd make a mess of his skin if he went digging for it later.

Fuck.

Goddamned body was always fighting back. Even as close as he was, even with his power at a monumental swell, he was being fucked with.

As Rade walked back to the bedroom where Janice waited, he considered undressing her. He liked the way her shirt hugged her chest, the way her breasts ballooned up and over the top of her bra. When he was tying her up, he watched them wobble beneath the fabric of her shirt; globules like one would see floating effortlessly in a lava lamp. His body was desperate for the shimmering warmth that flooded his legs when he ejaculated. When he released, the surge of endorphins and dopamine made the animal he'd beaten into submission cry with joy.

He had to admit, he'd indulged his body before.

Such decadence. Such deliciousness.

Stepping into a bedroom, Rade found Janice exactly as he left her: strapped with zip ties to a straight-back chair. She had run from the pharmacy during their shootout. He tracked her easily, though, and caught her in a parking garage at the university. She'd tried to shoot him after he found her trying to hot-wire a Prius. But she was too slow, too emotional, and he got the gun from her and sucker punched her into unconsciousness. Twenty years of looking and it was as easy as that. Knocked out, Janice's head hit the steering wheel. The horn blared before he dragged her out toward his rental car. It was sloppy work, nothing he was particularly proud of, but his body had been quite excited.

It was a thrilling moment.

The bedroom was on the second floor of an unfinished house. It stood on the edge of a brand-new development. Most of the houses were skeletal, their yards just rectangles of dry dirt. Tiny sprigs of trees had been planted in the yards. One day, Rade imagined, this might be a beautiful place. And the family who lived in the house would never know how much of Janice's blood had soaked into its floors.

Looking Janice over, Rade let his brain wander back through the fields of his memory. There were so many bodies there. He remembered fumbling in darkness on rain-soaked soil. His shape was hairier two hundred generations back, his limbs shorter and knotted with muscle. And his mind was a thing of simplicity, driven solely by the basest needs: to fill his gullet and fuck his balls empty. A few lives ago, as a young girl, he toyed with his genitals endlessly, could never scratch a desperate itch; her clitoris and labia were singed off by her grandmother in a strange ritual. Beyond that, the memories continued to tumble fast and loose. There were the mother and daughter whores in London who stank of spoiled milk. He drank up their scent as he sodomized them together. One with his cock, the other with a fat carrot the mother had delicately chiseled into the shape of a phallus. There was the young African man, who sucked on his cock with a violence he'd never before experienced. His previous self killed the man and wore his teeth around his neck. That blood, that power, it was Rade's first true taste of destruction. The ensuing addiction coursed through Darya and the lives that followed. Over a dozen lives, he whipped writhing bodies, pissed into the mouth of a fat woman with inverted nipples, and drank the blood of a Scandinavian prince, waking up with clotted blood matted in his pubic hair.

Standing across from Janice, Rade inhaled the stale, cedar-scented air of the bedroom and let the memories fade away. He was not frequently given to nostalgia. Though his body still enjoyed the queasy frisson of those memories, he largely found them quaint now—the dreams of a beast. As much as his flesh still wanted to quiver and cheat, he liked to believe he no longer fell for its tricks and illusions.

No. I won't touch Janice's body with desire.

I'll touch it with hate.

Rade pulled off his rubber gloves, tossed them to the floor, then tugged a new pair from his back pocket and put them on slowly. His eyes were glued to Janice's as he took off his hoodie, folded it carefully, and placed it on a gray athletic duffel bag on the floor under a cheap card table.

"Before you escaped," Rade said, "you told me you'd do everything you could to cure me. Like you were a doctor or something. How funny. I believed you. I was going to run too. But then I saw it."

He paused.

Then, shaking his head, he said, "I saw that same ruthlessness. You are truly your mother's daughter. More than you could ever imagine."

Janice said nothing, her expression stone-faced.

Rade walked around her, the lighting touching her shoulders.

"Back then, I felt abandoned. Lost in this world. It took time, but I came to realize that was for the best. Staying with the team . . . distilled me. And now, we've come full circle. You're the one who's been abandoned."

Back at the card table, Rade pulled a laptop from the duffel bag. He set it up on the table, logged into Skype, and then turned the laptop around to face Janice. On the screen were four open windows, stacked neatly in a row, faces appearing in each. Two men and two women, three of them in their midsixties; one woman was younger, possibly forty. They all wore business attire. The woman on the far right of the screen had thin blond hair pulled into a ponytail. She had green eyes and skin the golden color of lightly toasted bread. The woman was framed by a window, through which a hazy sky was visible. She toyed with an exceedingly expensive Aurora 88 Sigaro Limited Edition fountain pen.

Rade took his place standing behind the table, as if at attention.

"Dr. Sykes," he said, "if you could begin."

The blond woman looked directly at Janice.

"It's good to see you. You look well."

Janice ignored her.

Dr. Sykes twirled her pen and said, "Let's begin, Rade."

Rade removed a leather kit from the duffel bag; inside were hypodermic needles and syringes. He carefully filled a syringe with a clear liquid from a small glass bottle with a rubber stopper.

Then he walked over to Janice, carefully inspected the inside crease of her right arm, and injected the clear liquid into her accessory cephalic vein.

Janice didn't thrash; she didn't fight.

• • •

Janice had spent the last twenty years running from this moment.

She'd trained every nerve fiber in her body to resist what would come next and mentally walked herself through the worst pain imaginable—envisioning steel cutting, pliers pulling, hammers breaking, chemicals burning, and rope strangling. Janice knew that Rade would be the perfect torturer.

She insisted on being his most imperfect victim.

Seventeen seconds passed before Rade turned to the laptop.

He nodded to those assembled.

The show was about to begin.

29

AS RADE BEGAN to remove items from his black leather kit, Janice angled her head as best she could to see what he would be using.

Scalpels, knives, awls, augers, specialized surgical instruments.

But the last thing Rade removed from the briefcase was a cheese grater. The kind sold in stores catering to high-end chefs and most discerning foodies. The cheese grater was encased in a plastic sleeve to protect blades that Janice could only assume were exquisitely, beautifully sharp.

Rade walked over to Janice, the grater tight in the grip of his right hand.

"I need the solution," he said.

Janice spoke for the first time.

"No."

"I have all the skills you have. I know all the same escape techniques. The same survival strategies. I want you to make this easy. For me. If you give it to me, I will cut your throat. It will hurt but not for long. Not compared to the alternative. If you don't give me the solution, I'll have to open you up to get it."

Tears rolled down Janice's cheeks before she knew it.

God damn it, she thought. *Already . . . You need to be strong, girl. You need to show him he can't scare you. Don't want him getting off on this.*

"The solution," Rade said again.

"No."

Rade slowly slid the cover off the cheese grater. Then, stepping next to Janice, he placed the cold metal against the warm skin on her forearm. He wasn't sweating. She imagined his heart rate hadn't increased by a single beat.

"We didn't abandon you," Janice said.

Rade met Janice's gaze.

"We didn't," she continued. "We would never have forgotten you."

On the laptop, one of the women cleared her throat. The signal was clear. Keep going. Don't stop. This must be done and done now. Rade momentarily closed his eyes. Janice wanted to imagine he paused because there was still an emotional, feeling person at his core. He hadn't been totally erased. Of course, she figured she was wrong. *Do not hold out hope, girl. Can't have no faith in hope.*

"Tell me the solution."

Janice, her skin flushed, her nose running, eyes bloodshot, shook her head in defiance. She stared down the blurry faces on the laptop, sending them every ounce of hatred and rage she could hold in her gaze. She willed it to wither their souls.

"Fine," Rade said. "Fine."

. . .

Rade had used the grater before.

He saw the art in what it could do. It was such a simple tool, yet it was capable of unimaginable horrors. Watching someone's skin curl up through the grater's notches never ceased to amaze him.

When the grater slid across Janice's flesh she howled.

Her screams bounced off the walls like a car crash in an echo chamber.

Rade ignored it, kept working. When he'd removed enough of the first three layers of flesh, enough to see the fat globules and muscle underneath, Rade emptied a vial of silver nitrate onto her arm.

Then he stepped back from his work and looked upon it.

His hands, his forearms, and shirt were soaked with blood.

Janice coughed and spat, the thin drool dripping down her chin. Without looking up, she said, "When I had my little girl, I pushed for four hours straight with no meds. Not even a single Tylenol. I can push through this. I can push through anything you do to me long enough to make you understand: I won't break."

So Rade got back to work.

Over the next five minutes he carved through muscle, down to bone. He went slowly, enjoying the way the fat bubbled up through the grooves and the muscle curled tight. When he hit bone, he began shaving it down. Janice passed out. He woke her with smelling salts from his kit.

When she woke, Janice said, "You're being lied to."

Her voice was now a pale flicker.

Rade lowered the grater. He could see his reflection in the pool of blood on the floor beneath the chair. He got close, placing his ear a few inches from Janice's mouth. She wanted to bite his ear off, but she knew she didn't have the strength to move her neck. Besides, her words would be more powerful.

"They're lying . . . ," Janice repeated.

"Of course they are," Rade said. "That's never changed."

"Turn . . . turn off the computer . . . I'll tell you. . . ."

"Tell me what?" He leaned in even closer.

Over the weirdly antiseptic scent of fresh blood and raw flesh, she could smell Rade's antiperspirant. Floral hints, something citrus, something earthy.

"What she's hiding from you. . . ."

"She?"

"Dr. Sykes. . . ."

Rade stepped backward to the table and, still facing Janice, reached around and closed the laptop. He then removed a syringe from his kit. Then, crouching down in front of her, Rade prepped the needle and found a vein on Janice's right hand; one he hadn't gotten to yet with the grater. He injected her.

"Painkillers and norepinephrine," he said.

Then he said, "Talk."

Janice gave the drugs a few seconds to infuse her system. The heaviness in her head lifted, the fog in her eyes cleared. She met Rade's cold gaze with a glacial stare that suggested nothing of her former self remained.

"They built a new accelerator," Janice said. "They won't tell you it works . . . but it does. And I can get you in. You can be fixed. . . . No more medication. . . . No more torture and death. No more being their tool."

Rade cocked his head like a dog, curious.

Seeing his interest, Janice continued, making her mouth form words though her throat felt as though it were collapsing in on itself. "The machine is only a few miles away. It went . . . it went online a few months ago. You ensure my daughter is treated and released, and I will tell you where it is."

"Give me the solution and we'll go there now," Rade said.

"No . . . Not unless we have a deal. . . ."

Exploding into motion, Rade grabbed Janice's hair and wrenched her head back. It happened too quickly for her to scream, though the pain that shuddered through her body had shredded nearly all her resolve.

"I don't make deals," Rade said. "Tell me and I'll make sure this ends quickly. That's all I can offer. Nothing more."

Janice grimaced, her vision swimming, her skull in a vise.

"Fine," she whispered.

Rade let her go. Janice's head flopped down, her chin banging into her chest hard enough that she bit her tongue. The dull penny taste of blood was instantaneous. Rade walked over to the card table and opened up the laptop again. He leaned the screen back as far as it would go to see the windows, and their digitized faces, click back into focus.

"Everything okay?" Dr. Sykes asked.

"Listen," Rade said.

The laptop was turned to face Janice.

"Fifty-One," he said. "Give them the solution."

Janice closed her eyes and recentered. Then, with a broken sigh, she recited a long series of numbers and letters—a formula. *The solution.* Rade listened to it dispassionately as the heads on the laptop scribbled it all down. Smiles spread across their faces simultaneously. Finished, Janice looked up at Rade.

"I forgive you," she said.

"And what's that supposed to mean?" Rade asked.

"You can't help what you are."

Rade pulled a filleting knife from his kit under the card table.

Janice knew what it meant. The pain gnawing at the back of her brain, the stiffness in her limbs, all of it would come to an end soon. As Rade approached, Janice looked beyond him, beyond the faces on the laptop, at the wall. It dissolved away and Ashanique's smiling face materialized there. Janice laughed to herself, remembering how her daughter would dance in front of the mirror, wearing a scarf and sunglasses. Each little movement sent a jagged cascade of pain through her body, but each was worth it—while Rade's cocktail might have worn off, the endorphins that flooded Janice's body more than masked the pain.

Seeing Ashanique, feeling her daughter's warmth, she was at peace.

Janice said, "I see back . . . a million years . . . my line . . . continues. . . ."

Knowing he'd already lost her, Rade stepped toward Janice, and without hesitation, he slashed her throat in a clean line.

Before the blood frothed out of the wound, Janice mouthed something. It was not meant for Rade but the people, the lives, Janice saw beyond him. The walls of the apartment building dissolved away like sugar in water. The sun rose overhead and Janice could hear the ocean-wave rise, crest, and fall of cicada calls.

Rade could not hear it.

He did not need to.

"This is where you end," he whispered.

30

THE SOUND OF *the cicadas is deafening.*

It rises and falls like ocean swells, sweeping across the savanna, intermingling with the chatter of birdcalls and the grunts of grazing wildebeest.

The sun hangs directly overhead.

In the far distance, just over the mountains, the patriarch notices a thunderstorm. It will rain tonight, and he will need to move his family into the forests that surround the savanna.

A lion roars as the cicadas start up again.

The patriarch's family is sprawled in the shade at the base of a baobab tree, its massive branches sweeping out over the red dirt and small, thorny bushes. The matriarch to his left, her narrowed eyes are trained on the sunlit grasslands. Sitting in her lap is their youngest, a child of no more than eight, napping, her eyes rolling under her eyelids. To his right, his oldest son, a young man with long legs and a scarred left hand, sharpens a flake blade with a river stone. The young man's wife, a lithe girl with a dark stripe painted across her eyes, sleeps. Their children, toddlers, toy distractedly with the long-ago-abandoned shell of a tortoise.

They have walked for fifteen days straight, following the herds.

At the base of the mountains, where the rivers were at their wildest, the family hunted deer and boar. In the early evenings, when the moon was at its largest, the family swam in a shallow pool teeming with small fish and frogs. Now, in the buzzing heat, the patriarch licks his lips, recalling the sweet taste of the water. He thinks over the route they'll take south, through the river basin, before swinging back toward the northern forests. He plans to bring his family to the shallow pool again. Even if it means a day less on the savanna, a day less hunting, he knows it would be good for them. They have never felt as close, as much a family, as they did sleeping beside the pool.

The cicadas stop their relentless buzzing. The savanna is silent.

The wildebeest and elephant look up, instantly attuned to something the patriarch cannot hear. But he knows predators have moved in close. He grips his spear, fingers moving over the smooth surface. The matriarch stirs beside him, leaning forward to better watch the swaying grass.

Seconds later, the elephant and wildebeest lower their heads and feed again. The danger they sensed has passed. The cicadas start back up. The patriarch sighs and leans against the trunk of the baobab. As he does, he places his hand on the small of the matriarch's back, runs his fingers along the dull scars that dot her skin. He likes the feel of them—small, soft mountain ranges and valleys.

Still watching the savanna, the matriarch shakes a handful of dried berries from a small leather pouch she wears around her ankle. She chews them thoughtfully, enjoying the touch of the patriarch. They have been together for twenty years now.

She recalls the birth of their first daughter. The matriarch was in labor for two days, crouched and moaning beside a fire, while the patriarch rubbed smoothing clay onto her back. The baby was stillborn and she recalls crying silently after they'd buried the tiny body. The patriarch peeled the dried clay from her back, tossed it into the guttering fire, and then they moved on. Chewing the leathery berries, the matriarch takes her eyes from the savanna for a brief moment, to look down at the face of her sleeping child. The youngster awoke before dawn, crying and afraid. She could not explain why, but the matriarch understands that the visions during sleep are often frightening. She is eager to soothe the little one again.

The patriarch looks beyond the horizon. He imagines he sees many things in that gamboling haze—animals, people, faces of loved ones, faces of those who have died. A breeze rustles the leaves above his head. The branches sway. It brings a cool sensation that sweeps over the patriarch's face and shoulders.

He closes his eyes, one with the moment.

31

MATILDA SLEPT THROUGH the first three rings as her cell danced on her nightstand.

At the fourth, eyes still closed, she reached over, picked up her cell, and pressed it against her ear.

"Hello?"

The phone was cold. Matilda was under three layers of blankets and wore flannels; her fabric cocoon. Curled fetal, she wasn't sweating. She'd had a boyfriend in college, Oscar, who used to call her a caddis fly. He specifically meant the larval form of the caddis fly. A small, grublike insect found in fast-running, cold-water creeks and rivers. The creature builds a little house for itself out of pebbles, a sort of rocky blanket that it hides in before it's old enough to molt and take skyward. Despite the subtle gross-out factor (or maybe because of it), Matilda liked the nickname and she liked that he thought the insects were cute, snug in their stony burritos. After their relationship soured, and it really did, badly, she kept the nickname.

"Dr. Deacon. This is Detective Omaboe. Sorry to wake you."

"What time is it?"

"A little after two thirty. I wanted to talk to you about the girl."

"Ashanique? Thought you wanted to wait until tomorrow morning."

Matilda sat up in her bed, suddenly very awake and concerned. Her bedroom ceiling was crisscrossed with lines of light, reflecting off the snow and ice on the street two floors below. On the wall opposite her bed, she saw a

133

warped version of her pale face reflected in the television screen. She looked tiny, alone.

"Is she okay?" Matilda asked.

"She's in the hospital."

"I thought—"

"No," Kojo clarified, his disembodied voice so close. "I meant she's had some trouble. Another seizure. Doctors told me she's okay, but they don't know what brought it on. I thought maybe those pills her mom was giving her. They're running tests. I just figured you ought to know about it."

"A seizure?"

"Yes, that's what I was told."

"But she's okay?"

"She's asking for you. Doctors told her you'd be by to check on her in the morning, when visiting hours start up again."

"I'll go now," Matilda said, pushing off the blankets. "I have access."

"Now I didn't mean to get you out of bed and—"

"Why'd you call me then?"

Matilda didn't mean it in any accusatory way. And she hoped the tone of her voice made that clear. She wasn't sure why she cared if she'd offended Kojo, someone she barely knew. But she did, and it went beyond just professionalism. There was an emotion attached to her worry—she wanted him to like her, to trust her, to want to call her again.

Okay, she told herself. *What's that all about? This isn't just about Ashanique or . . .*

Matilda listened keenly to the silence on the other end as she grabbed a pair of green scrub bottoms from the floor.

Kojo cleared his throat.

"I was worried about her," he said. "Figured you might be too."

"Want to meet me there?"

Kojo paused again. "Been a long night already. I've got a ton of paperwork. Everyone hears about shootings and wonders about the investigations, how the cops follow leads and sort through evidence. No one ever stops to think about all the paperwork. That's just not sexy. Truth is, though, almost every case is broken line by line—we write the reports and find the answers there."

"You're right, doesn't sound sexy."

"Drive safe now," Kojo said. "I'll talk to you again soon."

Matilda put the cell phone back on the nightstand. She replayed Kojo's last words in her head in a loop. There was something there. She told herself that maybe, after Ashanique was okay, after the girl was safe and in a place where Matilda could really, truly understand what was going on in her head, then maybe this thing with Kojo could . . .

Ashanique needs you. That's it. That's the only thing happening right now.

Twenty-three minutes later, Matilda walked into the hospital.

She stopped by the nurses' station on the sixth floor and asked the on-call psychiatrist about Ashanique's condition. The psychiatrist wasn't too worried about the seizure (that was the domain of Dr. Olson, the neurologist on deck) but she had concerns about some of the things Ashanique had been saying. They went beyond post-traumatic stress. The psychiatrist tossed around words like *undifferentiated schizophrenia* and *schizophreniform disorder*. Matilda wasn't prepared to call it anything yet. Despite some reservations, the psychiatrist okayed Matilda to look in on the girl. Figured it would help for Ashanique to see a familiar face.

The curtains were drawn across the windows to room 623.

Inside, the only light emanated from a blinking call button hung over the edge of Ashanique's bed. The girl appeared to be asleep. Matilda closed the door quietly. She considered tiptoeing over to the uncomfortable recliner near the bathroom. She figured she could sleep there until Ashanique woke up. But halfway across the room, Matilda realized that might frighten her.

A soft voice called to her from the darkness.

"I'm awake."

Ashanique sat up. With her braids undone, her hair spilled out against a propped-up pillow in magnificent wild curls. Ashanique moved her feet out of the way so Matilda could sit on the edge of the hospital bed.

"How're you doing?" Matilda asked, sitting down.

Ashanique shrugged. "Fine."

"I heard about the seizure. Must have been scary."

"It wasn't. I'm worried about what caused it, though."

"Ashanique, do you know what is happening?"

"It's the memories. All those lives that are coming back."

"Like George?"

Ashanique nodded.

Though it was hard to see the girl's eyes, Matilda felt the weight of her gaze. She shifted and moved farther up on the bed, closer to Ashanique; she needed the girl to know she wasn't going anywhere. That she could be trusted.

As Matilda listened to Ashanique's breathing, images from the previous forty-eight hours flooded her mind. So much had happened. This little girl was in the hospital and her mother was missing, possibly dead; Clark's throat had been slit by some maniacal killer; Matilda herself had been only minutes away from death; and all of it had started the moment she walked into Ashanique's life.

"Did your mother tell you about George? Did she coach you?" Matilda needed to know the truth.

Ashanique seemed to sink into her bed. "You still don't believe me?"

"I'm not saying I don't. I just need to understand better what it is you're experiencing. I did some research on George Edwin Ellison. You got all the facts right; all the ones that I could verify. And the details were . . . remarkable. Whatever it is that is going on inside your mind, Ashanique, it makes you very, very special."

"It scares me sometimes," Ashanique whispered. "It's not seeing all the lives that came before this one. It's not experiencing them either. Some of them are really, really horrible, though. It's just that there are *too many*. I feel like . . . Sometimes I feel like I'm going to drown under the weight of all of them."

"I'd find that frightening too."

"You had that feeling ever?"

"Not like that, but I swam when I was in high school, and I once helped save one of my teammates. She'd been bragging about being able to swim the length of the pool, back, and then back again in one breath. Stupid stuff. She tried and almost made it. She sank to the bottom of the deep end and, luckily, I was over there. I pulled her up and the coach did CPR. She was okay, but afterward she told us what it felt like. Her head got light, fizzy, like there was soda bubbling around inside, she said, but her body got really, really heavy. She sank faster than she knew she could. Then it all went black."

Ashanique nodded as she listened to Matilda.

"It makes me feel like I might go crazy like the others."

Matilda leaned in. "What others, Ashanique?"

The girl's hands tightened on the bedsheets.

"My mom told me things when she was alive."

"Ashanique, we don't know that—"

"She's gone now," Ashanique said. "I don't know how I feel it, but I do. It's not so bad, though. Things were getting tough for her. She was really stressed-out. She's with the older ones now, with the other numbers."

Matilda propped herself up on her right arm so she had a better view of Ashanique. As she spoke, she ran her fingers along the girl's forearm. Even though it was very light, Ashanique seemed to relax instantly at the touch.

"That man who attacked us, he said he was looking for number Fifty-One. I assume he meant your mom. Do you know what that means? She was fifty-one of what?"

Ashanique said, "She didn't tell me. She didn't need to."

"Can you tell me?"

"Clarity. It was called Project Clarity. It was an experiment, a long, long time ago. But I can see it in my head. That's what I was drawing, you know? When you saw me in my room; that place in the forest and the snow. I was there, Matilda. I was part of it in a past life. In my mom's life and my grandmother's life. The Night Doctors did terrible things there. Terrible things, and they'll do them again if they catch me. That's why *he's* looking for me. . . ."

"The man at the pharmacy?"

Ashanique nodded.

"Listen, you're safe here, okay? There are policemen on every floor of this building. They're all here. And I'm here. You don't have to run anymore, Ashanique. You're safe. And I'm not going to leave you. No matter what happens."

Ashanique took Matilda's hand and squeezed it tight between her own. Her fingers were warm, and Matilda's were so cold.

"You heard my mom," Ashanique said. "I have to meet someone tonight."

"I know that's what your mom said, but this person—"

"Childers."

"Who is Childers?"

"I don't know. Someone who works for Dr. Song. We have to be in the library at the International Museum of Surgical Science tonight."

"Have you met Dr. Song before?"

Ashanique looked away, hiding whatever she knew. A moment later, she said, "I've never met him, but my mom told me he is the only one who can fix me."

"Why would you need to be fixed, Ashanique?"

"I already told you. Right now, the past lives that I can see are just a trickle. But my mom told me that more and more will come. Without the pills, they'll overwhelm me. Make me crazy like the others. But even the pills won't stop it all the way. It will get worse and worse as I get older. By the time it's done, I'll be insane."

Matilda knew the girl sounded delusional. Her story was the product of a severely ill mother to a daughter who had never known another life outside of the topsy-turvy one they inhabited. And yet, the pain, the fear, the profound anxiety in Ashanique's eyes were very real. Matilda knew she had to be careful. When used incorrectly, therapy can be more damaging than a weapon.

"How will Dr. Song fix you?"

Ashanique smiled.

"With the solution."

32

DR. HENRY OLSON was dictating when the detective asked to see him.

Dr. Olson was old enough to have grandchildren but he was the proud father of a seven-year-old girl. She'd run him ragged the last few days, between dance recitals and the art classes that his husband, Alex, insisted on signing her up for despite the fact that he couldn't take her. Dr. Olson's anger at having to drive across the city in rush hour dissipated the second he saw his daughter's first papier-mâché mask. He mounted it above the fireplace, the proud father of a budding artist.

But now, there was this impossible case of a girl whose mother had been feeding her cancer medications without any medical oversight.

Unreal.

Dr. Olson would have asked himself what the world was coming to, but it was actually much improved from when he was a young intern, when it felt like every other child was coming to the ER abused and abandoned.

In the few quiet alone hours that Dr. Olson had, usually when he was swimming at the rec center, he frequently drifted back to the faces of those broken children. He wished he could gather them up in his arms, give them those precious moments of happiness his daughter so enjoyed.

"What can I do for you, Detective?"

Dr. Olson leaned back in his office chair and undid his tie. He noticed the clock on the wall behind the detective. It was near three thirty in the morning.

Kojo said, "Any updates on Ashanique?"

Dr. Olson threaded his fingers behind his head.

"She seems like a healthy girl, and, considering what she's witnessed, she's doing surprisingly well. But that's not to say I don't have some concerns. First and foremost is the fact that her mother's been dosing her with an experimental cancer medicine, one that has never been properly studied in children and has some serious side effects in adults. The girl's blood sugar is also higher than I'd like. Could mean prediabetes; could mean something else. We're waiting on additional labs to come back. Any luck on finding the mother?"

"Still looking. You mentioned side effects from the medication."

"There're a whole host of things. Pain, nausea, headaches, blurred vision, anemia, lymphedema, restlessness, but I'm most concerned about potential liver damage. I haven't seen anything to suggest there's an actual problem, though."

"Why would the mother give her daughter something like this?"

Dr. Olson shook his head.

"That's the real question, right? Wish I had an answer. You wouldn't believe the things I've seen parents give their children. But I'm sure you've come across just as many horrors. I, uh, I honestly have no idea why she'd give the girl MetroChime, but I can tell you that it isn't exactly an easy medicine to come across. It's an experimental cancer drug, developed by a small British pharma company to treat leukemia but stuck in clinical trials. Average time it takes to get pediatric approval on a drug is thirteen years; this thing's been around at least that. Funny thing is, the mother had to work hard to track this stuff down. That suggests, to me at least, that it was more than deliberate. It was calculated. She obviously believed that this drug would help her daughter. Against what, your guess is as good as mine. Certainly not cancer."

"Any of these side effects involving mental disturbances? Seeing things, hearing things? Schizophrenic-like behaviors?"

Dr. Olson frowned. "Not that I'm aware of but . . . truth is, when a clinical trial is run, nearly every side effect is listed. Someone stubs their toe twice during a research study of a medication and it'll turn up on the warnings. Half the stuff on there is a sort of reverse placebo effect. People know they're taking a new med and will assign any negative health condition that arises to it. You enroll someone in a study who fails to mention he gets headaches every afternoon on account of the amount of caffeine he drinks, and guess what? Your drug now has a side effect of causing headaches. That's an over-simplification but not far from the truth. So, yeah, maybe psychological stuff is possible. We haven't done a full eval yet. What's got you concerned?"

"Some of the stuff she talked about. Said she hears things?"

"I leave most of that to our psychiatrists. I don't see anything in a neurological sense. No tumors. No apparent injuries. Nothing physical that might cause some of the things you're describing. However, the wheels of medicine sometimes move pretty slowly. I'll have a better sense of things when we get all the test results in."

Dr. Olson ended with his trademark "not much left to talk about" smile.

"Thanks, Doc," Kojo said. "Appreciate it."

"I'll call you when I know anything more."

• • •

Kojo told himself it'd be a good idea to check in on Ashanique himself.

He didn't mind seeing Matilda as well.

Kojo knew she was at the hospital. After his wake-up call, she wouldn't have been able to sleep. She was more than just transfixed by Ashanique. He had to admit, the girl held a certain fascination that went beyond the details of the case. Even Dr. Olson had confirmed as much.

Kojo took an elevator to the sixth floor, where he flashed his badge to the nurse working the desk. Kojo found the door to Ashanique's room open. He peered inside and saw Matilda sitting on the girl's bed.

Ashanique, awake, smiled and waved.

"Thought you had paperwork?" Matilda said.

"I was in the area, figured I'd stop by. Want to get a cup of coffee?"

Matilda turned and looked back at Ashanique.

Ashanique nodded. "I'll be fine."

Kojo and Matilda grabbed two cups of watery coffee from the cafeteria. The only people sitting at the tables were a handful of staff—nurses, medical assistants, and doctors—who talked shop over stale doughnuts and exceedingly thick slices of banana bread.

Drinks in hand, they made their way to a bench in the lobby. Through the floor-to-ceiling windows, they could see a steam vent sending weaving white serpents up into a night sky peppered with stars. The night was frigid and silent.

"You think she's special too, don't you?" Matilda asked Kojo.

"I think she's resilient."

"I mean, the stories—"

Kojo nodded. "The past-life memories?"

"Yes."

Even harried and exhausted, Matilda was a bright light. Kojo noted the brilliance in her eyes, a brilliance that suggested an unquenchable curiosity and a fierce intellect. He also noticed how incredibly smooth the skin around her neck was. He imagined touching it but quickly shook the thought loose.

"I'm not a scientist like you," Kojo said, "but my gut tells me there's something more going on here than just a girl telling stories. To be honest with you, thinking about this stuff gives me that same sort of overwhelming feeling you get when you think too hard about space. You know, about how it's infinite? How we're these tiny specks in the middle of nothing? You think too hard about that stuff and you feel crazy. I realize that's not a technical term. What about you?"

"I still don't know. If it's true, it flips psychology on its head. If it's not, it means she's some sort of savant. Either way, I can't help but feel—"

"That she's special?"

"Yeah."

Kojo shifted, stretching his back. It was a tell, an unconscious shifting of emotion. Matilda knew he was going to ask her something personal.

"I get the research," he said. "I get why you have an interest in Ashanique's case. But, there's something more to it, isn't there? This whole thing, the past lives, the idea that you can remember backward hundreds of years, it speaks to you. I mean, beyond the science of it."

Matilda said, "Is it that obvious?"

"No," Kojo replied. "I just pick up on things."

"My mother has Alzheimer's. Hers was early onset. My grandfather did too. I'm convinced, well, all the genetic science says, I'm likely to develop dementia. I've spent my career, most of it really, trying to find a way to stop the progression of dementia. Seeing it firsthand, watching how someone can be so utterly erased so quickly . . . I knew since I was in high school that I would make it my mission to find a cure. So I studied chemistry and psychology, and I've been trying to weave the two together. If we can understand the chemistry of how a memory is formed, of how the brain stores those memories, how it retrieves them, then we can figure out how to protect the process. How to fix it when it's falling apart. I have all these notes on the walls of my office, they started out as a way to try and see the big picture. You should see my apartment. Anyway, I thought that maybe immersing myself in it all would help guide that breakthrough. . . ."

"And did it?"

"No," Matilda said. "It wound up being a nest of sorts, a way to insulate myself in my own thoughts. I don't think I realized that until now, until Ashanique. I'm so scared that I'm going to lose it all, lose myself like my mother and grandfather, that I'm struggling to write all my thoughts and ideas down as fast as I have them."

"They all worth keeping?"

"Of course not. What happened this morning, it's helped me remember that all this stuff is only important if it truly helps other people too. Why bother solving the riddle of memory if you have no one to remember—"

Matilda's cell phone buzzed.

She pulled it from her purse. The screen read TAMIKO.

"A colleague," Matilda said, tucking her phone away. "She probably heard about what happened yesterday morning, wants to make sure I'm okay."

"Understandable, you had a rough day."

Matilda's cell buzzed again.

A text from Tamiko:

Just heard. Oh my God. Please call me. Or just stop by.

"Sorry," Matilda said, turning back to Kojo.

"Look, you've got stuff to do. I should get going anyway."

"Of course, all that paperwork."

"Yeah." Kojo smiled. "Always the paperwork."

He put out his hand. They shook.

Kojo noticed how cool her hand felt. He had the sudden, at the time inexplicable, desire to warm it. The shake lasted a little longer than either of them expected and ended with an awkward parting.

Kojo laughed. "Okay. Okay. I'll be in touch."

Matilda said, "Please do."

33

MATILDA WATCHED KOJO walk to the elevator.

As the doors closed, he looked at her and waved.

Matilda replayed their conversation as she walked back upstairs; she worried she wasn't as clear about Ashanique's uniqueness as she'd meant to be. At the same time, she wondered if it mattered. She could tell that Kojo recognized the strange, powerful aura around the girl—it was unmistakable.

Reaching Ashanique's floor, Matilda stopped by the doc box, where physicians and nurses gathered to chart and discuss cases.

There were a couple of residents charting. She didn't know either of them, and they both looked a good ten years younger than she was. Four in the morning and they were running on that superhuman energy that came with being twenty and on the verge of a new career. When Matilda walked in, they seemed surprised to see her.

"I heard what happened to Clark. So terrible."

Matilda just nodded. She knew they weren't sympathetic because of the affair. Clark had kept that as hidden as his empathy. But he was her boss, and in a tight-knit university community, the loss of a boss to something as horrible as a murder—*No,* Matilda mentally told herself, *it was a slaying*—was a tragedy no one could emerge from unscathed. Matilda needed to remain numb.

She needed to focus on Ashanique.

Matilda took a seat at a computer. As she logged into the system, she wondered: If what the girl had was something psychological—possibly a mixture of coaching and untreated illness—then it was unique, a condition she'd never seen before. Let alone read about. If it wasn't, then . . . Well,

Matilda knew she couldn't let her mind go there yet. All she knew with any certainty was that Ashanique's case was incredibly complicated. Whatever Janice had gotten into, it was ugly, and the girl desperately needed help to get out of it. Regardless of what the cops uncovered, regardless of whether social services could find the girl a new, safe home, there would be years of therapy required to work through the trauma—not to mention whatever underlying condition was causing the seizures and visions.

Matilda opened Ashanique's electronic medical record and asked one of the residents to take a look at the girl's labs. She knew the results weren't off—nothing elevated, nothing weird—but she needed corroboration. There were brain scans as well. The resident only confirmed what Matilda already figured: analysis of the girl's chart showed nothing physically wrong with her.

No tumor. No infections. No nothing.

God damn it. So much for the easy explanation.

Matilda went down the hall to Ashanique's hospital room.

She found the girl asleep. As the first beams of daylight softened the air, Ashanique turned, grimaced, and groaned. Matilda walked over, ready with a soothing hand, when her cell phone buzzed again. This time, it was a call from Canada and not a number she recognized.

Matilda answered the phone with a whispered hello as she exited Ashanique's room and stepped into the hallway.

"Dr. Deacon? This is Dr. Lane Foss. Did I wake you?"

"No, I'm awake. Who's this?"

"Sorry," Dr. Foss said; his voice had the distinctive speakerphone echo. "I don't know what time zone you're in. I'm one of the curators at the Canadian War Museum. You left a message about a pocket watch belonging to a British First World War soldier named George Ellison. . . ."

"Oh, yes. Yes I did."

"Well, we have the pocket watch in an exhibit here. It's on loan from the Imperial War Museum in Manchester. Did you have a specific question about it?"

Matilda leaned against a wall as two nurses passed her. One of them, a former student who had gotten terrible grades, waved, and Matilda nodded back with a smile. She couldn't believe the hospital had hired her.

"So, uh," Matilda said into the cell, "this is going to sound a little goofy, but is there any chance that there's a smiley face or a drawing carved onto the back of the pocket watch?"

"A smiley face?"

"Yeah."

Dr. Foss was silent. Matilda worried he was about to hang up. The request did sound ridiculous. But he didn't hang up. She heard a click as he switched off from speaker. His voice was suddenly closer, the phone rustling as he walked.

"I'll take a look," he said. "I'm right near the exhibit now. Can I ask what this is in regards to? It is an odd request."

"I'm working with a, uh, family member of Mr. Ellison. There is apparently a long-standing story that Mr. Ellison carved a face on the back of that watch. I told the family I'd inquire about it. That's the long and short of it."

"Well," Dr. Foss said, "I'm looking at the pocket watch now and I don't see anything. It's blank on the back. Just a metal case with, uh, no . . . There's no inscription of any kind. Guess we can put that family legend to rest."

Matilda glanced into the room at Ashanique.

The girl had rolled again in her sleep, covering half her face with the bedsheets as the light poured in. Matilda was convinced the girl wasn't making up the pocket watch story. It was such a strangely specific detail. And Ashanique seemed so confident of it. Still, this little girl had far bigger problems than dealing with a voice inside her head. Her mom had taken investigational cancer drugs for God's sake. There was a maniac trying to kill her. *Maybe*, Matilda thought, *it's just best to let this past-life stuff go. As convincing as Ashanique seemed, it isn't doing her any good to rehash it all. The girl needs real help, not your getting lost in her mother's delirium.*

"I'm sorry to have bothered you, Dr. Foss," Matilda said. "Thank you—"

"Hang on."

Foss's voice was distant again.

"There's something here," he said. "I need to use both hands for a second. Can I call you back in a minute? It'll be just a minute."

"Sure."

Dr. Foss hung up before he heard the reply.

Matilda stood in the hallway, confused about what was happening and checking her cell every few seconds for a message or an email. Nothing came. She sighed, leaned over to look again at Ashanique, and that was when her cell buzzed.

It was not a phone call, though.

It was a video call.

Matilda answered, and a video chat window opened on her cell. She saw a desk, blurry with motion for a moment, before it stabilized.

Dr. Foss's voice came in from offscreen.

"Sorry about the delay," he said. "This is kind of crazy, but I noticed the back of the pocket watch, the casing, had an edge to it. There was a layer of metal on top, a covering. So, I . . ."

The image shook again and Dr. Foss's hands appeared; he was holding a metal circle in his right hand. It was dull bronze.

"This was on the back," he said. "Sort of a cover, I guess. It was probably done when it was refurbished shortly after the war. I pulled it off. It just kind of snapped off. Anyway, I want you to see this."

Dr. Foss put the metal circle down on the desk and moved the pocket watch into view. The watch appeared quite ordinary. The kind of thing you'd find in the vest pocket of a hip businessman or the back pocket of a grandpa. Dr. Foss turned it over and Matilda gasped, nearly dropping the cell.

Engraved on the back of a pocket watch, faint but unmistakable, was a smiley face. It wasn't the sort of smiley face Matilda was used to seeing. Nothing like the spray-painted ones under overpasses or drawn with Sharpies in bathroom stalls. The head was blocky rather than round, the mouth flat. The impression it gave was less of mirth than longing—there was something undeniably haunting about it.

"I guess family legend trumps expert opinion," Dr. Foss said. "I would love to hear more about how you found out about this."

"Wow, uh, thank you," Matilda said, utterly stunned.

"You're welcome."

The call ended.

Matilda thought she might vomit.

34

RADE ENTERED the Lakeshore Gym through the revolving doors.

He was wearing a baseball cap with three LED lights sewn into the crown.

The lights were on.

A referral-only athletics center on the city's Gold Coast, Lakeshore was the fifth most exclusive club in the United States. Members endured a five-hour fitness evaluation before they could begin a customized training program in the gym's 150,000-square-foot indoor running track, five heated pools, twelve indoor tennis courts, driving range, and private changing cabanas. Annual membership fees typically ran close to $27,000. Retinal scanners restricted access on each of the gym's five floors. Only fifty members had admittance to the penthouse's private spa.

Rade was not a member.

But he was likely more familiar with the facility than even its staff. He'd surveilled the place on the few occasions he'd visited. He knew where the cameras were, their models, and how to fool them. The cameras installed in the club couldn't properly process bright LEDs, the ones sewn into his cap would conceal his face when anyone reviewed the video feed—he'd look like someone with a gleaming supernova for a head.

Rade also knew there was only a single, armed security guard on duty.

The young woman at the front desk wore a dark suit and had her hair pulled back in a tight ponytail. She was in her early twenties and greeted

Rade with a pearlescent smile. He noticed the tiny diamond stud in her left nostril.

"Good afternoon, sir. Can I help you?"

"Dorothy Sykes," Rade said.

The young woman shook her head.

"I'm sorry. Our membership—"

Rade pulled a Bren Ten 10mm pistol from the holster under his left arm and shot the young woman between the eyes. Blood Pollocked the wall behind her. Making sure not to get any of her blood on his fingers, Rade kneeled down over her body and carefully pulled her ID badge and then used it to swipe through the door behind the desk. The door led to a hallway lined with sitting couches and framed photos of tropical locations artfully blurred.

The security guard came running around the corner, face busy with concern. He barely registered Rade's presence before a slug popped through his chest. The guard hit the lushly carpeted floor face-first.

At the end of the hallway was an elevator. Using the receptionist's badge, Rade stepped inside and pressed the P button for the penthouse. As the elevator climbed, Rade tucked his sweatpants into his shoes. Then he unzipped and removed his hoodie and carefully folded it before placing it on the floor of the elevator.

Thirty-two seconds later, as the elevator chimed and the doors opened, Rade pulled on shatterproof athletic glasses and changed his latex gloves.

He stepped out of the elevator into the penthouse.

There was a reception area with leather chairs and courtesy health food—nuts, fruits, and bottles of water. Across the room was a door with a retinal scanner lock. There were two older men lounging about and watching a basketball game on a flat-screen TV; Rade shot them both—one in the head, the other in the shoulder. He grabbed the wounded man and dragged him over to the retinal scanner.

"Open the door."

"Jesus!"

Rade pushed the man's head against the scanner. It read his retina, and the door unlocked. Rade shot the man in the temple and let his body slump to the floor. He pulled open the door and stepped into a narrow hallway that led to a glass door indistinct with steam. Hidden speakers played Chopin.

Rade walked slowly, listening carefully.

The speakers were playing Chopin's Piano Sonata No. 2.

Rade pushed the steamed door open and stepped into a large tiled room. Chairs surrounded an opulent Jacuzzi, large enough to house an entire football team.

Three men and four women sat in the pool.

The men were half-submerged, their faces red and dripping with sweat. One of the women rested on the pool's edge, dangling her feet into the tumultuous water, the other, a blonde, was up to her neck, eyes closed.

Whatever conversation had been interrupted ceased immediately as everyone turned, bewildered, to stare at Rade.

He shot all of them but the blonde.

• • •

Dr. Dorothy Sykes sat frozen in the Jacuzzi, her recently reworked breasts bobbing in the froth.

She'd had her eyes closed when the shooting started. The bark of the Bren Ten violently jolted her from a healing daydream about a recent trip to Barbados. Thank Christ the shooting was over quickly. Dorothy opened her eyes to see the bodies of her fellow exclusive members bobbing in front of her.

The Jacuzzi water went from pink to bright red to deep red.

"That . . . ," Dorothy said, "was uncalled-for."

"You lied to me," Rade said. "That won't go unpunished."

"I didn't lie to you, Rade. And these people—"

"Rich scumbags."

"They had nothing to do with it! You're losing it, Rade."

Rade closed his eyes and rubbed his right temple.

"I'm not losing anything. . . . Maybe you've forgotten what I am, Doctor. I am not just some errand boy. I'm not a soldier driven by moral duty or blind devotion to an ineffable cause. I am what you made me: a weapon. You don't actually think the knife cares about whose throat it slits, do you?"

"This was wrong. This won't be an easy mess to clean up."

"None of them are." Rade stepped closer to the pool and pointed the gun directly at Dorothy's face. "There's a new machine online. I can be cured."

"Why would you believe Fifty-One?"

"I can tell when someone is lying to me. I'd peeled her like a grape. In a situation like that, I've found that people tend to be pretty honest."

Rade raised the Bren Ten, leveled it at Dorothy.

"Okay, okay," she said. "Can we talk?"

"Go ahead."

"Um, maybe I could get out first? I mean . . ."

Dorothy glanced down at the body of one of the murdered men floating beside her. The body spun in circles, buffeted by the jets. He had a Marine crest tattoo on his left shoulder, faded, the ink diffused under the skin. There was something so unnatural about his flesh in the water. It looked like rubber.

Dorothy had seen death before.

She'd inflicted it plenty of times. But those times had always been under contained, antiseptic circumstances. Always rationalized through careful process and design. While in high school at Dover Sacred Heart Academy, she wrote a report on *Dracula*. A curious girl encouraged by one of the school's more liberal teachers, she explored the real history behind the vampire mythology. She wrote about Vlad the Impaler, lingering on the more disgusting details, and Elizabeth Báthory, who bathed in the blood of virgins. Writing the paper, Dorothy had gotten an illicit charge envisioning a nubile countess sitting in a tub of gore. She felt filthy pleasure in the idea and punished herself with six Hail Marys.

In the Jacuzzi, her stomach turned.

She needed to get out. And quick.

"Can you please hand me a towel?"

Rade walked over to a shelving unit and tossed a towel to Dorothy. She stepped out of the pool and wrapped the towel around her chest.

Her skin glistened with pink water and tiny crimson bubbles.

"I didn't lie, Rade," Dorothy said as she sat in a lounge chair.

Rade leaned and crouched across from her, rolling his neck, working out a kink.

"There is a second machine but . . . ," Dorothy said. "But we've only had some early successes with it with primates. All of our tests with human subjects failed. We didn't—I didn't want to tell you until we'd perfected the procedure. Until the accelerator was ready."

"What's the holdup?"

"We're getting complex DNA damage. Can't repair it easily."

"Why? Homologous recombination isn't working?"

"No, it is. But it's inconsistent."

"So you mix it up. Try microhomology-mediated end joining."

"We have. It's— We think it's on the machinery end."

"I don't understand, Dr. Sykes," Rade said. "I gave you the solution."

"We ran it and there are still problems."

"What problems?"

Dorothy had spent the last two days in meetings. Sometimes meetings within meetings where she joined a videoconference call while in a departmental working group. She prided herself on being the leader, on being able to switch mental gears with surprising ease. Mostly, she liked how her quick thinking surprised people at the table or on the other end of the camera. There was a process to "thinking in three dimensions," that's what she dubbed the skill, and it involved focusing on the salient details first. Like speed-reading, Dorothy had taught herself how to pick out the imperative stuff and abandon the clutter in only a few seconds.

Thinking in three dimensions was a skill. And one that made leaders look good. But Dorothy knew that being a leader also meant looking like a leader. Staying fit. Staying strong. Talking like you mean everything you say. Regardless of whether you actually did.

"It's rather complicated," Dorothy said.

"Don't belittle me. I have a gun."

"Of course," Dorothy said as she stood and grabbed another towel from the shelf. "We can go to the facility now, if you'd like. It's probably best if you saw it all firsthand. You can see how the solution fits in for yourself and come to your own conclusions."

Dorothy looked to Rade for an answer.

"Fine," Rade said. "Hurry."

35

RADE ALWAYS HATED being in hospitals.

Yet it seemed a particularly cruel twist of fate that he'd ended up spending all his childhood under medical supervision and much of his adulthood walking down the quiet halls, passing through the antiseptic labs, and eating the near-tasteless cafeteria food of countless hospitals. He could live with the food, the sterile environment, it was the patients that made his skin crawl—hospitals traded in an illusion of cleanliness, when in fact they were bastions of unchecked disease.

Following Dorothy down a narrow hallway, he was keenly aware of everyone that passed him, every opportunity for infection. While Dr. Sykes was dressed in business attire and a lab coat with a stethoscope around her neck, Rade was garbed in a new tracksuit and hoodie. Per usual, he was wearing latex gloves, but he'd also pulled shoe covers over his sneakers and had a blue carbon-filter face mask.

As Rade feared, the hospital was crowded with the usual worrisome assortment: harried doctors scrambling to get from room to room, charts and clipboards in hand; jaded nurses in comfortable shoes; and, worse, waiting rooms filled with Vietnam-era bearded and scraggly men with their wives and the younger, straitlaced vets, many missing limbs.

Dorothy navigated the crowds carefully, weaving through doors she unlocked with a passkey on a lanyard, twirling the Aurora fountain pen in her hand.

153

Rade followed closely behind, ignoring the disabled, the ill, and the angry.

He felt like Lucifer among hell's teeming masses. An angel, albeit a rogue one, thrown down with the fetid hordes. He didn't walk past them so much as he walked above them. Poor pieces of shit were so mired in their animal selves that they didn't even bother to look up at him as he passed.

"This way," Dorothy said.

Dorothy stopped at a service elevator. Her passkey worked here as well, allowing them to access the hospital's private sixth floor. When the elevator arrived, Rade stepped inside first, eager to get away from the crowds.

When the doors opened again, Rade followed Dorothy down an empty corridor to a double door. The large room behind the doors felt like a factory. There were tracks on the floor and large blocks of machinery sitting about, all of them linked together by miles of wire, cable, and hawsers; people in scrubs and smocks milled about, comparing notes on tablets. Dorothy crossed the room to a linear particle accelerator—a LINAC machine. It resembled an MRI on steroids—its cyclopean eye stared down from the ceiling like the tail end of a telescope.

"Dr. Sykes?"

One of the people at the back of the room walked over. He had a mess of curly hair and large-framed glasses. His badge read ANNO. "The machine is calibrated," he said. "Still having trouble with the flattening filters but—"

"This is a cannon, not a scalpel. We agree on that?"

"Yes."

"Where's the patient?"

Anno pointed with his chin to a drooling and shaved man in a wheelchair. Two nurses stood beside him. They wore full face guards and elbow-length rubber gloves. Rade noticed the gloves were neoprene, black and shiny. There was something undeniably sexy about them. Rade typically used the nitrile powder-free gloves, the purple kind, because they were easy to find and comfortable. But he made a mental note to ask the nurses where they got the neoprene ones.

The man in the wheelchair had purple bags under his eyes, heavy with fluid. Rade guessed the man hadn't slept in a while. He was desperately near death.

"Begin," Dorothy told Anno.

Anno, in turn, signaled the nurses. They wheeled the ill man to a rough X marked by duct tape beneath the lens of the LINAC machine. The man sat slumped there, too sick to even look up at the equipment towering over him.

Anno handed Dorothy a tablet. She held it so Rade could see the screen. "This is Mr. Taylor Heyerdahl, aged fifty-six," Dorothy said. "He is of average intelligence and has undergone several days of thought-reform treatments including electroshock and hourly, regimented doses of temazepam and scopolamine. As you can see from his readings, there is still significant, though dulled, electrical activity in the fronto-striatal circuitry and the hippocampus. He's exactly where we've been stuck for the past twenty years. If the solution works, we'll see that neural activity skip a beat before we reset it."

Anno signaled the team manning a computer bank on the far side of the room. The LINAC clanked to life. The machine rattled and knocked like a metal poltergeist. The beams emanating from its lens were invisible but their effect on Mr. Taylor Heyerdahl was not. He spasmed in his chair and spat as his tongue protruded from his mouth. The sound he made was inhuman. All the blood vessels in his eyes popped simultaneously, painting his sclera bright red, before he died of a massive heart attack. With the test over, the LINAC machine instantly fell silent. Dorothy turned to Rade and shrugged.

"Fifty-One lied to you. To protect her daughter."

"The solution . . ."

"It's incorrect, very clever but incorrect. Maybe she changed one number? Maybe she changed ten? What she provided us looked like it broke the cipher but it didn't. It just gave us what looked like answers."

"I looked into her eyes. She wasn't hiding anything."

"She tricked you. Or she remembered wrong."

Rade pulled the Bren Ten from the back of his pants and shot Anno in the chest. Anno fell backward, his face registering nothing. His tablet shattered on the floor. Techs scrambled, ducking for cover. Rade tracked them with the barrel of the gun as Dorothy approached him, hands raised, desperate.

"Rade, please, you can't just—"

"Say that again."

Dorothy's face tightened but she relented.

"Please, Rade. Please stop this."

"The best and the brightest," Rade spat, "you love to tell me how you have to turn away every genius who comes to your door to work on this project. You're telling me none of these people can solve the problem? How many decades has this organization spent spinning its wheels and grinding gears? I'm beginning to think that Dr. Theriault was smarter than all of you combined."

"What do you want me to tell you?"

Dorothy stepped in front of Rade.

He pushed the gun to her chin.

Dorothy narrowed her eyes. She was brave, not like the techs and scientists who scattered across the lab at the sound of a single gunshot. Rade respected that about her. Willing to die for a cause.

"It isn't about intelligence," Dorothy said. "It's about technology."

"We're light-years more advanced now. Don't bullshit me."

"No, you're right," Dorothy said, "and that's exactly the problem. The math Dr. Theriault was doing was old-school. Artisanal. Everything was so . . . *compartmentalized* back then, it's a wonder we even know the answers we do. Over the past forty years we've broken only two of the ciphers she used for her journals. And none of those addressed the genetic issues we need answered."

"So you work backward, you reverse engineer it."

"What I'm saying is, we might know some of the answers, but the problem is we don't know what questions she was asking. We've managed, through brute force, to develop algorithms that buffer the areas. . . ."

Rade eased his finger from the trigger.

Nodding, Dorothy reached up and carefully pulled the gun from her chin.

"You see the machine is real," she said. "It functions. We can prime subjects with targeted treatments to block CRH receptors before hitting the dentate gyrus of the hippocampus. The beam is strong, but we can't get the wavelength right. As you can clearly see, Mr. Heyerdahl's brain was effectively fried. You are right: all these brilliant people can't solve this. Not like you can. You got us close with Fifty-One, but . . . for whatever reason, it didn't work. If you want to cure yourself and move this research forward, then I need you to get the girl. She isn't like her mother. The memories will be fresh. Her brain is malleable. Find her and we can wrench the real solution from her."

Rade tucked the Bren Ten away and Dorothy visibly relaxed.

"Fine," he said, "but the leash comes off."

"Rade . . ."

"I'm on my own."

"I cannot allow you to continue . . . this." Dorothy motioned back to Anno's corpse and the widening pool of blood coagulating under him. "Cleaning up your mess at the gym was more than enough. I'm not sure the city of Chicago will buy another crazed mass shooter—especially one who works for a Fortune 500. My God, Rade, I have to frame one of our investors. Do you know how bad that looks? And now this? A research scientist?"

"He killed himself," Rade said, walking away. "Happens all the time."

36

DR. TAMIKO KADREY opened her office door to find Matilda and a young African American girl waiting for her.

She looked taken aback, but considering everything that had happened over the past twenty-four hours, Matilda was sure she'd understand. While she wasn't a close friend, Tamiko was kind and respectful. Despite the fact that they didn't always see eye to eye on research—Tamiko was convinced there might actually be a biological basis for the inheritance of memory—they bonded over a love of loud music, bad men, and red wine.

"Tamiko," Matilda said, standing up. "Sorry to bust in like this."

"It's okay. I called you, remember? Are you okay?"

They hugged. The warmth felt good. It was crazy, Matilda thought, how a simple touch, just skin-to-skin contact, could instantly relax her.

"You heard about Clark—"

"Yes, I'm so sorry."

"This thing has been— I don't even know how to describe it. Roller coaster, earthquake, nothing really fits. And it's not over. There are people after . . . Well, we're just trying to get our footing again is all."

"People after you? This about Clark's murder?"

Matilda nodded.

"Jesus, Matilda, have you been to the police? You shouldn't—"

"We've talked to the police. There's a detective helping us out. Kojo something, I don't recall his last name. We're safe. We're okay now."

Tamiko didn't look especially convinced. She turned to Ashanique.

"And who are you?"

The girl gave a forced smile.

"My name is Ashanique Walters."

"Walters?"

"Yes, ma'am."

Tamiko nodded before she hung up her purse and settled into her desk chair. She seemed a bit stiff, a bit formal. Matilda knew Tamiko and her ex-husband had recently gotten into it over alimony payments. She figured things had gotten worse.

Tamiko turned to Matilda. "So how can I help?"

"I don't know how to say this without it sounding as insane as . . . well, as it is, but I'm convinced that Ashanique has the ability to recall past lives."

Tamiko looked over at Ashanique.

"Okay . . . ," she said. "Um . . ."

"We've run labs and scans," Matilda said. "Everything comes back negative. Every psych battery comes back normal. Ashanique isn't suffering from paranoid delusions or psychosis. And every historical detail, even the most impossible, has proven true. You have to trust me on this. She is remembering lives and experiences she can't possibly know about."

"Um, okay . . . Well, then, we should discuss our options. Tests reveal nothing?"

"So far."

Tamiko leaned back in her chair.

"All right, let's just talk about this. As you know, there have been some fringe theories about how this past-life thing could work. Engrams, the lateral interpositus nucleus, Purkinje neurons, but I haven't studied them all in depth. Could be a matter of genetic enhancers. Sometimes a mutated gene can intensify the phenotypes caused by another gene. That results in stunning effects. In labs, they've been able to create animals immune to certain neurodegenerative diseases or use the mutated genes to increase muscle mass. And this effect gets stronger as it's passed down. With each successive generation, it can take on new and more powerful properties. Relatively radical stuff."

Matilda nodded, understanding, but she wondered how much, if any,

Ashanique caught. She looked over at the girl. Ashanique seemed anxious to go.

Tamiko was just getting started, however. Clearly intrigued and excited by the concepts Matilda's visit had sparked.

"The most logical avenue for the transfer of memories, however, is something called the Morris hypothesis. It suggests that memories can be stored genetically and inherited from parent to child. Are you familiar with the planarian studies in the late 1950s?"

Matilda said, "No. I might have learned about it in college."

"It's pretty memorable."

"A lot of college was kind of a blur, frankly. First time away from home . . ."

Matilda glanced at Ashanique, hoping the girl didn't get where she was going.

Ashanique said, "I don't know what either of you are talking about."

"Okay, well, quick lecture then." Tamiko grinned. "There was a researcher studying these tiny aquatic worms called planarians. They sound gross, but they're kind of cute. Have little goofy eyes. Anyway, planarians have the amazing ability to regrow their bodies. If you take one and you cut off its head, it becomes two planarians. The head grows a new body and the body grows a new head. The researcher wanted to look at memory with planarians, and he ran this experiment where he taught some planarians how to navigate a maze. Then he put those planarians in a blender—nasty, I know—and fed their bodies to planarians that had never been in the maze. And guess what happened?"

"They threw up," Ashanique joked.

Tamiko laughed.

"No," she continued. "They knew how to navigate the maze. Crazy, right? The finding was shocking. It suggested that memory could be stored in the body and transferred. Alas, no other scientists were able to replicate the experiment. So it was dismissed and forgotten. But what you're suggesting is that there's a kernel of truth to the planarian idea—that the Morris hypothesis is correct and memories can be transferred. Only way for us to find out is to run some tests. I'd be looking for crazy electrical stuff going on in the hippocampus. Maybe signs of expanding neural networking and, well, something we've never actually seen before."

"Can you do these tests here?"

"Yes. But ideally we'd do genetic studies, with multiple generations of Ashanique's family. That would give us a clearer picture."

"I'm the only one left," Ashanique said.

"I'm sorry to hear that," Tamiko replied. "Well then, we'll just have to see what's going on inside your head and make deductions based on that information. What are the things you're remembering? Can you tell me some of the specifics?"

"A soldier dying in World War One," Ashanique said. "His name was George Edwin Ellison."

"Okay. Anyone else?"

"Dozens more. All sorts of people throughout history, like a boy who hunts a tiger in the jungle. There are people, doctors like you, at this military base in the forest. I see that a lot. In fact, I think you look just like someone who was there."

Tamiko smiles, turns to Matilda.

"I don't know. You're clearly convinced something is going on. I get that and I respect your judgment. So we'll do the tests—we'll do electrical stimulation on some particular parts of the hippocampus while running a few standard visual programs—and see what comes back. That sound good?"

Matilda nodded and looked back at Ashanique.

"I guess," the girl said, staring hard at Tamiko.

"By the way, why now?" Tamiko asked as she gathered up some papers. "Why would these past-life memories suddenly just appear two days ago?"

Ashanique looked down at her lap.

"My mom said because of my period."

"Your mom knew about this condition?"

"Yes. She had it too."

"One last thing," Tamiko said, standing. "If the Morris hypothesis is correct and memory can be inherited alongside genes, then how is it that Ashanique can remember the last moments of George Edwin Ellison's life? She claims to have seen his death but he never handed down those specific memories. He died with them."

"I experienced it," Ashanique said. "I felt it."

"And I don't know how that'd be possible, honestly. Even if we accept that memory can be transferred and, for whatever reason, Ashanique has been able to activate them, she's talking about memories she can't have. We can't know for sure, of course. But these inherited memories should only go up to the birth of the next generation, when the genes bifurcated. So Ashanique should only have her mother's memory up until her own birth."

Ashanique said, "I don't know how it works. But I know what I see."

"Well then," Tamiko said, grabbing her purse. "Let's go to the lab."

37

"TELL ME THE STORY of the girl again."

Brandon sat at the kitchen island and kicked the cabinet underneath.

When Kojo first remodeled the kitchen, Brandon would sit there and kick the newly painted wood with his shoes, scuffing the paint within seconds. Even though Kojo realized that few, if any, people would be looking at the cabinet doors beneath the island, the thought of those scuff marks drove him crazy. He couldn't convince Brandon to stop the kicking either—Dr. Landau, the boy's doctor, suggested it might be a repetitive behavior, an unconscious way to cope—so Kojo got his son some soft slippers, the kind with little stuffed animal heads on the front. His were teddy bears.

So Brandon's feet brushed against the cabinet doors.

The sound was soft, like wind rustling leaves.

Kojo actually liked the sound of it.

He was making eggs and toast, Brandon's favorite. Kojo tore a hole in the center of the bread and cracked the egg inside. He cooked them over easy. Brandon loved cutting into the egg and seeing the yoke soak into the bread.

He watched Kojo cook, legs pumping madly under the island.

"Story time," Brandon said. "The one with the octopus."

Kojo frequently told Brandon stories. It wasn't his thing; his tales were stilted and amateurish. Constance had been great at coming up with stories when Brandon was little. She'd just make them up off the top of her head: the one about a giant who uses a tree as a toothbrush, the one about the little girl who finds a hidden world inside a gleaming white cube—but Kojo couldn't.

When Kojo winged it, his stream-of-consciousness stories automatically became work stories. They'd end right there. Cut off before they became too unnerving. Like the one about the veinless junkie who got pregnant so she could shoot up in the veins in her engorged breasts or the one about the pimp who put out a cigarette on one of his girls' eyes. Not stories a child, or anyone for that matter, needs to hear.

So instead, Kojo told Brandon about Ashanique.

"Her special power is her memory," he said as he flipped the egg and toast. "She has this crazy ability to remember the lives of all sorts of interesting people. People from history, like kings and queens and soldiers."

"Like she's got all the books in her head."

"Exactly." Kojo nodded. "That's actually totally right."

"She's a special person. Like me."

Kojo looked up from the stovetop. Brandon gave his infectious smile, the smile he used on everyone he could. The woman who packed their groceries at the corner store called it the smile of a flirt. Ophelia said it was Brandon's purest expression.

"You certainly are," Kojo said. "You're why I get up in the morning. I want to make the world a better place for you. I want everyone out there to see you the same way I see you: a strong, beautiful, brilliant boy who believes he can accomplish anything."

Kojo glanced at the clock over at the fridge.

Ophelia's running late. Fifteen minutes behind already.

He walked through the various things he needed to take care of, the pending cases, the open investigations (all those lost souls, the bodies on ice). He needed to hit the grocery store too (they'd been out of milk for three days and there was one roll of toilet paper between two bathrooms). And now, again, Ophelia was late.

Couldn't she at least pick up one thing on her way over? Does she notice we're running low on milk and toilet paper? Good Lord...

"Ophelia will be here soon," Kojo said. "I need to finish getting ready."

"We should have another mommy."

"What?"

"Another mommy would help you."

Kojo's cell phone rattled the counter just as the front door unlocked and opened. Ophelia walked into the house with a grocery bag.

"Sorry I'm late," she said, closing the door. "I just stopped by the market to grab some milk. I noticed you were running low. A few supplies as well."

Brandon jumped down from his chair and ran over to see her.

Ophelia laughed as she put down the bag and they hugged.

Kojo smiled to her and waved as he answered his cell.

His boss, Chief Wittkower, was on the other end.

"You coming in today?"

"Yeah, just a late start."

Ophelia walked into the kitchen beside Brandon. He was holding her hand. Cell at his ear, Kojo mouthed *Thank you* to Ophelia as she started putting away the groceries.

She could have been Brandon's grandmother. In her midsixties, Ophelia wore a long, colorful skirt and a short-sleeved top. Though she'd been in the States a few years, she dressed as though she were going to work in Accra.

Chief Wittkower cleared his throat.

"Feds are here."

"Why?"

"Janice Walters case," Wittkower said.

"That doesn't make any—"

"It does when you find out who Mrs. Walters really is."

38

"IS NOW GOOD?"

Kojo rapped on the open door to Chief Toby Wittkower's office.

The chief was short and dense-boned. But despite outward appearances, the red cheeks, the straining eyes behind thick glasses, he was not volcanic. Wittkower was a pragmatic man, a balanced man. He had a finely tuned eye for organization, the kind of person who walked into a dinner party and rearranged the books and straightened the foot rugs.

"Come on in, Detective. Shut the door."

Chief Wittkower sat behind his immaculate desk, glasses perched on his nose, as he read through a rookie officer's report. "How is it possible," he said, "for one person to get 'its' and 'it's' confused in every single instance?"

Kojo sat across from Chief Wittkower.

"Probably just didn't care enough."

"Exactly what's wrong with the world today, no pride in people's work."

"You said the Feds are here."

Ready to rumble, always ready, this one. Chief Wittkower used to think Kojo's eagerness was due to being fresh, suffering from a bad case of rookie-itis. He quickly realized that Detective Omaboe wasn't trying to please anyone but himself. The eagerness was mistaken impatience; Kojo operated at another speed from the rest of the department, hell, from the rest of humanity. Everyone else was playing catch-up. Kojo exemplified the sort of behavior that gets a homicide detective a commendation. And a knife in the back.

166

Chief Wittkower wasn't going to be the one to put it there.

He figured he wouldn't likely remove it either.

"It's the case from the university. The Walters girl and her mother."

Kojo was confused.

"Mom's in on something?"

"Janice isn't Janice. She's Janet. Or Jill. Who the fuck knows who she really is? But her prints tell us she's been linked with some domestic terrorist incidents going back about twenty years. We're not talking anything with links to the Middle East or black nationalism groups; this is more cultlike, loony shit. Call themselves the Null Cohort. These cats don't leave calling cards or post manifestos. They're not out recruiting new members. From what I've been told, they target scientists, bureaucrats, and military doctors."

"Null Cohort? What the fuck's that mean?"

"I had no idea. So I used something called a dictionary. Amazing what you'll find inside an actual book. *Null* means 'nothing.' But in scientific talk, it means having zero value or producing no signal. It is what the researchers are trying to disprove. Or something— It gets complicated. *Cohort* is another fancy term, most of the time used in research. It means a group of people treated together. Like at the same time, in an experiment. Put them together and you get Null Cohort, a group of similar people who represented the opposite of what a research experiment would try to prove. But don't quote me on any of that, I barely understand it myself."

"So these domestic terrorists are what? Rejects from a study?"

"Got me. Feds ran the connections. All the best data people at Quantico can't find a link between the targets. Could be that's the point. Could be it's just a major fuck-you to the Man. Thing is, that sort of agenda almost requires posting manifestos or uploading videos. These guys? Mum. Maybe their name is a joke. Or a distraction."

"But we do know their name. That's something."

"Maybe. . . ."

Kojo asked, "What have they done?"

Chief Wittkower rubbed his eyes with his knuckles. He hadn't had any coffee in three hours. The single-serve coffeemaker in the hall outside his office was shit. One minute it overfilled the mug with watery coffee, the next it was spitting and dripping sludge. Still, he'd take it.

Hell is crowded with the ungrateful.

"It all started in the late 1980s. Their modus operandi consists of mail bombs and shootings. Only five casualties. Some injuries, one doc was blinded, and a woman scientist lost a hand. Not exactly top-tier stuff, but considering how long it's been going on, the Feds sniff out any and all associations."

"And Ashanique Walters's mom is part of this?"

"That is what I've been told. We've been asked to gather up everything we have on her, going back at least ten years under five different aliases. It ain't much, tell the truth. Outstanding warrants for trespassing, breaking and entering, and shoplifting. But whoever Janice is, she's excellent at getting out of trouble. And fast."

Kojo nodded, he seemed to be getting it.

Of course, Wittkower thought, *if anyone got it, it'd be him.*

"How about the girl? Anything on her?"

Chief Wittkower thumbed through a neat stack of papers on his left. Pulled out one and skimmed it over briefly before turning back to Kojo.

"You probably already know more than me. She's in middle school, gets decent grades but nothing spectacular. Misses a lot of class due to some sort of illness. A lot of notes from the school nurse about pain here and there. A lot of calls from the mom letting the school know she's out sick."

"So you going to show me what you have on Janice?"

"Time's tight. You can take the stack here but . . ." Chief Wittkower opened a desk drawer and pulled out a videocassette and file folder.

He handed both to Kojo.

"There's a TV with a built-in tape player in the back office. In the folder you're going to find a note from Dr. Shapiro, the police shrink who interviewed her. Half the shit he says isn't important, but you'll want to read it anyway."

· · ·

Kojo located the TV/VCR in a storage room near the showers.

It hadn't been touched in at least ten years.

He grabbed a towel from the locker room to wipe the thick film of dust from the screen. Kojo plugged the TV in and dragged over a stool with a warped leg.

Before he popped in the videocassette, he opened the folder to read Dr. Shapiro's note. The ducts overhead came on, and cobwebs, blown free by the ensuing breeze, drifted lazily onto the pages.

39

Note from Dr. M. Shapiro

I wanted to include a personal note with this file. I'll admit at the outset that I might have let this case get to me a little. Excuse the informality; this is primarily for my own benefit, as Mrs. Olander's case is complicated.

Much of this is summary of the interview tapes, but it provides an excellent background on Mrs. Olander's paranoid delusions—perhaps enough material for a case study (?) or white paper (?).

Mrs. Janet Olander (a suspected pseudonym) was apprehended during a sweep of a suspected drug-manufacturing lab in Pullman. The owner of the lab, Mr. Datlow, is also suspected of being involved with an obscure anarchist group called, variously, NULL or NULL COHORT. Though both, of course, deny any and all involvement. While Mrs. Olander was caught in the sweep alongside two other women, Mr. Datlow was not. As of the time of this note, all four are suspected of having fled the state. The files have been turned over to the FBI.

Those are the facts. What I found most fascinating about Mrs. Olander's case was everything else: she talked of conspiracies inside conspiracies—really detailed stuff that, honestly, I had not encountered outside of some of the major literature (Dagnall, Parker,

Van der Linden). So I jumped at the chance to go deep
on it. If anything, it makes for some stirring reading.

NOTE: It should be mentioned that Mrs. Olander only
volunteered this information because she thought I might
be able to help her and she claimed to be suffering
from a medical ailment that was impairing her judgment
(more to come). She was hesitant at first and suggested
there would be "deadly" repercussions but eventually
relented. She was evaluated for intoxication—labs were
run—but proved negative for any recreational or prescription drugs that might have affected her. Oddly,
we did detect the presence of a cancer treatment medication, new to the market, but it was found in only
faint traces.

Here are the bare bones as far as I can work them out:

Janet claimed to be tangentially involved with a group
called NULL or NULL COHORT. She was evasive about the
mission of this group and her involvement. From what
I can glean—interviews and FBI insiders—this group,
classified as anarchist, has been targeting scientists,
military officers, and psychologists with mail bombs.
As far as I can determine (and I'm not alone), there is
no correlation between those people targeted—no common
places of work (as listed) and no common interests.

- There were seven victims of Null over the past twenty-
  odd years. They are below, with notes when available.
  All of the victims suffered burns and/or lost a hand,
  fingers, or eyes/eyesight. There were two fatalities.

    Dr. Owen Wendt—Tallahassee, FL. 1987
        Retired primatologist, formerly at Fort Detrick
    Adm. Frederick Cook—Silver Springs, MD. 1989
        Retired chief of naval research, stationed in
    the Western Pacific

Dr. Joseph Curwen—Joplin, MO. 1989 (fatally injured)

> Former Duke professor; author of "The Lupine Papers," a '60s-era study into altering consciousness via light deprivation

Dr. Lisa Kubie—Seattle, WA. 1991

> Research scientist associated with Dr. Curwen

Dr. Carolyn Barnes Speer—Taos, NM. 1994

> Physician at Taos' Addiction Control Center

Stanley Bennett—Washington, DC. 1998 (fatally injured)

> Retired engineer, developed medical imaging technology

Sgt. Julian Marchetti—Dallas, TX. 2000

> Former associate of deceased bacteriologist Frank Olson

Though there is no documentation to support Janet's accusations, she claims all of these people were involved in a covert CIA mind-control program similar in nature to the infamous MK-ULTRA. In fact, Janet claims that this project—she would not give its name—was an offspring of ULTRA itself. So, in her mind, the Null are getting payback—punishing scientists and military personnel involved in a clandestine experiment. One that I can find no evidence of.

- Here's where things get interesting. According to Janet, the purpose of this experiment was to take the lessons learned in the "Magic Room" and apply them in a new, more technologically advanced setting.

    What is the Magic Room? Good question. It took me several weeks to track the information down. Below is an excerpt from a letter I received from Dr. Franklin Gross, a history professor at Wash U. A good summary.

"What you have to know is that our world came within seconds of Armageddon in the 1950s. A nuclear holocaust seemed inevitable. The only thing keeping it at bay was knowledge. If we knew what our enemy knew, then we could be one step ahead of them. We could get our finger on the launch key before they did. But, of course, the knowledge we needed was inside the heads of people who didn't want to divulge it. We had to make them talk; we had to bring them over to our side. It was the same on the other side too.

We toyed with truth serums, LSD, electroconvulsive therapy, none of it worked as efficiently as we'd liked. Some scientists, particularly in Eastern Bloc countries, explored the outer limits of pain as a means to gain mental control. That was effective up to a point but the results were short-lived. But in 1954, we learned of a new technique.

The Magic Room.

It was the invention of some very enterprising psychiatrists in Hungary—in particular, a Dr. László Németh. The room itself was in a prison. It was unusual in every facet of its design. Twelve feet by fifteen feet in dimensions, however, it was not rectangular but oval shaped. The walls curved outward. There was a bed. Easy chairs. A desk. A toilet and sink. All told, the Magic Room looked quite comfortable for any political prisoner who was used to being shoved into a room the size of a sardine can with ten other inmates.

But that deception was core to the purpose of the room. The bed was sloped, it touched the ground at the end. Nearly impossible to sleep in. All the furniture was likewise uncomfortable. Built at odd angles or with exceptionally rough *materials. And all of it was covered in a highly reflective material. This is because of the lights. All the lights in the Magic Room had rotating lampshades. They were painted in bizarre clashing colors, and as the lampshades turned, they pro- duced bizarre—you could say, psychedelic—patterns on the walls. Well, on every surface of the room. It was like being in an ever-shifting, red-hued underwater grotto. Enough to drive anyone to mad- ness within a few days. But Dr. Németh wasn't after madness, he was after truth. He wanted to control his patients' minds. To do that, he used the silver beam. What was the silver beam? Pos- sibly just a bright light but it might also have been something more. . . ."*

That "something more," according to Janet, is a linear particle accelerator. Yeah. There are many of these in use—you can look up the basic physics of how they op- erate, but they essentially generate X-rays and high- energy particles for research and medical treatments.

- This covert research program used a linear particle accelerator (or LINAC, as they are known) to brain- wash experimental subjects. That's what they tried. I should mention briefly who "they" are: the HED, or Human Ecology Division. As near as I can tell, the HED is a study group—associated with several universities and medical schools—that focuses on cross-cultural research and is interested in "the relationship between man and his environment and the neurological dimensions of adaptive processes." Whatever that means. Janet claimed the HED was re- ally a CIA-funded group running "brainwashing" (she called it "thought-reform") experiments on unwilling participants. Mostly orphans. That part gets me too.

- According to Janet, most of the study's subjects were taken from orphanages. Though some were actually lifted right off the street. The dates of these experiments are a bit tricky—she talks on the tapes of 1970s-set experiments but claims it began decades earlier. Regardless, the children were transported to a remote facility where they were tortured, abused, and experimented on using LINAC machines. The purpose of all this awfulness: to break their wills, erase their minds, and then plant new memories.

- Janet was one of these orphans—only she wasn't really. She was the daughter of the lead experimenter (!!??), a particle physicist named DR. CELESTE THERIAULT. (I can find no record of a scientist by that name.) Apparently, Dr. Theriault believed that the then-burgeoning technology of particle accelerators offered deep insights into how memories were formed and stored in *human DNA*—the Morris hypothesis. She aimed to prove it was true and wanted to use it for the aforementioned mind-control programs they were developing.

- While they successfully used the accelerators to erase memories, rewriting them with new ones became problematic. The scientists couldn't get the process to work, though Dr. Theriault labored tirelessly to crack the complicated mathematics. She committed suicide sometime in 1979. Leaving Janet with the HED.

- It is unclear exactly what happened next. Janet was experimented on with the rest of the remaining orphans at this clandestine facility. How Janet got out is also unclear, but she has been on the run ever since. Apparently, there is something of an underground network, shuttling various survivors around—from city to city—to hide them. Janet claims a good number of these people are in the network, but there are some who are outside of it, completely hidden (off the grid, so to speak). Further, she claims that the HED is still active—not only pursuing her but also continuing to run secret, dangerous experiments without government oversight. She supposes that their techniques have advanced significantly over the ensuing years and that they have, potentially, gone even further underground.

- Last, but most important: Janet claims there was a curious side effect in a small subset of the subjects—dubbed the "Null" by the researchers. These Null subjects were able to access latent memories of past lives that were encoded in their DNA. Some of the Null could remember back generations, through hundreds, sometimes thousands, of years. Maybe even millions?

  The Null "Cohort" (note that it's the same name as the anarchist group) have been damaged to the point that they require ongoing medication—the aforementioned cancer drug—to avoid losing their minds. Why isn't exactly explained, but I suspect it has something to do with the past-life memories that are invading the brains of Null members. This, Janet explained, is why she was acting as though she were high—she was, in fact, overwhelmed by her "past-life memories."

I could go on and on. I haven't mentioned the business about the creation of AIDS using particle accelerators (apparently one was also used to cover up the murder of a promising young scientist in the mid-1960s), or the equally outlandish claim that the HED employs people known as "Night Doctors" to capture their unwitting subjects—these Night Doctors, apparently, are something of a historical boogeyman largely afflicting African American communities.

You can see why I got so wrapped up in this thing. It writes itself!

Martin Shapiro, PsyD.

40

KOJO PLACED THE PAGES on his lap and stared at the videotape in his hand.

Clearly, Ashanique's mother had paranoid delusions. And clearly, those delusions had found their way into her daughter's mind. It also made the madness of feeding her kid experimental cancer meds more palatable—the woman was insane. She'd been insane for years. Somehow, she'd hid it really well.

Kojo considered stopping there.

Do you really need to see this videotape? What more is there to know?

Call it a detective's instincts, or call it morbid curiosity, but Kojo needed to see Janet say these things. He needed to hear it for himself.

Kojo pushed the videotape into the ancient TV/VCR.

Then he pressed play.

A black screen filled with "burned in" white text; identifying date, location, names, and tape details appeared first. Then, the image cut to a blurry shot of Janet, looking haggard and thin, sitting at a police table, a blank wall behind her.

Dr. Shapiro, offscreen, spoke first.

```
NAME: "JANET OLANDER"
ADDRESS: UNKNOWN
AGE/DOB: 36/UNKNOWN
PLACE AND DATE OF INTERVIEW: Station 302—June 12, 2005
TIME: Commenced 1323. Concluded 1451.
TAPE REFERENCE NUMBER(S): 1/1, 2/1, 3/1, & 4/1
```

INTERVIEWING OFFICER:

  Det. Chief. Supt. 2812 ROGERS

  Dr. SHAPIRO (lead)

  DECLARATION: This transcription of the video recording consisting of five pages is the exhibit referred
  to in statement made and signed by me.

  SIGNATURE of physician

  _____

  SIGNATURE of officer preparing record

  _____

TAPE 1

00:01:15

  DR. M. SHAPIRO: This interview is being videotaped
  and audio recorded and is being conducted in an office at the Chicago Police Station. I am Doctor Martin Shapiro of the Chicago Police Twelfth District.
  The woman across from me is Mrs. Janet Olander.
  Would you please pronounce and spell your last name
  for me?

  J. OLANDER: O-L-A-N-N-D . . .

  DR. M. SHAPIRO: Are you having difficulty focusing,
  Mrs. Olander? Would you like a glass of water?

  J. OLANDER: I'm fine.

  DR. M. SHAPIRO: Are you sure?

  J. OLANDER: That I'm fine? No. I need those pills—
  the yellow-and-white ones you took off me. They
  help . . .

DR. M. SHAPIRO: You're talking about the cancer medications? The MetroChime?

J. OLANDER: Yes.

DR. M. SHAPIRO: I'm afraid I can't do that. Those medications were stolen and, as far as we can ascertain, you do not currently have or are in remission from cancer. Can you explain to me why you think you need the medication?

J. OLANDER: Look at me. Listen to me. I'm struggling.

DR. M. SHAPIRO: Have you taken any other drugs tonight? Either over-the-counter or illicit, or both? Anything we should know about that might help us make sense of what you told the officers who picked you up earlier this evening?

J. OLANDER: My urine is clean. You already know that. Listen, I—I'm sick, okay? That's all. I was a police officer once, you know? I get how this works—how this whole thing is supposed to go. You need to get me those pills.

DR. M. SHAPIRO: You were an officer? Where?

J. OLANDER: San Francisco. A long time ago.

DR. M. SHAPIRO: Mrs. Olander. I can't give you those pills. But you're here now to tell me about tonight's incident. Can you tell me what exactly you were doing at, uh, at the residence of one Mr. Datlow, 400 South Corliss Avenue?

J. OLANDER: I was visiting.

DR. M. SHAPIRO: This address is a suspected drug lab. Do you know what was being made there?

J. OLANDER: I know you do not want to go down this rabbit hole, Dr. Shapiro. You'll regret it.

DR. M. SHAPIRO: Why is that?

J. OLANDER: They'll come for me. It isn't safe here.

DR. M. SHAPIRO: Who will come?

J. OLANDER: Don't do this, Doc . . . I don't feel well.

DR. M. SHAPIRO: In addition to the chemical compounds and equipment associated with the suspected manufacture of drugs, there were also many weapons and bomb-manufacturing materials discovered in Mr. Tyler's residence. When you were visiting, were you aware of these items?

J. OLANDER: I don't think you're listening to me, Doc.

DR. M. SHAPIRO: I believe I am. I think you're just not willing to answer my questions. I'm not here to assess your innocence or guilt; I'm here to assess your mental status. You told the arresting officers some very concerning things. Can we talk about them now?

J. OLANDER: You think I'm a terrorist.

DR. M. SHAPIRO: I don't make any assumptions about you. I am here, working for the Chicago Police Department, to evaluate your mental status at the time of arrest. You told the arresting officers that you were part of an experiment, is that right? That you had escaped?

J. OLANDER: I wasn't myself then.

DR. M. SHAPIRO: Were you on drugs at the time?

J. OLANDER: Sure.

DR. M. SHAPIRO: Okay. Let's start over. Can you tell me anything about the place you escaped from? The experiment?

J. OLANDER: It was a lab. In a remote location. Way off the grid. Military at the time. The people who ran it, they were doctors with a group called the HED.

DR. M. SHAPIRO: HED?

J. OLANDER: It stands for the Human Ecology Division.

DR. M. SHAPIRO: And what exactly do they do?

J. OLANDER: You ever heard of MK-DELTA or MK-ULTRA? The brainwashing experiments they did? How about the Lupine Papers? Or Dr. Joe Curwen at Duke University? He ran parapsychology labs that did covert research on something Curwen called the Fold. And those were just the programs that came to light. They were dinosaurs; the agency stumbling in the dark to try and tap into here— (J.O. points at her left temple.)

DR. M. SHAPIRO: Agency as in the CIA?

J. OLANDER: Yes.

DR. M. SHAPIRO: You're suggesting it was a mind-control program? Something like brainwashing?

J. OLANDER: I'm not suggesting, Doc.

DR. M. SHAPIRO: And you were part of this program?

J. OLANDER: Not at first, I wasn't. My mother was. But—(long pause as she closes her eyes and leans back)—um, here's the rub, Doc, my mom, she was in charge. The whole thing was her idea. I was just along for the ride.

DR. M. SHAPIRO: This program, what was it designed to do?

J. OLANDER: Terrible— Terrible things. To children.

DR. M. SHAPIRO: Like what, Janet?

(J.O. holds her head and mumbles indistinctly.)

J. OLANDER: . . . genetics—they had an accelerator— Mom did the math, you see. It's— It's all about memory.

DR. M. SHAPIRO: Like memorization?

J. OLANDER: No. Like targeting glurr (sp?) pro- teins before—before they form ampahs (sp?) . . . They called it Clarity . . .

DR. M. SHAPIRO: Tell me what that means, Janet.

(J.O. slowly sits upright, with her face forward. Her eyes are locked on Dr. Shapiro's eyes. She appears lucid. She leans in with her eyes still on his.)

J. OLANDER: Do you know what it's like to hunt an- telope with spears in the Carpathian Mountains? To slaughter Spanish soldiers in the surf of Melilla?

DR. M. SHAPIRO: No. I do not. Janet, you said you're on the run. Can you tell me why they are chasing you?

J. OLANDER: We're the ones who got away. They hunt us because if the world finds out we exist it will destroy everything they've been working toward. And . . . (J.O. leans forward) I know a secret. The key to a code that they want to crack so, so bad. A few years ago, if they'd got it, it would have

worked, but the technology hadn't caught up. Now
that it has, my mind's too fragmented to remember it
all. Ironic, right?

00:11:45

End Tape 1

41

ASHANIQUE SAT STILL as Tamiko placed an ECG cap on her head.

They were in her lab on the fifth floor, and the ECG cap resembled a shower cap, skintight, with dozens of electrodes protruding from the surface. The electrodes were connected to thin white wires. They, in turn, led to the machines that read the electrical activity in the brain.

Tamiko seemed satisfied.

Sitting on a rolling chair nearby, Matilda gave Ashanique a thumbs-up.

She swung a bar across the front of the rather ominous chair Ashanique had been placed in. It had a plastic chin rest and a rubber-coated forehead brace. Slowly, gently, Tamiko moved Ashanique's head into position—her chin on the rest and her forehead pressed up against the brace.

"Are you comfortable?"

Ashanique said, "Not exactly."

"But enough?"

"Yeah. Enough. How long does this test take?"

"Only a few minutes. You shouldn't feel anything."

Tamiko rolled a monitor on a cart up in front of Ashanique. She adjusted the height of the cart so Ashanique could look directly at the monitor without moving her head. Tamiko explained that the monitor would display a series of images and words. She wanted Ashanique to read them to herself. The ECG would register the electrical swells and dips associated with each image or word.

"This will show us exactly what parts of the hippocampus are most active. We'll be able to target those specific neurons associated with long-term memory. The images will guide the process. Best to just ease into it, okay?"

"Okay," Ashanique said.

Matilda gently rubbed the girl's shoulder.

"You'll do great," she said. "There are no wrong answers here."

The lights were dimmed and Ashanique felt like a guinea pig, her face pressed up against the plastic guard, her head immobile under the weight of the ECG wires. She stared at the monitor as it suddenly flickered to life. At first, she thought it would be like watching TV. Maybe she'd be shown one of the Disney Channel shows she remembered from third grade. Ashanique imagined it wouldn't be so bad if she was just shown a funny TV show and the computers tracked the electrical output of her brain while she was laughing inside.

But Ashanique knew that wouldn't happen.

Out of the very corner of her eye, she saw Matilda sitting with her arms crossed and looking worried. The same look Ashanique's teachers had when her mom would come to the school for parent-teacher conferences. The teachers were always the ones on the defensive. Janice showed up armed with every assignment Ashanique had completed and an excuse for every day she missed or was late.

Ashanique understood why when the first image popped up on the monitor.

"What is this?" Ashanique asked loudly.

Tamiko said, "Just watch the images. React inside your head. Don't speak."

The first image on the screen was a short, looped video of soldiers running over a barricade made of loose stone and dirt. The footage was grainy and jumped. Speckled with age. Ashanique recognized this war; she'd seen it in vivid, crystal-clear color. Her pulse quickened and she heard her heart in her ears.

And just like that it ended.

Ten seconds later, a series of photos flashed across the screen. They were Polaroids of handwritten calculations. Numbers scrawled on a sheet of paper. Ashanique didn't know what they were, but her body did. She felt every muscle tighten and started to grind her teeth. Whatever this test was meant to do, Ashanique didn't want to participate any longer.

"Is this almost over?" Ashanique asked Tamiko.

Tamiko seemed irritated. "Please, just finish the test."

"Maybe there's another test we can run," Matilda jumped in. "Something a little less invasive."

"This is hardly invasive," Tamiko said.

Glancing away from the screen, Ashanique could see Tamiko staring at the ECG readouts as she thumbed through them. Her expression was incredulous.

"Keep going," Tamiko said. "It'll be over soon."

On the monitor, more video footage rolled. It was a shot from the hood of a car as it drove along a rutted, narrow road through a snowy forest. Ashanique knew this was the same place she'd drawn, the place she'd seen in her memories. But instead of watching the footage, Ashanique was desperate to close her eyes. She felt sick to her stomach. She felt like she was going to pass out.

"My head hurts," Ashanique said, breathing hard. "I have to stop."

"You can't stop now."

Matilda lurched from her chair. "Tamiko. Stop this."

"My head . . . ," Ashanique moaned.

On the monitor, the video footage of the car in the forest sped up—double time, then triple. The forest flashed by, a smear of green and white. Ashanique couldn't tell if it was getting faster and faster on purpose or if it was just her mind losing its focus. The monitor was so close to her face. She felt as though she were about to fall into it. She could practically smell the pine aroma of the forest. She could actually hear the car's tires grinding on the road.

Ashanique slumped forward, her limbs too heavy to move, her eyes rolling. "Please . . . Stop this. . . ."

"You have to push harder. We need to see this through," Tamiko said.

Matilda had seen enough.

She stood and moved to pull a limp Ashanique away from the monitor. But Tamiko beat her to the punch, sticking a Taser into Matilda's right side, just below her breast. Eight million volts of electricity forced her body rigid.

Matilda fell to the ground, unconscious.

Tamiko ignored her and pushed Ashanique closer to the monitor.

"You are unique," Tamiko said. "You're the only child of a Null we are aware of. In the lab, we saw the Clarity develop only after weeks, sometimes months, of heavy testing. Heavy exposure. But you, Ashanique, you're not like the others. They had to be awakened by forceful prodding. Not you, you awoke on your own."

Wide eyes glued to the flashing screen, Ashanique's eyes rolled to white. She sank into herself.

And saw the life just before her own. . . .

42

WINTER IS JUST *loosening its grip on the mountains.*

Parts of the earth tumble, rocks and low-slung shrubs, toward a slate-gray bay. Fog rolls in ropy coils across the water, shrouding the remnants of an old gold rush town. It was a desolate land then; it is even more desolate now.

The roar of an engine breaks the heavy silence as a camouflage Humvee tears down a twisting, narrow dirt road at the water's edge. Mud-spattered and worn, the vehicle is tattooed with military insignias and an American flag.

Inside the Humvee a long-limbed but reed-thin African American girl sits between two soldiers. The one behind the wheel has a mustache and red cheeks. His name is Morton. By the window is Phillips, a tall black man with steely eyes and a habit of rolling his cigarette lighter between his fingers in a fluid, hypnotic arc.

"We're going to see my mom, right?" Janelle Walters asks the soldiers.

She is six years old.

Morton and Phillips are silent. They've been silent much of the three-hour drive from the airport. Phillips said a few words to Janelle when they stopped for a snack in a small town with only one gas station. She had to pee something fierce, and he walked her to the restroom and told her to make sure to lock the door behind her. When she was done, she unlocked the door and peeked outside and saw Phillips standing there, still as a statue, with his hand on the gun on his hip.

After they'd climbed back in the Humvee, Morton handed Janelle a bag of chips and a Tab cola. He told her to make sure not to make a mess, the only words out of his mouth the whole time. Then he looked at Phillips, and Phillips shook his head.

"Man, least we outside and stretching our legs."

Janelle knew they were talking about "babysitting" her. When they met her at the airport, Morton had been in a funk. Janelle figured out quickly it was because he hated being around kids. The idea that he had to pick up this brat from the airport and drive her across the island made him surly. Phillips tried to calm him down, but no matter what he said, Morton just shrugged it off. Janelle thought Morton was an angry person, and she didn't like the idea of sitting beside him. What would he do if she talked too much? Or asked too many questions? Janelle's mom said she had a mouth on her. It took everything Janelle had to keep quiet for that first hour. But then she had to pee.

Finally, they're getting close.

Janelle can sense it in the men. The whole way up until now, Morton was driving with both his hands on the steering wheel. Gripping it like he was trying to strangle the life out of it. Now, he's leaning back and his hands are loose. Phillips is doing that thing with the lighter. Janelle's fascinated by it.

"It's been two weeks since I saw her last," Janelle says.

Phillips says, "She'll be glad to see you, I bet."

"Kinda cruel," Morton says.

Judging by his tone, Janelle can already tell he's about to say something mean. Something that will likely upset her. But she's close to seeing her mom now, no matter what Morton says, she's determined to not let it dampen her mood. Not one bit.

Phillips says, "Don't start this. The girl ..."

Morton gives Phillips an ugly sidelong look. "That's my point exactly. It's like bringing your lap dog to the pound to visit all the other poor fuckers. Rubbing it in their faces, you know?"

"Boss wants to see her kid. And watch your mouth."

Morton scoffs. Janelle has heard worse.

"All I'm saying"—Morton continues his tirade—"seems kinda sick. Makes me wonder what the real reason is. Maybe she just wants to see her kid. Maybe she's got something else in mind. I don't care what they tell me, how they talk all

big and fancy about revolutionizing warfare, what they're doing in that base is just a few steps above what we saw gooks doing. Some of that shit . . ."

"You're gonna scare her," Phillips says.

Janelle says, "You can't scare me. I know it's all just talk."

Morton laughs. It's a hollow sound, like a rock tossed into a well.

The Humvee screams around a corner. A half mile ahead is a checkpoint with a rolling fence. It is topped with razor wire like Janelle's seen in the movies about prison escapes. All she can think is that her mother is safe behind those fences. Out here, in the middle of nowhere, it makes sense to have the maximum protection. Who knows what runs up and down these mountains in the darkest part of night? Janelle certainly doesn't want to know.

At the gate, Morton flashes his badge at a waiting soldier.

"We got Dr. Theriault's kid here."

The rolling fence opens, and the Humvee roars through. Janelle doesn't speak for the rest of the ride; her eyes are glued on the road. Her whole body is alive with expectant electricity.

The dirt road twists for another five miles inland before the base materializes from the surrounding evergreen forest. It is black and squat and parts of it are covered in camouflaged tarps. Janelle knows that if they'd approached the building from any other angle, it'd evaporate into the trees. How cool? Not only did Mom get to work at a lab tucked into the mountains, but it was a secret lab.

The Humvee stops in a rock-strewn lot a few yards from what Janelle assumes is the front door to the place. Morton gets out first and stretches. Before he opens his door, Phillips turns to Janelle.

"Your mom's missed you," he says. "Been talking 'bout seeing you for a long time. Can't get her to shut up about it, to be honest."

"Really?" Janelle asks, the surprise in her voice obvious.

Phillips smiles and nods. He's never spoken to Dr. Theriault in his life. She doesn't pay any of the military staff any mind. He's never seen her in the commissary, and she doesn't ride the elevators like the other scientists. When she's passed him in the halls, she's as cold as the air on the top of the mountains. Phillips knows he's a ghost, so are all the other soldiers. He also knows Dr. Theriault will only break this little girl's heart. Morton's right, she shouldn't be here. But she is.

"She's been real busy, though," Phillips adds. "She might be busy still."

"My mom's always busy. That's her job."

Phillips laughs. "That it is."

Stepping into the base is like stepping into an electronic cave. She knows it's made of concrete, but she never imagined it'd be as dark as it is. At the university lab, the walls are white and the floor is an endless stretch of tile. The place is cleaned every single day and the people there wear white coats and laugh a lot. Two breaths into her mom's forest hideout and Janelle knows that nobody laughs here. A bowling ball solidifies in her stomach. She worries it'll be there for the rest of her visit.

Janelle follows Phillips down a narrow corridor where the lights are embedded in the center of the walls, not on the ceiling. She doesn't ask why. But she counts each one she passes and she's at fifty-two before they take a left turn to a spiraling concrete staircase. The only other people Janelle sees as they walk downstairs are men in military fatigues and a handful of people in scrubs. Several of the women who pass her smile, but no one says anything. Janelle gets the impression that this place must be sacrosanct. It certainly has the heavy air you find in a church or a cemetery. She wonders what sort of experiments her mother is working on here. She wonders why Morton thought it was cruel for her to see the "poor fuckers." Who are they?

At the bottom of the stairs, Phillips swipes his badge to unlock some metal doors. They click unlocked and he holds them open for Janelle. She steps into another corridor lined with the same lights just like the one up above. They walk to another door. He unlocks it, but before he opens it, he looks down at Janelle.

"Yer momma tell you 'bout the other children?"

"The 'poor fuckers' Morton was talking about?"

"Now, come on . . ." Phillips fights to hold back his laughter. "They are children, but they're not children like you, understand? They've got some medical issues. They're here to see if they can make things right with them again. Because of that, they're kept separate. You know, kept in their own rooms."

"My mom worked with kids at the university. Lots of sick kids."

"So you understand how this is gonna look."

Janelle nods and acts confident, though she's not sure she actually does understand how this is going to look. The children at the university, they were in hospital beds and wore thin hospital nightgowns. Some of them had their heads shaved and needles in their arms. But they were always children like Janelle. Just children who didn't have the health or the mind she did. As Phil-

lips opens the door, Janelle is worried about what she's going to see. Are there monsters in here?

They step into a large circular room. It has high ceilings like a missile silo that Janelle read about in school once. Doctors and nurses stand around machines and desks in the center of the room. Janelle doesn't see her mother, not at first. She's too busy looking for the monsters they're hiding in this place.

Janelle follows Phillips into the room, and as they walk across the concrete floor—she notices they are scuffed—she eyes the fifty-odd doors set into the walls. They look like prison doors. Thick and steel, each is painted bright orange. There are no windows on the doors, but there are numbers stenciled in white paint. She notices 32 . . . 33 . . .

"Janelle?"

A young Korean man with a thin mustache and glasses walks over, hand extended. Janelle smiles shyly. She shakes his hand. "I'm Dr. Hyun-Ki Song. But you can just call me Dr. Song. I work with your mother; she's looking forward to seeing you."

Dr. Song escorts Janelle to a subbasement via a series of winding hallways and wide concrete staircases. Her mother, Dr. Celeste Theriault, six years older than the fresh-out-of-school Dr. Song, sits at a lab bench in a long, narrow room crowded with scientific equipment and silent technicians. Janelle is reminded of walking into a library.

Janelle runs up to her mother and hugs her.

Dr. Theriault turns and looks down at Janelle with a cool, detached smile. "Hey there, Janny. Good to see you." Janelle keeps hugging her mom, so happy to be nuzzling her warmth, but she senses there's something wrong. Her mother is rigid, cold.

"Honey," Dr. Theriault says, "I need you to let me go now."

Janelle pulls away, tries to hide her disappointment.

"I know you're busy, the men said so."

"Yes, but I'll visit more with you later. Dr. Song . . . ?"

Dr. Song takes Janelle's hand and leads her back upstairs. As they walk, Janelle turns and looks back at her mother, who is bent over the microscope again. She wants her to look back, but her mother doesn't. Janelle heads upstairs, heart breaking.

They pass a room with the steel doors open. Inside, Janelle can see a small, frail boy strapped down on a gurney beneath a massive metal cylinder. Janelle thinks it could be a telescope, but it's squat and the eyepiece is too big. The machine hums. The skinny boy wears a boiler suit like a prisoner and the number 19 is stenciled on the pant legs. He shakes, then the humming stops. Janelle stops to watch.

"Is he going to be okay?" Janelle asks Dr. Song.

"He'll be fine," Dr. Song says. "Just running tests. Come on now."

"Let me just watch a little longer. . . ."

Dr. Song reaches for Janelle's arm but stops himself from pulling her away.

The two soldiers wheel the boy from the room. He looks drugged out. Delirious. Janelle and Dr. Song walk alongside them for a moment before the soldiers turn the cart into another room where two women in white coats wait with several men in scrubs. One of the female doctors is Japanese. Her face is half covered by a medical mask, but her badge reads, DR. TAMIKO KADREY. *The woman next to her is older, maybe in her late thirties, and her badge reads,* DR. DOROTHY SYKES.

The soldiers wheel the boy up in front of Dr. Sykes and she cracks open a vial of smelling salts. The boy suddenly rouses. Dr. Song puts his hand on Janelle's shoulder.

"We really should be going," he says.

But there is no way Janelle is going to move. She stands firm. She needs to see what's going to happen with the boy marked 19. The boy stops trembling. Dr. Sykes asks him to tell her what he's seen. His voice sounds like a little boy's, but his words can't be his own.

"Dobroye utro," he says.

Janelle has no idea what it means.

"What is your name?" Dr. Sykes asks the boy.

The boy turns to her.

"Anastasia Tschaikovsky."

Dr. Song pulls Janelle away from the door and drags her back down the hallway. Janelle tries to comprehend what she's just seen.

She's frightened, her eyes darting.

She wants to go home.

She's desperate to see her mom again, to drag her mom from her microscope and this horrible place. . . .

43

ASHANIQUE RETURNED to herself.

Her mother's memories faded at the back of her mind like ice melting on her tongue. Lingering only for a single nostalgic moment. The monitor was blank now. The buzzing sound had ceased. Tamiko sat beside her. Leaning forward, Ashanique couldn't see Matilda. She knew Matilda wouldn't have left her alone.

Something was wrong.

"What is the solution?" Tamiko asked.

Ashanique shook her head.

"I don't know what you're talking about. . . ."

"Your mother hid something from us. It's a series of numbers, an answer to a complicated math problem. You know what she knew. You must see it."

"I don't see any numbers," Ashanique said. "But I did see you."

Tamiko blanched.

"Saw me what?"

"You were there, Dr. Kadrey. You were very young. I don't know why you believed so deeply in something so wrong, but you did. You're here now, in this hospital, doing all this research, but that place never left you. Did it?"

"I need the solution, Ashanique. I'll let you go."

"No you won't. The Night Doctors never let anyone go."

As Tamiko turned, reaching for her purse, Ashanique saw Matilda lying on the floor just beyond the desk. She looked as though she had fallen asleep, her body relaxed. But the way she lay, sprawled out, told Ashanique every-thing she needed to know: Matilda was hurt, and Tamiko was dangerous.

Something heavy, awful, settled onto Ashanique's chest.

If Matilda is hurt . . .

Ashanique watched carefully as Tamiko reached deep into her purse, past the handle of the Taser, and wrapped her fingers around the grip of a Colt Mustang handgun. Ashanique knew this was her one moment, her only chance.

Wrenching her head free of the brace, Ashanique turned and kicked Tamiko out of the chair. As Tamiko struggled to get up, Ashanique leaped on the purse. Its contents spilled out across the floor, clattering against the tile.

Tamiko was slow to move.

When she finally rolled over, she saw Ashanique had the Colt leveled at her.

"Wake her up."

Ashanique motioned to Matilda.

"There are smelling salts by the door," Tamiko said.

Keeping the gun on the good doctor, Ashanique backed up slowly toward the door. She locked it before she pulled the medical kit from the wall. She slid it across the tile floor to the doctor's feet.

"Wake her," Ashanique said. "Now."

Tamiko opened the kit and dug around for the salts.

"She trusted you," Ashanique said. "You were her friend."

"I'm a colleague."

"And you'd kill her, just for . . . some stupid numbers."

"Those numbers could change the course of history. They could end wars, end violence and criminality. With those numbers, we could unlock all the secrets of the human mind. Imagine the things we could do."

"Wake her."

Ashanique tightened her grip on the gun. Janice had taken her shoot-ing at least twice a month. They shot targets, bottles, pumpkins, and scrap metal. But this was different. This was a person; a real, live person. Ashanique thought her hands would be shaking. She was surprised they weren't. She was also surprised there weren't alarms going off and cops rushing into the room. The Colt was lighter than the guns she was used to firing. Almost too light.

She wondered if it could truly stop Tamiko.

"Okay," Tamiko said, cracking the salts. "Okay."

Tamiko held the pungent white sticks under Matilda's nose.

Matilda began to cough, her eyes racing behind her eyelids.

Ashanique exhaled; Matilda was going to be all right.

· · ·

"Tell me what that place was," Ashanique said, her voice trembling more than her hands. "What happened there?"

Tamiko looked up the Colt's barrel to the girl's eyes.

"You already know this."

Ashanique said, "I see things, I don't know what they mean yet."

She pulled the trigger and the Colt bucked. The bullet sped over Tamiko's left shoulder and punched a small hole into the wall twenty feet behind her.

Tamiko started talking.

"Project Clarity was an experiment to alter memories," she said. "Your grandmother led the project, and your mother was a subject. You have their memories inside you, carried in your genes. I know you only just went Null four days ago. The memories are fresh. They might be overwhelming now, like a dam has burst in your head, but it will only get worse."

"Null? What does that mean?"

"That's what we called them, the ones in the study who had what you're having now. The memories. It's a stupid name, really, but . . ."

Ashanique grimaced as pain swelled in her head. She thought she heard distant voices like the ones she heard in the static of the noise-canceling headphones. They might have been panicked patients or security guards racing toward the lab. Or they were deeper voices, awakened lives.

"And my mom was right? This is because of . . ."

Tamiko stepped toward Ashanique, hands raised.

"Puberty," she said. "Your body is transforming. Even though you don't sense it, not explicitly, you are becoming another being. The foundational pieces of your body are changed. Along with the hormones is a cascade of neurotransmitters that wash over your brain. Glutamate receptors—"

"GluRs?"

"Yes." Tamiko smiled. "You remember. Yes, that's it."

"And AMPAs . . ."

Tamiko nodded. "Amino-hydroxy-methyl-isoxazolepropionic acid receptors. AMPAs. They are chemicals crucial to memory formation. Listen, Ashanique, you have the cure—the way to stop what's happening to you— hidden inside your memory. Let me get it out. Let me find the solution and we can cure you."

"You mean symbols that mean different letters and numbers?"

Tamiko nodded again.

"This can all be over if you just tell me what your mother knew," Tamiko begged Ashanique, her hands shaking.

Matilda sat up; eyes opened wide, she took in the scene with horror.

"Ashanique . . . What is this?"

Ashanique kept the gun leveled at Tamiko.

"They're going to kill you, Dr. Kadrey."

Tamiko turned to Matilda, desperate like a drowning swimmer searching for anything, anyone, to grab hold of. "Let me help."

"I think you've done enough," Matilda said as she stood.

"You okay?" Ashanique asked.

"I'll be fine," Matilda said.

"We can't trust her."

"I know."

"We have to tie her up," Ashanique said. "Use that tubing."

Ashanique kept the Colt on Tamiko as Matilda wrapped her hands with oxygen tubing from a package on a lab bench. Then she tied Tamiko to a water pipe in the corner of the room. As she worked, Tamiko fumed.

"She's not like the originals, Matilda. She isn't going to last very long. She's already got obvious synaptic degradation. Very advanced. Even if you can get ahold of MetroChime, it'll only slow the process. With the best treatment you can find out there on the run, she'll be dead within a year. But I'd give her a month."

Tamiko flashed a knowing grin.

The look terrified Ashanique.

She wanted to fire again and not miss.

"They know for sure you exist now. They'll come after you and they won't stop until they have you. They see everything. They hear everything.

Everyone you know, everyone you love, will be crushed. Running will only make it that much worse."

Matilda finished, the knot looked solid.

"She'll scream," Ashanique said.

Matilda grabbed medical tape from a desk drawer and wrapped it around Tamiko's head, covering her mouth in two long strips. The whole time, Tamiko stared at Ashanique like she was trying to see into the girl's very soul.

"We have to go," Matilda said.

. . .

Stepping out of the room, Ashanique and Matilda found a nondescript hallway lined with doors.

They moved quickly toward the end of the hall and a sharp left turn. Rounding the corner revealed an elevator bank. Men and women in scrubs and lab coats stood around, waiting for the doors to open.

Ashanique tucked the Colt into the back of her pants, and she and Matilda moved quickly to join the scrum of researchers. As they stepped up to the nearest elevator, the doors to an elevator two over opened and disgorged a group of passengers. Among them was the bald man who'd come to kill Janice.

The man's head gleamed in the artificial light.

His hands were encased in purple latex gloves.

Ashanique hid her face as the elevator doors in front of her whooshed open. She grabbed Matilda's hand and pulled her inside, squeezing past an irritated man on a cell phone. As the doors closed, Ashanique briefly glimpsed the bald man walking down the hallway toward Tamiko's lab.

She knew they would have only minutes to escape the building.

44

RADE FOUND TAMIKO tied up in the lab.

He looked gravely disappointed.

It was as though Rade always assumed Tamiko would fuck this up; that despite her advanced degrees and cool composure, she was never really part of the team. The fact that Rade couldn't even be bothered to scream at her said it all.

He locked the door behind him and squatted down beside Tamiko.

Rade pushed the hair from her face and straightened the collar on her lab coat. He did it gently but not out of any concern for her. He just hated how messy she looked in that moment.

"What did she tell you?" he asked.

Then, without an ounce of sympathy, he tore away the medical tape.

Tamiko's lips were red and puffy, irritated by the tape.

"The girl has Fifty-One's memories," Tamiko said, "but she denied knowing the solution. But . . . her readings were some of the most exaggerated I've ever seen. Even the initial imagery, only piecemeal and suggestive, was enough to trigger explosive activity in her hippocampus. She is more sensitive than any of the previous subjects. Maybe it's that I have refined equipment or maybe it has something to do with the strength of her genes but . . . she's incredible. You have to understand, she's the first new generation we've seen."

"And the solution?"

"Ashanique needs focus, a little more time, but it's in there."

"But you didn't get it?"

"Like I said, she's . . . This has just happened. Only days ago, Rade. . . . We've never had success with a Null in that short a time span. The electrical activity doubles every few days. It's only a matter of—"

"Where are they going?"

"I don't know. They didn't—"

Rade dragged a straight razor from his hoodie pocket.

Tamiko scrambled. "A detective . . ."

"Yes?"

"Matilda mentioned a detective looking out for them. He was investigating the shooting. I think Matilda and the girl are going to try to get in touch with him. If you find the detective, you can find them. My purse . . . on the floor . . . He talked to everyone after the incident. Handed his card around."

Rade stood and walked over to Tamiko's purse. Using the straight razor, he poked through the purse's contents as though he were an Old West tracker, the kind from classic Western films, digging through the remnants of a fire pit, looking for clues.

He uncovered several business cards.

But only one of them read CHICAGO HOMICIDE.

Kojo's card.

Rade picked it up and turned it around.

"That's the one. Find him and you'll find them."

Rade walked back over to Tamiko and kneeled beside her again, the straight razor hanging between his legs. Its metal tip scraped the tile floor.

"HED will coordinate the search with local law enforcement. We'll find them within hours," Rade said. "The truth is, you aren't privy to the inroads they've made over the past decade. The technology has taken this whole thing much further than a few . . . hired hands out in the field. It isn't like before. We're not detectives. But all those fresh faces they have, the ones watching the video feeds or scraping social media, even the researchers designing the next generation of tests, they don't know what we know. . . ."

Tamiko nodded a bit too forcefully.

It smacked of desperation to Rade.

"They don't have the insight we have, right?" Tamiko said. "They haven't had the setbacks we had to work through. All those years of trial and error with the orphans, all those millions of dollars spent chasing our tails on—"

"I wasn't talking about research. I'm talking about the Null. You, Dr. Sykes, the rest of the team, none of you know what the Null know."

Tamiko swallowed hard.

"Please, Rade," she said. "I have always been loyal—"

"Yes. You have."

"And I'm useful. I designed the protocols for the initial tests. I oversaw the data collection for the first cohorts. I was the one who recognized the first changes. It's in the notes. You can call Sykes. I can do that again. Even from here, I can help them to fix what isn't working."

"What isn't working here is *you.*"

Tamiko closed her eyes.

Rade's razor flashed faster than even he could see—merely a spark, like stone striking stone. It cut through her blouse; blood spilled from the tear, running in rivulets onto her lab coat and pants.

Rade's gloved fingers explored the edge of the cut. It was very deep. He'd sunk the blade between the third and fourth ribs, slashed through the pericardium, and sliced into her heart itself. Rade knew, from experience, that Tamiko would bleed out within seconds, each heartbeat emptying her body.

But Rade wouldn't even allow her those precious seconds.

"We have seen everything," he said as he leaned forward, staring deep into Tamiko's quickly dilating pupils. "And we know the secret at the heart of our consciousness. You've spent your whole life looking for the answer, looking for a way to explain why humanity is so very special."

Rade caressed Tamiko's head, running his gloved hands through her hair.

"I'm going to show you now."

He pulled her hair back and cut open her throat.

45

HAND IN HAND, Matilda and Ashanique ran across the campus.

While Matilda worried they looked too obvious running through the crowds of students and patients, no one stopped them; no one really even batted an eye. Truth was, Matilda thought, most people avoided drama at all costs. Too much hassle. Too much worry. Good thing a surging panic pushed Matilda on. She was amazed she wasn't winded.

She had never been much for running.

Swimming was always her thing.

Matilda found being submersed was not only relaxing, it was also restorative. In water, sound traveled differently, light bended and warped, and her mind shifted into another gear. One she hadn't known existed until she'd started doing all her heavy thinking underwater. Meter by meter, kick by kick, she could scroll through her research. Isolated in the pool, complex chemistry made more sense—swimming, she could synthesize peptides and catalyze enzymes with ease. It even had the benefit of being healthy, according to her personal physician, it was the best low-impact activity she could do to strengthen her heart and oxygenate her brain.

But on land, scrambling across campus, dodging passing students, she was weaker than she expected. The air was heavier, the ground that much harder.

"You okay?" Matilda yelled to Ashanique as they rounded a building.

Ashanique grunted a yes.

202

Matilda could feel the girl holding back. She assumed Janice must have trained her to run, to escape and survive.

Ashanique could shoot; she certainly could sprint.

Breathe in and breathe out. Keep the time. Match the crunch of your feet on the sidewalk with the thump of your heart.

A minute later, they cleared the corner of the bookstore and stepped out onto South Ellis Avenue, where a passing cop car slowed. The cruiser's lights were on. The bulky cop behind the wheel leaned his head out the window.

"Everything okay?"

"There's a man," Matilda began. "He's chasing us. He has a gun."

The officer got out of his car with his hand on his gun.

"Go on, get inside."

As they ran around the cruiser and climbed into the back seat, he reached in through the open driver's-side window and grabbed his radio.

"Car Twelve to Control."

A woman's voice came over the radio. "Go ahead."

"Four-Adam-Sixteen on scene at university. Possible Ten–Thirty-Two. O-R."

"Control to Twelve, I read you. Possible Ten–Thirty-Two. What is your location?"

The cop looked back at a street sign.

"On campus, South Ellis near the intersection with East Fifty-Eighth Street. I don't have a visual. Got two females, one white, one black, a preteen, in my car. Say there's a man after them. No visual. Over."

"Stand by."

The officer got back into the patrol car and hung up the radio before he closed the door. He turned around to Matilda. His name tag read GOMEZ.

"You two all right?"

"I think so," Matilda said, barely controlling the panic in her voice. She didn't feel safe, even in the back seat of the cop car. She wasn't sure she'd ever feel safe again. "He's in the hospital. If you haven't gotten the calls already, they're going to be coming in fast. It's the same guy from the university a day ago. The same man."

Before Matilda could go on, the officer turned to the front.

He pulled his cell phone from his shirt pocket and flipped it open. He dialed a three-digit number. "I have the girl," he said into his cell.

Matilda stopped breathing.

"Understood," Officer Gomez said.

He hung up his cell with a sigh.

Matilda put an arm across Ashanique as the cop turned around with his gun. The only thing separating them was the mesh partition and three feet of humid air.

"You went for my weapon," Officer Gomez said. "I had to defend myself."

"No—"

A jagged sound split the air as something smashed into Officer Gomez's forehead. The gun dropped from his hand as he slumped against the steering wheel.

Ashanique lowered the Colt into her lap.

"He was going to kill us."

Stunned, Matilda silently glanced through the mesh at Officer Gomez's body. The morning had left her mind scrambled. Her world was not so much turned upside down as it was turned inside out. She had been right after all; she wasn't even safe in the back of a cop car.

There is no safe place now. Tamiko told you as much, Maddie. They will come for Ashanique; for you. They control everything and everyone.

"We have to get out of the car," Ashanique said. "Matilda?"

Matilda felt like screaming.

"We have to get out of the car."

The doors were locked, so Ashanique lay back and kicked at the left rear passenger window until it shattered. She toppled the loose glass and then reached, gingerly, through the frame to open the door. With a click, it swung wide.

Ashanique pulled Matilda out after her.

"We have to leave now, Matilda. We can't call anyone. No police. There's no one we can trust. We have to find a place they're not going to be looking for us. A place to hide out until tonight."

Matilda thought immediately of her mother.

It wasn't so much that she considered Stonybrook necessarily a safe place. Or that she always turned to her mother in times of deep confusion and stress. It was concern. She had to warn the facility. She had to get her mother to a protected place, locked away until this was over. Somewhere out of town. Somewhere they could all hide. Truthfully, she didn't consider the ramifications—she only knew what she'd seen and she knew she never wanted to see that again. Her overriding instinct was clear: Go to your mother; make sure she's safe.

"I know a place," Matilda said.

They flagged down a cab on East Fifty-Ninth Street and barreled into the back seat. Three blocks away, cop cars, their lights blazing and sirens rending the air, charged onto campus. The cabdriver, the ID posted on the Plexiglass partition gave his name as Jasper Adeyanju, turned around and asked where he was supposed to be going.

Matilda said, "Braidwood. Stonybrook Assisted-Living Facility. It's on South La Grange. I-80's probably fastest."

"Okay. . . . It's your money."

Jasper started the meter and turned up his music, a rollicking Nigerian "highlife" pop song, before easing the cab into traffic. In the back seat, Ashanique lay back and sighed. Matilda saw tears welling up in the corners of her eyes.

"It's okay. You just saved our lives."

"I haven't killed anyone before," Ashanique whispered. "Not in this life."

"You did the right thing—"

Ashanique turned away, wiping her eyes.

"That's not it. There is no right thing. No wrong. There are only actions and repercussions. And all the bad things, all the cruel consequences, come from fear. Maybe that cop was scared. Maybe that's why he was about to kill you. I'm not sad about him losing his life, though. He made that choice."

Matilda didn't know what to say. She nodded, trying to be sympathetic.

"Are you afraid, Matilda?"

Unsure of how to answer, Matilda took a moment. She saw Rade cutting Clark's throat. She saw his blood splash onto the floor. She saw the cop's head being blown open. She saw again the horror in his eyes.

Yes, Maddie. You're afraid. Very afraid.

"Don't be," Ashanique said. "I know the secret now."

46

WANDERING THE AISLES of the gas station, Ashanique picked up a bag of salt-and-vinegar chips, a package of strawberry licorice, and a root beer soda.

She met Matilda at the checkout counter.

Matilda paid cash for the food, two touristy ball caps, two cheap pairs of sunglasses, a pair of kitchen scissors, and two prepaid smartphones.

Walking back out to the cab, Matilda pulled the SIM card from her cell—the one she'd had for two years, filled with un-downloaded photos of Clark—before she tossed the phone into a trash can.

She handed the SIM card to Ashanique.

The girl bent it before it snapped in half.

"We have to be smarter from now on, like my mom taught me," Ashanique said, dropping the pieces of the SIM. "No credit cards, no logging into accounts, we're going to have to look different too. Cut our hair and change our clothes."

The cab took I-90 out of the city.

The sun was hidden by churning clouds that turned the humid air a sickly yellow.

As the cab idled in traffic, Matilda took Ashanique's hands. They were cold but not shaking. Not like her own.

"Everything that is happening," Ashanique said. "It was because of an experiment. That's why I'm like this. Why I can remember other lives."

206

"You were in this experiment?"

"No. But my mother was."

Ashanique glanced up at the rearview mirror and caught the cabdriver's eyes beneath the bill of his cap. He immediately looked away.

"It was in the late 1970s. In Alaska."

"And you saw what they did there? To your mother?"

Ashanique nodded. "There were fifty children, all of them orphans; some taken from hospitals, others from orphanages. A few of them snatched right off the street by the Night Doctors, or so they were called. The Night Doctors name was a boogeyman thing. Rumors swirled around, you know? People in poor neighborhoods were scared. Kids had gone missing."

The traffic cleared and the cab sped up.

"That's how they got their name. But the thing is, the Night Doctors aren't maniacs. They're scientists. Smart people who got caught up in something so complicated, and so important, that they can't see how destructive it is. Matilda, if you want to understand this, you're going to have to forget what you think you know. . . ."

"About what, Ashanique?"

"About everything."

Ashanique turned and looked out the window at the quickly darkening world. The sun had been banished. The shadows were so long, they swallowed whole buildings. For a second, the world looked like it was being erased.

"Why do you care about me?" she asked.

"I made a promise to your mother that I'd keep you safe," Matilda said. "And . . . I—well, you're amazing, for starters. I've never met anyone like you. And—well, actually that's not true. A few years ago, I saw a patient who said a lot of the same things you've said. This man came to me because he was worried. He knew he wasn't ill, not in the clinical sense, but he didn't know how else to handle the things he was seeing in his head. He came to me for help and opened up. This patient told me something I couldn't believe at the time. I was blind and stupid and I let him down. I'm not going to do that again."

"Did he remember past lives?"

"Yes, he did."

"He was the man I saw the picture of in your office, right?"

"Yes. His name was Theo," Matilda said. "And he talked about the Night Doctors. He talked about being taken by them into a lab. About being experimented on . . ."

"They called us the Null," Ashanique said.

"The Null?"

"One of the doctors, I think it was Dr. Kadrey, said it as a joke. She said that if they weren't careful, we'd become the null hypothesis. The null thing stuck. What she really meant was that we were a side effect. Project Clarity wasn't about making people like me. We were the mistakes. The insignificant. The Null."

"If you were the mistakes, were there any successes?"

Ashanique couldn't stanch the tears welling up.

Her mind was changing so quickly. With every new memory that appeared, it felt as though new neural networks had been formed. Synaptic connections that had lain dormant since birth suddenly thrummed with electrochemical life. Neurohormones that had drifted aimlessly in the intracerebral space found themselves drawn, like iron shavings, to the magnetic pull of newly awakened nerve cells. The feeling was like a neural thunderstorm, every burst of synaptic energy a bolt of lightning. And with each new image came a new emotion. Even the slightest recollection added to the density of her thoughts.

Ashanique could feel her thinking transform, even when she spoke to herself—in that eternally quiet voice—the words were different. She used bigger words, crafted more complicated sentences.

The past was colonizing her.

Gifting her with its boundless store of knowledge.

Successes.

"When I hear that word I want to picture people breaking the tape at the end of a marathon. I want to see people smiling and laughing. Instead, I see the blank stare of the brain-dead boy, his spinal cerebral fluid leaking from his ears."

"I'm sorry, Ashanique. I'm so sorry you have to feel all that. Having to experience all those things firsthand must be so difficult. No one should have to witness so much suffering."

"Beauty," Ashanique said, wiping the tears away.

"What?"

Ashanique took Matilda's hands in her own and squeezed them tight.

"What they did was horrible. The successes were the worst. But what the Null discovered, what we became, is beautiful. It's difficult to put into words but when you see your past lives, when you see down the chain of genetics, through all those people, all those experiences, you realize something profound."

Matilda couldn't look away.

Ashanique needed her to hear this.

"We are forever, Matilda. We think it ends the minute our eyes close and our hearts stop but . . . it doesn't. There isn't heaven, not like they say, but we do live on. I see all the way back, all that history, all that knowledge, it's right in front of us the whole time."

47

AS MATILDA SIGNED IN, Ashanique made her way into the foyer where Rosa was watching TV and Francine sorted through another stack of *National Geographic* magazines.

The receptionist, in scrubs, smiled at Matilda.

"Your mother's in the memory-care unit sitting room," she said.

"I'd like to check her out for a few hours. She doing okay today?"

The receptionist made the *comme ci, comme ça* hand gesture.

"She got confused at breakfast. Do you know anything about a hairpin? She thinks her neighbor might have taken it."

"The hairpin's with my uncle. I explained this to her nurse."

"Sorry," the receptionist said. "I'll make a note of it in her chart."

"I think the nurse already did."

"Anyway, it might not be a great day to take her out. You guys going to lunch or . . . ? Let me put in a call to Dr. Chaudhary. He and you can talk about how she's doing. I'm just saying it might not be the best day to have her out. He'll call us back and then I'll patch the call through to the memory unit and you can talk to him there."

Matilda met Ashanique by the muted TV.

The receptionist waited for the call, scrolling through her social media feeds.

The TV was tuned to CNN and continuous coverage of the second university shooting. Matilda didn't think it was such a good idea for Ashanique to be watching it, but then a photo of Tamiko popped up; she was smiling in her lab coat, and the scrawl on the bottom of the screen read: *Noted professor found dead in laboratory . . . suspect still . . .*

"Terrible thing," Rosa said.

Francine shook her head as she flipped through the January 1988 issue.

After thirty seconds of digging around the couch, Matilda found the TV remote and changed the channel to a *Law & Order* rerun. She took hold of Ashanique's hand and led her toward the back of the facility.

"Come on. I want you to meet my mother."

After the receptionist punched in the code to unlock the door to the memory unit, Ashanique followed Matilda inside. They took a wide hallway to a sitting room as the door clicked shut behind them.

Lucy was in a rocking chair, rocking slowly, staring outside at the empty bench where several Stonybrook employees took personal calls and smoked.

She was cradling a well-worn baby doll.

Matilda leaned down beside Lucy and placed a hand on her shoulder.

"Mom?"

Lucy turned and examined Matilda's face.

"Hello," she said. "Do you know what time it is? I feel like I've probably been wasting most of the day just looking out the window and daydreaming. Did you know I was a professor?"

"Yes. At Colgate."

"Oh," Lucy said. "We've met before? I'm so sorry."

"Mom," Matilda said. "We need to go out for a bit, okay?"

"We're going somewhere?"

"Yes. Just for a little bit."

Lucy looked around Matilda at Ashanique.

"Who is that?"

"This is Ashanique."

Lucy looked Ashanique over and nodded, more to herself than Matilda.

"Yes, yes. I've met her before. She comes regularly to visit her grandmother."

"This is my first time here," Ashanique said.

Lucy screwed up her face, confused.

"No. I've met you before. I think . . . No, no. You were a student. Yes, you were one of my very best students. Do you remember the lesson? We have a test today. I hope you came prepared."

"Mom," Matilda began, "we have to start packing."

Lucy waved her off. Then, smiling to herself, contentedly ensconced in the memory of a long-ago lecture, she started speaking in French.

"Qui était au Sénégal . . . ils ont vendu les esclaves au port . . . on en parle aujourd'hui à voix basse mais ça s'est passé . . ."

Curious, Ashanique pulled a stool over from under the window and sat across from Lucy. She leaned in and listened carefully as Lucy mumbled. Matilda watched, impressed with how gentle Ashanique was but unsure of what the girl was doing.

"It's okay," Matilda said. "She has these moments. It'll pass."

Ashanique touched Lucy's knee.

"J'étais autrefois un Igbo."

"Qu'est-ce que vous avez dit?" Lucy asked.

"J'ai été volé de mon peuple," Ashanique continued. *"J'étais sur un très long voyage. À travers l'océan. J'étais à bord de l'Henrietta Marie . . ."*

Lucy gasped.

"Il a coulé dans une tempête . . ."

Matilda hadn't studied French in fifteen years.

She was in shambles when she tried to speak with any fluency, but she could still read the language. She got the gist of what Ashanique and Lucy were talking about. Lucy was fully absorbed in the conversation. Matilda had not seen her mother that focused, that attentive, in nearly a decade. She couldn't help but cover her mouth as she watched the two of them converse. Lucy with her flourishing hand gestures and wide-eyed amazement, and Ashanique with a knowing, nearly wise modulation and tone.

This is miraculous. I am witnessing the miraculous.

But as miraculous as it was, they had to get moving. Matilda knew it was only a matter of time before the people coming for Ashanique tracked them to Stonybrook. She'd taken a huge risk coming to the facility, but it wasn't until she'd watched her mother conversing with Ashanique that she truly realized the enormity of what she was doing.

Why didn't I just check us into a hotel? Or go to the bus station? Because you're human; you're flawed. Where do people turn when they're in trouble?

*Where do they always eventually run? Home. They always go home, Maddie.
And home, for you, is your mother. Now get her the fuck out of this place.*

Matilda stood up, interrupting the conversation.

"I need to get her stuff packed, okay? We should leave soon."

"She's coming with us? Isn't that—" Ashanique asked.

"We'll drop her with a friend on our way out of town."

Ashanique turned and looked toward the entrance to the memory unit.
She was listening for something.

Matilda only heard the sound a few seconds later. She made no mental
connections to the noise. She didn't associate it with anything more than
the usual sounds of daily life—a car backfiring, a balloon popping, someone
clapping.

But then she heard the screaming and she knew.

He was here.

48

RADE WAS STRUCK by the smell when he stepped into Stonybrook.

He stood by the receptionist's desk and inhaled long and slow, catching the scent of something nostalgic. But there were no real memories associated with the chemical lavender smell of the facility. It was what bubbled up from underneath: the paradoxically clean smell of a clinical death.

To Rade, this was a place where malfunctioning people went to spend their last years—their bodies being slowly dragged into the abyss by the weight of their crumbling minds. This was the end of all tethered flesh. The place stood as a stark reminder of just how much *more* he is than the average person.

He wondered, momentarily, about others like him—surely there must have been at least a handful? How did they die here? Were their brilliant, pure selves entombed in an animal grave? The concrete shoes of flesh?

How horrible.

"Excuse me?"

Rade turned to the receptionist as she removed her headphones.

"If you're here to visit a resident, I'll need you to sign in and I'll also have to see your ID."

"Deacon."

As a matter of habit, the receptionist stood to walk around her desk and take Rade's ID. She paused midway. She looked beyond him, outside the front doors. He knew she'd noticed something lying just outside. A coat. And shoes. Maybe she'd even felt that tickle crawling up her spine, spilling over her shoulders, as she realized she was looking at a body. That was when she saw the blood.

The receptionist spun around, her mouth open in a silent scream.

Rade's first round hit her neck. It severed her headphone wires before punching a nasty hole in her carotid. She hit the floor, bleeding out. Reaching over her desk, Rade grabbed her ID badge. Her name was Becky.

"What was that?! I heard—"

An elderly man tottered around the corner, waving his cane.

Rade shot the man in the gut.

He stepped over the body and walked into the TV room, where an older woman turned to glare at him.

"Where is Dr. Deacon?" Rade asked.

The woman was too terrified to speak; the words just wouldn't form in her gaping mouth. Next to her, another woman, oblivious to everything as she turned the pages of the November 1990 issue of *National Geographic*, paused to fix her hearing aid. Deaf as an adder, she turned to page thirty-two of the magazine.

"You know that murder I told you about?" she asked loudly. "Well, this is going to sound a little bit like I'm cuckoo in the cuckoo head but . . . I don't think I actually did read about it after all. As crazy as it seems—"

Rade killed Rosa and Francine with two shots each.

Then he walked to the memory unit and studied the keypad.

Some of the keys were darker than others. He knew that was from finger grease. No one usually notices that kind of thing—on this keypad, the 3, 6, 9, 0 were the darkest. Rade stood there, staring at the numbers, working through the various combinations in his mind, when he was interrupted by the arrival of two police officers.

"Drop the weapon!"

Rade stood still, the gun tight in his right hand.

"I said drop the fucking gun!"

Rade turned slowly, glancing over his shoulder at the cops.

The first officer commanded again: "Drop the gun, asshole!"

Rade wasn't going to comply.

He moved, faster than either officer expected.

Rade's first bullet hit one of the cops in the left leg. As she fell, the second officer fired. That slug slammed into Rade's right side, shattering his tenth rib before exiting through his back. Briefly spun by the force of the impact, Rade recovered.

Sharpened by pain, he returned fire with deadly accuracy.

The second officer was hit first. The bullet entered his chin, passed up through his tongue, and lodged itself behind his eyes. Before the first officer, now on the ground, could get off another round, Rade shot her in the neck. She crumpled, pressing her hand against her vertebral artery to stanch a pulsing gush of blood.

Pushing his left hand flat against his wound, Rade walked over to the cop.

She tried to speak.

Tried to plead.

He shot her in the head.

49

"MOM, WE'VE GOT to go."

"Why now?" Lucy asked, reaching for Ashanique. "We're talking."

"Mom—"

The shriek of alarms answered.

And as sound obliterated the normal hum of the memory unit, the residents began to panic. Nursing staff and medical assistants ran to calm them and organize them for evacuation. An old man with a prosthetic leg stumbled over a stool. A woman in a wheelchair held her hands over her ears and screamed.

The door to the memory unit opened and Rade stepped inside.

Matilda stood frozen.

Again, she saw Clark's throat being slashed.

Rade's murderous wink replayed in slow motion.

Ashanique grabbed Matilda's hand tight. The sensation snapped Matilda from her paralysis and she turned and took Lucy's arm. She and Ashanique ran with Lucy toward the back of the unit, down a long, twisting hallway lined by framed photos. Lucy cried and muttered. She told Matilda that her arms were being hurt, that she was being bruised. Matilda wanted to cry, to apologize, but if she said even one word she knew it would slow them down. Rade was likely only yards behind them.

If you don't run, you'll all die.

As they passed her bedroom, Lucy wrenched free of Matilda's grip and ducked inside. She slammed the door behind her and quickly locked it.

"Don't come in!" Lucy shouted from the other side. "I don't know who you are but I don't want you to come in!"

"Mom! It's me!"

Matilda banged on the door with her fists. Even as her brain was going into paroxysms of anxiety, she clearly recalled when Lucy still lived at home and would accidentally lock herself in the bathroom. She'd cry, trying to get herself out. Matilda would calmly explain to her how to open the door. It never worked. Matilda would always have to use a knife to pick the lock and open the door. She'd find Lucy calmly sitting on the toilet, smiling like a child.

"Next time, sweetie," Lucy would say, "please knock before you come in."

But this time, Matilda knew she wouldn't get the door open. And she knew her mother couldn't be calmed on the other side.

"Come on!" Ashanique pulled at Matilda. "Please!"

"Mom!"

Matilda slammed her body hard enough against he door that the wood cracked and splintered. She did it again. And again.

Still, the hinges held.

• • •

Rade moved slower than he would have liked.

It'd been a while since he was last shot.

Each step he took, the broken bones ground together and tiny slivers stuck deeper into his left lung. He could count at least seventy-eight similar injuries over his lifetimes. In one of his bodies, he'd had his right hand severed by an enraged husband. In another, an arrow gouged out his left eye. When he was born again the next time, the injuries had healed; the flesh was intact. Rade tried not to think of the animal encounters—so many maulings, so many bears.

Rade rounded the corner in time to see Ashanique point the Colt at him.

She fired, the shot went wide, but he didn't flinch.

"I won't hurt you," Rade said, doubting she could hear him over the screech of the alarms and the wailing of confused residents and terrified staff.

. . .

Ashanique fired again just before Matilda dragged her clear of the hall.

A framed painting of a bucolic farm shattered just over Rade's head.

"Come on!"

Matilda took Ashanique's hand and together they ran toward the rear doors of the memory unit, the ones that led outside to the courtyard. But when they reached it, the door was locked. They were trapped. Sirens deafening, a strobe light flashed wickedly above their heads.

"We have to get to the museum!"

Ashanique struggled with the door, desperate.

"How many rounds do you have left?" Matilda shouted over the noise.

"I don't know," Ashanique said. "Maybe five?"

Matilda said, "Use them all."

Rade appeared at the end of the hall. The reflective strips on the sides of his pants flashed in the strobe light. Despite his injury, he walked quickly.

Ashanique fired the Colt, rocking her back into Matilda.

A light fixture exploded over Rade's head.

"I'm going to cut you apart," he said, step quickening. "Just like your mother."

Ashanique began to cry as Matilda pushed hard against the door with her hip. She was able to glimpse daylight through a crack at the bottom of the door and tried to widen it with her foot. Kicking at it, the door seemed to loosen in its frame. Though it was unlikely that she'd get it open, Matilda had to believe she could.

Come on, Maddie. Push this fucking thing!

Behind Matilda, the Colt shook in Ashanique's hand as, now only fifty feet away, Rade raised his gun, his grip strong, his hand steady.

"Put the gun down, girl," he said.

"Please," Ashanique begged through tears. "Please . . ."

There was a sudden clang of metal before the door moved and Matilda stumbled forward into the wan daylight. Pulling the door open, Kojo stepped inside, 9mm in hand. He moved in front of Ashanique and fired five rounds in quick succession at Rade. Rade, in turn, fired back as he wove and dodged.

"Hurry!" Kojo shouted back to Matilda.

But she was already outside with the girl, running to Kojo's idling car.

Two feet from the vehicle, a sobbing Ashanique faltered. Matilda caught her and helped her into the back seat. As soon as Ashanique was lying down, she began to seize.

"It'll pass." Matilda climbed in and held her. "It'll pass. . . ."

As she gritted her teeth, Ashanique said, "I don't want it to."

"What?"

"These memories . . . They . . . They . . ."

Ashanique passed out seconds before Kojo barreled out of the building and climbed into the driver's seat, slamming and locking the door.

"Hang tight."

Kojo slammed his foot on the gas pedal.

The car lurched forward, nearly throwing Matilda to the floor.

"That asshole must've been hopped up on something," Kojo said, looking in the rearview to see if Rade had emerged from Stonybrook after them. "I hit him. No doubt about it. Didn't seem to slow him down any, though. I should go back in, make sure he doesn't kill—"

"We have to get her out of here," Matilda said, holding the girl.

Ashanique continued to seize in Matilda's arms.

Glancing over his shoulder, Kojo asked if Ashanique was going to be okay. "Her doctor said she has seizures," he said. "We need to get to a hospital, right?"

"No hospitals," Matilda said. "We can't trust anyone."

"Ashanique doesn't look okay. She needs help."

"She has help. Please, just get us downtown."

As Kojo radioed in the shooting, he pushed the car down a suburban street as fast as it would go, fishtailing around corners.

In the back seat, Matilda pulled Ashanique closer.

The girl's convulsions slowed, their violence diminished, but still her eyes moved in frantic arcs under her eyelids.

Matilda wondered what new nightmare she was seeing.

50

JANELLE IS ELEVEN and she follows her mother through deep snow.

The sky is translucent, the no-color of water. But the sun is nowhere to be seen. Janelle assumes it's hidden behind the towering fir trees that they're walking between, but every time she looks, she can't see it. They are both wearing snowsuits; the crunch of their boots is the only constant sound. They've been walking for nearly twenty minutes.

A crow croaks somewhere closer to the mountains, and Janelle is glad to hear it. Dr. Song had explained to her that they're some of the smartest creatures besides people, dolphins, and apes. He'd pointed up at a tree that was filled with crows—a murder cawing in the dusk—and told her that they were social, just like people. Crows can remember faces and voices. They're always watching because they're infinitely curious.

Janelle and her mother come to the edge of a rocky escarpment, and her mother stops.

Below them, the waves crash against black, jagged rocks that look like giants' teeth. Janelle once called them the Nephilim's Molars. The first time she saw them she wondered how many ships had been chewed up there. Surely there were just heaps of old shipwrecks under the water. Janelle imagined scuba diving down there and picking through the wreckage. She'd find cannons and crown jewels, just like the explorers in the pages of National Geographic *did.*

Her mother kisses her, bringing her out of her daydream.

"None of this is going to make sense," she says. "But if you survive what hap-

pens next, then you will be stronger than I ever was. Don't let them break you, okay? Promise me you won't let them break you."

Janelle has no idea why her mother has taken her out into the snow.

She doesn't understand what her mother is saying.

Truly, none of it makes sense.

. . .

Dr. Theriault is exhausted.

She's been sick to her stomach for five weeks straight. She hasn't slept in three days and she's been seeing things—not people or imaginary beings but distortions, wavy lines and shifting ripples of light. She knows the problems are in her visual cortex; lack of sleep and never-ending stress will do that. The visions are warning signs. It's her brain's way of putting the brakes on thinking, the brain's way of protecting itself.

And Dr. Theriault knows it'll only get worse. At this point, there is no way to stop it. Every passing minute, her body fights to pull her back into the lanes of sanity.

Not now, though.

Standing two hundred feet above the raging ocean, the hallucinations have stopped. Maybe it's the fresh air, but her stomach is no longer trying to turn itself inside out. Her mind is clear. Her daughter will be just fine. She is strong enough.

With that last certainty, she runs and jumps.

She expects gravity to kick in quickly. Throw 142 pounds over the edge of a cliff and it will fall fast. But there is a fraction of a second where Dr. Theriault feels weightless. Like maybe she will blow out across the sea.

The sensation doesn't last. It's a trick, another of her mind's contortions. She plummets too fast to even cry out. She doesn't hit the water. Her body shatters against the rocks before it is caught up in the churning darkness.

A single thought burns before her soul powers down:

Coral. We are coral.

. . .

For Janelle, it happens before she can even process it.

Her mother is there and then she is not.

Janelle steps to the edge of the escarpment and looks down into the ocean. There is no sign of her mother. Janelle knows that they won't recover her body.

Her mother did exist, she is certain of it, but outside of whatever few pictures remain, there is no evidence now.

Janelle stands there, staring, and the snow starts to fall.

She is still there when the snow stops and the sun cuts through the clouds. It illuminates the faces of the men, soldiers from the base, who crash through the forest and sweep Janelle up. One of them carries her like he'd carry a newborn. He says something about hypothermia, about how her lips are blue. Janelle tries to imagine what that looks like. Mostly she pictures the women with funky makeup she saw in a fashion magazine once. She tries to laugh but no sound exits her mouth.

Back at the base, Dr. Song wraps her in warm blankets and plies her with hot tea. It's sweetened with a ton of honey, something her mother would never do. She'd only add milk and tell Janelle that was enough. Janelle doesn't want to think about outside—about the ocean and the molars that ground up her mother. She wants to be warm and sip tea. For the first time in a very long time, Janelle honestly thinks that people like her. Why else would they do all this?

That's when it hits her: the other children, the damaged ones behind the numbered doors, don't ever feel this. Even though her mom and the other scientists explained it to her, saying that those children needed help, that they were sick, she knows that sick, damaged children need comfort too. Suddenly the tea she's sipping isn't sweet. The warm blankets feel like wet sheets.

She kicks them off and puts the tea down.

The numbered doors don't have windows, the experimental subjects can't see her, but Janelle feels terrible being in front of them like this. Carrying on like she can't help herself, like she doesn't have free will. Though she came to the facility a visitor, she's become a patient, just like them. And her mom must have known. Janelle realizes that the stuff her mother was saying near the cliff— about being strong, about not breaking—that was in preparation for this moment. Janelle realizes that she needs to be strong, not just to survive this place but to ensure that what happens here never happens again. Janelle also knows that the comfort, the kindness, won't last.

She will be next.

Sometimes the universe makes everlasting decisions in the blindingly brief segments of time. In less than a fraction of a fraction of a second, whole stars can evaporate and massive black holes can come into existence. So it is with Janelle, in between heartbeats she becomes the fighter she knows she'll need to be.

Janelle doesn't have to wait long. She sleeps terribly that night, her dreams clotted with visions of her mother floating and falling, floating and falling, in a terrifying loop. And she wakes frequently as the scientists fight just around the corner. They're arguing about where to go next. About how everything might be lost because Dr. Theriault, "the damned bitch," took the solution with her.

Without that, they may as well start from scratch with a new method.

Though Janelle only hears bits and pieces, it is enough to convince her unconscious mind that she needs to leave. When they come for her, soldiers dragging her out of her sleeping bag at two in the morning, she is ready for them. She fights, her nails raking Morton's face. He howls and hits her hard in the stomach. Stuck gasping, she is dragged on her back down the hallway to the machine.

Morton presses an old napkin from his pocket up against the angry scratches on his face. He flicks Janelle off while two soldiers hold her down and Dr. Tamiko Kadrey injects her with a stinging liquid that burns as it runs into her veins. Seconds later, Janelle goes woozy. Her brains turn to wool, and her body evaporates around her.

Dr. Dorothy Sykes materializes.

She stands over Janelle, hands clasped before her like she's going to ask a favor. Which is silly. She's in control here. "You know what we do here," Dorothy says. "You know how important our work is. I need you to help us, Janelle. You can be a part of what your mother was trying to accomplish. You don't want to see all of her hard work, the work she lived for, go to waste, right?"

Janelle feels herself nod.

"This is a waste of time," Tamiko says. "We can pull the information."

"Pull it how?" Dorothy barks. Her voice softens as she addresses Janelle again.

"Good. That's excellent. Your mother, sad to say, left some unfinished business. She was working so hard; maybe she just forgot to let us know how to continue her work? We need some numbers, very, very important numbers. I need you to think back to every conversation you had with her, every conversation you overheard, every note you might have seen, every paper of hers you might have colored on the back of. You're a smart girl, very clever, do you think you can go back through all those memories?"

"Yes," Janelle says. It comes out as "Yesh."

"Good. Good."

Dorothy kneels down beside Janelle and strokes her hair. Dorothy's hands are too cold; they feel like icicles scraping across her scalp. "I need you to search your memory for numbers and letters, a formula like in chemistry, and it's associated with a complicated series of words that go in short palindromic repeats. Do you understand?"

"Yes. But I don't . . ."

"Don't what?"

"I don't have any memory of anything like that."

Tamiko stomps over. "This is absurd. She won't remember this way!"

"What if she's not one of them?" Dorothy asks Tamiko. "What then?"

Tamiko says, "We make her one."

Dorothy glances over Janelle, at the scientists on the other side of the room. They all look at one another, uncertain, before they nod.

Tamiko looks closely at Janelle and says, "She's healthy enough that we can increase the wavelength without doing much damage to the neurons. We give her an extended exposure and we do it until we see the activity. Truth is, the mechanics of activation in the Null Cohort is unclear. Could be it's not a mutation, could be it's just something natural that's been reactivated, atavism, in a way. We all carry the DNA to have tails but it's not activated. I honestly think we might be seeing some deeper process with the Null—some underlying memory system that most humans have either lost or, possibly, sublimated. If I'm right and we can pinpoint the source of this archaic memory network, then we can not only reactivate it but also alter how it functions. This might not be unique, with enough prodding, so to speak, we might be able to make anyone Null."

Dorothy doesn't need to think it over.

"Get her ready."

Fifteen minutes later, Janelle's head is shaved and she's in one of the jumpsuits that all the experimental subjects wear. She's one of them now. As they wheel her to the LINAC machine, she sees two of the soldiers spray-painting the number 51 on an empty cell door. Her new home. Her head is still as light as helium, her body still stretched out and rubbery as chewing gum.

In position beneath the machine, Janelle closes her eyes.

Dorothy gives the signal, and the LINAC is turned on.

There is an industrial thunderstorm overhead before . . .

51

MATILDA PICKED UP the Colt from the floor of Kojo's car.

Ashanique had fallen asleep in Matilda's arms but it wasn't until the seizure had ended that she was able to ease the girl over onto the seat. Ashanique slept deeply, her head resting against the window. The cold glass was pressed up against her forehead. Matilda didn't want to move her; Ashanique needed every second of sleep.

"I'm coming up to talk to you."

Matilda climbed up into the front passenger seat and buckled in. She had the Colt in her right hand and tried to keep the gun leveled at Kojo.

But her shaking hand belied her anxiety.

Holding a gun on a cop? Good move, Maddie.

Kojo clearly saw the gun but said nothing. He kept his hands at two and eleven, eyes on the road. Surely, Matilda assumed, it wasn't the first time he'd had a weapon pointed at him. Still, it was a tremendous risk.

"I need your cell phone," Matilda said.

"I've already called in the shooting," Kojo replied. "Your mom will be okay."

"You don't know that. Give me your cell. Please."

Kojo pulled his cell from his coat pocket and handed it over to Matilda. She rolled down the window and tossed it outside.

"Seriously?" he asked, slowing the car.

"Keep going," Matilda said. She pulled out the second prepaid smartphone they'd bought at the gas station and handed it to Kojo. "It's already activated."

226

"This is ridiculous," he said, looking over the phone.

"This is life-and-death."

"You know, you don't need to keep that on me," Kojo said, eyeing the gun.

"I'm sorry, I can't trust anyone."

"I know you've gotten yourself mixed up in something ugly. I never said you wanted any of this. Or any of it was your fault. But you're in it now. You should try to let me help you get out of it. Help you and her."

Matilda glanced back at Ashanique.

"Everyone who's tried to help us has also tried to kill us."

"I haven't," Kojo said.

"You haven't *yet.*"

Matilda shifted her weight, uncomfortable in the seat. She felt beaten. Scarred. Existentially confused about everything that had happened. After Clark was murdered and the cops came onto the scene, she held out hope that her world could be righted again. She honestly believed that things could get back to normal—or some semblance of normal. All of that evaporated the minute Rade showed up at Stonybrook. It was as Tamiko had warned—there was no escape, no safety. Matilda was determined just to survive the evening, long enough to get Ashanique to the museum and the mysterious Childers. Whatever happened after that would be out of Matilda's hands—her job, her only job, was to ensure the girl got there.

"Let me take you two back to the station, Matilda. You'll be safe there. We can forget you put a gun on me. We can get her some help and figure out what's going on together. I'm sure if we compare notes, we'll—"

"It's getting late. We have to be downtown."

"The girl's clearly sick, she's got real problems."

"No, she's . . . she's something *more* than us."

· · ·

Kojo watched Matilda sidelong.

He was struggling to stay on top of all the information being thrown at him—the day had begun with the confusion of the videotape, more than enough to keep his mind busy for weeks, before exploding into a bloody shootout.

He had no idea what to expect next, but he couldn't stop himself from formulating new outs—talking Matilda down, convincing her to let him take the girl to the hospital, or, worse, overpowering her and getting the Colt. He had time—the interstate was congested and it would likely only be even more backed-up as they got closer to the city.

Kojo could sense Matilda was serious.

It was the same sensation he'd had in the offices at the university during her questioning. She had a profound empathy—something inherent, something integral to who she was. That was the deeper reading—the emotional brain. And yet, other, deeper parts of him saw something else. Even with the exhaustion, even with the panic, she had an unidentifiable sexiness.

He hated thinking the word, but it was true.

Get your goddamned head back in the game.

Two things that needed to happen: he needed to get that gun from Matilda, and he needed to convince her to trust him. He wasn't sure which would come first.

"What's downtown?" Kojo asked.

Matilda seemed to weigh the question carefully.

"Museum," she said. "It's the International Museum of Surgical Science. And, before you ask, no, I've never heard of it either."

"It's on North Lakeshore Drive. Right by Burton."

"There's someone she can trust there. Someone who'll meet us."

"You talked to Ashanique's mother, right? She kicked you out of the apartment when she found out you were interviewing the girl. What's your read on her? Why's she dosing her daughter with cancer meds?"

Matilda said, "What's happening to Ashanique happened to Janice."

Kojo nodded; that seemed to make sense.

"Janice was arrested thirteen years ago," he said. "She was swept up in a raid on a suspected drug lab. Feds have linked her to some terrorist group targeting scientists and military officers who were part of a project—"

"The Clarity," Matilda confirmed. "Crazy as it sounds, Ashanique has seen it, because her mother and her grandmother saw it. And I'm convinced that's real. Somehow this Project Clarity unlocked memories—possibly even as a side effect of some larger experiment—and Ashanique has inherited her mother's predisposition for activating those ancestral memories. She's going to lose her mind if we don't get her to that museum and get her treated. Take a look at her, Detective. You saved our lives back there. You've seen what we're running from."

Kojo glanced at the rearview mirror.

Ashanique was breathing heavily, slowly. He had to admit she looked worse than the last time he'd seen her. He turned back to Matilda.

"What happens at the museum?"

"Ashanique's not the only one with this. I don't know how many there are, but Janice was in touch with a group—"

"The Null Cohort," Kojo said, putting it all together for himself.

"There's an underground and a doctor, Dr. Song, who can help them."

"He can cure her?"

Matilda said, "I don't know. Janice seemed to think so."

Kojo thought it over, looking back at the girl again. Ashanique looked fragile, that tough, spirited instinct—that survival kick—that had gotten her this far was clearly draining. Maybe Matilda was right, maybe this was the result of some fucked-up experiment, but in the end it didn't matter. What mattered was that there was a sick girl in his back seat, a girl who'd die without his help. Ignoring the procedural voice that droned in the back of his skull about rules and regulations, about job security and making his mortgage, Kojo knew what he had to do.

"Okay. I'll take you."

He pulled a hand from the wheel. "I just need to get that cell you gave me. It's in my coat pocket right here. I have to call home to make sure my boy's okay, all right? He was expecting me."

Matilda thought it over.

"I'm being real," Kojo said. "No tricks."

Matilda motioned her okay with the gun.

Kojo carefully pulled the cell from his front pocket. He called Ophelia, and as he waited for her to pick up, he glanced over at Matilda. For the first time, he noticed that the hair on the underside of her ponytail was scarlet.

"Mr. Omaboe?" Ophelia answered the phone.

"I'm going to be a little later than expected. Are you okay watching Brandon past dinner? Really sorry about this."

"I do have an appointment with my sister at eight but . . ."

Kojo turned to Matilda.

"I will be home as soon as I can. Thank you, Ophelia."

52

ASHANIQUE AWOKE TO find the car idling, pulled into a parking spot along-side the colonnaded International Museum of Surgical Science building.

Both Kojo and Matilda turned around in their seats to look at her.

"How you feeling?" Matilda asked.

"I'm okay, I guess. Little headache but . . ."

"But what?"

Ashanique thought for a second before she spoke. "While I'm scared I'm losing myself, I don't think these memories are such a bad thing. Not the way my mom made them sound. I mean . . . It doesn't feel unnatural. For her, they were nightmares. Terrible things she didn't want to see, even when they were good. She said they clogged up her thinking, made her feel like she was going crazy. But not me. These memories . . . this sounds stupid, but even when they hurt, it feels like I'm being put back together. Not pulled apart like my mom felt."

"You know what I think?" Kojo said. "You should have some water."

He turned to Matilda. "There's a bottle under your seat."

Keeping the gun level as best she could, Matilda reached under the front passenger seat and pulled out a blue thermos half filled with lukewarm water. She handed it back to Ashanique. The girl took several long gulps.

She handed it back.

"Keep it," Kojo said. "She needs it more than me."

"I'm not talking this way 'cause I'm dehydrated," Ashanique said. She took another drink before she looked at the museum. "I need to meet some-one named Childers here. Childers will take me to Dr. Song."

"And you honestly believe Dr. Song is going to fix this?" Kojo asked.

"Dr. Song is the only person who knows what's going on inside my head. This is what my mother wanted, Detective. This is what she fought for."

Ashanique turned to Matilda. "Is Lucy okay?"

Matilda nodded. "Yes, thank you. I called a few minutes ago. She's shook up, which is to be expected. I can't believe I put her in that situation—"

"You didn't know," Ashanique said. "How could you know?"

"I was running on adrenaline, just going with my gut."

"Going home." Ashanique smiled.

"You're something special," Matilda said, reaching back and squeezing Ashanique's knee. "I hope you know that."

Matilda wanted to say more, to tell the girl again how sorry she was for everything that had happened. And how determined she was to make sure Ashanique was safe when all the horrors had passed. But she wasn't sure that would happen anytime soon—if ever. Matilda prayed the girl couldn't read that worry, that clouding pessimism, in her eyes. She needed Asha-nique to stay strong.

"Should we go in?" Kojo asked.

Ashanique nodded.

. . .

Kojo flashed his badge to a security guard at the museum's entrance. He told the woman they were there to talk to someone—the guard didn't ask questions and waved them through the metal detector.

"I don't have to fill out anything about this, right?" the guard asked.

"You're cool," Kojo said. "We'll only be a little bit."

"Museum closes in less than an hour."

They made their way through a few exhibits—a cabinet with old-school prosthetic limbs, an iron lung, eighteenth-century medicines—before reach-ing the second floor. There, they entered the library. Kojo walked around the room first, scanning the place in officer mode and seeing nothing that raised his hackles, before he motioned for Ashanique and Matilda.

"No one's here," Ashanique said.

"Maybe we're early?" Matilda suggested.

Kojo said, "Just be on guard."

The room was relatively small. It had a marble floor and ornate wooden bookshelves lining the walls. There was a single large table in the center of the room and twelve leather chairs seated around it. As Ashanique made her way around the bookshelves, leaning in to read the titles behind the glass, Matilda and Kojo peeked into an adjacent room. It contained an exhibit and was empty as well.

"So what time is Childers supposed to be here?" Kojo asked Ashanique.

"By four," she said, still looking over the books.

Kojo walked over to a window and looked out at the ground below while Matilda sat at the table. She called Stonybrook again to follow up on Lucy but the signal was busy. She scanned her cell for news about the shooting, but there wasn't much information available. She doubted the killer had been caught.

Kojo walked over and leaned up against the table.

"I'll get follow-up alerts," Kojo said, noticing her cell screen.

"I just . . . God, I don't even know what I'd do with myself."

"Hey. No, it's not your fault, okay? You were doing good. This guy—"

"His name is Rade," Ashanique interrupted. "He's one of us."

"One of you but he works for them?" Kojo asked.

Ashanique nodded before she went back to looking at the books.

Kojo pulled out a chair and sat down beside Matilda.

"You did pretty amazing today," he said. "Considering the chaos you've seen over the last two days, you seem very in control. I'm impressed."

"I'm about two seconds from falling apart."

Kojo laughed.

"Nah, nah. That's not you. I can see you're strong. Got that look in your eyes. You might not know your way around handling a firearm, and I was a little concerned in the car, but . . . I could tell you were in this all the way. You care about her and, even more, you believe her. That's saying something."

"You convinced?"

Kojo rolled his neck as he considered.

"I'm gonna be honest with you, I don't know. I know that whatever is going on has a whole shitload of people upset. That guy back at the nursing home, the cop Ashanique killed—"

Matilda recoiled hearing that.

"—in self-defense," Kojo clarified. "I'm not gonna judge you two on that. You say he was going to shoot you—"

"He was going to kill Matilda," Ashanique said across the room.

"And I'm trusting you on that, I am. All I'm saying is that this thing, it's complicated. This goes beyond just a Chicago homicide detective, a university psychologist, and an eleven-year-old girl."

"What are you saying?" Matilda leaned forward.

"I'm saying we need help. The police—"

"Tried to kill us," Ashanique scoffed.

Kojo continued, "And the FBI. Homeland Security, I don't know. But I'm telling you that we're gonna need assistance to get out of this. We both want that guy—the guy called Rade—taken out. We also both want to get Ashanique some help. I get that you're following what Janice said, but what if no one shows up here? Or, worse, what if Rade and ten of his best, baldest friends walk in that door? Can we please agree that if no one walks in here named Childers in the next fifteen minutes we'll leave?"

Matilda looked to Ashanique.

The girl shook her head.

"I've got no other place to go," she said.

"That's what I'm trying to fix, but it—"

Kojo didn't finish his thought before he jumped out of his chair, gun pulled and leveled at the young woman who'd just walked into the library.

The young woman placed her hands in the air.

She was exceedingly tall and thin, wearing leather pants and a jean jacket. Her lips and nose were pierced and half her head was shaved, the other a swoop of black hair that fell across her left eye.

As she walked closer, Matilda saw she had green eyes.

"I'm Childers. Who the fuck are you?"

"You armed, Childers?" Kojo asked.

Childers nodded.

"Okay," Kojo said. "Take out your piece and put it on the floor."

Childers rolled her eyes before, using only her right hand, she pulled a Glock from the back of her leather pants. She placed it on the floor carefully.

"There's no time for this," she said. "The girl needs to see Dr. Song now."

Kojo said, "We'd all like to see Dr. Song."

"Nope," Childers said. "Just Ashanique."

"No deal," Kojo said.

"You're wasting time."

"How can we trust you?" Matilda asked, hand on the Colt tucked into the back of her pants.

Childers locked eyes with Ashanique.

"When your mother was found in the snow, Dr. Song put a blanket around her shoulders. He gave her hot tea with honey. She'd never had honey in tea like that before. You know how that felt, don't you? How it felt to be cared for? And when things changed, he was the only one who tried to help. Dr. Song is waiting for you, Ashanique. But you need to come alone. These people, they don't understand."

Tears bathing her eyes, Ashanique looked over at Matilda.

"It's true," the girl said. "I need to go alone."

Kojo shook his head. "This is a big, big mistake."

"I trust her," Ashanique said.

Kojo wouldn't let it go. "Matilda, you yourself said these people are capable of anything. They got into the university, into the nursing home. How'd they find you? How'd they track you across the city? This group, the Human Ecology Division, or whatever it was called, they have deep pockets and all the connections."

"Childers knows things no one else knows," Ashanique said.

"And she could be faking," Kojo said. "Maybe there's a file on your mom. Maybe she just pulled all this information from it. How do we even know there is a Dr. Song? I'm telling you, I've been doing this thing for a long time, and I've never seen bad people with this much power. We're not handing the girl over alone."

Childers said, "You're making this worse. For all of us."

"Please," Ashanique begged. "I trust her."

Matilda stepped over to Kojo.

She placed her hand on his arm and slowly forced him to lower his firearm.

"This is wrong," he insisted. "Don't let her just walk out of here."

"It's okay," Matilda said. "She understands."

Kojo just kept shaking his head, disbelieving.

"Thank you," Ashanique said.

She walked over to Matilda and hugged her. As they embraced, Matilda slipped her cell phone into the girl's coat pocket. Ashanique noticed and looked up at Matilda. Matilda mouthed, *Trust me.* Ashanique nodded.

Ashanique crossed the room to Childers. The older girl opened her backpack and pulled out a metal detector wand. She scanned Ashanique. The wand was silent. She put the wand back as Ashanique turned to Kojo.

"Thank you," she said. "Take care of Matilda."

Childers picked her Glock up off the table.

"You did the right thing," Childers said.

Kojo and Matilda followed Ashanique and Childers to a staff elevator. Childers inserted a key, and the elevator doors sprang open.

She stepped inside after Ashanique.

"I'm going to be okay," Ashanique said to Matilda. "Dr. Song will fix me."

The doors closed.

Ashanique was gone.

53

"GIVE ME YOUR CELL."

They were back in Kojo's car, and he was furious.

Matilda asked again. "Please. Hurry, I need your cell."

Kojo couldn't believe he'd allowed Matilda to let Ashanique go like that. *With some random punk girl?*

He held in his rage and handed over the prepaid smartphone, eyes glued to the outside of the museum. He assumed that if Childers and Ashanique came out the front or side, he'd see them. Even if they ducked into an alley behind the building, they'd have to walk back to the street to get anywhere.

"Why do you need my cell?"

Matilda said, "Watch."

Kojo turned his attention to the screen as Matilda logged into a tracking app. A window opened displaying a map of Chicago.

"I slipped my cell into her coat," Matilda said. "We can follow them."

She held up the cell phone so Kojo could see two little blue circles positioned close together on the digital map. One of them was moving down East Burton Place toward Astor. He assumed that was Ashanique. The other, them, was stationary. Somehow, despite his watching, Childers and Ashanique had snuck past.

"Are you waiting for a green light?"

Kojo cleared his throat.

"Nah, I'm ready."

He fired up the car and pulled out into the late-afternoon traffic. They followed the tracking signal down North Astor Street before it came to a stop near an alley. Kojo pulled the car over and together they watched the screen for a few seconds. Ashanique's blue circle wasn't moving. It was sitting in the entrance to an alleyway.

"We're about to be ditched," Kojo said.

He kicked the car into gear and back into traffic.

Kojo knew the city well enough to not even bother looking at the screen. When Brandon was just a preschooler, two years before Constance died, Kojo had made the force and was determined to show his first partner, Bob, a fat racist from Michigan, that he wasn't there because of affirmative action. He wanted Bob to know he was as invested, if not more, in the safety and security of the city he called home. Bob couldn't divorce Kojo's dark skin or his "crazy-ass" name from the fact that he'd grown up in a blue-collar neighborhood and went to a decent high school. The way Bob saw it, Kojo had just swum over from Ghana and was two paychecks from joining a terrorist cell. So when Kojo's shift ended, his education began. Kojo could cite rules and regulations till he was out of breath, but none of it meant anything to Bob—only thing he understood were the streets; for Bob, if you knew the streets, you knew the town. So Kojo spent hours getting lost—mostly in his car, sometimes on his bike or on foot—and finding his way back to where he'd started. He memorized every street around the station house within a fifteen-mile radius. That included every alleyway and parking lot. First time they chased down a fleeing suspect together and Kojo navigated without assistance, Bob was impressed. He said nothing, but Kojo didn't need the words. He could see it in Bob's eyes. Bob had a heart attack five months later at the police gym and died facedown on a treadmill. Kojo went to his funeral with Constance. When his widow told them that Bob had only great things to say about him, Kojo nodded appreciatively and said, "I'm so sorry for your loss. He was a great cop."

The street Ashanique stopped on was one of those Kojo had memorized so many years ago. He hadn't been down it in well over a decade, but he hadn't forgotten any of its particular quirks either. He swerved the car right up to the gutter alongside a parking garage and jumped out. Matilda followed.

"There," Kojo said as they entered the garage.

Matilda's cell lay on the concrete near an SUV. She picked it up. The screen was cracked, but otherwise the cell looked okay.

"You think they got into a car?" she asked Kojo.

"I think they're still nearby," Kojo said.

"Why?"

"You want me to say it's a cop's second sense, right? That'd be kinda cool. But, no, it's actually the fact that Ashanique left us some clues."

Kojo pointed to one of the girl's bracelets. It was the yellow one, lying on the ground beside a steel door that was slightly ajar.

Smart girl.

Gun drawn, Kojo opened the steel door. The entrance was clear. He motioned for Matilda to follow him up a staircase to another door marked, in faded letters, NEW BEGINNINGS REHABILITATION. The door was locked. Kojo tried it twice.

"Come on, we'll have to go around."

The entrance to the building, just on the south side of the parking garage, was a series of brick steps that led to glass double doors. Both of the doors were marked with the swirling blue New Beginnings Rehabilitation logo. This was a drug-treatment facility. Kojo knew the place well. His neighbor's kid had wound up here trying to get clean.

Kojo and Matilda walked inside.

"How can I help you?" a middle-aged receptionist asked from behind a small desk lined with fake flowers. He was in his midsixties and had pierced ears.

Kojo flashed his badge.

"We need to take a look around."

The receptionist hit a buzzer and the door to his right unlocked. Passing through the door, Kojo and Matilda made their way down a wide hallway lined by residents' rooms. Most were the size of an average hotel room, with two beds and two dressers, a curtain on a track to separate the sides.

Kojo checked the rooms on the right, while Matilda glanced into those on the left. Most were empty—the in-patient residents out at group time or in the dining area starting dinner or playing cards. Flyers on the wall announced there was going to be a screening of *The Wizard of Oz* in the break room. Popcorn would be served.

They came to the end of the hallway, where it split left and right.

"You head right; I'll take left," Kojo said.

"I'm not exactly trained for this."

"We're trusting Childers, right?"

"No," Matilda said. "We're trusting Ashanique."

54

ASHANIQUE SAT ON a folding chair in a bare concrete antechamber.

At one time it might have been a furnace room, but it had clearly been remodeled to look like a bunker. The kind of place George would have hidden in during a "kraut" shelling. The ceiling lights were inset. The door was burnished steel. After she'd taken Ashanique to the room, Childers told her to wait, that she'd be right back with Dr. Song.

The waiting was hard.

Ashanique didn't want to panic in the room. But it made her claustrophobic, it reminded her too much of the Clarity base in the snow in her mother's memories. The feeling of being caged, of being kept, reminded her of the videos Tamiko had shown—those flashing images seemed to hit nerves she didn't know she had, triggering a cascade of emotions she couldn't control. Ashanique couldn't go back to that space—she had to focus, to calm herself. But thinking about Tamiko only led to thinking about Rade and that made the muscles in Ashanique's jaw clench and ache.

So she took a deep breath and scrolled back through her mother's life.

Her mother had used so many names, but they didn't confuse her. Janelle, even though she'd really only just remembered it, sounded much better than Janice. Janice always felt like a name she'd been given at work. It was too perfunctory, too formal, and didn't fit with who her mother had been. But Janelle, there was something organic about that name. It matched Ashanique's memories—it felt right for her skin tone and her hair. Ashanique repeated the name over and over in her head; there was magic in it. It was a name to fit a mantra.

There was a knock on the door.

Childers stepped inside.

"You ready?"

Ashanique stood up and followed Childers into the corridor outside the room. It was lined with pipes. This was what Ashanique imagined a subbasement looked like. She'd heard of basements beneath basements, and always imagined they were choked with pipes and wires and rats. She prayed there were no rats in the corridor with her. She also prayed the lights didn't suddenly go out.

George had seen rats in the trenches.

There was an instance at the Battle of the Somme where he was walking through a narrow trench, past the bodies of fallen regiment men who were injured but dying. George knew they were beyond medical attention—their only hope would be a quick salvation. The dying men plucked feebly at his pants legs. They begged for water. For help. One man begged him to kick the rats away. He said they were chewing through his boots to his toes.

The rats in the trenches . . . so many rats . . .

Stumbling, Ashanique closed her eyes to push the memory away.

She knew she was getting worse.

Dr. Song had to help her soon.

Childers stopped at a door with a biometric lock. She leaned up against it so the sensor could perform a retinal scan. The door unlocked with a heavy clank. As Ashanique passed through the doorway, she felt like a fairy-tale character. The girl who wandered into Blue Beard's hidden room. She'd never heard that fairy tale before, but somehow she knew it. It was from an earlier life, a quieter life.

The room wasn't dark or filled with cobwebs.

It was not the subbasement torture dungeon filled with rats.

Rather, it was a clinic. Modern and relatively clean; it was a large, rectangular, and windowless room with low lighting that buzzed from a dozen or so flat-paneled lights inset in the walls. There were cameras and sensors in the corners.

But it was what was hanging in the middle of the room that caught Ashanique's attention first: there were people suspended from the ceiling.

Three people, in fact—two men and one woman.

All of them hung supine in mesh hammocks from the ceiling, their bodies about three feet off the floor, roughly at waist height.

Around them, medical equipment beeped and droned.

Ashanique had seen this equipment in Janelle's memories of Alaska— these were heart monitors and oxygen sensors. The people in the hammocks didn't move; they barely seemed to breathe. All of them were connected to IV drips, the clear plastic bags hanging over their heads like jellyfish floating in the digital glow of the machines. Even though she wasn't going to take their pulses, she could sense that these people were alive but in deep, deep comas.

"This is the legacy of the Clarity."

The voice was brittle but familiar.

Ashanique turned around to see Dr. Song standing behind her. He was much, much older. The years had worn him down like rain wearing the side of a mountain. Deep wrinkles etched his face and neck. He wore a lab coat with stained sleeves and an out-of-date skinny tie. He exuded an air of age and comfort. Even the lenses of the big glasses perched on his nose were smeared.

"Welcome home," he said.

"Who are these people?"

"Those are the survivors," Dr. Song said. "They're dreaming. The man to your left is Terry. The woman is Alice. The other man is named Hugh. You know, you are the spitting image of your mother. It is amazing to see her . . . you, again."

Ashanique ignored Dr. Song's comment.

"Will these people wake up?"

"That depends," Dr. Song said.

"Depends on what?"

"On what you have inside your head."

55

THERE WAS A dragging sound as the door to the clinic opened and Childers appeared.

"Sorry, Dr. Song. I tried," she said.

Childers stepped aside, and Kojo and Matilda stepped into the clinic behind her. Kojo had his gun drawn and Childers's Glock tucked into the front of his pants. He pointed to a corner, and Childers obediently walked over to a wall and crossed her arms. Dr. Song shook his head.

"No need for this," he said. "We're all friends here."

Matilda ran to Ashanique and they embraced.

"You need to let me do this," Ashanique said.

"I need to know what *this* is first. I made a promise, remember?"

Kojo passed Childers's Glock to Matilda before he crossed the room to a folded wheelchair in the corner. He unfolded it, then rolled it over to Dr. Song.

"Have a seat," Kojo said.

The wheelchair creaked as he sat.

"Talk," Kojo said. "Who are these people you're hiding down here?"

"These are some of the Null," Dr. Song explained. "Like Ashanique's mother, they were members of an experiment that began fifty-two years ago."

"Project Clarity. The Human Ecology Division. CIA mind-control experiments," Kojo said. "I know what Janice Walters thought was going on. And I'm not dumb enough to ignore that good people, well-meaning people, can do terrible things. You were part of Clarity as well?"

"Yes, I was a young neurosurgeon at the time, and you're right, our intentions were beneficent. You have to understand, when Clarity began, it was an attempt at understanding how the mind functioned to improve people's lives. But, sadly, it devolved into something I'm quite ashamed of."

"I'm guessing you're going to tell us that the bald cat—"

"Rade. Number Nineteen."

"—that dude, yeah. You're going to tell me he's out there cleaning up whatever mess Clarity left behind. Removing witnesses like Ashanique's mom. What I need you to tell me is how we're going to make this girl well."

Dr. Song cleared his throat, his eyes on Ashanique.

"The particular condition she has is irreversible. The memories that are flooding into her brain are not going to stop. They will continue to enter her consciousness and overwhelm her. It has happened with every Null since the very first we . . . created."

Hearing this, Ashanique felt a lump form in her throat. She didn't want to cry again, certainly not in front of Dr. Song. Her mother had taught her that crying was natural, normal, and to be appreciated but that many people saw it as weakness. Her mother told her those people, the ones who saw it as a negative, would all cry eventually, and when they did, they'd nearly burst.

Ashanique didn't want to look weak in front of Dr. Song and Childers.

She needed them to know she was strong.

"Janice Walters seemed to be functioning pretty well," Matilda said.

"She was taking MetroChime regularly," Dr. Song said. "So is Rade. But it's only a stopgap measure. It all depends on the neural activity associated with the hippocampus. . . ."

Dr. Song took a moment to reconfigure his thoughts.

"You are familiar with cyberattacks, correct? How hackers will bombard a website with incoming traffic from thousands, sometimes millions, of interlinked computers. Basically, a denial-of-service attack. The same thing is happening in Ashanique's brain. All those memories, going back to the very ascendance of our species, are awakening. All of the Null eventually go insane; no human brain is able to process all that data. This process can take years, decades even. But Ashanique is different. She's the daughter of a Null, the first that I'm aware of, and that makes her quite special. I can slow the attacks down with the medication, but eventually, even that fails. With the others, at that stage, there is only one option. . . ."

Dr. Song rotated in the wheelchair to look at the people in the hammocks.

"They are in medically induced comas. It is the only way."

"Fuck that," Kojo said. "You're not putting her under."

"No, of course not. I want to fix her. Clarity was a tragedy. Our whole network, the former guards and nurses finding and saving the Null, the former subjects who gave their lives to get Ashanique here, they all want the same thing: forgiveness. They found me first."

Dr. Song pointed back to one of the comatose men.

"Thirteen; his name's Terry. He and number Twenty-Six, Alice over there, found me a decade ago. Came to my lab. I don't know how they tracked me down. They'd been taking all sorts of drugs, sharing them with the other Null. They had this whole revenge thing going. They were sending mail bombs to former Project Clarity researchers and staff. I refocused their energies on prolonging their lives and turned them on to MetroChime. But for a lot of them, the damage had already been done. Theo, number Seven, killed himself a couple years back."

Matilda gasped upon hearing the name.

"Vang?" she asked.

Dr. Song nodded. "Theo Vang. I couldn't save him."

"I tried, but . . ."

"It's okay," Dr. Song said. "You couldn't have known. I'm only thankful that there were so few subjects. We were making such great progress, I had hoped we could help the Null when we'd completed our primary goals, but then Dr. Theriault killed herself. She was our guiding light, you understand? The only way we were going to make thought reform a reality was with her research. But she felt like she was getting nowhere. . . ."

Matilda kneeled down beside Dr. Song, level with his face.

"I'm going to assume you're telling us the truth. That you and Ashanique's grandmother spent millions of dollars and did unthinkable things to children just to get at a truth that most people can read on someone's face for free. No tests required. No drugs. Just using the most human of skills: empathy. I'm going to assume you've already realized this, that you're truly trying to atone for it, and accept your word. But comas, drugs, that's not going to do. Tell us how we fix Ashanique."

Dr. Song took a moment, pulling several folded sheets of paper from his pocket. He held them up for everyone to see. They were photocopies of a journal. The lined pages were filled with complicated diagrams that were surrounded by passages written in a strange symbolic language.

"This, Clarity, is all about mind control. Since time immemorial, there's been a concerted, though usually secretive, attempt to develop techniques to erase and reprogram people's minds. From poisons and electricity, to mysticism and the occult. With the advent of modern medicine, however, new avenues have shown significant promise, mostly pharmacological, but sometimes surgical. Dr. Theriault focused on epigenetics, engrams, and mutation. She believed that the core of a person's . . . identity, so to speak, centered on the hippocampus. If you could ablate, essentially, reprogram the mind. She recorded the process in a series of encrypted journals. She was paranoid, delusional. We were never able to decipher the encryption—the process she'd developed was incredibly complicated. Under their breath, some of the Clarity researchers took to calling her journals the Voynich notes, named after the infamous, un-crackable medieval manuscript. The solution is the key to unlocking those notes. Because Ashanique has Dr. Theriault's memories, she knows the solution. With the information, we can reprogram a linear particle accelerator and fix Ashanique's mind. Stop the voices. Make her normal."

"But Janet had her mother's memories too, right?" Kojo asked. "Why couldn't she have given you the solution? Why wait till now?"

"Her real name was Janelle," Dr. Song said. "And memories fade. Even though Ashanique's are vivid, it is because they are fresh. And some people deal with afflictions differently. Unlike her daughter, Janelle fought the memories that flooded her brain. She drowned them with drugs, alcohol, and rage. She likely didn't know what was hidden there. And if she did, she certainly wasn't willing to delve into it. We tried to convince her to try. We begged and pleaded. But more than anything, Fifty-One wanted to forget. And when she had a daughter, her life was transformed, renewed, and we all hoped—Janelle most especially—that what she had forsaken, Ashanique might embrace."

Matilda looked back at Kojo.

He nodded and lowered his weapon.

"Okay," Matilda said. "Where do we start?"

Dr. Song stood and motioned to the door.

"Down the hall is a washroom. There is a cabinet with hair dye and trimmers. I'd suggest that you lose the beard, Detective. Matilda, you should cut and color your hair. Ashanique will need a makeover as well. Childers will help out, I'm afraid I'm not very good with . . . this sort of thing."

56

RADE STEPPED OUT of a rented Honda Civic and surveyed the house across the street.

Kojo's house.

It was evening, and most everyone in the neighborhood was home for supper or already full and gorging themselves on TV. The block was largely quiet save for the incessant barking of a drop-kick terrier stymied behind a vinyl fence.

Over his lifetimes, Rade has had many dogs.

He loved all of them. When he lived in the Caucasus Mountains as a trapper, he had a borzoi that would hunt alongside him. The dog had no name; it never needed one. They would spend days wandering mountain trails in search of game—brown bear was a particularly challenging and thrilling quarry.

Rade ignored the barking dog and walked up to the front door of Kojo's house. He was limping from the bullet wound in his side and the spot where one of Kojo's rounds had grazed him on the thigh. Rade was adept at sewing flesh. He'd stopped by a Walmart, grabbed supplies, and then did a little self-surgery in a bathroom stall next to a man evacuating his bowels between pained groans.

Ten stitches, six butterfly bandages, no big deal.

Reaching Kojo's front door, he rang the doorbell and waited, looking over the house carefully. It was not a place he'd ever have chosen to live. It was

247

too old; there would be too much upkeep. Rade was good with his hands. He prided himself on mechanical skills. But spending his weekends repairing siding and replacing roofing tiles would sap his energy. He had a hard enough time keeping his own body at bay—he didn't have a second to waste on some crumbling pile. But he did find it odd that a detective lived in the house. It seemed a bit cultivated for a police officer. There was an art to the place and, briefly, he wondered if he'd been underestimating Kojo.

The door finally opened, and Ophelia appeared behind the screen door. "What can I do for you?"

She didn't open the door. Didn't even unlock it.

"This is Detective Omaboe's residence, correct?"

. . .

Ophelia crossed her arms.

She was in no mood.

After Kojo's brusque phone call and Brandon's difficult afternoon, the very last thing she wanted was to deal with some weirdo. Twice a week this seemed to happen. Someone rapped at the door and stood there expecting to talk with the police detective as though he'd be willing to solve any problem in his off-hours.

In her hometown of Assin Foso, there were people who would show up at the priest's house at all hours of the day. They would show up and demand, yes, demand, special attention. A prayer for their sick cousin, a petition to the Lord Jesus that their daughter gets good grades in school despite her attention deficits, or a plea to God to ensure that their grandmother finds her way into heaven. Here, it seemed, the police were like the priests. So long as they weren't in their cars patrolling, they were the ones everyone turned to when they needed guidance.

"He is not available at this time," Ophelia said perfunctorily.

She found the man's demeanor strange, but the look of him was even stranger. Her first thought was that he must be suffering from cancer. Ophelia had several good friends who'd undergone chemotherapy treatment. A few of them wore their bald heads as a badge of courage, a fist to the cancer attempting to destroy them. This man, however, was as bald as they were (it seemed even his eyebrows were missing as well) but he didn't appear ill.

If she were forced to say, she would have concluded it was a fashion statement. If that was indeed the case, it was a poor choice. Ophelia considered the man hideous.

"Oh, I remember now," Rade said. "He's across town."

Ophelia moved to close the door but she was too slow, hesitant even though she was unnerved. Rade sliced through the screen door with a box cutter that he seemed to pull from nowhere and, in one fluid motion, grabbed Ophelia by the throat. He squeezed until she couldn't breathe. Her head swam as carbon dioxide instantly began its deadly buildup in her blood.

"Who is at the door?"

Brandon's voice bounced from behind Ophelia.

Oh, God, he needs to run and hide!

Scramble as fast as he can up the stairs and lock himself in his bedroom.

Ophelia wanted to scream to him: *Don't come any closer! Go to your room, right now!* But she could barely get a sliver of air down her crushed windpipe. Ophelia knew she'd lose consciousness in a matter of seconds. Desperate to forestall the man entering the house, she tried to grab his arms, to dig her long nails (just shellacked yesterday) into his flesh. But her vision was dimming, and the screen door was still in the way. Her nails raked the metal mesh. Before she blacked out completely, the man pulled her closer, dragging her face through the screen door; the sharp edges traced a bloody grid across her chin and forehead.

"You will pass out," Rade said. "And I will take the boy."

Ophelia's body went slack; the sensation was like being dunked in freezing water. Her toes and then feet went numb. Her fingers and hands followed.

Finally, emptiness swept up through her burning chest and into her head.

She was almost thankful when it extinguished the furnace of pain and grief raging inside her oxygen-starved brain.

Then a sweet, effortless darkness overwhelmed her.

* * *

Brandon was frozen to his spot on the stairs.

He couldn't take his eyes from the pale man stepping through the ripped screen door and into his house. The pale man closed and then locked the front door. He had a knife in his hand; the blade glimmered in the half-light like one of those deep-sea fish that Brandon saw on a Discovery Channel show once.

Brandon had seen a horror movie once too.

His dad didn't know, but one time Ophelia left the TV on when she thought he was asleep. He was thirsty, so he crept downstairs to get a drink of water and that's when he saw it. On the TV there was a man with no hair and deep black eyes. He had a knife and he chased two teenagers through a dusty old room.

The pale man looked like the same man from the horror movie.

He had a knife.

Ophelia was lying there, bloody and dead.

"Hello," Rade said. "You and me are going to take a little drive."

57

ASHANIQUE FELT LIKE she hadn't eaten in forever.

"Come on, in here."

After Childers had done the girl's hair up in cornrows, she directed Ashanique to the concrete room she'd arrived in. Dr. Song had set up a folding table in the middle of the room. Sitting there, waiting for the food Childers had promised to bring, Ashanique looked around the room and remembered something her mother had told her. She said that the other people who were on the run, the ones who could see things other people couldn't, were excellent at hiding. They could hide almost anywhere. For Ashanique, those words conjured up images of people hiding in the forests or on boats in the middle of the ocean.

But now she knew the truth.

They were hiding in the basements of drug rehab centers.

They were in cramped, nasty basements with roaches and silverfish and people hanging in sad hammocks.

Ashanique's stomach rumbled. She wondered about what sort of food Childers could possibly get. *Maybe McDonald's? Maybe a submarine sandwich?* Ashanique hadn't had one of those in years. The last one she'd eaten had ham and tomato and a ton of mustard. She devoured every inch of it—even the pieces of bread that were soaked in mustard and had no meat or even tomato to squeeze between them.

Childers walked in with a small plate of food and a bag of maxi pads.

She put the maxi pads down on the table first and then positioned the tray right in front of Ashanique. Apparently, Childers didn't have to go far to get the food. It was from the cafeteria in the treatment center fifteen feet overhead. The night's dinner was turkey with stuffing, mashed potatoes and gravy, a side of green beans, and a thing of bright orange Jell-O. Ashanique was hungry enough that she wasn't going to complain about not getting McDonald's. She'd never really been a fan of Thanksgiving food, though. At least there weren't cranberries in the stuffing.

"Thank you," Ashanique said.

"Sorry," Childers replied, reading Ashanique's less-than-excited expression. "It's pretty much that or some saltines and peanut butter."

"No. This is great, really."

Childers turned to go, but Ashanique cleared her throat and asked, "Do you mind? Just sitting with me for a little bit?"

.   .   .

Childers hadn't spent more than fifteen minutes talking with anyone other than Dr. Song for nearly three months.

Even though she wasn't exactly the most extroverted person, she found she craved some casual conversation now and again. Even from the Null. Childers wasn't like them, but she wasn't like Dr. Song either—neither fish nor fowl, as her religious and long-dead mother would have said. Childers tried to look that expression up once. Apparently, it wasn't biblical at all but some sixteenth-century monk claptrap. Regardless, it fit Childers to a T. That was another of her mom's expressions.

Ashanique took a few bites and chewed them slowly.

She swallowed and sipped some water before she asked, "You watch TV?"

"Sure," Childers said. "You?"

"Yeah, it's kind of stupid, but I like cartoons."

"That's not stupid."

"I'm eleven."

"Cartoons aren't for babies. Some of them are pretty clever."

"You don't watch them, though."

Childers didn't have a childhood that included cartoons. When she was little, still a boy and called Caleb, a name she always hated because it sounded harsh, like a weapon, Mom forbade any and all filmed entertainment. No TV, no movies. Plays were okay, so long as they were religious. Childers's dad was only a photograph and a blurry one at that. Her mother said he was a great man and nothing more. For a while, when she was in middle school, Childers wondered if maybe—just maybe—her father was an angel.

How else to explain a girl being trapped in a boy's body?

Surely, there had been a divine mistake. Perhaps her father had been a rogue angel—one of the flukes from Genesis, the messiest part of the Bible. The first cartoon Childers saw was at a shelter. She was fifteen and she'd run away after her mother found her wearing a dress in her room. All it took was a single glance; the rage in her mother's eyes was enough to convince her never, ever to look back. And she hadn't. Shelters, couches, excruciating acts, one underground—the "trans" express—led to another: Childers met Dr. Song at a shelter in Logan Square.

Well, *met* was wrong.

She'd been threatened by another resident—a skinhead with a thing for curb-stomping "homos"—and ran to hide in the basement. That was how she found the sleeping Nulls and Dr. Song. Turned out he needed help, after twenty-some years on the run, his body was finally showing the wear and tear. She offered. He accepted.

Over the last five years, they'd moved in and out of eight different facilities. Childers had never seen the agents of the HED (or the bald man Dr. Song seemed to fear the most) but she didn't doubt their existence either—she'd seen enough of the horror of the world to know that people were capable of the worst possible acts.

"Those people in the other room . . ."

"Yes."

"How long have they been sleeping?"

"Two of them for at least three years."

"That's not good for them, right? To sleep that long?"

"They don't really have a choice."

"But that's going to change," Ashanique said. "I can fix them."

"That's what Dr. Song tells me."

"You don't believe it?"

Childers took a moment.

"Dr. Song's told me all about the science of it. Even though I don't exactly get all the words, I get the core of it. And it makes sense. I'm a living example of how wires get crossed and things don't exactly turn out the way they were supposed to. Same time, it has me worried. How often do you go to the doctor with a cold and he gives you another cold to fix it?"

"The solution is different."

"You remember it now?"

Ashanique nodded. "I think so, but . . ."

"But what?"

There was a knock at the door. Matilda stuck her head in. She'd dyed her hair blond. Childers thought it looked good, though it was something of a sloppy job. Kojo stood behind her, clean-shaven. He looked different. More refined.

"Sorry to interrupt," Matilda said. "Do you guys mind if we come in?"

Ashanique finished her meal with her plate on her lap as Dr. Song, Kojo, and Matilda joined her and Childers at the folding table.

Dr. Song spread some file folders out before he passed out key cards and badges. None of them had Matilda's or Kojo's or Ashanique's face on them, but there were two for Childers and Dr. Song. He also had a duffel bag. Inside was a Taser, a few rounds of 8mm ammunition, and several coils of rope.

"I can get us into the facility. When the LINAC went live a few months back, I made some, uh, reconnaissance missions over there. That makes it sound like spy craft, but really, it was a matter of sneaking into HR and convincing them I was still an employee. The best thing about HED is that it's far too big for its britches now. You picture these conspiratorial groups as being highly sophisticated, lean black ops machines that can turn on a dime. They're not. They're just as clumsy and overburdened as the rest of the government. Unlike Health and Human Services, however, the HED has a team of hired hit men."

"What's your game plan?" Kojo asked as he thumbed through the things on the table. "We're all just going to follow you in?"

"It's a hospital. We can get in just fine. But we'll need a vehicle to load up the Null patients. Something like a van."

"I can get that," Kojo said. "Matilda and I will go."

. . .

On her way out, Matilda found Ashanique in the clinic with the sleeping Nulls.

She was standing by Alice, staring down at the woman's slack face.

"I remember Twenty-Six," Ashanique said. "My mother always worried about her. She was so slight, such a pale and sickly looking little girl. Who knew she'd be one of the few to make it this far? Twenty-Six was from a warm climate. None of the kids could remember where they came from; electroshock and drugs took care of that. Well, until the machine awoke their memories. But some of their likes and dislikes, those things were hard-wired. Electroshock and drugs couldn't remove them. Twenty-Six had this thing about the color yellow. She just loved it and used to talk about wanting to live in the mountains so she could watch the Aspen trees change color from green to yellow. I wonder if she ever did after they got out?"

Matilda kissed Ashanique's forehead.

"I'll be back soon. Then we're going to get you well."

58

KOJO AND MATILDA rode down Lake Shore Drive in a rented commuter van.
The back was spacious, enough to fit three wheelchairs comfortably.

Outside, the clouds had cleared and the moon was perfect and bright.

Anxious to hear from Ophelia, Kojo phoned the house. It rang five times
before he heard his own voice. *You've reached the Omaboe residence, please—*
Kojo tried Ophelia's cell.

She rarely kept it with her, preferring to have it in her purse because she
read somewhere on the Internet that cell phone signals could give you brain
cancer. It drove Kojo crazy, but he'd never doubted her commitment. She
might be late here and there, and she didn't always answer the phone, but
Brandon was so deeply happy when he was with her. The call went straight
to Ophelia's message. Kojo hung up and slid his cell into his pocket.

"Tell me about your son," Matilda asked.

Kojo smiled just thinking about him.

"Brandon, his name's Brandon. He's twelve going on thirty-five."

"A handful, huh?"

"Yeah. But not something I can't handle."

Matilda glanced at Kojo's left hand again. Not only was there no wedding
ring, there was no evidence of him ever having worn one.

"Twelve is a tricky age for a boy. Lot of changes going on."

"Brandon lets me know. He's good about that." Kojo looked over at
Matilda, seeing if she was getting him. She was.

He continued, "If anything, I raised him to be vocal. To speak out, you

256

know? He's proud and he ain't shy. Something has him freaked out: he's going to tell someone. Either me or Ophelia. . . ."

"His mom?"

"No, his mom's dead. Five years ago. Uterine cancer. No, Ophelia is his nurse. My son's got Down syndrome. It's not that— It's not that he can't take care of himself. Just the other day I found him in the kitchen making his own version of tacos. He had the beans, the cheese, was using tortilla chips and gluing them together with the bean paste to make a shell. He can take care of himself, but he needs help, you know? He's got the confidence, just needs the guidance. And, unfortunately, I can't be around as often as I would like."

"I've worked with a few cops. It's a tough life. Lot of stress."

"Stress I've got under control. Don't take me wrong, I don't sleep well, and I have some anger issues; most of that I chalk up to the job. But, uh, I have my outlets."

"Okay . . ."

The way Matilda said it, Kojo knew she thought he was drinking or popping pills to see himself through his day. He didn't blame her. When someone was a shrink, he or she saw the world through that lens. Everyone was screwed up in one way or another. Kojo knew she was programmed to do it. Same way he read people on the street; same way he scanned their eyes, their features, their hands. Maybe he carried a gun and maybe she's got an advanced degree, but what they did was fundamentally the same. They read and they reacted.

"It's not like that," Kojo clarified. "I do woodworking. Have a setup in my garage. I'm not gonna say I'm anything great. I'm no Wendell Castle. I make furniture, mostly end tables and chairs. I don't sell 'em. Just give them to friends and family. You know, holiday gifts and such. Any weekend I'm off, that's where you'll find me, covered in sawdust."

Matilda laughed.

Kojo wondered if she pictured him sweaty and shirtless, working the tools. It was a funny image, not something he associated with himself, but he sort of wanted her to picture that. Hearing her laugh, seeing those dimples, Kojo couldn't help but feel a bit giddy; a lightness in his head, an effervescence. Before meeting Matilda, he hadn't felt that sensation in a very long time.

"I'd love to see some of your stuff," Matilda said.

"Sure. I could send you some pics."

"It'd be nice to see it in person. Just, I don't know, sometimes it's hard to tell with furniture unless you're right there. Able to touch it, feel the wood . . ."

Matilda trailed off. Kojo realized he was staring at her. The moment of silence grew like a bubble around them. Drowning out the traffic and the infinite thrum of the tires on the asphalt. Matilda broke off eye contact first, looked at her lap.

"So, um, how exactly did you pick up woodworking?"

Kojo cleared his throat, turning his attention back to the road.

"My grandfather, back in Ghana, he was a woodworker. Pretty good. Used all the traditional tools and stuff. And, no, he didn't make spears."

Kojo shot Matilda a look.

She recoiled.

"No. No, I wouldn't have—"

Kojo laughed. "Relax, just a joke. People make so many assumptions about me 'cause of my name. They hear my parents were Ghanaians, they think maybe I was raised in a thatch hut. Had goats as playmates. Went hunting lions with long spears. You know, that kinda bullshit. My dad was a doctor. My mom was a teacher. They moved to the States two years before I was born. I'm as American as it gets. How about you? From Chicago?"

"Yeah, native girl. My mom's had a hard time the last few years, but she was wonderful when I was growing up. Really caring, devoted to me with everything she had. No way I could ever repay her for everything she sacrificed to make sure I turned out halfway decent."

"I'd say you're more than halfway decent."

"Thanks."

"Not much more," Kojo jokingly clarified. "But a little. How about your dad?"

"He was never really part of the picture. He and my mom met while she was in grad school. She said he was handsome and collected books. Beyond that, he was pretty much an asshole. Minute he found out she was pregnant after three months of dating, he took off. And not like stopped calling her but basically up and disappeared, moved to a new town and left nothing behind."

"Asshole."

"Pretty much exactly right."

"You ever try to look him up?"

Matilda shrugged. "When I was younger and trying to figure out who I was—you know, the whole early-twenties soul-search thing. But I never got anywhere. After a few months, I stopped trying. I realized I'd have nothing to say to him. But you're a good dad, I can tell."

"Thank you. How? I don't always feel like a very good dad."

"You're patient but interested, polite but firm. Maybe it's the whole woodworking thing that's blinding me, but I feel like you've got what people call an old soul. There's a sophistication to you, a maturity, that most people rarely achieve. It's amazing how the slightest thing—a missed appointment, a bounced check, a single ugly glance—can turn some people completely upside down. I've worked with patients whose lives have fallen apart, like completely, because of the most trivial thing snowballing into an avalanche. But you, you seem really even-keeled, like you know exactly who you are and you don't need to prove it. Like I said, that's the makings, at least in my book, of a good dad and a good person."

"Thank you. I . . . I try."

They rode on in silence for a moment before Matilda said, "You could have taken that gun from me anytime, right? Just ripped it out of my hand?"

"Yeah."

"So why didn't you?"

Kojo sank back in his seat, cracked his knuckles.

"I can see Brandon in Ashanique. She's got his same tenacity. And she believes in people, in the goodness of people, the same as him. I believe her. I do. All the memories she says she has. None of it makes sense when Dr. Song talks about it, but Ashanique knows, and I can tell."

Matilda reached into her purse and pulled out a folded Post-it Note and a pen. She used the window to scribble something on the note, a few words in shorthand.

"I say something that memorable?" Kojo asked.

"No—I mean, no, you just reminded me of something."

"I saw your office. Wasn't prying. It was part of the crime scene, right? I noticed the notes taped up everywhere—"

"Hard not to," Matilda said, a bit embarrassed.

"Talk to me about that. All those notes on the walls and doors, is that research stuff? Solving the chemistry of memory? Or is it, I don't know, like you're putting your brain on the outside? Just to see it all more clearly? That sounds really stupid, but I think you get what I mean."

"Doesn't sound stupid. It's hard to explain—"

"You don't have to. Just was asking."

Matilda reached over and touched Kojo's shoulder.

A shiver of electricity rippled through his muscles—the comforting power of human touch, the flood of oxytocin and endorphins. Even though he wasn't normally a touchy person, he found the warmth of that contact instantly soothing. It grounded his thoughts and solidified his feelings.

Kojo slowed the van as they came to a light.

He'd found Matilda attractive at the university but that was reflexive, the sort of double take you do when you see a physique that checks those mental boxes, a muscle memory.

Sitting in the car, just the two of them in their bubble of silence, he found her beautiful. It was her mind. Her words. Her boldness. The way the fading light played in her eyes and the condensation on the window that created a halo around her hair. Kojo was exhausted, he'd broken the law and probably lost his job, but he wanted nothing more than to kiss Matilda.

He didn't.

"Ashanique puts everything in perspective, doesn't she?" he said.

"She's changed my life."

The light flicked to green and Kojo pressed the pedal down.

59

KOJO PULLED THE VAN up to a loading bay just off the kitchen of the rehab facility.

Childers was there with the three comatose Nulls. They were wrapped in thick coats and propped up in wheelchairs.

"They going to be okay for a while?" Kojo asked Childers as he got out of the van.

"Yeah. They're just asleep is all. We drive safe, though, okay?"

"Of course."

As the Nulls were moved to the van, Matilda headed inside. She found Ashanique pale and shaken, sitting in a wheelchair. She hurried over to the girl and kneeled at her side. Dr. Song was nowhere in sight.

"Ashanique, you okay?"

The girl moaned. "My head hurts."

"Shit," Matilda said, looking around the room for MetroChime. "Did Dr. Song give you any medication while we were gone? Did you tell him you weren't well?"

"He knows," Ashanique said. "Can't do anything about it now."

"What do you mean?"

Dr. Song appeared in the doorway. Matilda stroked Ashanique's hair and then kissed her forehead before she walked over to Dr. Song.

"She's getting worse. Can't you do anything for her?"

Dr. Song pulled Matilda into the hallway.

261

"The condition is progressing more rapidly than I'd expected," Dr. Song said.

"Why?"

"She's different from the others. All the Null I've seen have been directly involved in the Clarity experiment. The past-life memories flooding their heads are a direct result of exposure to the LINAC. But Ashanique inherited what happened to her. For her, the mutation is inborn like albinism or some regressive gene."

"You're saying she can't be cured?"

"We don't know that. She's different. I believe that if the Null could be activated the way they were, then it stands to reason that Ashanique can be deactivated in a similar fashion. It's merely a matter of reapplying the suppressor system that was already in place. But only the LINAC can do it."

Matilda stepped to the side and glanced in at Ashanique. The girl seemed to be getting paler, sicker, by the moment. Matilda didn't want to take any risks.

"She's not well enough to travel."

"We don't have a choice," Dr. Song said. "I can pump her full of Metro-Chime but, at this point, I'm not sure what good it will do. If we wait more than a few hours, I think the most logical step is to ease her into a medically induced—"

"No way. You're not knocking her out."

Dr. Song shook his head.

"Then she has to go now, the sooner the better."

"How certain are you that this solution is going to fix everything?"

"Trust me, Matilda."

"I can't."

"Don't trust me then," Dr. Song told her. "Trust the science."

As she looked in at Ashanique, the girl managed a slight smile.

It was enough.

"Let's go," Matilda said.

60

THEY WENT INTO the hospital through the loading bay.

Wearing scrubs, their hair changed, the idea was to avoid anyone scanning the monitors, whether they were normal security or working for the HED. Matilda wasn't sure if they were distinguishable anyway.

Kojo pulled the van in while Dr. Song and Matilda unloaded the comatose Nulls. It didn't take long before security showed up: a guard doing the rounds, a flashlight at his hip beside a gun that had likely never been drawn. He rapped a knuckle on the windshield of the van.

"No unloading here, bud," the guard said. "You need to move."

Kojo rolled down the window. "Sorry, what?"

The guard, getting pissed, practically stuck his head in the driver's-side window. "I said . . . ," he began. He stopped short when Kojo pressed Dr. Song's Taser into his neck. The guard's knees buckled, he fell backward, where Childers caught him. She lowered him to the ground and bound him with the rope. She also took his ID badge.

Childers gave a thumbs-up to Kojo.

The badge opened a door to a supply room.

They were in.

Wearing the proper garb and pushing the three comatose patients, Matilda, Kojo, and Childers looked like they belonged. Even with Ashanique trailing behind with Dr. Song, none of the nurses and techs they passed blinked an eye.

263

"There is an elevator to the left," Dr. Song directed. "We'll need my badge."

Two elevator rides and fifteen hundred feet of hallway later, they approached the doors to the room that housed the HED LINAC machine.

An armed security guard sat at a small desk to the left of the door. He looked up at them, his face illuminated by the tablet in his hands. Recognizing them immediately, the guard jumped up. The tablet clattered to the floor. He drew his weapon and, without a word, began firing.

A window to Kojo's left exploded. He dived to the ground, pulling his sidearm, as Matilda and Dr. Song guided the comatose Nulls toward the wall. Ashanique scrambled behind Matilda, her heart racing. The sound of the shots reverberated around the hallway like boxed-in explosions.

The guard kept shooting as he walked fearlessly toward them. A ceiling light burst over Matilda's head. Hot shards of glass rained down into her hair. Dr. Song cried out as a bullet tore through his left foot. Kojo steadied his weapon and fired once. The bullet screamed into the guard's forehead, sending him spinning to the tiled floor, where he twitched once before lying still.

Kojo ran over to Matilda and Ashanique. "You okay? Anyone hit?"

Matilda, Childers, and Ashanique were uninjured. Amazingly, Terry, Alice, and Hugh remained unharmed as well. Dr. Song stood and steadied himself, trying not to put weight on his foot. Childers looked the wound over.

"I'll live," Dr. Song said. "We need to get inside."

Kojo shot out a video camera over the guard's small desk as Dr. Song scanned his badge on the reader next to the door. It beeped but did not unlock. Dr. Song tried it again, but again it failed. He turned back to look at Childers, shaking his head.

"I don't understand . . . ," he began.

He stopped when he noticed Ashanique pulling the badge from the dead guard's belt. She stepped up beside him and calmly held the badge to the reader.

There was a metallic clank as the door unlocked.

They made their way inside quickly. The door closed and locked behind them before Dr. Song flipped on the lights. The LINAC was revealed. Ashanique walked across the room to look closely at the machine. It reminded her of a squat telescope and seemed to hover eight feet over the floor. It was bigger than the ones she'd seen in her mind. Sleeker. Recalling the one her mother had been subjected to, and how loud it was, Ashanique wondered what sort of sound this one was going to make.

"Ashanique," Dr. Song said. "Please, we don't have much time."

He pointed to a whiteboard opposite the LINAC machine before Childers eased him into a chair. As Ashanique walked over to the board, she noticed that Dr. Song had made bloody left shoeprints around the room.

"Can you write it out for us?" Dr. Song said.

Ashanique grabbed a dry-erase marker from the shelf on the whiteboard and took the cap off the marker. As everyone watched, unconsciously holding their breath, Ashanique began to write.

She began to cover the whiteboard with symbols.

Next to them she wrote numbers.

And then beside those she wrote another series of symbols.

"Incredible," Dr. Song said.

·   ·   ·

Dr. Song was desperate to believe that this would be his absolution.

He had long dreamed of the moment he'd see the solution. Even more, he often lay awake at night imagining how he'd use the resulting code to program the LINAC and cure Terry, Alice, and Hugh. It was a video he had played and reversed over and over during decades of long nights in dozens of dank basements. Curing the Null would maybe erase his past crimes. Dr. Song imagined the hate, the bitterness, would be washed away like caked-on mud. Then, when Terry, Alice, and Hugh had been cured, he would find the others; he would walk every continent if he had to. And when that was accomplished, when the madness had finally vanished, then maybe, just maybe, he would feel good enough about himself to wish for a normal life. A life he didn't think he'd ever deserve again. At sixty, he knew he still had time left to begin again, time enough to forge a new soul.

As Ashanique covered the whiteboard with symbols, letters, and numbers, Dr. Song was stunned to see she was using Dr. Theriault's handwriting. Watching it in real time, he realized Ashanique wasn't channeling the intellect of a dead woman; she was reaching into the depths of a mind that stretched into infinity. For all intents and purposes, Ashanique was Dr. Theriault, just as she was Janelle.

Alarms began to sound outside the room.

Dr. Song knew the guard's body had likely been discovered. The doors to the lab would be kicked in within a few minutes' time. Ashanique ignored the blare of the sirens and kept writing. She finished twenty seconds later and turned around.

"There it is," she said.

Dr. Song pulled the photocopied journal pages from his back pocket. He unfolded them and began to translate the passages in his mind, scribbling with a pencil on the margins of the pages.

"Amazing," he mumbled.

"Doctor," Kojo said, eyeing the door. "We don't have much time."

Dr. Song looked up at the whiteboard. He knew this process might take an hour, possibly even longer. He was going to suggest they barricade themselves in, prepare to be overrun, but he didn't, because Ashanique put her hands on the LINAC control panel and turned on the machine.

"You don't need to decipher it now," she said. "I can do this."

"You remember it all?" Dr. Song asked, stunned.

"Yes."

Matilda touched Ashanique's arm. "Are you ready?"

"No," she said, "I don't want to lose them. I know what they knew, my mother, my grandmother. All those other lives. I— They're a part of me. I don't want to give them up. If I do, they'll be gone forever. Silenced the same way as they are with . . . with everyone else."

Behind them, the LINAC machine came online. It buzzed and rattled. Metal knocked against metal, loud enough that Dr. Song was surprised the comatose Nulls didn't startle in their endless sleep.

"Put Terry beneath the machine," Ashanique said.

Childers wheeled Terry under the LINAC and put the brakes on his wheelchair. She looked up into the dark eye of the machine.

Ashanique asked everyone to take a step back.

They did.

"I don't want you to be accidentally exposed," she said.

Just before the test was activated, the door to the room swung open.

Rade stepped inside and shot Terry in the chest.

Blood blossomed under Terry's shirt. The force was enough to knock him out of the wheelchair. His head hit the linoleum floor with a sad, hollow sound. Rade turned to the other two comatose Nulls and shot them both as well. Alice and Hugh were blown backward and their locked wheelchairs overturned. The tiny front wheels turned in useless silence as the echoes of the gunshots faded.

"No one move," Rade said.

· · ·

That's when Kojo saw the worst thing he'd seen in all his decades as a cop.

Every other horror, every awful act humankind was capable of, none of it compared to the sight of Rade holding a Sig Sauer P938 handgun to his son's head. Brandon was beyond crying. His face was a sheet of pure terror. His eyes seemed enveloped in psychic pain.

"Drop the gun," Rade said.

"Okay. Okay."

Kojo carefully pulled his revolver from his belt and laid it on the floor. Then he kicked it over to Rade. Rade stepped on it with his left foot. Brandon squirmed and moaned. Rade looked over at Ashanique, then turned to Matilda and Childers.

"Empty your pockets," Rade ordered.

Matilda, Childers, and Ashanique turned their pockets inside out.

Satisfied, Rade let go of Brandon and pushed the boy to Kojo. Brandon collapsed in his father's arms. Kojo held him close as Rade walked across the room to the whiteboard. He looked over Ashanique's work, studying it carefully.

With Rade briefly preoccupied, Childers looked around for a weapon. Any weapon. She saw a scalpel in a pocket of a lab coat on a hook two feet away. She plucked the scalpel from the coat and removed its protective plastic sheath.

Kojo noticed and shook his head.

Childers put a finger to her lips.

Shhhhh...

61

RADE TURNED THE Sig Sauer on Dr. Song.

"Does it work?"

"We— We were just readying the first test."

"Hurry up."

Rade stepped toward Dr. Song just as Childers ran at him with the scalpel. She'd had enough. Seeing the Nulls shot down so helpless broke something inside her. As she ran, Childers thought back to when she was in the ER after being jumped by some creeps near the train tracks. While they bandaged her up, she watched a junkie come in practically dead. But the doctor grabbed an AED and jolted the junkie's chest. Her body danced before the junkie bolted upright, mouth wide-open and eyes bugging out like she'd just seen the Four Horsemen ride past her. Whatever the AED did, Childers felt its organic equivalent—an uncanny boost that turned her into a killing machine.

Rade clearly wasn't expecting her to be so bold.

He swung toward Childers just in time to get a scalpel across the cheek. The narrow blade cut a thin line through the subcutaneous fat. It was deep enough that it tinged across Rade's teeth. The sound was oddly pretty.

"Fuck!"

Rade spit blood onto the floor.

Childers, impressed with her own speed, slashed again.

This time, the scalpel didn't clear the space, however, because Rade put a bullet in Childers's gut. Childers stumbled backward into a row of file cabinets.

She was stunned, surprised to see the quickly spreading stain of gore soaking her T-shirt. The light in the room appeared to quickly fade, retreating like a film reel run in reverse. As everything darkened and the sounds of the room dampened to a fuzzy mush, Childers glanced at Dr. Song. She couldn't see his face clearly, but she could tell he was panicked. Brandon was crying.

Childers's last thought was simple:

It would be nice to see the sunrise right now.

. . .

Holding his bleeding cheek, Rade pointed the gun at Dr. Song.

"Does the *fucking* solution work?!"

Dr. Song nodded, before pointing to Ashanique.

"I don't know how. Ask Dr. Theriault."

Rade turned to Ashanique and narrowed his eyes.

Then he chuckled. "Okay, you tell me."

"Put the gun away first."

Rade walked up to Matilda and pressed the muzzle of the Sig Sauer against her forehead. "Tell me. Now."

Ashanique said, "It restructures the suppression system in the hippocampus. The first tests, at Project Clarity, they activated cell regeneration on an expanded rate, one that led to increased neural connections along older, abandoned pathways. But the generation of these new networks didn't stop there. With the Null, novel neural root systems appeared. Those are the source of the memories. I don't know how exactly they are coded but they're in the junk DNA. The process my grandmother developed clips the newly developed neural root system like yanking a weed from your lawn. When you undergo the process, it will remove all your genetic memories."

"And new memories?"

"Shouldn't be affected. This is targeted; that's the brilliance of it."

Rade dragged Matilda over to Ashanique.

"What if the HED gets this? Can they do what they want the first time?"

"Maybe," Ashanique said. "With certain modifications, it could work. For those who aren't Null, and we don't actually know what percentage that could be, the revised procedure would likely suppress the hippocampus's activity to the point that we could rewrite the memory there."

"The answer is yes," Rade says.

"With some qualifications, yes."

"So Dr. Sykes lied to me."

Rade pulled the gun away from Matilda's head. He turned to look at the LINAC machine humming in the corner, then glanced over at Childers's corpse. A pool of blood congealed under her chest, sticking her clothes to the floor.

"The police will be here soon, Nineteen," Dr. Song said.

"My name is Rade. Nineteen doesn't exist anymore. And there's no one coming to save you here. We own the police."

"You don't own me," Kojo said.

Rade shrugged. "You're nobody."

"Rade," Ashanique said, "I know what was done to you was unconscionable. That the memories awakened were horrific. But you can be fixed. They can be erased. I want to show you, but first you need to let these people go. They don't have anything to do with it anymore. Just you and me, we'll fix you."

Rade shifted his gaze to Kojo and Brandon. The boy was sobbing. Rade considered putting a hole in the boy's stomach and watching his expression as the pain seized him. He decided against it.

"Everyone group together," Rade said, motioning with the gun. "Knee to knee, arms intertwined. I see any of you move, I will shoot the children first. Understand?"

Rade let Matilda go. She walked over to Dr. Song and, together, they sat down beside Kojo. Matilda linked elbows with Ashanique and Kojo.

Kojo then wrapped his arms around Brandon.

"Keep your head down," Kojo whispered to his son. "Just keep your eyes on the floor, okay? We're going to stay real still and we'll be fine."

Moving the gun hand to hand, Rade took off his blood-soaked hoodie and the white tank top underneath. While the slice in his cheek had clotted, the red streaks of dribbled blood ran down his neck across his chest and ribs to his waist.

"Don't fuck this up."

Rade sat cross-legged on the floor beneath the LINAC. He trained the gun on Brandon. His hand was perfectly still, his eyes as sharp as acacia thorns.

"Go ahead, Doctor. . . ."

Rattling sounds pinged around the room as the LINAC started up; the racket sounded as though someone had dumped all their loose change into a dryer and run it on high. The clanging was thankfully short-lived, however, only seconds in duration. As the LINAC moved into position over Rade's head, it angled downward in a smooth, silent motion.

The room filled with an anxious energy as the air pressure fell.

As the LINAC quieted, Ashanique said, "We tried to save you before, Rade. I'm sorry you're still so scared and so hurt."

The LINAC fired.

The Sig Sauer dropped to the floor as Rade fell forward, convulsing. . . .

62

A BLIZZARD ROARS over the Three Saints Bay facility.

Five inches have fallen in the past forty-seven minutes, and the lights inside the base flicker as the generators are strained. The hallways are empty. The staircases as well. The soldier manning the desk at the entrance doesn't play cards. He doesn't clean his gun or thumb through the stiff-paged girlie magazine that Morton stashed under the file folders in the desk's bottom drawer. Instead, he sits and listens to the storm grinding its way across the invisible landscape beyond the walls. He thinks back to being a child in Louisiana and hearing the relentless reverberation of hurricanes.

In the central housing unit, the experimental subjects' doors are all shut. They are silent inside their rooms. Some of the orphans sleep. Too drugged-out and delirious to hear the blizzard overhead. Others lie idly in their beds, staring at their nails or chewing on their hair. Waiting, always waiting. The Null, however, sit with their ears to the steel doors of their cells. Each and every one. They are ready. . . .

In the medical unit, Dr. Song and Dr. Sykes perform an autopsy. Thirty-Three died during one of the aerobic sessions on a treadmill. She was fifteen and appeared fit. The records indicate that she was taken from an orphanage in Taos, New Mexico. Thirty-Three was Latina and quite short. Dr. Sykes is convinced she had an underlying heart condition—one that Dr. Song should have picked up on right after they recruited her. As Dorothy removes Thirty-Three's

272

heart, she turns the bruised raw organ around in the antiseptic light. Nothing evident.

"Three treatment failures in three weeks," Dr. Song says, his mouth hidden by his medical mask. He keeps his eyes on the corpse. "I'm worried we're pushing—"

"More will die," Dorothy says. "They will keep dying until we get what we want. Did Joe Curwen at Duke stop after he lost a couple subjects? Absolutely not. And he sure as hell got a lot closer than we have. If Dr. Theriault thought she was saving these wretches from suffering by tossing herself into the ocean, she was sorely mistaken."

Dr. Song looks up to meet Dorothy's gaze.

"Get Janelle ready."

All of this is heard by subject Nineteen. He sits in his cell, ear to the door, just like the other Null. Nineteen is an eight-year-old boy, his thin frame lost in the bagginess of his boiler suit. His name is Rade Gavrilovic. Unlike most of the orphans, he remembers his parents. He vividly recalls the alcoholism and abuse. And he remembers the day he was taken. It was the first and only time his mother, high on methamphetamines and reeking of cheap liquor, had taken him to the playground in the park near their apartment. She dozed off on a bench while he played on the jungle gym. There were no other children. It was the middle of the day on a Wednesday. He played for only twenty minutes before the soldiers came. They gave his mother cash, he couldn't see how much, and then led him to a waiting car. That was it.

When Rade hears the door to Janelle's cell open, he is ready.

He digs at the thick callus on his left heel. The skin is white there, as hard and white as the snow pummeling the world above. Two days ago, as soldiers were escorting Rade from the medical center, he stepped on a hypodermic needle. He did not cry out. He did not even limp. Rade knew he needed to keep that needle in his flesh. It was a key. Though the pain is delicious and his bloodied fingers have trouble grasping the end of the needle, he manages to pull it from his heel.

Rade uses it to unlock his cell door.

Unlike some of the other Null, his past-life memories include many thieves. There was once a blacksmith. An African man who plied his trade in eighteenth-

century Paris. He was good at locks, and Rade remembers exactly how they were constructed. The technology hasn't really changed. Using the needle, it takes him thirty-seven seconds.

The door swings open. Outside, the main room is empty.

Ignoring his bleeding foot and knowing that it will only be a matter of seconds before the soldiers watching the closed-circuit televisions upstairs see him, Rade scrambles to the cell next to his. He unlocks it, opens the door, and slips inside.

A ten-year-old girl with bruised eyes sits on her cot.

She is Eighteen, and that is all that is known about her.

"Time to go," Rade tells her.

Together they run out of the room, bare feet slapping the concrete floor. They run across the main floor to the hallway opposite just as a soldier comes barreling in. Rade is on him faster than he can pull his sidearm. The soldier, only ten years older than Rade, has a face blurred by acne. He screams when Rade plunges the hypodermic needle into his right ear. The drum bursts. Rade gets the soldier's gun and shoots him in the chest. Then shoots him again in the back of the head.

"We have two minutes," Rade says, handing the gun to Eighteen.

She gets into position: gun outstretched, both hands on the grip, as Rade makes his way to the other cells. He unlocks as many of the Null as he can. Twenty-Two, Twenty-Three, Thirty, then back to Fifteen and Ten. By the time the hallway just outside the main room fills with the tumbling crash of boots, Rade has freed twenty-four of the experimental subjects. They all have a role to play in what happens next.

"Hurry," Eighteen shouts as the first soldier runs in.

Eighteen drops him with a shot to the forehead.

Rade wrenches a fire ax from the wall outside cell number 40. He uses it to gut a soldier as he stumbles down the stairs into the main room. Rade slides the ax to another Null and grabs the soldiers' semiautomatic weapons. He opens fire as another two soldiers run into the room. Their blood sprays across the faces of the panicked scientists who scramble into the room behind them. One of the Null orphans smashes the butt of an assault rifle into a steam duct. The main room fills with a billowing miasma of steam as more soldiers and scientists rush inside, all of them screaming.

Everyone is engulfed in hot fog.

Rade's memory of what happens next is piecemeal: As soldiers material-ize from the team, he shoots them. Every adult face he sees, he blasts. They fall away, their blood spatter mingling with the mist. As he moves, he comes across numerous tableaux of violence—an orphan hacking off a scientist's head here, a soldier shooting a Null subject in the face there. Rade finds Forty-Two in the fog. He has two access badges and hands one to Rade.

"This is it!" Forty-Two screams before a bullet severs his vocal cords.

Rade runs with the ID badge to the first in a series of locked doors. He swipes the badge, and the door opens. He's not thinking while he does this. He's not wondering when they're going to shut the whole place down, maybe pull the plug on the power, or set off the sprinkler system, or just shoot up the hallways. Rade moves on instinct, driven by more than a million years of neural activ-ity surging through his brain. He isn't running down these hallways, leaving bloody soldiers and doctors in his wake, as a boy—he's doing it as everyone who came before him. He's killing as Darya. He's running as a Trojan warrior. This moment, this bloodthirsty now, is the first time that Rade recognizes his own ascendancy. He knows he is better than every throat he cuts.

As Rade and Forty run through the third set of doors, they pass a room where Janelle lies bruised and bloodied on a folding cot. Rade stops and helps her up. She's barely conscious, her left eye bruised shut. Dorothy has been frus-trated. She's lashed out at Janelle but never struck her directly. Apparently, Rade thinks, that has changed.

"We need to go now!" Forty yells.

Rade helps Janelle navigate a series of stairs and narrow hallways before they are joined by a mob of the Null subjects on the ground floor of the facility. Twenty strong, they kick down a supply room door and grab every available coat, hat, and pair of gloves that they can find. Someone, maybe Sixteen, tells the group that there are rafts with outboard motors a half mile from the facility. She overheard two soldiers say they're moored to a dock and never guarded.

The mob, dressed for the cold, streams through the final set of doors. Morton and Phillips are waiting there, guns at the ready. They don't warn the orphans that they're going to open fire. They just do. The guns chatter, and their bullets rip through the first five Null subjects. Blood sprays across Janelle's face. She tastes it. But the group surges forward, unstoppable. Morton goes down first and is torn apart. Phillips, mercifully, takes an ax to the neck. In the chaos, Seven, one of the oldest Null boys, a Hmong kid everyone calls Vang, though no one knows if that's his actual name, is hit in the face with the butt of a rifle. It's an accident. He's delirious and blood oozes from his nose. Twenty-Two grabs him and helps him up.

The door to the outside is opened and snow blasts inside. It swirls in blinding clouds across the faces of the Null subjects. They run into it, gleeful, laughing. Yards from freedom, Forty is shot in the leg. She falls. Rade runs back to her. Janelle stops and yells for Rade to get up. "Come on! We have to go now. This is our only chance!"

Rade glances back at Forty, struggling to stanch the wound in her calf.

He turns and looks past Janelle at the night landscape behind her. The snowdrifts as tall as houses, the towering pine trees bent near sideways. He drops the gun in his hand. He drops the needle in the other. Janelle shakes her head before she's pulled out into the night by one of the other escapees. She vanishes into the winter blur.

Rade spins around to help Forty up but one of the soldiers is already there. He shoots her in the forehead and Forty's blood sprays in a perfect arc across Rade's bare feet. The warm blood drenches his toes and makes it look like he's wearing red socks.

That is when the memory fades.

It disassembles like wet gauze. Rade watches as Forty's body dissolves into the floor and then the floor dissolves as well. He is suddenly no longer in the HED facility but in a street.

There are people marching around him, waving banners, lit by torchlight. They are washed away, fading like overexposed photographs. The marchers step into shadows and never reappear. . . .

The memory is gone.

Rade is in Russia, he sees himself in a mirror. He is Darya, but only for a second. Her face fades away. The mirror becomes shadow. . . .

The memory is lost.

Rade is in a forest, drinking from a stream, his hands chapped and the sound of fire rushing overhead. It goes too. . . .

A thousand lives slip past him.

A thousand lives evaporate until . . .

63

RADE WOKE UP to find he was bound with computer cable.

Kojo stood over him, the Sig Sauer in his right hand.

Only a few minutes had passed.

Rade said, "It worked."

He heard the words come out of his mouth, but he wasn't certain what exactly he meant by them. Rade searched his mind, gathering up crumbling lumps of memory, but they fell apart before he could get a clear look at them.

All that was left were sensations . . . running . . . hurting . . . fear . . .

Now, the furthest back his memory went was a decade. But instead of being filtered through the rage and pain, it was focused. Like a spotlight tightened down to a pinpoint. It was just as bright. Just as powerful. But not burdened by all the residue of the past. Rade had been working his way toward ascension, pulling every hair from his body, scrubbing his skin free of useless cells, and clearing his mind of base contemplations. He had been engaged in a never-ending series of skirmishes; taking ground slowly, inch by neural inch. Up until that moment, staring up at Kojo's fierce eyes, Rade was ready to continue that fight and win on his own personal terms. But the solution gave him a weapon he never could have imagined: an atomic bomb of simplicity. Erasing his mind, breaking the bonds of all those other lives, finally, truly made him perfect.

"They're gone," Rade said. "You understand?"

Rade rolled onto his side and looked over at Ashanique.

"It worked. The memories are gone. Let me go now."

"Why?"

"I can stop the HED. I know where they are."

Ashanique turned to Kojo.

"Fuck that," Kojo said.

He glanced across the room at Matilda. She sat beside Brandon. He was calm but clearly desperate to leave.

"We need to hurry, Ashanique," Dr. Song said. "The machine is ready."

"Ashanique . . ." Matilda took the girl's hand.

"I'm not like the others," Ashanique said. "I don't need the capsules."

"You've been so sick. The meds work."

"They don't. I've been pretending to take them. I put them in my mouth and leave them behind my teeth. Then, when no one's looking, I spit them out. Usually into my hand where they crumble and I just drop the dust."

"Why? Dr. Song says—"

Rade laughed.

"Dr. Song is wrong, Matilda. I'm different. The machine only fixes people damaged by the tests, by the experiments. Not me. I was born this way. If I just have the time, I can integrate the memories. Maybe my mother, maybe Rade, they weren't ready. But I'm ready. Don't you see what this is . . . ?"

Matilda shook her head.

Ashanique said, "I am everyone who came before me, just like all of us are. Only, I've been given a gift, a way to see into those souls. Please, Matilda, let me use this gift. I can change the world with it. If I go into that machine, it ends."

.   .   .

Matilda read Ashanique's face, her eyes.

Every microexpression—the lifting of her eyebrows, the curl of her lips—told Matilda that Ashanique was in complete and utter control, all of the subconscious tells had been erased. Matilda had never seen a face as perfectly at peace. There was no internal conflict, no suppression of emotion.

"Do you believe me?" the girl asked.

Matilda could see Ashanique was reading as well. Matilda felt naked, her soul exposed. There was nothing she could hide from Ashanique's eyes.

Matilda simply nodded.

Ashanique turned to Kojo. "Untie him."

"You don't know what you're saying. . . . He's a killer."

Rade scooted closer to Kojo so that he was at the detective's feet.

Kojo backed up and put both hands on the gun.

"No one else can stop this," Rade said. "You have no idea how much money and power are wrapped up in this thing. If a single document leaks, entire branches of government will be wiped out overnight. If you bring it to the press, if you drag the machine out of this room and have Ashanique and me testify, nothing happens. There will be no investigation because there can be no investigation. Let me be your tool. Let me be your weapon."

Ashanique pushed Kojo's gun down. He let her.

"This is crazy," Kojo said.

"This ends tonight," Ashanique replied.

She pulled the scalpel from Childers's dead grip and used it to cut through the ties on Rade's hands. As he sat up, rubbing the chafed skin on his wrists, Ashanique placed a hand on his shoulder.

He shuddered under her touch.

"It isn't true," she said. "My mom would never have abandoned you or Forty."

Rade looked up at her confused.

"I have no idea what you're talking about."

64

MATILDA SAT ALONE in an interview room.

It was small, with a little half desk that was stuck to one wall. The walls themselves were pale yellow in color, and the overhead lighting made every-thing look washed-out, like the tanned paper around the pictures in Lucy's photo albums. Matilda had been in this room for over an hour. She knew Ashanique was in another room. Dr. Song in a third.

When they'd first arrived at the station, there was a brief interview with a detective. He mentioned he was a friend of Kojo's but walked that back a few seconds later, realizing he'd made a mistake.

No one else had come in since.

Matilda noticed a bruise on her right arm. It was in the shape of a human hand, fingers outstretched. She'd gotten it at the VA hospital.

Seconds after Rade slipped out of the LINAC room, the door was kicked open and SWAT officers stormed in. Matilda held hands with Ashanique and they both got down on their knees; she didn't hear the shouted orders, at least not that she could remember. But her body heard. Letting go of Ashanique's hand, Matilda threaded her fingers over her head. She closed her eyes and loosened her limbs as the cuffs went on. The half hour that followed was a tumult—she'd been pushed into the back of a squad car, dragged back out, and then hustled into the department before being tossed into the interview room. Alone with herself for the first time in days, Matilda was desperate for another person's presence.

Eight minutes later, Kojo walked in.

Matilda couldn't help but jump up and hug him. She felt her eyes tear over and wiped them prophylactically. Kojo felt so solid, the weight of him grounding her. She never wanted to let him go.

"It's okay," Kojo said. "We're okay. I had a friend switch the cameras off before I came in here. We have a couple of minutes before they figure it out and my ass is hauled out. So let me talk first, and then you can ask me a question if there's time."

Matilda nodded.

"These people Rade worked for, the HED, they're going to try and bury us. We've got to go underground. FBI is already here; I can't trust anyone in the department, we already know that. I can get you and Ashanique out, though. But you can't go home. Ever. Understand?"

Matilda nodded again, tears rolling down her face to her chin.

"I have a place for you to go. It's not long-term but it'll be safe for a while. You'll fly out tonight."

"How is Brandon?"

Kojo said, "He's all right. Gonna take a long time to recover from this, though. There are a couple of psychologists in with him. They haven't told him about . . . Ah, man. Officers found Ophelia at my place. She survived but she's gonna have a long road to recovery. I'm not sure when Brandon can know that. He's a strong kid, though. You saw it. You know."

"He is, like his dad. How's Ashanique?"

"You're not going to be shocked to hear this but she's doing surprisingly well. They have a few people in there, people that I know. Psychologists walk out shaking their heads, can't believe how smart she is. How tough. I think she's going to be fine."

Kojo held Matilda in silence for a second.

"Here's the thing," he said. "I'm not going to pretend that I get exactly what went down. Dr. Song can show me papers and explain it all till he's out of breath, but there's one thing that I can't make sense of. I get the genetic memory piece. I get the experiment. What I don't get is how Ashanique remembers that World War One—"

"George."

"Yes, George. How can she remember his death?"

Matilda wiped her nose and pulled far enough away to look Kojo in the eyes. She did not, however, let go. "I've been thinking about that too," she said. "I think Ashanique already told us the answer. We just— Well, I just didn't want to hear it. Maybe I'm shell-shocked, definitely sleep-deprived. Beyond exhausted, really. But I think it's that we're all one. All part of a single— Goddamn, this sounds silly."

"Go on. Nothing else makes sense."

Matilda said, "There's this thing I remember from college. They say that all matter can't ever be truly destroyed. Every particle that exists has always existed. It takes on new forms, passing from one to the other. It's a plant, then inside a cow, then a person, then back to the soil. What if human consciousness can affect that process? What if... what if we can influence it? We know Ashanique and the other Null can remember their ancestors' lives. It's coded in their bodies. But maybe they can also remember other people's lives."

"Okay. How?"

Matilda thought back to when she and Ashanique were in the cab. Ashanique had cried, thinking of the beauty she'd seen, the splendor at the heart of being Null.

"The collective unconscious is real. I don't know how they're stored; I don't know how they're transferred, but George's memories, his very last moments, wound up inside Ashanique. They're probably inside all of us. She and the other Null can access them. Maybe it's something quantum. But the only way it makes sense is if we're just like she said: We're more than disparate individuals. We're all connected in a collective and shared neural history. Humanity has a source code and Ashanique's found a way to tap into it."

Matilda took Kojo's hands and held them tight.

"She's the first," Matilda said, her voice charged with astonishment.

Kojo whispered, feeling a sudden solemnity.

"First of what?"

"Something remarkable."

65

RADE PULLED A new hoodie over a bulletproof vest.

Standing outside his rental car in the HED parking lot, he laced up the Nike Blazers he'd picked up at a mall in Aurora. They looked good in the sodium lights. It was late on a Thursday night and there were only seventeen cars in the lot.

Rade knew each and every one.

He was there to kill their owners.

As Rade crossed the lot, he slipped on his wireless headphones. He'd already prepped Philip Glass's "Island" and turned it up as loud as it would go. The song was his driving music. When he listened to it, he saw all sorts of swirling colors in the corner of his vision—ribbon-thin spirals of red and gold slowly unwinding, spinning out into infinity. He considered the synesthesia just another manifestation of his perfection—a sign that his brain had moved into a different gear. Despite what he'd read online in New Agey scientific journals with names like *Advancements in Human Achievement* and *Journal of the Mind-Boxy Praxis*, he did not consider himself a more advanced human. In Rade's mind, there was no further evolution to be had in the human form—he was greater because he simply wasn't human.

And the HED was where he would demonstrate it.

You are finally ready now.

The Human Ecology Division building was a low-slung, two-level brick affair that wouldn't have looked out of place in the pages of a magazine extolling the virtues of midcentury modern architecture. It was built in the midfifties and intended to be utilitarian—originally purposed as a school, it was remodeled in the 1970s as a research facility for the Army Corps of Engineers. The Human Ecology Division, flush with renewed CIA funds, moved into the building in 1985. Though the organization's various bureaucrats had all tried to put their mark on the place—breaking up the floors and adding a spiral staircase in 1990, installing a sleek, modern lobby in 2006—the building had never lost its rather banal, practical look.

Rade walked into that sleek lobby and tossed a grenade.

It bounced behind the receptionist's desk and rolled to the older man's feet before it exploded in a tarry fireball. The alarms went off, sprinklers followed. Rade pulled both of his Glocks from his track pants and started shooting.

The first people he encountered were the three security guards on duty. Though they had nothing to do with Project Clarity, likely hadn't even been born when he escaped the facility, he knew they'd die. If he didn't kill them here, quickly, they would die when the CIA's sweeper unit came through. Even though it had a building and a parking lot, the HED was a place that didn't technically exist. When it burned, everyone in it would burn too.

He shot the men as they rounded a corner, radios squawking in panic.

Rade had brought fifteen grenades.

He tossed one into each lab he passed.

By the time he was on the second floor, he'd thrown ten grenades and, despite the sprinkler system, smoke choked the hallways. Rade had killed eight scientists. Some of them were new, some he'd seen in videoconferences. Two of them, assistants to Dr. Sykes in the late 1970s, actually recognized him. They were smart enough to know not to try and fight back; both of them closed their eyes before he put an 8mm round in their heads.

At the north end of the building, Rade tossed two grenades on the spiral staircase after he ascended it. He actually waited to see the damage they did. The staircase shuddered, its lower half falling away first. He was coated in drywall dust and wondered how many carcinogens he'd inhaled. As the last pieces of shattered, steaming-hot metal pinged against the linoleum floor, Rade took a long, deep breath. The smell reminded him of something, though he wasn't sure what it was. A memory teasingly played its fingers along the base of his brain, tickling like a failing sparkler.

That was when someone stabbed Rade in the back with a pair of scissors.

He felt them go in deep. Ripping through his hoodie, cutting through one of the vest's straps, before it plunged through his left trapezius muscle. One of the blades chipped his spine. He didn't need to see it to know it was one of those heavy-duty scissors, the metal ones with painted black handles. Rade turned to see a cowering scientist in a lab coat. The man was young, maybe late twenties, and he actually mouthed *Sorry* as he backed away, hands raised.

Rade shot him in the nose.

He continued on, inhaling too much smoke, feeling the sooty deposits building up in his lungs, and wondering if he should have brought a respirator.

No time for that now. No time for second-guessing.

Rade tossed his last grenades into two rooms thrumming with computers. He also threw in the Glocks before he stopped at Dr. Sykes's office door. He had decided earlier in the evening that he wasn't going to shoot her. He had other plans.

Dr. Sykes's door was locked, so he casually knocked.

Dorothy opened the door with a Colt revolver.

She fired twice before Rade smacked the gun from her hand. One bullet hit the vest, and the vest did its job. The second hit him in the neck. He felt the instant warmth of an arterial gush as the blood burbled out and poured down his side, under the vest, and into his pants, where it was wicked up. Rade clamped his left hand down on his wound, but he knew he had only minutes before he bled out.

• • •

Dorothy considered herself a perceptive person.

She'd spent forty years in biomedical research, to the detriment of every other aspect of her life. Four years of medical school, a residency in surgery, another in neurology, then four years for the PhD in biochemistry—she was not a stupid person. But she'd also left behind two failed marriages, three children who hated her—children she hadn't seen in nearly a decade—and lived in a small apartment with no artwork. As she backed away from Rade, his face paling by the second from blood loss, she couldn't help but think of the fact that she used to love art.

In school, when life was simple and seemed so full of meaning and purpose, she would go to the Art Institute and stare at the Postimpressionist paintings, losing herself in their vivid colors. At the time, nearly thirty years ago, she imagined they perfectly captured the swirling complexity of the human brain's neural network. Cheesy, yes, but on point. She hadn't had time to look at art, or even think about it, since then. Funnily enough, Dorothy couldn't help but see the contrast of Rade's bright red arterial blood against his pale skin and think . . . *It's kind of pretty.*

"You lied to me," Rade gurgled.

"I never lied. The machine didn't—"

"Not the machine."

Dorothy moved behind her desk. Her eyes scanned across the papers and laptops, looking for anything sharp. She just needed to keep him at arm's length for another minute and thirty seconds or so. He was bleeding out bad.

Goddamn, Dorothy thought. *Going to the shooting range on weekends actually paid off. This fucker's just failed.*

"Then what, Rade? I never, ever lied. They left you behind, remember?"

"No."

"I trained you. I showed you how to learn from the memories, how to mine them for skills. That ruthlessness, that cunning, I gave it to you. For twenty years, we've been a team. And I've never let you—"

Rade suddenly lurched forward with an unexpected burst of strength and kicked the desk, pinning Dorothy against the wall. Textbooks tumbled from a bookshelf, pages coming loose and floating about.

The door to the hallway still open, smoke poured into the room, clouding the ceiling. Dorothy could hear sirens outside.

This is almost over. Hang on.

"About what we are," Rade clarified.

"I don't understand. What—"

Rade spat a wad of phlegmy, clotted blood onto the desk, clearing his throat. "Null aren't freaks. . . . The machine didn't activate old nerves. . . . It plugged us in . . ."

•   •   •

Rade could feel his body slipping.

He kicked the desk again, crunching Dorothy harder against the wall.

The smoke spilled in faster.

"Plugged you into what?" Dorothy asked between gritted teeth.

"The rest of us," Rade said, delirious now. "We are legion."

Rade coughed, the blood spurting wildly from between his fingers. Dorothy saw her moment and pushed the desk back against him.

Rade stumbled backward but caught himself on her lab coat with his filthy, blood-coated right hand. Dorothy grabbed at his hand to wrench it off. In the corner of his vision, he saw fire trucks and cops pulling up outside.

He could feel her body tensing. He figured she was considering jumping. From the room's height, she might break a leg, but it must have seemed worth the chance—it was only thirty feet, and there were bushes just below the window. People had certainly survived a hell of a lot worse.

Holding on to her lab coat as tight as he could, he freed his left hand and, stretching as far as he could, snagged Dorothy's Aurora fountain pen from her breast pocket. She stared at him, befuddled, as he ripped the cap off with his teeth.

Dorothy clearly didn't realize what he was doing until he did it.

"You end here," Rade said.

With a final burst of vigor, the very last ounce he possessed, he dragged her down and slammed the tip of the Aurora pen into Dorothy's right eye. It pierced deep. Cutting through the gelatinous vitreous body before cutting through the optic nerve and shredding the blood vessels. Dorothy fell backward against the wall, screaming, as Rade tumbled back in the opposite direction.

He hit the floor and found fire.

As the quickly spreading flames licked the clothing from his body, Rade realized that this was the moment he'd been preparing for—he was transforming.

Embrace it; embrace the conversion.

All the animal skin peeled away.

The heavy, burdensome bones fractured and the marrow steamed. His organs boiled, and then, as the last few pulses of bioelectrical energy crossed his synaptic junctions, Rade became a being of light.

And ash.

66

AN OLD WOMAN *makes her way up a winding path that coils across the face of a mountain.*

The clouds eddy in the valleys below her. She is dressed in colorful woven fabrics and moves slowly, relying on walking sticks to help her over obstacles like tree roots and stones. She glances up at the top of the mountain where a monastery sits. The old woman has been walking for five days. She takes two breaks a day, once in midmorning when the sun casts short shadows and once in the early evening. She does not eat much, some dried meats and nuts, and her legs are strong. The old woman has been walking for most of her sixty-two years, she doesn't believe in riding horses or sitting in the backs of wagons. Her feet will get her where she needs to go and, already, the world is moving far too fast.

The old woman reaches the monastery late in the day.

The sun sets over the mountains at her back, bathing them blood red. She pauses a moment to look out over the valley through which she's walked. The old woman recalls the path—the muddy creek she forded, the antelope bounding in twitchy anxiety over stubbled hills.

As with all the journeys she's taken, she sees the beauty in the process.

The old woman turns and opens the wooden door to the stone monastery and steps inside to see monks in supplication. They look like puddles of orange, still and silent on the stone floor. She makes her way down the aisle between them to the abbot at the front of the sanctuary. Seeing her approach, he rises and takes her hand.

"Mother," he says. "It has been so long. I was worried you would never allow me to see you again."

She nods as she fights back tears.

"Many cruel things were said," the old woman whispers. "I have forgiven them."

Together they walk carefully up a narrow flight of stairs to the roof.

"How are his pains?" the old woman asks.

"They come and go. There has been only mild pain today."

"And it is in the stomach?"

"As well as the legs."

The old woman is silent as she considers this.

"Does that worry you, Mother?"

"He is also my son. All of it worries me."

They reach the roof and step out on the ceiling of heaven. The view from here is stunning; the whole of the world below is spread out at their feet.

The abbot escorts his mother to a monk lying on a platform. She sits down beside the monk as the abbot chants prayers. The old woman pulls several small cloth bags filled with cinnabar, mercury sulfide, and dried herbs from a satchel.

Unrolling several strips of "eating paper"—digestible rice paper with magical incantations handwritten on them—the old woman feeds them to the ill monk before she takes her sons' hands—the monk's and the abbot's.

"It is so good to see you both again."

"Yes, Mother. Anger has made us ill."

"It is over now."

The abbot and his medicine woman mother bow their heads in prayer as the ill monk opens his eyes to see the sweep of the sun overhead.

He grips his mother's hand as tightly as he can and weeps. . . .

67

ASHANIQUE'S EYES fluttered open.

For a second, she wasn't sure where she was.

But she knew she was safe.

Ashanique sat up. She was in bed, a twin with a down blanket and a folded quilt on the end. Sunlight poured through the window opposite, illuminating a small bedroom with late-morning light. The closet door was open and she could see new clothes hanging inside. On the love seat was a backpack, also new.

Ashanique got out of bed, pulled on a sweater, and made her way to the kitchen. The smell of coffee and toast quickened her step.

The house was a two-story and barely decorated. Some leftover art, mostly landscapes owned by the previous tenants, dotted the walls. As Ashanique ran down the stairs, she caught sight of snow-peaked mountains through the windows. They were visible only briefly before towering pine trees blocked the view.

"Good morning."

Ashanique found Matilda in the kitchen. She'd cut her hair short and dyed it red. She sat at the kitchen table—another leftover—sipping coffee, a laptop open in front of her. Ashanique saw Matilda was talking to Kojo on a secure video call. He was sitting in his living room. Brandon was in the background singing. The boy walked into view and waved when he noticed Ashanique. She leaned in and blew a kiss.

"How're you, Ash?" Kojo asked.

"Good. Slept in, though. Makes me kind of wonky."

"You enjoying school?"

Ashanique shrugged. "It's school."

She waved goodbye and walked across the small kitchen to pour herself a cup of coffee. Matilda watched her, then looked back at Kojo.

"So two new Null kids will be coming by next week," she said. "They're twins, thirteen years old, mom is number Twenty-Seven. She died two years back and they've been in foster care ever since. We'll see what we can learn."

"How the hell did you find them?"

"With the HED broken and Congress investigating, a lot of paperwork has made its way online. Dr. Song's been coordinating some of those releases. Most via offshore leak sites but at least it's out there. He was contacted by other survivors. People like Janice, people who've spent the last forty-some years in hiding. They feel safe enough to reach out. The network is still active. Dr. Song's busier than ever, trying to get people where they need to be."

"To the LINAC machines?"

"Some of them," Matilda said. "The original subjects who are still around."

"And their kids?"

Matilda smiled. "They're mostly like Ash. They don't want to forget."

"By the way, you look at the link I sent?"

"Yeah. It's all anonymized. Hard to say if it's real."

Kojo leaned in, face closer to the camera.

"Excited for our visit?"

"Of course."

Matilda sipped her coffee. As she did, her bathrobe slipped off her shoulder, revealing a hint of pale skin and a curve of cleavage.

"Hang on," Kojo said as she straightened her bathrobe. "Got to let me at least enjoy the peek."

"Stop it, you two," Ashanique said as she sat at the table. "I need Matilda."

"Fine," Kojo said. "I'll call you two this afternoon."

Matilda smiled, puckered. Then: "Don't forget."

"I wouldn't."

"And say 'bye to Brandon for me. Excited to see him."

"He loves it up there. 'Bye, babe."

Kojo logged out, and Matilda turned her attention to Ashanique. "Okay," she said. "You've got another one, right?"

"You're going to love it."

"This is, what? The—"

"Eightieth."

Matilda smiled as she opened a program on the laptop and began recording.

"So," she said, "tell me about this life."

Ashanique began with the old woman's journey across the desert.

She went into great detail, mostly about the feel of the dry air and the smells of the high mountain desert, painting a vivid picture, before she described the touching reunion between the medicine mother and her sons.

As she listened, Matilda glanced over Ashanique's shoulder to the window just above the kitchen sink. There, she could see the back of Lucy's head as the old woman slowly rocked back and forth on the porch glider.

Lucy's eyes were turned to the mountains and the bright sky beyond.

POSTSCRIPT

68

13:09:23 PM INTENZE_DEVICE: There were more. You on?

Changed status to Away (13:11:34 PM)

Changed status to Online (13:15:09 PM)

13:15:16 PM NULLHYPE: yes

13:15:17 PM NULLHYPE: who is this?

13:15:21 PM INTENZE_DEVICE: Alaska was the fifth site. I have a list, hacked it after the fire. All systems down.

13:15:32 PM NULLHYPE: what sites?

13:15:37 PM NULLHYPE: where is the list from?

13:15:42 PM INTENZE_DEVICE: Don't believe me?

13:15:45 PM INTENZE_DEVICE: Project CLARITY

13:15:48 PM NULLHYPE: hacked HED?

13:15:51 PM INTENZE_DEVICE: Yes. Ten sites total. I got files go back to 1960s and more. Things you don't know, things you would never believe. Examples:

13:15:53 PM INTENZE_DEVICE: Taos

13:15:55 PM INTENZE_DEVICE: Chattanooga

13:15:56 PM INTENZE_DEVICE: Miami

13:15:58 PM INTENZE_DEVICE: And project MINISTRY

13:15:59 PM NULLHYPE: who is this?

13:16:02 PM NULLHYPE: ?

13:16:05 PM INTENZE_DEVICE: Rade wasn't alone

13:16:06 PM INTENZE_DEVICE: Lock your door. I'm coming.

Changed status to Away (13:16:08 PM)

ABOUT THE AUTHOR

KEITH THOMAS worked as a lead clinical researcher at the University of Colorado Denver School of Medicine and National Jewish Health before writing for film and television. He has developed projects for studios and production companies and has collaborated with writers like James Patterson and filmmakers like Paul Haggis. He lives in Denver and works in Los Angeles.